FALLEN ANGEL

Fallen Angel

C. L. Hartley

YELLOWBACK MYSTERIES
JAMES A. ROCK & COMPANY, PUBLISHERS
FLORENCE • SOUTH CAROLINA

Fallen Angel by C. L. Hartley

is an imprint of JAMES A. ROCK & CO., PUBLISHERS

Fallen Angel copyright ©2017 by C. L. Hartley

Address comments and inquiries to:

YELLOWBACK MYSTERIES
James A. Rock & Company, Publishers
1937 West Palmetto Street, #248
Florence, SC 29501

E-mail:
jarrock@sprintmail.com   lar-rock@earthlink.net
Internet URL: www.rockpublishing.com

Paperback ISBN-13/EAN: 978-1-59663-797-9

Library of Congress Control Number: 2007928489

Printed in the United States of America

First Edition: 2017

This is dedicated to
those in my life
who encouraged me
to finish what I had started,
and had faith that
it would be worth
the effort

Chapter 1

I STOOD ON THE SIDEWALK in front of a small coffee shop downtown. It wasn't that I hadn't expected to feel totally out of place; I had. I didn't belong here anymore. I just hadn't expected this creepy sense of déjà vu. It was making my skin crawl.

This is an old city and this particular section of town used to rely heavily on manufacturing. Now there seemed to be an inordinate number of vacant brick buildings, all with big "For Sale or Lease" signs on them. Some of the old buildings have been converted to condos or renovated for new office space. It wasn't exactly the city I'd grown up in; it had changed substantially in the twelve years I'd been gone. Unfortunately, it hadn't changed nearly enough to suit me.

I looked both ways and crossed the street. My brother owns one of the independent insurance agencies here in town. To my knowledge he doesn't particularly care for insurance; it's more that it pays the bills and isn't a "family" business. With a wife and three kids, I guess those items have to take priority over personal happiness. He was always the responsible one.

The front door of the insurance office gave a small beep when I entered. The office itself was an eighties throw back. Everything was done in either mauve or gray and a cheap imitation Barry Manilow was playing in the background. Pink and gray was bad enough, but obsolete elevator music, now that was just beyond my comprehension.

The first thought I had upon entering was "ick." The second was "How the hell has Marty worked in this place every day for the last fifteen years?"

I slid my black Ray-Ban Predators (aptly named, I might add) up to hold my hair away from my face. My hair was now so long that it came to the middle of my back. It was as straight as any straightening iron could ever produce and as black as my Ray-Ban's.

I looked at the large blonde woman sitting behind the front desk, a new addition (the blonde, not the desk). She was at least fifty pounds overweight and even her blonde hair was big. The hair was a testament to the capabilities of ultra-strong, super-hold hair spray and her dark roots were her own testament. Not a pretty picture, but not shocking in this town, or neighborhood, for that matter. I suppose I needed an attitude adjustment, but home always brought out the worst in me.

The blonde stammered. "Can … I … help you?"

I have a tendency to make people nervous. Of course, I try to make people nervous. Being scary takes work. Not as much work as it used to, but who's going to be afraid of a five-foot-three-inch tall, 110-pound, cherub-featured brunette? Nobody, that's who. So it has taken me years to perfect an aura that matches my personality. Bitch.

"I'm Ace. I'm here to see Marty. Is he in?"

Ace had been my nickname since I was a kid. Angelica Cynthia, had turned into A.C, which had been altered to Acey and now just about everyone in the family called me Ace.

I didn't smile at the woman. I didn't make pleasantries. Why should I make people feel good about my return? I didn't feel all that happy about it, and misery does love company. Besides I thrive on fear and misery. Or at least that's what I'm told and most of the time the as-sessment was probably accurate.

Misery may love company, but right about now it could also use a good stiff drink. I know, it's only ten-thirty in the morning and I'm thinking about a couple shots of J.D. But between the mauve and the blonde and my forced return … it just wasn't a good sign for the day.

The blonde nodded and buzzed to let Marty know I was there. He walked out immediately. He was probably afraid that his assistant would quit if she spent too much time in my presence.

Marty got all the good Italian male genes. He's well over six-foot looks like a Greek god and don't think he doesn't know it. It really isn't fair that I got stuck with our mother's gene pool and he got our father's. Daddy's tall, along with all of his side of the family. My mom is short, along with every other female member of her family. I guess it was just destiny. Marty was responsible and incredibly sexy, I was short and the family nightmare. Go figure.

"Hey there, you made it. I was beginning to think you were going to blow us all off." The key word left off of that statement was "again."

He was grinning from ear to ear. He really had missed me and was genuinely happy to see me. We've kept in touch over the years. I send gifts to his kids twice a year, birthdays and Christmas. I was the missing Aunty Ace that everyone referred to in hushed tones at family gatherings. Or at least that was Marty's take on things.

Whenever we spoke, Marty discussed the kids and his work. I always discussed current events. I couldn't exactly discuss my kids—I don't have any. And as for my work … well, let's just say it was always either classified or illegal. I never thought sharing that sort of thing was going to keep my brother safe or make him overly secure about my personal safety.

"Yep, here I am. Do you have any idea why? I do have other things to be doing. It isn't like I enjoy being here, as you well know."

Marty appeared disappointed with my attitude. Par for the course, I suppose. No one I was related to ever looked happy with me. Happy to *see* me maybe, but never happy *with* me. That is, except Uncle Tony. And I might add, he was the only reason I'd come home.

"You could at least pretend to be glad to be here. I mean, no one actually expects you to be, but think of the pure bewilderment on their faces when you appear to be pleased about the prospects of seeing everyone. It'd really be a shock. You might even give Aunt Ruth a real heart attack."

Marty was being a smartass, of course. Our Aunt Ruth is one of those people who is always sick, in the head maybe. But she complains about everything and is one the toughest old ladies around. She'll outlast all of us, but unfortunately, for the rest of the family, they'll all have to listen to her hypocondriatic crap until they die.

"I may have been summoned by the overlord himself, but I don't have to be happy about it." Uncle Tony was "the overlord" I'd mentioned. He's our grandfather's youngest brother on our father's side. He was only a few years older than our father.

Uncle Tony liked me. Always had, or at least that's what he claimed. I was never sure where I stood for real, but since I was probably the only kid born into this generation of the Pascoli family who shared any of Tony's personality traits, no one ever questioned our relationship—the single exception being me. We were both absolutely ruthless and irritatingly intelligent.

Uncle Tony has an IQ close to mine. When I was tested in the eighth grade I scored 148. That was on an adult scoring level, not an eighth grade level. I was pushed up two grades after the testing. They couldn't exactly just hand me a diploma and send me on my way; I was only fourteen. When I started working for the U.S. government, I was around twenty-two. I was tested again. This time I scored 180.

I graduated from high school at sixteen, went to college and finished my first master's degree by the time I was twenty. I studied criminal psychology. I thought it might be useful for self-study more than anything else. I finished my second master's at twenty-one. This time I studied law. But inevitably I had to get out of this town, so I applied to the FBI.

It seemed appropriate considering my academic background and criminal knowledge—not to mention my own criminal inclinations. Uncle Tony was not pleased. He told me the Pascoli family and the FBI were, more or less, opposing forces in the scheme of things. He may have been right, but I went anyway.

I didn't stay with the Bureau. They wanted me to do more paperwork than field work. I hate paperwork. It only took two years to find another government agency that was far more appropriate for my skills. Thus was born The Fallen Angel. But I left full-time government employment several years ago and became an independent contractor.

When I was growing up my teachers had considered me something of a child prodigy, although my parents considered my intellect and abilities a nuisance. I tended to get into trouble—a lot of trouble. Uncle Tony, on the other hand, had stated early on that he considered me his successor. Tony had said, even back then, that it was my intelligence, skill and my drive to protect what was mine that made me the right choice for the position.

In light of my current line of expertise, I suppose it wasn't that hard to see the correlation. But I didn't want to move back here in order to be a successor. Besides, the responsibility that goes with that job is a bit more than I think I want.

I've been living in southern Italy for the last four years. I don't like the cold. I don't like cities and I don't like people knowing who I am. This automatically makes me less than thrilled about my summons. It gets very cold here; it's a huge city and everyone who's anyone knows me.

Marty looked from me to his assistant and said, "Why don't we walk down the street to Starbucks and get a coffee? We can talk on the way."

I turned and started for the door.

"Cathy," Marty advised, "we'll be back in a little while."

He followed me out the door and, once outside, looked at me sideways.

"What?" I scowled.

"Ace ... uh ... is that a gun?" His line of vision was focused on the small bulge at the lower part of my back.

Well, duh! "Of course!"

He didn't look thrilled.

"Let's look at this from my point of view," I said, "shall we? I have no idea why I'm here. I have no idea who knows I'm here. I have no idea what's expected of me and I don't trust anyone. It seems safer for me to carry, than to not carry. Besides, I always carry. You know that."

"Well, yea, but ..."

"No buts. I was once supposed to be Tony's successor. I have no intention of showing up here for a family gathering and getting shot down by one of his rivals because I make them nervous. Forget it. The gun stays."

That wasn't really much of a possibility, of course. The families had all been in a quiet alliance for years. But that didn't mean I was willing to take my chances either.

"I guess I see your point. Have you gone to see the overlord yet?"

I smiled—the first since I'd crossed the city limits. Occasionally I called Tony the "overlord." Marty never did. He was afraid of Tony and rightly so. I, on the other hand, never showed any fear. But just because I didn't show it, didn't mean it wasn't there. It was always there. However, hearing Marty refer to him as the "overlord" made me want to chuckle. Well, almost.

"No. I wanted to know if you knew what was going on. Do you?"

He shook his head and looked down at the sidewalk. "I'm not sure, but I think he's retiring. He looks tired. I saw him a couple of weeks ago when he swung by the agency. He wanted information on you and what you'd been up to. After the conversation, I walked away with the feeling that he wants you home to take over."

SHIT!!! That is exactly what I've been afraid of. Now that just sucks! I wanted to scream. My adrenaline was churning and I wanted to hit something—*someone,* actually, would have been better—but I'd settle for something. I always managed, somehow, to stay calm on the outside. No need for anyone to see my hysteria, right?

"You sure?" I probed. "I mean, did he actually *say* that? Or did someone else say something?"

"No, you know Tony tells absolutely no one what he's thinking. He plays it close to the vest, always has. He never gives anything away."

Well, that sounded far too familiar. "I guess, then, the only way I'll find out is to just go see him. I hope you're wrong. I don't want to have come back here."

"It isn't *that* bad."

I stopped and looked at him. "You listen to elevator music all day. You sit in a pink and gray cloud with a fat blonde and you tell me it isn't that bad? What the hell is wrong with you?! It is *that* bad! No offense Marty, but it's depressing. I can't move back here!"

"Okay, so my office is incredibly depressing and I need to do something about it. But you don't have to sit in my office, and you don't get a choice of whether or not you're moving back either. And you know it."

We started moving again. He was right. Too many people relied on Tony, or at least the position he filled, to take care of them. They needed him to ensure they had jobs, to feed, house and clothe their families. Jumping ship would make my life better, but it would royally screw almost every other member of my extended family.

When we reached Starbucks I looked at the doors and then kept going.

"Where are we going?" he demanded.

"Mario's. I need a *drink*. Coffee is not going to do it."

Mario was our second cousin. And Mario's was family-owned. I could go in there at seven in the morning on a Sunday and get a drink if I wanted it. Nobody would tell me otherwise.

"It's not even eleven yet."

"I don't care. Besides, Mario won't care either. Life sucks at the moment and I need a couple shots before I go to Tony's."

He gave me a look, shook his head and followed me. "I hope you haven't turned into an alcoholic while you've been gone."

Smartass. "I didn't need to be an alcoholic before I came back, but I might just turn into one if I stay too long."

Mario's didn't actually open until three, so when we got there and the door was locked, I wasn't deterred. I pounded on the door and a young man answered. I gave him my scary aura and asked for Mario. It worked like a charm. He let us in.

Marty leaned into me and whispered. "How do you do that? You seem perfectly normal one minute and the next thing I know you're hell's spawn."

I slid off my glasses and looked up and back over my shoulder at my brother. "It has taken years to perfect. But intimidation and fear are actually pretty easy for a woman. We generally refer to it as PMS."

That got me a smile. "Remember, you said that, not me."

The young man walked us in through the darkened restaurant. It was always dark in Mario's, but when no one was here it was even darker because none of the candles on the tables were lit. I walked over to the bar and took down two stools.

I stared at the young man. "Tell Mario we're here."

He hesitated, as if worried he'd offend me. "Who … should I say is here?"

I slid off my leather car coat. It was really warm enough to go without it, but I had to cover the gun outside if I was going to carry it. I walked to the backside of the bar. I grabbed the bottle of J.D. and two glasses. The kid had gotten a good glimpse of the gun. That was good. Mario would know it was actually me.

"His cousins, Marty and Ace." I walked back around and gave a glass to Marty and poured both of us a drink.

I was blending really well with the dark. I was wearing a short black tank top that showed part of my tattoos—a large one on my back and the same tattoo, mirror-imaged, on the front. A smaller version rested next to my right hip bone and a belly ring with a charm concluded the lot. All angels. All custom designed.

My black low rise, boot-cut jeans helped with the height issue by making me look taller. This was also assisted by the two-inch heels on my black cowboy boots. I needed all the help I could get.

Tentatively, Mario approached. Apparently the kid had told him about the gun.

"Ace, is that really you?"

He had a faint accent still. He'd moved here with his parents when he was about ten. They had lived in *Florence* for most of his first ten years, but since the rest of the family had come to America, they'd decided to join them.

I chugged my third shot. "Yep. It's me. Sorry to break in so early, but I needed a fix." I held up the bottle of whisky. That got me a big smile and a hug. I'm not a huggy person, but my family is really into it.

Mario hugged Marty and they discussed some work pleasantries. I was proud of Mario for holding himself in check for as long as he managed it. It took almost five full minutes.

"So, have you seen Tony yet? He knows you're home?"

"He's the one who called me home, but no I haven't been there yet. I wanted to check in on my brother first."

Mario was looking antsy. He was thinking that if he didn't call Tony right now, he might regret it. I could see it all over his face, or should I say, the little vein just above his eye. It ticked every time he was uncomfortable, lying, or put on the spot. And considering the topic, I decided to put him out of his misery.

"You can call him," I said, "if it makes you feel better. You look like you're going to have a coronary. But in the meantime, is there anyone back there cooking? I'm starved. I'd settle for some bread if it's been delivered." He looked visibly relieved. You could see the stress drain from his entire body.

I usually eat in the morning, but I'd only had coffee earlier due to my distress of being home. I decided it wasn't wise to be drinking whisky on an empty stomach followed by a visit to Tony. I might say or do something stupid.

"You just make yourselves at home and I'll have something brought out. I'm certain they can put something together. And I'll call Tony. He'll be pleased that you came. I think he was worried you wouldn't come back."

So he had already told the others he'd requested my presence. Now that was … unnerving. "He's never told me to come home before." I replied. "I think he didn't want to be the boy who cried wolf."

They both stared at me, but it was Marty who asked what I was talking about. I had to wonder—was I the only one in the room who had heard the fable? Instead, I shook it off.

"I think he didn't want call me home regularly for unimportant crap—family gatherings, weddings, funerals, you know … crap. He may have been afraid that I wouldn't show when he really needed me, thinking it was just more of the same. I'm more apt to show up if he only calls once, rather than repeatedly, over the years. It means he needs me here for a reason." I took a chug. "Not crap."

It could mean a couple of other things as well, but I really didn't want to consider them.

The only reason I came back was because it was *Tony* and he represented my responsibilities here. Nobody, not even my parents, could have gotten me back here. This place made me claustrophobic as a child, and I'd already seen that the reaction hadn't changed.

When Tony called, I think he mentioned living up to my "family obligations." In my family that could be anything from killing off an entire group of rival business owners to taking Aunt Cassie to church on Sunday. You just never know when it's Tony. But he wouldn't have called if it weren't important, or if he weren't trying to reinstate a family hold on me for a reason. That last part made me nervous.

Mario and Marty exchanged looks and Mario left.

I took another shot. I had an iron stomach. I could drink with the best of them. Unfortunately, that means I need more to get me to a state of comfortable warmth. That nice glow doesn't show for at least six shots, even on an empty stomach, but with every chug I was getting closer.

Mario returned and told us he'd spoken with Tony and he'd be by for lunch in an hour. Mario said he'd bring us appetizers but would serve lunch when Tony arrived. That meant I was expected to stay but Marty could leave if he did so before Tony arrived.

Almost an hour later, Marty and I were finishing our bruschetta. "Are you staying or going?" I asked. "You need to decide—it's almost noon. He'll be here shortly."

"You going to be okay if I go?"

A big brother to the end. Of course he couldn't exactly defend me if anything happened, but it was nice that he thought he should. "I'll be fine. Tony and I are more equals these days than you might like to think."

He nodded and stood up. "Give me a call when you find out what's going on." He stopped and thought about it. "That is, if you can. I know, with Tony, things get … well, you know what I mean."

I took a sip of the red wine Mario had served with the bruschetta. It had less kick than the whiskey and, thanks to the bruschetta, I was feeling straight again, but comfortable.

"Yep. If it isn't a big secret, or if I can give you a *Reader's Digest* version, I will. I'll talk to you later. I have to go see the parental units anyway and I don't want to have to do that alone."

"And why would you?" The voice was thick with accent and coming from the other side of the darkened restaurant. I'd know that voice anywhere. It had scared me since I was a child and cherished me for the same length of time.

It was Tony.

I stood. Something I learned early in life—showing *respect* is not the same thing as showing fear. They can go hand-in-hand, but they don't have to. There is nothing wrong with being respectful to your elders, even if it is a lot like butt-kissing.

I held out my arms as I approached him. It was expected. We embraced. "You look good. You've been out of state for a while. I can see that tan even in here."

He gave me a little laugh. I glanced over at Marty who was now wondering why he hadn't left when he had the chance. Tony and Marty embraced as well. When Marty pulled back I decided Marty's torture should end, he didn't need to be here.

"Tony, you must excuse Marty. He's been neglecting business to keep me company this morning and he'll have to do it again later to go to our parents'. I really don't want him to lose any business on my account."

"Of course, my little angel. If that's what you'd prefer." He took off his coat and sat in the booth we'd been sitting at.

"I think it's best."

"Very well, it was good to see you again Martin. You look wonderful. We will see you later. You are coming to the family party at the end of the month? I do not recall receiving your confirmation back." He was pressuring. I'd seen him do this a thousand times and at least three quarters of those were directed at Marty.

I knew the problem. We'd been discussing it for the past twenty minutes. Cara. She's Marty's wife and his life. She had a lot of problems with Marty's "family" connections.

"Marty'll be there," I assured Uncle Tony. "But I don't think Cara will be able to make it. Marty said she's been going crazy keeping up with work and things. She doesn't have a free minute. Besides, if they come together, there is always an issue with having to find a babysitter. And with the family attending, it makes it even harder to find a suitable sitter. There are some really dangerous people in the world. You can't trust just anyone these days to watch your children." Hell, we should know.

"That is unfortunately true. Well, if Cara can't come I am sorry, but I would still like to have Martin there. You will join us, won't you?" It sounded like a question, but it wasn't. Marty nodded and said good-bye.

After he was out the door, I turned to Tony. "Why do you do that? You know you scare the shit out of him. Isn't that enough?"

I shook my head and sat back down in my seat. I was about the only person on the planet who would speak to him like that, and I never did it in front of anyone. That would be disrespectful and then it would have to be addressed.

"Your brother has left the safety of the family. It would be better if he started re-associating with his own," he said, arranging his napkin across his lap.

"He did that to protect his kids and his wife. Staying out of family business is best for them. Ignorance is bliss and all that. You shouldn't push him back in. It isn't fair to him or Cara. You know how she feels about it."

"He should have chosen a wife who was more … suited to his family. He chose unwisely."

Mario brought our food, did some effective ass-kissing and left.

"I think you're wrong about Cara." That got me a full-on stare. It wasn't exactly a challenge, but like I said, no one talked to him like this. "She's *good* for him. She's a good wife, she's a good mother and she is tolerant of her in-laws for the most part. She just doesn't want her husband getting killed or arrested. She doesn't want her children growing up fatherless. I don't think that makes her an unwise choice. It makes her the perfect choice. Besides, you know as well as I do that Marty isn't … cold enough—I think that's the best way of putting it—to be involved in family business and not have it bother him. He'd have to change his entire personality. He's too honest and too nice. Honest and nice are not the traits of great wise-guys."

Tony smiled. "You're right. But he should have been toughened up a long time ago." He sighed. "It's too late now isn't it?"

I gave him a slight nod.

"Very well. We'll have to settle for him at the party alone, that is if you can actually get him to attend."

"I might even be able to convince Cara to attend but I don't know why you want them there. If the reasoning is significant enough, I could possibly persuade her. It isn't like you make her do this often."

Every family has obligations. Ours just seem to stretch beyond the average. Cara would consider it, if it were important.

He took a bite of his chicken scampi. "It is to announce your engagement. I think it would be best if your brother and his wife were there."

CHAPTER 2

THE BITE OF FOOD IN MY mouth just fell to the plate. I was in shock.

Engagement? I wasn't getting *married*. I didn't think so at least. I would have *remembered* an engagement, a fiancé.

"What the hell are you talking about?! I am *not* getting married!" The emphasis was on "not."

"Have you lost it? You're delusional! Who the hell would want to marry me? I'm a freaking assassin, for kripe's sakes! I *kill* people! No man, even remotely in his right mind, would ever consider it. And by that logic he'd have to be damn near certifiable! I can't marry some *crazy* person!"

Now I just wanted to vomit. The problem was Mario and Tony's guards had overheard me yelling at Tony. This wasn't done, at least not if you planned on living though the day.

Tony just continued eating. It was as though nothing had happened.

I looked to Mario and then to the others. I stood up, unclipped my gun from the back of my pants and laid it on the table. That got only a mild look from Tony, but he wasn't concerned. He knew I wouldn't kill him. If I did, then that left me in charge of the family—a job I certainly did not want (especially without any notion of how to do it).

We always had a guaranteed standing with each other just because of this. I needed him alive and running the businesses, so I didn't have to, and he needed me alive and available to take over. This kept both of us alive, pretty much no matter what we did, but neither of us ever really pushed it. Of course we both had different acceptability levels on what was "pushing it".

"Would you three please leave us alone?" I said. "This discussion is private." Mario did as I asked immediately. Tony waved at the other two and they went to the front of the restaurant.

I started pacing. "What are you thinking? You can't marry me off. You know that. I *know* you do. Did you promise me to someone already? I can't believe you'd do something like this without discussing it with me first."

I continued to rant and rave for at least another ten minutes while Tony ate. It was as though he expected this reaction … and he *should* have expected it.

Finally he spoke. "Sit down." He dabbed his mouth with his napkin. "Your food is getting cold."

"I'm not hungry." But I sat.

"Very well. You will be getting married. It is a family matter, not a love matter. You don't have to even like him as far as I'm concerned. You don't have to live with him either, although it would look better if you did. We'll just get you a large house so you don't have to see each other. And you cannot kill him. That should be understood before we even begin."

He shifted in his seat. "There are three prospective grooms. You will select one by the end of the month. I have set up meetings with each. By the end of the month you should have spent sufficient time with each to decide what you think of them. I doubt it will take that long. You never did have problems deciding who you *didn't* like fairly quickly." Tony started to call Mario.

"Oh, no," I protested. "It isn't that easy. I want to know *why*. What is the point in this? I am not saying 'I do' to some macho jerk just because you tell me to. Things are not as they were twelve years ago." Hell, twelve years ago he couldn't have gotten me to do this without an explanation either. "I've grown and changed and I'm not getting married just to make you happy. I want to know *why*."

"Fine, I will tell you. But I would like my coffee if you don't mind."

I nodded and he called for Mario who came running like someone had set his ass on fire. Tony ordered coffee and desert. Mario left.

"Well?"

"I will be retiring. I can't keep doing this forever and you are my primary successor, as you well know." The coffee came and he stopped. He started pouring the cream.

"Con-tin-ue." I was frustrated and he knew it. He was enjoying this because I had flipped out earlier. I never explode like that. I always had that calm thing going.

"You need an alliance with one of the other area families. It may be old-fashioned and in your case stupid, but most will view the Pascolis as weak to have a woman running things." He waved his hand at me. "Yes, don't bother getting all women's lib on me, there's no point. I can't change the perception of others without you killing people. And to keep the body count down to a minimum, you need a husband."

"Why right now?" I whined. "Why can't it wait until I've had a chance to really look my options over? I'm not going to risk, not only me, but the entire family by marrying the wrong one. I don't think I can get all the info I need in just a few weeks."

"If I gave you six months you would have ignored it and waited until the last four weeks." I started to protest, but he cut in. "I know you. Don't even bother denying it." He sipped his coffee. "Besides, you have a good eye. You'll know."

"Why these three? Who are they?"

He nodded and took another sip of coffee. "Derek Sampini, Alfonso Merek and Anthony Sheppa. They were chosen because they were single, direct blood to the heads of three of the local families, and not at all unmanageable. You are actually more than capable of running the family on your own. I just want you to have a secondary source of strength. You can run these gentlemen as well as the family."

It made sense, but there were several names that could have been added to that list, providing they weren't married yet ... or dead. "What about Peter Torra, David Merek and Thad and Alex Sevelli?"

He looked disgusted. "Peter got married. David is dead and the other two are in jail. Besides, you would have problems controlling Alex."

Peter getting married was a shock. He was one of the biggest philanderers around. David being dead was even more so. But Thad and Alex's being in jail was beyond my comprehension. Alex was so careful.

"What do you mean jail? When did they end up in jail?"

"Thad was weak, you know that. He sold out Alex and their father for a plea bargain with the state. It still has to go to trial, but there isn't much chance either of them will get out. It's sad really. Roberto is a decent man; played by the rules and always held his territory. He also had a good sense of humor. He won't survive jail." Tony sighed. "Children can be so ungrateful."

I stood up, ready to go. Tony'd finished his dessert and coffee and looked ready to leave as well. I gazed over at him while he put on his coat.

"And you want me to marry a weak man so I can control him? You may want to rethink that." I shook my head. "I'll meet the prospects, but don't cross Alex off the list. As far as I see it, he's the best option I have in this, even if getting to him is a pain in the ass. And if that's the case you may have to delay the announcement a couple weeks."

"How would you get him out? They are using his brother as a witness, and there is a truck load of evidence." Tony stopped and thought about it for a minute. "If you could get them out, Roberto and Alexander, it would probably be a good thing even if you don't choose him. They would make good allies. However, I don't want you getting yourself into trouble to do this."

What was he thinking? I'm one of the best. Get in trouble, my eye. Then I noticed him picking at his watch—it was a sign he was lying about something. But God only knew what. With Tony, it could be anything.

"Do you know where the evidence is being held?" I asked.

He nodded.

"Do you have someone on the inside who could get a note to Alex?"

Again he nodded.

"You should send him one. Make sure he's alright with disposing of the witness. It is his *brother,* after all. I'd hate to overstep my boundaries by killing Thad and then find out that Alex wanted him alive."

"He should have taken care of it himself," said Tony, "before it got to this point. There were plenty of reasons. But he let his brotherly love get in the way. He risked everyone in the family for that one brother who has now sold him and his father out. It isn't good to risk the many for the one. Do you agree?"

He was so right. "I agree, but sometimes it takes a little stay in jail to realize it. Cleaning your own house isn't easy. I'll get him out. It won't even be that hard. Most likely, they only have three copies of the evidence, if that. One in the D.A.'s office, one at the Sevelli's attorneys and then the one in the evidence locker at the county courthouse. That is where it is, isn't it?"

"Yes, but what I'm wondering is how you're going to dispose of them."

He had to have known what I was capable of. This was a walk in the park for me. "Two robberies and a fire. That courthouse is ancient—an electrical fire would be far from surprising and you'd be amazed how quickly an electrical fire can destroy an entire floor of a building predominately full of paper. But I'll try not to take out the floor. I don't want more destroyed than necessary. The law offices will be a piece of cake."

"And our witness?"

"Well, that will require some finesse, but I'd say that brain aneurysms come so unexpectedly and work quickly once they start. One could die without any preexisting signs … or evidence."

"It could be done?"

I nodded.

"We may delay the party then. I want you to meet the other three. If they do not meet your approval …" He stopped as if thinking about it, but then began fidgeting with that damned watch band. "I hadn't even considered the possibility of tying you to a liability such as Thad turned out to be. You're right. It could be a bigger problem to align the family through a weak link."

I was having problems believing that he hadn't contemplated that thought previously, especially with such a recent reminder (and one that should have hit too close to home to be easily overlooked). But if he said so, I wasn't going to contradict him—even if I knew he was lying.

"I'm more concerned," I said, "with the idea of tying me to someone who can't fill my place if I leave town for a while. I need someone who will be almost as strong as I am. Someone the family can turn to if I continue doing contract work occasionally."

Tony shook his head. "I don't approve of your continued work in that area. However, you are right. Your husband must be able to fill your place if you aren't available—even if it's only for appearance sake." He shook his head again. "I don't know what I was thinking."

He leaned into me and kissed my cheek. "I'll send the information through my channels at the prison to Alex and find out how he feels about taking the next step. I will mention to him that you are in need of additional alliances, possibly through marriage, and see how he responds."

Tony and I walked out together. I was pretty sure he was up to something, but no point focusing on it. He wouldn't tell me until he was ready and I knew better than to push.

Tony told me I was scheduled to meet one of the possible future grooms tonight, but I wasn't overly pleased at the prospect. I asked about appropriate attire and he looked me up and down. I think it was the first time he'd paid any attention—I'd always been one of the guys.

"You should probably be a bit more feminine. Not extremely so, that displays weakness, but something a bit more … dressed might be better. You look like one of my enforcers, with a much better figure."

I smiled. "I used to be one of your enforcers and I would hope I have a better figure than Franky or Barry." They both had to weigh in the neighborhood of two-fifty to three hundred pounds. It was a big neighborhood. They're big guys.

He kissed me on the cheek again and climbed into the back of his Caddy.

On the way back to Marty's office I tried to remember what Alex had looked like the last time I'd seen him. He wasn't fashion model good-looking, more like scary good-looking. Not *me* scary, and not *Tony* scary. Tony and I are pretty much the same type of scary. It's an image based on intimidation, and shear force-of-will type scary.

Alex, as I recall, was about six-three and built like a professional weight lifter—not the kind that gets all big and bulky. He was more the well-defined and sculpted weight-lifter type; the kind of man, who, when he wears a T-shirt, he really *wears* it. He was also the sort of guy you know could kick your ass if you didn't fall into line.

Most of the times I'd seen him in the past, he'd been of a brooding nature and it was written all over his features, right up to his eyes. Olive skin tone and dark hair—at least it used to be dark. That was about thirteen years ago.

I could be slightly off by all this. I was younger than he was and always looked at him as a far greater force to be reckoned with than myself. Thinking back, there were only a few actual events that led me to believe that, but when you're young you tend to blow things out of proportion.

The force-to-be-reckoned-with image was the reason Tony had said I'd have problems handling Alex. He was right. In some areas, Alex would be difficult; but in others I think I could probably hold my own now.

To my knowledge he never abused anyone who didn't have it coming, never sold drugs, and didn't have his hands in anything related to child abuse. Thank God, because I can't abide drugs, or any form of child-related abuse. I'd have to kill him instead of getting him out of jail if that were the case.

I know Alex was married once. She was killed about fifteen years ago. Strange thing about this, though—so was her golf instructor. Golf can be a really *dangerous* game … especially when you play with someone else's wife … in the winter … at one of the local motels. Both were shot once in the head. It was never very thoroughly investigated. Go figure.

You would think information like that would make me nervous, but oddly it didn't. In fact, it was actually somehow comforting. I understood the motivation. When the motive is unclear—when it's just for games of power—then I find this behavior disturbing. He'd never married again and had to be in his early forties now. That's a long haul for staying single.

I finally reached Marty's office. It was just about one-thirty. I walked into the office, removed my glasses and the secretary smiled at me this time. She knew I was Marty's sister now, I could tell by her demeanor. He'd tried to reassure her I wasn't some scary nut. Considering, I think he was doing her a great disservice.

"Marty in?"

"Yes, Ms. Pascoli, but his wife is in with him and the children. I don't know if I should disturb them." She was making this little grimace. I'm sure she thought it was cute, but I found it irritating.

"Yes, you should disturb them. I need to speak with both of them and I'd like to see my nieces. Just ring in and let them know I'm here."

She did as I asked. Thinking ahead, I pulled out my gun and placed it on top of the filing cabinet. Jumping and tugging on me (my nieces, that is) was probably a bad idea with a gun at my back—especially considering their mother's feelings on the whole killing-people thing. I liked Cara and didn't want to end up on the same side as Tony where she was concerned.

Marty came out of his office, followed by three wild little girls. They were chasing after him and screaming "Auntie Ace!"

Just then I was attacked by a herd of munchkins. They tickled and wrestled me to the floor. I caught the look that Cara gave Marty. She would have been happier if I weren't there, but she had seen the gun on the filing cabinet and was pleased that I'd at least made the effort to present myself as an appropriate aunt figure.

She didn't want her kids exposed to any part of the family life, including even the "knowledge" that we carry. I could respect that, in the future I'd make an extra effort if I knew the kids would be around.

When the tickle fest was over, I heard about each of their schools and their friends and after school activities. It was about three when someone actually came in to do insurance business. Marty needed to work and the kids, Cara and I all tried to behave in the conference room.

Cara came right out and asked what was going on. I wasn't at all surprised. She was a very direct person, almost as direct as I am. I explained everything, just as I would have given it to Marty. Nothing about Alex, of course, or the activities discussed—just the need for a marriage, Tony's retirement, and who I was supposed to be meeting for matrimonial possibilities.

"So you're really going to take over? I thought Marty was kidding." She looked sick. I knew that fear—it was all for Marty.

"No, sadly it isn't a joke. Most people believed I would, eventually. To be honest though, I thought it would have been a little further in the future. I'd almost convinced myself that he'd given up on me and found someone else. He never mentioned my coming home, even once, in all this time. He wasn't happy I'd gone to work for the government, but there isn't much in the way of replacement material in the family these days. Tony's in his late fifties and he doesn't want to deal with it anymore, or at least that's what he says. I can't blame him … if he's telling me the truth that is. It's a lot of responsibility and work. But it is necessary, or I wouldn't be doing it. I don't want to take over—there just isn't anyone else."

"Couldn't you just let it go? I mean why run the family at all?"

She had a point and I understood it.

"First, because not all of the businesses are legitimate. It would be much easier if they were. I could basically let managers run the businesses independently which, for the most part, I believe the legitimate ones do. But it's the others that are the problem. If I stop protecting them, or shut them down, then the families that rely on that money to pay their rent, feed their kids, and so forth … well, it becomes a problem. And remember, they're not all capable of being legitimized. That means finding jobs within the legitimate businesses for those presently working on the illegal side of things.

"Ideally, that is where I want it all to go, although Tony doesn't know it. I don't like the idea of running a crime organization, but I can't stop it all at once either. The second and most disconcerting reason is territorial disputes. If I don't take the reigns, people will know it—people who are our allies and those who aren't. It would leave everyone in the family exposed to territory wars and vendettas for events that happened under Tony. I can't do that."

"But you want to clean it up? You aren't just going to continue like Tony?" She looked down and shook her head. "He keeps trying to pull Marty back in. He scares both of us. We've talked about moving, but both our families are here. I just wish he'd leave Marty alone."

"I know," I said sympathetically. "He can't seem to help himself. I yelled at him for it today. He was trying to do it at Mario's."

She looked astonished. "What?" she gasped. "You *yelled* at Tony? Nobody yells at Tony." True and smart girl for knowing she shouldn't try it.

"Yes," I confessed, "but, just as I need him, he needs *me*. I am probably the only person alive who will stay alive after yelling at him. He actually got a lot of it today. But I think we came to some understandings—besides he was expecting my explosion. He just sat there and kept eating."

She smiled. "Any of these understandings about Marty?"

"Yes, but he'll still try, even though I've told him to knock it off. Like I said, he can't help it. He knows where I stand about Marty's place with the family. He's a member of our blood family, but not the business family. He doesn't have any obligations there and I don't want him to. It's good for the girls if he stays away from it. He isn't up to family work; it isn't in him."

She nodded in agreement.

"The life you two have now is good for him. That said, he does have responsibilities, like any member of any family. There are times when he has to attend family functions. And the truth is, it would be better if you were with him. I understand not wanting the girls there. Exposing them to some of the family might not be a great idea if you want them to grow up ... well-balanced. But he needs support in dealing with our relatives. They can be ... overwhelming. When the announcement is made at Tony's party, about my marriage, it would not look good if the two of you weren't there—just because he's my brother and you're my sister-in-law and no other reason. Do you understand what I'm getting at?"

I was doing my best to choose my words carefully. I didn't want her any more freaked out about things than she already was. The truth is that my family is more than just overwhelming. They can be suffocatingly oppressive at times and that can have an adverse affect on adults as well as children. At best, a child could end up in therapy for years with a family like ours—dead or in jail were the far more common results. I didn't want that for my nieces any more than Cara.

She nodded. I looked at my watch and it was heading for three-thirty. "I'm supposed to be at Tony's at five for cocktails with the first prospect. We'll see how it goes. Would you let Marty know I won't be going out to the parents' place tonight, so he's off duty?"

I gave the girls each a hug and headed out to the front office for my gun. I had to get a chair to reach it—how embarrassing—and in front of the big-haired blonde. She looked at the gun in horror and then tried to cover it up by pasting on a big smile. I shook my head and left.

You'd think no one in this city carried a gun. Ha! I know better. Practically half of the adults carry, even if they don't have a permit. And I don't want to think about how many underage thugs were wandering around armed.

CHAPTER 3

TONY LIVES IN WHAT MOST would call a mansion. It's really overpowering. It screams money and power. I was sure he did that on purpose. My style is a bit more subdued.

When I arrived, I parked my Cooper out front, put my gun in the glove box and walked to the door. Tony doesn't allow his guests to carry guns when they enter his home. Personally, I think it's a good policy.

Tony's guy-Friday, Jason, was expecting me since I had to be buzzed-in to get through the gates. He looked at me approvingly. Apparently I'd chosen my wardrobe correctly.

I hadn't brought much, but I had brought a variety. When Tony summons, you just never know what's expected of you. I could have been storming a fortress, attending a charity function, or my own wedding.

Okay, that last thought was a little depressing. I still didn't want to get married, but maybe I'd change my mind. Maybe one of these guys would be so great I couldn't contain myself. Yeah, right, and maybe I'd see a cow jump over the moon on my way back to the hotel. No point thinking about it. I couldn't change it, so I might as well go with the flow.

I was announced in the library by Jason and went into the room. I was dressed perfectly, considering those who'd already arrived. I was wearing straight-leg black silk pants, a red silk button-down blouse, unbuttoned about half-way, and four-inch black heels. My jewelry was always kept to a minimum—basic pearls, earrings and choker. It gets in the way in a fight. And you just never know …

I had pulled my hair up into a chignon to keep it off my neck. Besides, it looks dressier than leaving it down.

"Angelica, so good of you to make it. You're just a few minutes late." Tony was making a point that I knew he would before I walked into the room. His guest was there so I couldn't be nasty about it—and he knew that as well.

"Well, it's fashionable for a lady to arrive several minutes late; it builds anticipation." I walked over and poured myself a glass of scotch. I was going to need it, especially if the young man sitting in the wing-backed chair was one of the prospectives. He didn't look like he could be more than seventeen, but I'm sure he was or he wouldn't have been considered. But I have noticed, as I get older, that people under twenty-five look like teenagers to me.

Tony walked around his desk and approached me. He leaned in close and whispered, "You shouldn't drink too much. You need a clear mind for this."

I whispered back, imitating a kiss on the cheek. "Yes, but I may need it not to kill the little weasel. He looks a bit younger than I had expected."

Tony smiled and pulled back. "Angelica, sweetheart, this is Alfonso Merek. I believe you remember his brother, David. David is, sadly, no longer with us—such a shame."

It was then that I looked directly at Alfonso. He was young, yes, but there was something in those eyes when David was mentioned. David had been stronger than average in personality; attractive and loyal to the end. I'd been raised with David as my counterpart in the Merek family. He was three years older than me and ready to take over his family even before I'd left twelve years ago.

Alfonso was something else entirely. If I didn't know better, I'd have said the look on his face was one of faint amusement; like he was gloating, or proud of himself. Within seconds I knew what it was. He hadn't even spoken and I'd known. He'd killed David to gain his position in the family.

I turned to Tony. "I don't mean to be rude, but would it be alright if I spoke with you alone for a moment. Maybe we could offer Alfonso a drink while we're gone. It will only be a moment." I smiled graciously at both of them and Tony conceded. He took my arm and we stepped down the hall to another doored room. It was a large parlor.

"You know he killed David, don't you ... for his place in the family?" I hissed. "It was right there on his face when you mentioned David's name. His eyes were shining, gloating, reflecting pride in his accomplishment. This is a very sick young man and there is not a chance in hell I'm tying myself to *that*."

He looked like I'd slapped him. It was suddenly clear to me that Tony hadn't known.

"I didn't know," he confirmed. "He hides it well. If his father had known he probably would have killed Alfonso and passed the position to another family member. But," he beamed, "I knew this elimination process would take you no time at all." He smiled. "We must make the appearance, but we'll get rid of him in an hour or so. Just go through the motions. You are scheduled to meet the second one at seven." He started to leave.

"You mean you've scheduled me to meet all three this evening, haven't you?"

He nodded. "I thought it best to get this out in the open as soon as possible. I don't like pulling strings for long. People in positions such as this do not like being puppets."

I frowned. "Do they *know* why they're here? The marriage I mean? And have you told any of them you are planning to retire? It could make a difference in the interest level." Also in how badly they'll feel when they're rejected.

"I have told the fathers of the candidates that I would like you to marry. I have not told them that I am so close to insisting on it. And no one knows of my retirement, with the exception of yourself and, I assume, your brother?" He knew I'd tell Marty that much.

"And Cara," I said, nodding. "I asked them to keep it quiet until things are announced. I think they both felt better about my being called home when they found out the reason."

"Good. We must go now, before our friend gets anxious."

Wasn't that the truth … we didn't want an anxious killer on our hands, now did we?

I spent the next hour and fifteen minutes being polite, smiling and gracious. I really hate having to pretend to be someone I'm not. If I were myself, however, no one would be interested. And at that moment, I was thinking that might not be such a bad idea, especially considering the present company.

Finally Alfonso took Tony's hint from fifteen minutes earlier and left. Tony walked him out and I went to the piano.

I had played since I was a child and, like my education, I had taken to it like a duck to water. My teacher thought me a prodigy and in this my parents, or at least my mother, held hopes of my becoming a nice, feminine, classical pianist. I loved music, but it just didn't have the adrenaline boost I craved.

I had played for a good ten minutes before Tony returned. He sat in front of the fireplace and watched me. It was something he had done even when I was young, so it never made me overly self-conscious. When I stopped he met my gaze.

"Who's next?"

"Anthony Sheppa. Are you absolutely certain about Alfonso?"

"The longer I watched him, the more sure I was. He is egotistical and self-involved. He seems to have no real interest in the welfare of his family's developments and he behaves like he's acting all the time. It isn't real. What he's showing on the outside is completely and thoroughly false. But what's underneath … it isn't good. He wouldn't feel the need to hide himself so completely if he had anything worth showing. He's ambitious, but not in a good way. He has no intention of working for the good of the family, just his own self-interest. I think he'd sell his mother out. And I'm positive he killed his brother."

Tony chuckled and took a sip of his drink. "I take it you didn't like him?"

I started playing again softly. "No. I wouldn't even consider bringing him into the family. He's a dangerous choice for everyone concerned.

Especially since you made it clear I couldn't kill him."

The next prospect was invited to stay for dinner. Anthony Sheppa was a nice guy—too nice if you ask me. He gave the appearance of being weak. To be perfectly honest, he reminded me of my brother. He didn't belong in this business, but he'd been pushed and prodded and here he was. I would have bet my eyeteeth he had a nice girl he dated regularly and was hoping to marry.

Obviously, my marrying him would have been a remarkably bad idea. Not just for Anthony's sake, or his girlfriend's, but for my own and the family's. He didn't have the spine to make the kind of decisions a leader is required to make. This was the reason I continued to support Marty's wish to stand outside the family lines. They both needed the instincts of a tiger but, sadly, had only those of a pussycat. They'd be eaten alive (and they probably knew it).

I liked Anthony Sheppa, but he wasn't for me. He and I would see each other again and I was glad. Like I said, he was nice. But not husband material. We said our goodbyes and Tony came into the library after me.

"So, when is number three expected?" I asked.

"Nine, for drinks. You haven't said how you feel about Anthony. You seemed to like him."

He was fishing. Did he really believe this was even possible? I was starting to wonder about Tony's judgment when it came to people. I knew, deep inside, that his judgment had always been sound. Therefore, he already had to know the answer. Maybe this was some sort of test.

"I really don't mean to be disrespectful here, but did you completely miss it?" I replied.

He just smiled.

"You did see it," I confirmed. "He isn't *family* material. How can he possibly be a direct line to inherit if he's so … nice? He reminds me of Marty. We can't tie *me* to nice. I have enough *nice* to protect. If we do, I'll be running his house, as well as ours," I said.

"Yes, but he is a better choice than Alfonso, true?"

He had a point there. Being married to a brainless gorilla would be better than Alfonso. "Yes, but only because an alliance with Alfonso would be worse than staying single. I honestly don't think either is appropriate." I thought about what I'd just said. "And to be truthful, if we don't find an appropriate fit, single may be a better choice than Anthony as well. Running one family is hard enough. If I have to take over the Sheppa's businesses, it would be far more than I could handle alone and Anthony isn't up to it."

"You may be right," he agreed but he didn't look happy. "But, let's not give this up yet. We still have Derek, and at worst, there is always Alex." He studied me. "I don't like the idea of Alex, but he may actually be a much better husband for you. You have changed, as you said. You picked up on things I completely missed about Alfonso and Anthony, at least on my first meetings with them. Alex could run things in your absence and he commands respect. But this, of course, is contingent on getting him out, and your ability to handle him. I don't want you under his thumb."

I almost laughed. "That makes two of us."

The third one arrived at nine o'clock on the dot. The only word I can think of to describe him is "greasy." He talked about business, which was good, but when we dipped into the "detail" information, I discovered the little shit had conned me. It takes a lot to con me.

He had no idea, whatsoever, about running any business, much less a family business. When I discussed present socio-economic issues with him, he looked like I had slapped him upside the head. He didn't have a clue when we discussed a number of other topics that I happen to find interesting: books, music and art. We soon found that Mr. Sampini didn't read. He could read, thank God for small favors, but *Playboy* seemed to be the extent of his reading pleasure. He liked hard rock and rap music and, as far as art went, I would have to say that *Three Dogs Playing Poker* and Elvis on black velvet would be his type of thing.

I'm not a snob, but there is no reason, in this day and age, that a person can't learn to appreciate the niceties that life has to offer. Mr. Sampini was, for lack of a better word, tacky.

When he left I was exhausted from having to be polite to an idiot. I know that shouldn't take work but, for me, it takes more work to deal with a moron for twenty minutes, than to run five miles. I just don't have it in me; it's just another one of my major faults.

I was getting another drink and this time I didn't have to stay sober. There were no more prospects. That was a blessing and a curse. There was no way I could marry any of them. I heard Tony walk in.

"He's an *imbecile*," I growled. "There is no way I can possibly stand in front of a priest and swear to take care of that man. I'd kill him by the end of the second day … and I believe that my *not* killing the new husband was one of your restrictions?"

He was almost as annoyed by the last one as I was. I caught him several times, pasting on his diplomatic look. I know that look. It's the one he uses when dealing with people he doesn't like. He poured himself a drink, his larger than mine and took a big swig.

"You can not possibly marry that. He was stupid, downright stupid. Where do these people get their education? Finding you a husband was supposed to be easy. It should have been. You're incredibly intelligent, attractive, resourceful, experienced in dealing with family matters. You know how to behave … even when you don't want to. You are a perfect wife for someone in our family's line of business. But these men are awful."

He moved across the room and sat on one end of the couch. I sat on the other. "I was thinking while the last one was jabbering along," he mused. "I couldn't even think of one who's married who would be a good choice."

He shook his head. "We have to get Alex out of prison. I just hope he agrees to the terms."

What the hell? "Terms? I thought you weren't going to levy terms. I thought it was just going to be a general alliance for assisting him, and then if things looked promising, we'd pursue it."

"I know, but you just saw the alternatives." He waved his hand toward the door. "Trust me, at a distance they all looked much bet-ter. It's too bad Anthony doesn't have more backbone. He was at least pleasant and well educated."

I couldn't argue. He had been very pleasant. "I'm betting he has a young lady—probably a nice respectable one. He, most likely, got thrown into this by his father. I'm not the one for him, but I don't know about promising anything to Alex. It might be best to offer him release in exchange for an alliance, then discuss a marriage after he and I have had a chance to feel each other out."

Now that just didn't come out right at all and it got me a raised eyebrow from Tony. "That wasn't what I meant. I mean he's a *little* intimidating and it might be nice to know if I can handle …" Damn, almost did it again. "… his personality before we commit to marriage."

"I see your point. But what if we get him out and he then refuses? He isn't known for wanting a wife. I'm sure you know his first marriage didn't work out so well."

I nodded.

"And he already has a sizable organization of his own. He doesn't need to marry. You do. "

"I thought you said you didn't want me under his thumb and you wanted me to be able to manage him?" Things were now freaking me out a bit. Spending the rest of my life attached to one of the scariest people I'd ever known, at least as a teen, was making me panicky.

"Figure out how … you're a smart girl. I've never overestimated you. I have on occasion underestimated, but never *over*. I think you can manage Alex. But it will be work."

I took a deep breath and blew it out. On that note Tony stood up and said good night.

Okay, that was it, end of discussion. I was marrying Alex, whether he wanted a wife or not. This should be interesting, especially considering I hadn't seen him in thirteen years. What if he was bald and fat and … ? Well, one trait would definitely still be there—he'd be scary, as always. Pissed as well, since he'd been tossed in jail. Not a good combination for a future groom.

CHAPTER 4

IT WAS FOUR DAYS LATER THAT Tony and I were sitting across the table from each other for breakfast. I'd moved into his house, mostly for convenience. Tony thought it didn't look good for me to be in a hotel. He said it was un-familial ... right, my ass! I swear the man just wanted to keep his eye on me. Every time I came in or left it was documented with his security people. This un-familial thing had forced me into the life I'd had as a fourteen year-old. It really sucked.

Jason came into the breakfast room with a note for Tony. After reading it, Tony looked to me. I, of course, was shoveling in my scrambled eggs. "Well, Alex has agreed. He wants the matters we discussed taken care of." With that said, Tony went back to his breakfast.

I wondered at times if the man knew the meaning of the word communication. He was often abrupt and, as Marty said, he kept it all close to the vest. So there were times, like now, when you had to pry information out of him. "You're sure he knows that ..." I glanced over to Jason.

Total trust ran between us, but I didn't want to incriminate myself either. Jason was loyal to the end, but under interrogation ... well, he might not be quite so steadfast with the possibility of a long prison sentence looking him in the eye. So why take the chance?

"Jason," I said, "would you please get me a cup of hot tea from the kitchen, milk only please." He nodded and left. I looked back to Tony. "He knows I'm getting rid of Thad? I don't want there to be a misunderstanding on that." Tony handed me the letter to read for myself.

Dear Friend,

I was pleased with the possibilities you mentioned. I have not seen Ace since she was in her late teens, but the prospect sounds conducive to both families. Dad isn't as physically fit as he was at one time. This place is taking its toll. T. can no longer rely on family connections. And I myself am more than happy to completely sever them. I should have taken care of the problem myself before it came to this. Hindsight has always been clear, but I can do little about it from this location.

Please consider this an agreement to all previously mentioned stipulations, including all necessary removals and the union.

I look forward to hearing from you soon.

A. S.

Blowing out a sigh, "Well, I guess it's time for me to go to work." I looked up and Jason had returned with my tea. "Thank you, Jason." He set it down and I took a sip.

It was an odd thing, that I'd developed such a fondness for tea—not to say I didn't still love my coffee. However, I was stationed in *England* for almost a year and that one little piece of English routine had stuck with me.

Jason left, as I hoped he would, but knowing the real reason I had asked him for the tea. Again, I trusted Jason, but it's never a good idea to mention more than necessary in front of anyone, even those you trust.

"Do you have everything you need?" Tony asked.

"Yes, I called in two favors and the removal situation shouldn't be hard. I'll be given access to a secure location and I have the necessary chemical. It came yesterday. It's a topical—just a touch on the skin and it's done. It isn't fast. It'll take several days, but it can't be traced in an autopsy and no one will ever connect it to me—not even the person who lets me in.

"The other locations have to be timed, but I have a couple days." I took another sip of the tea.

Over the rim of my cup I lifted my eyes to Tony. "When everything is done, Alex's attorney is going to have to make a stink to get them out, and an even louder stink to get them to release his land and personal holdings. They may release him and then stumble around, hoping to get something else on him, so they can put him back in prison before they release his finances." It was fear of flight—not that I, or anyone else in the families, would ever expect Alex to run from a fight. It just wasn't in him.

"They won't want to," I continued, "but without evidence or a witness, they can't hold someone or his material possessions for long. Alex is also going to have to make sure nothing can be found. He may want a couple of his people do some cleaning up, if it hasn't already been done. The D.A. is going to be desperate."

With a slight nod he responded. "I'll make sure he knows. So what are you doing today?"

"Well, I have three locations to case, so I think I'll start with the easiest first. Alex is using Max, right?" Tony inclined his head just enough to be interpreted as assent. "I think it would be best if people thought we were planning to announce our engagement prior to his incarceration."

"And why is that?" he inquired.

"For two very good reasons. First, we don't want the other families offended that I rejected their offspring. Second, it won't blatantly look as though I had anything to do with getting Alex and Roberto out. Because I've left them there this long, no one would *openly* infer I'd done anything to get them out now. So, you may also want to let Alex know about that as well."

"So you are off to Max's?"

Max was easiest access for me and I was taking advantage. I nodded. "He isn't the enemy. I'll simply stop by his office, say hello and introduce him to the idea that I'm Alex's fiancée. Give him some nice excuse like I'm looking for a mailing address, or have questions regarding Roberto's health issues. Max goes to his file and, *voilà*, I know where they keep the file. Besides, Max and I have a history. He'll make it easy on me. I think I'll check out the county courthouse afterwards. Is the D.A.'s office still located in the courthouse?"

"They moved across the street," said Tony. "They're now in a large old brick building that's been renovated for offices. They're located on the second floor."

How convenient … Possibly, I can get the two evidence sets out of the offices *and* set the fire all on the same evening—right after Thad is taken care of. Not bad for one night's work. Of course I needed to consider the ramifications; no one with any brains does something like this without research.

"Good. I can check out the alarm system while I'm at it. Maybe find out who installed it—that might be useful," I muttered, thinking I needed to get going.

"Cheeper's Alarms installed it," Tony grumped. "Cheeper" wasn't just his name. He was also more than a little thrifty when it came down to his security systems and he often installed pure crap. "Montgomery Cheeper was bragging to anyone who would listen about all the municiple jobs he gets. That office was one of them."

The average systems are a couple of *real* cameras, a number of fakes, and a basic alarm that goes off if doors or windows are opened. But alarms don't go off when windows are cut out and climbed through. You know all the laser beams and high tech floor plates and heat sensitive stuff you see in movies? Well, most of that is much too expensive for real companies with everyday businesses. You have to be a very safety-conscious organization or totally paranoid to install something like that.

Municipalities are not paranoid and they have a budget, usually a small one. And that, alone, explained how Cheeper had gotten the job. The only place where I might have a problem with the security was at the county courthouse evidence lockup. But the building was old. Truth be told, it was on the town historical ledger. It was an original piece of the town's architecture and that was good for me. It may have been a pain to wire an alarm in the basement where the evidence lockup was located. That means as long as I can handle the cameras, no problem, I'm in.

I changed into a black business suit, white silk button down, with the top three buttons open, and four inch heels. I pulled my hair up into a chignon again and headed for Alex's attorney.

✳ ✳ ✳

Parking in the building's parking garage; I took the elevator to the fourth floor where the law offices reside. Alex's attorney was Max Dressari. He's an older man and has been a family lawyer, including the Pascoli's for at least twenty-five years.

He's tall, thin, with a receding hairline (mostly silver now) and very Italian. He's kind of crass and harsh at times, but when you think about the people he spends his days with, it isn't really all that surprising. The guy had wise-guys popping out of the woodwork.

I spoke with the front desk receptionist and she buzzed Max. I was glad I had just popped in—it looked better than making an appointment. That way, I wouldn't have a scheduled appointment in their books if anyone bothered to check.

"Ace Pascoli, I haven't seen you in at least ten years!" He leaned over me and gave me a hug.

"It's actually been closer to fourteen. I believe that was the last time you got Franky out of trouble before I left." The oaf had broken some guy's arm in a bar brawl and Max had to smooth things over with him to keep him from pressing charges. It would have almost certainly been a last-straw-event for Franky. He'd been in trouble so much during that period that a judge, even a family-friendly one, would have probably given him a minimum of a year behind bars just to make a point.

Max invited me back to his office. It was a nice office. Lots of beige and black, accented with nice wood pieces, paintings and a sofa. He was doing well. But then again, successful criminals do pay well when they need his services.

"So Ace, what are you doing here? You look amazing by the way. You haven't been home in years from what I understand. What's going on … of course, you know anything you tell me is strictly confidential, as always."

He had a point. This was completely confidential and he never repeated anything. He had a jaw of iron—nothing leaked. I knew that, as did every other criminal in town. Otherwise he wouldn't be sitting across the desk from me. He'd be long dead. Blabber mouth lawyers and family don't tend to do well together ... if you get my drift.

"Well, this is the general situation. I'm engaged to marry Alexander Sevelli. It was arranged prior to his ... unfortunate incarceration. The marriage was arranged because Tony's considering retirement and there is an overall need in the family for me to have a strong marriage connection." Just saying this made my stomach clench ... *marriage*.

"I had no idea you and Alex had this arrangement. He never said anything." He glanced down at his hands on the desk and then back up at me. "To be perfectly honest, considering the present situation, and his brother's testimony, you and Tony may want to find another association."

I looked him directly in the eye. "I don't think so. He was carefully selected and I'm not all that worried about Alex's present situation. I'm a little more concerned with his father's, though. I know this is a little out of the ordinary, but I was wondering if you have anything in the file about Roberto's health. I know that Alex mentioned that he wasn't taking well to prison life. We really don't want anything happening to him."

His face lit up like a kid at Christmas. "So you don't think this will come to trial?" I couldn't blame him for his curiosity. I was betting Alex was a good client.

"I'd be very, very surprised if it did." I glanced about the office. I couldn't help looking at the paintings on the far wall; they were quite good. I loved art and had been collecting it for years. "Did you know that I have a license to practice law in New Jersey?" He shook his head. "Yes, well, I finished my master's in law just before I left. I sat for the bar and was licensed in all the states I thought I might need to be, hence, New Jersey. Do you know I've never been given a full tour of your facility? If you have time, I'd love to see where your archives and file logs are kept. I bet with all the cases you've worked on there's a small mountain of paper work hiding around here someplace." I gave him my best pretty girl smile ... it sort of hurt. I don't use it often.

I was fairly certain I'd gotten my point across by the twinkle in his eye. He shook his head and continued. "Ace you have always astonished me. Maybe we can have a look in the Sevelli folder and see if there is anything on ... Roberto's health." He stood and walked to the door. "Are you really a licensed attorney?"

I nodded.

"You scare me sometimes. You and Alex are really perfect for each other." He held the door for me as I walked out.

"I'll take that as a compliment."

He gave me a very thorough tour of the office and offered me a job if I wanted it.

I thought that might actually be interesting. A criminal defending criminals—what a novel idea.

"When will I be hearing from you again?" he asked speculatively.

Good question. "I don't know that you will. You'll receive an invitation to the engagement party, naturally. I'll expect you to make sure that the groom-to-be gets there when things become a little more pliable."

He nodded, but looked concerned.

"Don't worry; you'll know when they've become pliable. It was very good to see you and I'll think about the job offer." I turned on my heel and left.

One down, two to go. The county courthouse and the municipal building are located just two blocks down on the same street. Still, quite convenient.

I made my way through the front doors of the municipal building. They'd done a great job restoring it. It looked almost new, but still retained a feel of history. I walked down the main hall looking at the various bulletin boards, pretending to be interested in a large garage sale taking place next weekend. I noticed there was only a minimal security system on the main doors and windows. There was only a single camera on the main entry door as well. However, it still might be better to make my entrance from the offices above.

A quick ride in the elevator to the second floor gave me the opportunity to casually examine the layout of the elevator security. Again, there was a single camera and nothing else. I made my way to the District Attorney's office. At the backside of the building I noticed a small window at the end of the hall.

There was a camera on the same wall as the upstairs back window, facing away from the window. It would be possible to come through there and never be seen. Cheeper should be sued for putting a camera in a position like that on the backside of a building. It was asking for someone to break in. But I had to wonder, did the nice man screw up anything in the office itself?

When I walked through the office doors, the receptionist was having an argument with someone on the phone. It sounded a lot like a boyfriend argument. I sat in the chair in the main lobby, closest to the inner hall entrance that led to the back of the office. I picked up a magazine and began flipping pages. When she turned slightly in the other direction, during an intense exchange with her other-half, I slipped into the main office. A girl can't ask for anything easier than that.

There were several cameras in the main office. They were all very small, well hidden, and chances were that the employees didn't even know they were there. Hell, they were probably making notes on who stole pens and paperclips from the office. I made a very quick round and slipped out a side door from the back area. It had all gone very well.

This wasn't anything a climbing rope, a glass cutter and a black mask couldn't take care of. I needed to find out if they employed a guard at night, but I doubted it. If they went with Cheeper for their security system, they weren't taking their security very seriously … or they didn't have any money to spend. I'd bring my infra-red glasses just in case, but with the minimal security on the windows and doors, the chances of needing them would be negligible.

Crossing the street, I spied the windows to the basement where the evidence lock-up was maintained. They were extremely small, about two-and-a-half feet by one. I walked around to the back of the building to get a better look, hopefully, without being noticed.

I was right. The windows had a basic latch connection, recognition type of alarm set up, but the glass was free of alarm triggers. I could cut out the glass and climb right through. But if I were going to make it look like a wiring problem, I couldn't very well cut the glass—that would sort of give it away. I could, however, reroute the window trigger. It was a simple process and I would have no problem getting through the little window.

Getting to any of it without someone knowing, until the day I went in for the actual job, would be impossible. This was annoying, but not all that troublesome. I'd just have to locate the appropriate evidence pile, start the fire close and help it along, if necessary. I knew the building wouldn't burn to the ground—they'd have a decent sprinkler system. But in that area of the basement I may have to disconnect it to get the effect I needed.

I didn't need pictures to work from. I just needed time to think about all of the possibilities. I also needed to prep for my trip to see Thad.

Chapter 5

IT WAS TEN IN THE MORNING when I sat on a picnic table bench in the prison courtyard. Larry would make sure Thad came to see me. He'd made me promise I wasn't going to kill Thad there in the courtyard. He didn't want to take the heat. I couldn't blame him. If the situation were reversed I'd feel the same way. But it wasn't a problem since it would take several days for the effects of the poison to take.

From a distance I saw Thad approaching. I hadn't seen him in years and he looked very little like Alex, at least as far as my memory recalled. He was thinner, not as muscular and didn't give off an impression of overwhelming power. He was merely a guy. Not an impressive guy. Not even an attractive guy, just an everyday schlep.

Now, I normally fully investigate any contract I take. I'm particular as to whom I kill (and don't kill). I have, although not with anyone's knowledge, ensured that certain contracts are never taken, or that the contractor was eliminated instead. Not nice I know, but sometimes necessary.

This all started when a drug dealer attempted to hire me to kill a priest. At the time I was still on the government "Company" payroll, but I tended to freelance occasionally. Apparently, the priest was trying to get the local kids off drugs and involved in the community. He was having a high success rate with the kids and a negative effect on the dealer's income. Sorry, but I don't take out members of the clergy.

I'm not overly religious. I was born and raised Catholic, but I haven't been to mass since I was in my teens (and forced even then). However, there are so few people who go out of their way to really help others that I look at them in the same way I would any other endangered species.

Unfortunately, eliminating possible employers is looked down on in my line of business. It would make people reluctant to hire me, so I try to keep that little piece of info under my hat.

As with all of my previous contracts, I investigated Thad. He had been a junky for at least six years and heaven only knew what detox in prison was doing to his system. He'd sold out his aging father who was now retired from family business. He'd also sold out his older brother who had tried to protect him, and he had made the family that had raised and cared for him vulnerable to outside aggression—not to mention that the family had lost a critical leader with Alex in jail.

All of this bothered me, but I think what really bothered me is that he did this because he'd been caught with enough heroine to get the entire city of Trenton high for a month. It was found in the back end of his SUV during a routine stop for a speeding violation.

He was dealing without the knowledge of the family. Alex would have forced him to stop if he'd known, but Thad had to feed his habit somehow, and my guess was he'd been way beyond the limit with regard to Alex's understanding and compassion. From my point of view this was going to be a mercy killing all the way around.

I glanced over at Thad who was making his way toward me. He didn't recognize me yet. I was wondering if I'd have to force physical contact. It wouldn't look good to Larry if I did.

I was wearing my black car coat and black leather gloves, under which I wore plastic gloves, since I didn't want to kill myself in the process of administering the poison. It was in my pocket and needed to be applied just to the underside of my glove. I slid my hand under the table, took the vial out, poured a small amount into my palm, rubbed it into the glove, and put the vial back.

Thad was smoking and his movements were jerky. Well ... I could see detox was progressing nicely. "Thad, how are you?"

He gave me the jackass smile that said, "Hey, I know I'm hot"... *not.* Clearly, he was still a cocky little prick. I leaned into him, took his hand in mine and kissed him on the cheek.

The deed was done—no force necessary. Once applied to the skin, the poison reacted to body heat and was absorbed into the blood stream. It would take several days for the full effect, but it would be untransferable in a few minutes. Now I had to sit here and have a conversation with him. That was the sucky part.

"Come, sit down." I gestured to the picnic table.

He joined me on the bench. "Ace? When did *you* get back? Nobody's heard from you in years. I thought you went to work for the government."

Now see, that *was* a good cover and I hadn't even thought of it. I must be losing my touch, or was it just my mind … ugh! This whole marriage thing was throwing me off.

"Yep, it's me. I just got home. I heard through the grapevine that you'd turned state's evidence and I thought, since I was in the area, I'd swing by and see how things are going." I glanced around the prison yard. "I know it isn't *The Plaza*, but it isn't *Siberia* either."

He took a long drag off of his cigarette. He was looking me up and down. That's one thing I hate about dealing with prisoners—they don't get to see women for long hauls, so they tend to be a bit sexually starved.

"Yeah, I only have to stick it out until the trial—then I'll have served all my time. But if Alex or Dad has his way, I won't make it out of here. It's a good thing I stashed some cash 'cause I'm gonna need it when I get out. I'm gonna have to disappear or I won't live long. You know how Tony is? Well, Alex is worse. Seriously vengeful, you know? Hell, he killed his own wife. I mean, he stood there and pulled the trigger himself."

Only way to go as far as I was concerned; you should never ask someone else to do what you aren't willing to do yourself. Just my opinion of course, but some people don't have the stomach for it.

Thad let out a long exhalation of smoke. I don't usually smoke anymore, but today I could use one myself. I sat with him for another half hour before Larry said time was up. I kissed Thad on the cheek and said good-bye for the last time. Okay, maybe I was having a slight twinge of guilt. I don't get it often but, as a rule, I don't personally know the individual I'm offing either. However, I think it had more to do with how scared he seemed of Alex. The truth was that he *did* deserve this, so I needed to focus on that.

As soon as Thad left, I removed my gloves, turning them inside out. I tucked them in the little plastic bag which held the vile, sealed it, and put it in my pocket.

Well, that much was done. Within the next four days, the rest would fall into place.

Chapter 6

IT WENT WITHOUT EVEN THE slightest hiccup. Thad was gone three days later—peacefully from what we understood. He died in his sleep from natural causes. I removed only the necessary information from the two law offices, deleted the computer files and set the fire on the fourth night. The fire only managed to consume three groups of evidence; one of those was the Sevelli's. And, as I'd suspected, Max went to work on getting a family-friendly judge to release Alex and Roberto based on lack of evidence.

After the robberies, I'd kept the evidence, stashing it in one of my homes. Actually, it was a house I'd once used as my office, way back when. Now it was more or less empty, with the exception of stacks of banker boxes containing my old leasing agreements, tax returns and other miscellaneous paperwork. The boxes made great camouflage—it was like hiding a needle in a haystack. Anyone snooping would become thoroughly frustrated. After the first thirty or forty boxes, they'd give up.

On the other hand, I didn't want to lose track of the information about Alex in those evidence files. It never hurts to know your future husband's bad side as completely as possible. Not that I couldn't guess (and that was continuing to make me nervous). But in case my imagination was playing tricks on me, physical proof just might come in handy at some point.

The stink Max made was truly impressive. I had a new-found respect for him. He dug out precedents from places I wouldn't have even thought to look. Three weeks later, the Sevellis were released from jail, but the D.A.'s office was still holding their property and money. I believe they said something about paperwork and six to eight weeks. Max would fight that with all he had to get it done more quickly.

The D.A.'s office was furious, but couldn't do a damn thing about it and had no evidence against anyone, including me. There were two videos of a male, about five-feet-six-inches tall, dressed all in black and wearing a mask, but they couldn't use it to identify anyone. Chest taping may not be comfortable, but it works like a charm for gender confusion, and lifts were great for throwing off height perception.

The party was set for Saturday evening and the Sevellis were to be released on Friday morning … talk about cutting it close.

Personally, I was a nervous wreck. I'd be seeing Alex tonight for the first time in many years. He and Roberto would both be staying at Tony's because of the property-release problems. They could have stayed with other family members but, because of the engagement announcement, they decided to accept Tony's offer.

I was sitting at the dining table, eating breakfast, across from Tony. He and I had discussed a number of family operational details over the past few weeks. Taking over for him was going to be difficult. He had his hands in everything from industrial theft to toasters that fell off the back of trucks—the broadness and width of the theft spectrum amazed me. There was money being laundered through the few family businesses that were actually legitimate, like Mario's. I was going to have a time sorting through it all and restructuring. What a freaking nightmare!

"I thought we'd start with the imports we deal with today, if that's fine with you?" Tony supplied.

"I think I need a day off. I'm feeling fidgety and I don't think I'd be much good for working today. I wouldn't be able to focus." I was having problems getting food down, much less anything else.

With a slight nod, he said, "It's Alex's release. You're understandably worried about what you've gotten into. It will be fine." He sounded very calm but I knew he was as worried as I was. The difference was that he could distract himself with work. I preferred other things.

"Maybe, but I won't really be alright with "all this" until Alex and I spell out the terms of our marriage. I really want to know where we both stand." My stomach was churning and I wanted out of here—now. "I think I'll take one of the dirt bikes up to the hills today. It'll distract me and give me a chance to relax. Besides, if the state runs its prisons like the rest of the legal system, it will probably take all day to get them processed out."

"You have a point," he agreed, gruffly. "However, I would like you home for dinner. Hopefully, they will have arrived by then and you and Alex can speak."

"Remember, he's been in prison for over a month now," I reminded Tony. "I doubt he's has a decent night's sleep since he went in. It might be good if you let them go to their rooms and rest a bit, before you start badgering them with that family dealing and agreements thing. Alex isn't known for his smooth temperament. He's easily annoyed, even with sleep. He'll probably be a bear without it."

That got me nothing more than another nod. "If you are going riding, please take someone with you. I don't want you to hit a tree or something. And try to be careful. Remember when you broke your leg and arm two years ago? I know you enjoy living dangerously, but sometimes you take it to extremes."

He was right. But he must have heard about the incident from Marty. I didn't remember sharing that event with him.

That whole incident could have been avoided if I'd just kept my mind on what I was doing instead of getting cocky. I hate to say it, but I deserved what I got. Just as I was leaving the scene of a job, the police actually caught up with me—very poor planning on my part. I took my bike off the side of a bridge abutment that ran over a major highway and landed on top of a semi, about number six in a long convoy of trucks headed south.

Amazing as it may seem, that wasn't a problem. Even jumping the bike off the front of the truck and onto the road didn't present any problems, other than maybe giving the driver a heart attack. The actual crash came much later when I reached the road a mile from my house.

I skidded out on a dirt patch—pure stupidity on my part. I was so high from the adrenaline rush after the "semi jumping" that I got overly-confident. Arrogance can get you killed if you're not careful.

"I can take Jason. I'm sure he'd like out for a while, or I can call one of the Peretti boys. I'm sure they're up to it."

"No Perettis," he growled. "You are getting married to Alex and those three all look at you like you're a piece of … cheesecake. They have since you were a teen. Forget it."

Like I'd give any of them the time of day, "That was years ago," I countered. "Besides, aren't they all married now?"

"Two are married, one is divorced. And, to my knowledge, marriage has never stopped any of them before. No, you can take Jason. He won't be needed until later. And you're right, he could use some time out." Tony stood to leave the room. "I thought I should let you know. Alex will be put in the bedroom that adjoins yours. I think it best that the two of you have access to one another."

I was about to protest that this was a marriage of business, not love, but Tony held up a hand to ward off the statement. "You two have not seen each other in years and you also have not discussed marriage terms. You both have very strong … personalities. It would be best if everyone else in the house didn't have to listen to the two of you during negotiations. And, I am fairly certain that whether or not he shares your bed is going to be up for discussion."

"You think he's going to want us to have a *real* marriage? Not just business?" Now, this was the first time he'd implied anything of this sort.

"You are an extremely attractive woman. He is not an unattractive man. The two of you are possibly compatible, even with the age difference. I believe there are only eight years between you. You have similar personalities, likes and dislikes. And most of all, Alex has no children. I believe he wants them. It was the reason he married the first time."

He waved his hand as if to underscore the unimportance of what he'd just said. "You wouldn't have to actually raise them if you didn't choose to. I know you're not exactly maternal, but as his wife, having them may be a term of his negotiations."

Okay, the idea of reproducing just sent shivers of terror through me. It wasn't the sex, it wasn't getting fat, or even the birthing. I can take pain with the best of them. It was the idea that two of the scariest people ever born in this city would be reproducing together. That sounded like a really, really bad idea to me.

"Do you really think that a gene pool like mine should be mixing with his? Those kids would be so messed up from the start, they wouldn't have even a fighting chance?" I asked with a scowl.

Tony gave me an all-out laugh. "You *do* make a good argument. Just be back at a reasonable time in order to get ready for dinner. The terms the two of you set are between the two of you. *I'm* not marrying him. *You* are. I'll see you and Jason later."

Jason and I have always had an unusual relationship. I'd saved him from being beaten to death, literally, by a gang, when I was nineteen. He was closer to fifteen. There were five guys beating the crap out of him in a side alley when I came along and ended the altercation.

When I found out that he was one of ours, some generations removed (fifth cousin), I brought him to Tony. Tony gave him a job working at his home and he has been there ever since. He and Tony get along. Jason keeps his mouth shut and does what he's asked. Everyone seems happy with the arrangement.

Jason moved out of the main house and was given the guesthouse to live in when he married. Ellen knows how to behave and reaps the benefits of living in Tony's house. I think, from what I've seen, she's happy, but she doesn't like the way her husband looks at me. It isn't lust—it's more like awe—but I think she *mistakes* it for lust. When I'm married, I hope her dislike of me will end.

Jason and I spent the day riding and jumping in the hills. It was amazing. Before I knew it, it was three o'clock and Tony was going to be pissed if we didn't get back. We packed our stuff and headed home exhausted, happy and covered in dirt, literally caked on in layers.

It had rained two days before, so the ground was muddy and the dirt bikes kicked up everything. Each time we jumped a mound, the mud splattered. It was really a lot of fun, but Tony wasn't going to like me traipsing my dirt through his respectably immaculate house. Oh well.

Chapter 7

AS I WALKED IN THE FRONT door onto the pristine marble tiled floor lined with cream tone walls and perfect white hardware moulding, I did my best to be quiet. I didn't want to deal with Tony and his Mr. Clean sensibilities. He had a thing about dirt. Maybe that was why everything was white or light colored in his home.

From down the hall I heard, "Angelica, can we see you for a minute?!" It was a loud and demanding call, not to be considered a question.

Well, damn, so much for *sneaking* upstairs. "Tony," I replied, pleasantly, "I don't think you really want me coming down the hall like this." And, if he had any idea what I looked like, he would completely agree. Hell, he'd probably make me go outside and strip down before entering his sterile home.

"Don't be silly," he chided. "Get in here!" Again a command. It carried a certain level of affection, but it was a command not to be ignored.

My Levis, what was once a red shirt, and work boots were hopelessly filthy. In fact, it was possible that I wore more *mud* than clothes. It was everywhere.

"Okay," I called out gaily, "but remember I warned you." I walked down the hall and stepped into the library where he was holding court.

His eyes flashed as he looked in my direction. "Oh, dear God!" he moaned. "What the *hell* have you been doing? Did you bring the hills back with you? You're a mess!" Tony sputtered furiously.

52

Alex, on the other hand, who was sitting slightly to Tony's right, seemed to think it was funny and was clearly trying not to laugh because it would be rude.

"I warned you," I said, indignantly, "but you wouldn't take no for an answer. Now, if you'll excuse me, I think a shower and clean clothes are in order." Glancing around, but not moving any further into the room, I looked past Tony and said, "Alex, I see you made it. Is your father alright?"

It was a straightforward question; no lilt in the voice, no evidence of emotion, one way or the other. I was maintaining my calm façade, no matter how sick my stomach was feeling.

"Yes, thanks. You probably ought to go change before you start to take root. I believe dinner is scheduled early this evening," Alex replied, smiling.

My eyes refocused on Tony. "You have an hour," he declared. "See if you can fix yourself in that amount of time. And we'll be having additional guests. Is Jason with you? Does he look like that as well?" he asked, disgusted.

I leaned forward, kissed Tony on the cheek, and whispered in his ear. Then I beat it.

As I left I heard Alex ask, "Was that little display of affection for my benefit?"

Tony replied, laughing, "No, it was for mine. Jason is changing in his quarters and I was told to get a grip and stop being so anal. She's the only person I know who can get away with talking to me like that. And it always makes me laugh. But she would never be so disrespectful as to allow anyone else to hear a such a comment ."

✳✳✳

While I showered and changed, I thought about the prospect of spending the rest of my life tied to the man downstairs. I had many reasons to be nervous, but for the family's sake I needed to try working at this idea. Alex appeared to be unchanged—almost the same as I remembered him, all those years ago.

There were a few more lines on his face, and I noticed they didn't look like laugh lines. There was some gray in his hair, mostly at his temples. His hair was still short, almost military, and he was still built incredibly well. He still looked like a marauder of sorts. If I were a romantic I'd say he looked like a pirate. Luckily I'm not all that romantic or I'd be in more trouble than I already am.

I mean, how was I going to negotiate with a pirate? They aren't known for their negotiating skills—they don't negotiate. Last time I checked they plundered and pillaged, I don't ever recall hearing about Blackbeard negotiating.

I turned off the shower when I finally felt presentable and went rummaging through my closet. I had to wear something that screamed power … but in a casual way. A little bit sexy wouldn't hurt either. Hell, a lot sexy, but tasteful, of course. I'm supposed to marry this man. I need all the leverage I can find in this situation.

When I finished dressing I didn't think I looked bad at all. Casual meant pants—or at least to me it did. So I chose my brown suede. They were low rise and straight legged, almost chocolate in color, with no button or belt loops—just a zipper on my hip. I wore matching boots with four-and-a-half inch heels. It made me look tall—and for me, that's almost impossible.

Then I topped it with a cream colored semi-see-through chiffon single button tunic. There was only the one button and it fastened right between the base of my breasts, just covering the skin-tone bra. Almost everything was visible, and yet not. That was the idea. A thick gold chain, large gold hoop earrings and a ring that Tony had given me years ago made a good contrast with my olive skin.

I curled my hair for a change to make myself look a bit more feminine. I added a little makeup and there I was. Not bad considering I was scared to death to leave my room. I *looked* confident and that was all that mattered, right? The tattoos and belly ring always make me look confident, even if it's just total bull. Once again, I reminded myself—if you swim with sharks, you better look like one of their own or they'll gobble you up and spit you out. I had to look as though I was on the same level as my future husband or he might try to run me over.

It occurred to me that maybe I was overreacting. Maybe he wouldn't be a monster … and maybe I was better off preparing for the worst just in case.

Tony said we'd be having guests, which meant more than just the two Sevellis at dinner. I was betting on several of their family members, since they'd only been released today. There had to be any number of the family who'd want to check on them and make sure they had faired reasonably well behind bars.

I was certain that Roberto had taken some time to rest before dinner, but I hadn't heard anyone in Alex's room. I was hoping that he'd arrived early and taken some time to regroup because the questions would start flying tonight in the presence of his family and not stop for several days. He and I still needed to talk, but I figured we could B.S. our way through dinner.

Having taken forty-five minutes of the hour I was given, I was thinking it was about time to start down. If I didn't show up soon, someone would come to get me. Tony would make sure of it. I put on one last swipe of lip-gloss and the knock came.

"Coming."

I walked to the door. It was probably Tony. When I opened the door, the first thing I saw was … nothing. There was no one there. Then there was a second knock. It was the connector door.

It wasn't Tony.

It was Alex.

And I obviously wasn't thinking or I would have noticed.

I told myself, "Okay, calm down, this is perfectly fine. This man is going to be your husband and you had better get used to him." I walked to the connector, took a deep breath and opened the door only to discover that it was unlocked. Actually, studying it now, it looked as though the lock had been removed. Tony had been doing a little more than making Alex and me accessible for talking.

"Sorry, I didn't expect anyone at this door." I looked up into his eyes. I could see he was exhausted. "Come in," I held the door open and he walked through. "I know it's none of my business, but did you get any rest today? You look beat." I watched him walk over to my bed and sit; then lie back, throwing his arms over his head to stretch.

"No. I didn't want to rest before. I was antsy and now I'm not going to get the chance for at least a couple of hours. And for the record, I *feel* beat."

He sat up and looked at me. He'd even been too tired to put up that power field of his, and I'd been too distracted. That was becoming a predominate theme in this "getting married thing" … or was it the "being home" thing?

"You look amazing," he said.

Sexual tension suddenly flared in the room, a sensation that was obvious to us both. This was not going to be a strictly business marriage, there was no chance in hell. He was incredibly sexy. Scary, but sexy. I had the feeling that the scary part might just go away when we got used to each other. I could hope, right?

He was dressed all in black—a lightweight black v-neck cashmere sweater and black dress pants. His shoes were obviously expensive, and also black. He looked like a bad girl's dream. And I am nothing if not a bad girl.

"Thank you." I said, turning away so I could try to catch my breath.

The longer we looked at each other, the more I wanted to jump on the bed with him. Bad idea. I still must negotiate with him. I needed to appear only semi-interested, if that were at all possible.

Just as I was reapplying my mascara, which I didn't need, but I had to do something to distract myself, I felt him standing behind me. He slipped his hands under the backside of the tunic and lifted it slightly. "What's the tattoo? It's not exactly small is it?"

The tattoo is at least six-and-a-half inches wide and more than that long.

I glanced back over my shoulder. "The artist named it The Avenging Angel. I have that one and a smaller, mirrored version on my hip. It's a one-of-a-kind and was designed especially for me."

I felt his hands stop dead. He had to have recognized it. People in his line of work are usually familiar with my reputation—and my call sign—even though they don't have an actual name to go with it.

"Is that a sickle and a sword she's holding?" he asked, with no apparent emotion in his voice.

I nodded.

"And you're an assassin? That's what Tony said."

I nodded.

"You know, there's a fairly infamous person in your line of work who has this same type of tattoo. Or … two of them. You just mentioned that you have two of them."

I nodded again. He suddenly seemed very distant and concerned.

"Alex," I said, calmly, "I'm not here to kill you, so you can relax. But, to answer your question—yes, I am The Fallen Angel. On occasion, I'm also referred to as Lucifer's Mistress and as The Angel Divine. They are, all three, me. I've used the three names for my various ventures and they suit my purposes. But none of this is public knowledge, of course. When I'm in Tony's house, I'm Ace, Angel or Angelica, his niece … and reluctant successor."

"Why didn't Tony tell me this? He didn't say anything today when we discussed your work."

He was nervous. Good. I finally had one up on him. My guess was that it wouldn't last long, so I should probably savor it.

"Honestly, I don't think Tony has ever made the connection," I replied. "We rarely discuss my work. There are too many ears. Besides, I occasionally do government work and that's classified, of course. The other jobs are considered … controversial. And I'm not sure that our moral and business platforms would be compatible."

"Moral and business platforms? From the stories I've heard, you've been known to take out entire compounds, like *Rambo* or *James Bond.*" He sounded tired, confused, and slightly pissed that no one had told him who he had actually agreed to marry. "Is any of it true?"

I turned and looked up at him. "If you believe everything you hear,

I actually have wings. I can fly. I'm invisible and move at the speed of light. I can shoot lightning from my fingers. And I believe someone once said something about me being able to lift a car over my head. You might as well forget *Rambo* and *James Bond*. Hell, let's just say I'm *Superman*."

That at least got a smile. I sat down beside him on the bed. It was best to keep the channels between us as clear as possible. I didn't want any misunderstandings. "I'm an expert marksman. I do have several black-belts in various martial arts disciplines. I am an *Olympic* quality gymnast, even at my escalated age. I have little compunction about killing people who deserve it. I have a full training and understanding of drugs, torture and weaponry in general. I can pilot anything that flies and I can drive anything with wheels and ride most things with hooves. Although," I paused for effect, "I've found that some things with hooves don't go quite as fast as others."

His slight smile widened a bit.

"What else do you want to know?" I asked.

"The moral platform," he said.

"That's hard sometimes," I admitted. "It depends on the circumstances. I stopped working for the government because I didn't have a say in the targets. It's not a good feeling to suspect that you're bumping off some little girl's daddy simply because he doesn't agree with the country's foreign policy. It bothered me."

I shrugged. "So I went to work for myself. Now, I pick and choose. As a rule, I select those who really deserve to be wasted—and, if the job pays well, so much the better. On the other hand, I've been known to protect the person I was hired to kill… and to kill the person who hired me. I've even been known to kill people for free if it suits my moral platform. I don't always play by the rules when it comes to my contracting business.

"This information, however, is pretty confidential. If it got around, it could be bad for business."

I shifted and looked up at him. "As for the *platform* itself, it has various aspects. But, what it basically comes down to is that I kill *bad* people. That's pretty much it. And I need to really *believe,* based on my own moral code, that these people are bad. I have removed several child molesters and I'll take almost anyone associated with abusing children. I kill murderers and even other assassins on occasion.

"I have killed terrorists and individuals I consider criminally insane, on occasion drug pushers and growers. I don't like drugs. I don't kill clergy … unless there are special circumstances, like child abuse. And every case is examined carefully. I never accept a job until I've thoroughly researched the target. So," I concluded, "does that answer your question?"

He nodded.

There was a knock at the door.

"Come in."

Alex answered the knock, not me.

It was Jason and he looked a little disconcerted to find Alex in my room.

"I don't mean to interrupt, but Tony wanted me to check on you. He'd like to know when you'll be down. There's a group starting to gather and it would be best if you could join them … soon." He emphasized, ever so slightly, the word "soon."

He was looking at me. He was avoiding looking at Alex. Alex probably made him nervous. But then again, why should *he* be excluded? "We'll be right down. Just tell Tony we're getting to know each other and I'm sure he'll calm down about our being late."

Jason said thanks and left.

I turned back to Alex. "We should go down soon before Tony comes up himself."

"Is that a possibility?" He sounded as though he didn't believe it.

"Hey, with Tony, anything is possible." I looked at him again. "You *really* look tired. I'm not picking on you—I just know how it is when I'm tired and have to spend time with family … well, let's just say they can be exhausting, even when you're fully rested. I usually have a major outburst once the family 'life-picking' starts. It's never pretty."

"Life-picking?" he asked. There was a smirk in place now.

"Oh, *you* know … 'Why aren't you married yet?'; 'When are you planning on having a real career?'; 'How come you never went back to music like we'd always hoped?'; 'Isn't there a nice someone in your life yet?'; 'When are you going to grow up?'; or 'When are you going to settle down?' You know—life-picking."

Alex and I both stood. He was still grinning. "I don't get a lot of that except from my aunts—everyone else is too scared to broach those subjects. But your outbursts sound promising.

I started to open the door to the hall. I hesitated and looked at Alex. "Have I managed to scare the hell out of you yet? Will you be running for the hills before tomorrow night?"

He slipped his hands under the backside of the tunic. They were very male hands, warm, slightly callused, and large. Both of them together could cover pretty much my entire back. He pulled me close, bent down and kissed me. He was so much taller that, without these boots, he might have had to pick me up to kiss me.

The kiss was slow and warm …it picked up pace, gradually. He eased one hand along the curve of my back, moved it down to my buttocks and gave me a playfully squeeze. I let out a little groan. My hands were slowly making their way up along his chest. It was solid, under his black cashmere sweater. It was so soft over all that hard. And he smelled wonderful.

We continued groping and pawing at each other until we heard, "Hmm, hmm." We both looked up and saw Roberto standing right outside my doorway.

It was Alex who spoke. "Dad … we were … uh … just coming down."

Roberto was smiling and shaking his head. He mumbled something that sounded like "unbelievable" with a heavy Italian accent and then left.

I looked up at Alex and laughed. The lip-gloss was now all over him. No wonder his father was mumbling. "Wait here. You have a face full of gloss." I slipped under his arm and went to my side table for a tissue. I wiped it off and then returned to the makeup table to reapply.

"Don't put that crap back on," he said. "It doesn't taste that great. Besides, you have enough color to your lips now."

I looked in the little mirror and he was right. That kiss had done quite a job. "So when it fades do I get another one?"

That got me grabbed and kissed again. This time, a bit more abruptly and fully. I felt it all the way through my body this time. His hands did a bit more exploring and so did mine.

When we finally pulled back we were both panting. We had to get out of this room or there wasn't going to be anything to negotiate about this marriage. If he got me in that bed, I might just agree to anything.

"We need to go down." I sounded much calmer than I was.

"You're right. We can pick this up later after we get rid of my family." He slipped away from me, but left his hand at my back to usher me out of the room.

CHAPTER 8

WHEN WE ARRIVED DOWNSTAIRS, his hand was still at the bare skin of my back. As we entered we both put up our guards—almost simultaneously. It was suddenly like the room was significantly fuller.

There were approximately fifteen people in the living room and most had sensed our entrance and glanced in our direction. The majority were from the Sevelli family. I recognized two of Alex's aunts and several cousins. Alex's much younger brother Mike was also in attendance.

Mike was Alex's half-brother. They shared a father but had different mothers. Alex and Thad were in their teens when Roberto married Laura. The marriage only lasted a couple of years but their son, Mike, was just now getting his feet wet in his father's business. He looked a lot like Alex, but much younger. By the way he held himself, I was certain he would be a force to reckon with in a few years.

Unfortunately I also spotted an uninvited guest. Alfonso Merek was turning into a real pain in the ass. I suppose I should be grateful that Derek hadn't decided to join the party as well.

I leaned back into Alex's hand and looked up at him. "I don't know how much Tony's told you about Alfonso and Derek, but they are turning into real pests—Alfonso, especially, he is far worse than Derek. I've told them both that I don't feel we'd be well-matched. I think Derek is being pushed by his father. But Alfonso is definitely pursuing me on his own. He's ambitious and I think he's hoping to impress his father by making a significant alliance."

We both walked to the bar while talking. Alex made me a drink as well as one for himself. He glanced at me as I took my first sip and asked, "Why did you consider them poor choices? I know why *I* would think so, but why did you?"

Apparently Tony had shared something regarding the other three candidates, but heaven only knew what. We moved away from the bar and migrated in the direction of the piano. During most family occasions I make my way to the piano. If I play, I don't have to make small-talk or listen to the life-picking. It always seemed to me to be a pretty good trade-off.

"Derek isn't very bright," I replied, "but he is a good con-artist. He had me going for about a full six minutes, thinking he knew what he was talking about—of course he didn't. Alfonso, on the other hand, is devious and conniving. I sense that his ambition ultimately outweighs his common sense. I believe he did away with David. I can't prove it, but when David's untimely demise was mentioned on our first meeting, I would swear he gloated." I took another sip. "He makes my skin crawl."

"Wasn't there a third?" Alex asked.

Ah, yes. "Anthony Sheppa. He wasn't exactly family material—he's much too nice. I hope he never actually takes over the Sheppa's businesses. If he does, he won't live long."

Alex was now looking over the people in attendance. I eased in the direction of the piano bench. "Well, you have to do the family thing, so I think I'll play. It keeps me from having to be too social."

Alex put the stone face in place but the dark circles under his eyes gave away his fully fatigued state. "You should take advantage of making the rounds now. Then, if you decide to skip out early, no one will think you didn't appreciate their attendance. Besides, we'll see them all again tomorrow."

He nodded, ran his hand over my back, leaned down and kissed me on the cheek.

When I glanced to the right, Alfonso was glowering at us, looking like someone had stolen his prize dessert. Close enough to the truth I suppose. I set my drink on the piano, sat down and began to play.

I watched Alex making the rounds. He did it with expert precision. He would linger and chat with a small group for a short time and then move on. Presently, he was with his father, both aunts and Tony. I glanced at the door and found Jason standing there. I nodded. He approached and bent down to hear me over the piano.

"What's up?" I asked.

He looked slightly distraught. "Dinner's ready, but your fiancé makes me nervous. I have to tell Tony, but he seems ... involved."

I looked back at Tony and Jason was right. He did look involved. Still, that was really no excuse.

"How have you managed this house all these years," I asked, "but can still get all worked up over little things like announcing dinner?"

Jason rolled his eyes. "As a rule, I don't. But things have been tense around here since just before you came back and I don't know what's up. I feel like I'm sitting on a pinhead all the time. If I don't behave properly, someone might knock me off, especially with a visiting family here. You know? I don't want to overhear anything and get killed—all for announcing dinner at the wrong moment."

I laughed. "You worry too much. I'll take care of it."

I ended the song. I left and joined the group and by the time I arrived, so had Alfonso. I sidled in between Tony and Alex. I slipped my arm around Tony's waist and whispered that dinner was ready.

"Good, I'm starving." He then announced that we should move towards the dinning room for dinner.

I guess Alfonso was staying. Crap!!

I moved to follow Tony but Alex took me by the elbow, sliding his hand back under the backside of my shirt. We paused while the others began to depart. He leaned down and whispered in my ear. "I think you may be right about that little cretin. I mentioned Dave and he *did* look smug. I liked Dave and was sorry when he died. He would have made a good leader. That little shit doesn't stand a chance."

I frowned at him. "I think you may be underestimating his ruthlessness—irritating and skuzzy, yes—but he's ruthless and ambitious. I think he'll kill anyone who gets in his way."

I thought about that for a minute. Maybe I'd just put Alex in his way ... not good.

"You may want to watch your back," I suggested. "When it's made public that I intend to marry you, he may feel that action is necessary."

The room was now empty. He stepped back and looked at me. *"Now* you mention this? You could have said something upstairs."

I shrugged. "It just occurred to me. Being back home seems to have messed with my reasoning and ability to concentrate. I keep getting distracted. I think I need to get settled again. Living in someone else's house, not feeling like I can be myself all the time, and this marriage thing isn't helping." We started toward the dining room.

"Speaking of that, we need to discuss our expectations from the marriage and the business," he commented.

"I think maybe we should wait until tomorrow morning, after we've both had a good night's sleep. That way we're both thinking clearly. I don't want either of us agreeing to something we're not willing to live with." Truth be told, he wouldn't like that either.

As we entered the dining area, I noticed there were two empty places but they were at opposite ends of the table. One of them was next to Alfonso. Alex leaned into me from the back when I came to a slow stop. "We can discuss actual terms in the morning, but don't be surprised to find me in your bed this evening."

His hand was still warm on my back. "And I'll take the seat next to the little worm. I don't want him pawing at my future wife. It's bad enough that he leers."

Who was I to argue? I couldn't stand "the worm" and, besides, Alex would also be seated next to one of his aunts. I claimed the other open seat, near the end, right next to Tony. To my left was Alex's cousin, Anna. She seemed nice and had come with her mother, Katrina, Roberto's youngest sister. Anna was attractive—short dark hair, sharp nose, thin and well-maintained. She was somewhere in her forties as I recall.

Dinner went well. We all managed friendly exchanges. The meal was five courses so there was plenty of time for chatting and small-talk.

I was full by the end of the third course and I had to pick my way through the rest. Alex's family seemed pleasant enough. We finished around eight-thirty and adjourned to the living room. I headed straight for the piano but I was waylaid by Alfonso, of all people.

"I feel like you're avoiding me, but I noticed that you and Alex seem to be very friendly." He sounded agitated. "I was surprised he managed to get himself out of jail," he said, sneering . "He isn't particularly well-connected to professionals who specialize in that type of work. Do you know how tough it is to "create" an electrical fire? I mean, from what I've heard, no one can't prove it wasn't. Now, that takes some skills. And Thad—now that was slick. There was no suspicion of murder but, of course, it was a very convenient death." He turned and glanced at Alex. "I wonder how he did it?" he mused. "Shit, they had to be *real* professionals."

Of course it was *professional*. What the hell? Do I look like an amateur?

"I'm not avoiding you," I demurred. "I just don't normally circulate at family functions. As for Alex and me ... well, he and I have known each other for years. His family and ours have been in a comfortable arrangement for a long time, although you can probably see that by the way everyone gets along."

I looked around hoping someone would come rescue me. Yes, I can extract myself from any number of terrible situations, but I can never manage to disengage myself from an unwanted conversation. Truth is, I'm not a great "people" person. I kill them. I don't socialize with them.

"As for Alex's connections," I replied, "I don't know much about them. He's even more closed-mouthed than I am and Tony and I think it would be a little rude to ask."

I stood rooted to the spot but Alfonzo had managed to maneuver himself to my side, our backs to the room. As I finished my statement he tried to slide his hand in behind my blouse as Alex had done earlier.

I jumped.

"I'm sorry," he cooed. "I didn't mean to make you nervous."

Jerk!

"Your hands are cold," I said, avoiding eye-contact, and began to move away slowly. Put some distance between us so he didn't feel I was inviting that sort of attention from him. I needed rid of this sleazy letch and the sooner the better. Suddenly, I felt Alex. He had to be about eight feet behind me, but I was in his focus and I could feel him closing the gap. I didn't bother turning around. "Alex?"

When his arms came down, possessively, around me I wasn't all that surprised. "It's late. I think it's time you went up. I'll say our good-nights and be right behind you." He had said it just loud enough for Alfonso to hear. He was making a point.

I'm not usually good about people telling me what to do, but I'm also not good at family politics. That was one of the many reasons I'd left, years ago. I hated this crap. But it was an excellent reason to marry someone who *was* good at it. I might even pick up some pointers, eventually.

I looked up at him. He was stone-faced, tired, and the look in his eyes said pissed. He must have seen the letch trying to touch me. He leaned down and kissed me on top of the head. I turned in his arms and whispered, as close as I could to his ear from my height.

"Remember, you're tired. Don't say anything you'll regret to-morrow." That got me another kiss, this time on my forehead.

"I'll make our apologies to Tony for retiring early," he said, reassuringly.

I turned, saying nothing to Alfonso and left, heading straight out the door, up the stairs, and to my room. Odd thing was, when I reached my room, I noticed there were bags in there that weren't mine. I walked to the connector and tried to open it. It was locked, which I knew to be impossible because I'd looked at it just a few hours ago and there was no locking mechanism … not then, anyway. Looks like Tony had a locksmith in while we were downstairs; sneaky old bastard.

Okay, so Alex was now going to be my roommate. Well, I could think of worse things. And he did say I shouldn't be surprised if he was in my bed tonight.

One would think I'd be better with a man sharing my room. I mean I'm dangerous, right? He should be the one who was nervous, not me. When it comes right down to it, I'm sure I've actually hurt and killed far more people than he has. But the idea of that huge man sleeping in the same bed as me—it scares the hell out of me.

I decided getting ready for bed was the best course of action. I walked to the dresser, picked out my pale yellow chemise with the brocade lace trim. It matched my robe. I changed, took off my makeup and sat at the dresser table to brush my hair.

Fifteen minutes after my entrance, Alex walked in. Then he turned to lock the door.

I glanced at his reflection in the mirror. He'd completely dropped his menacing presence. It took a lot of energy to maintain it, no matter how natural it might seemed. He then sat on the bed, the side closest to the door, and removed his shoes. He looked like he could sleep sitting up.

"Did you manage to politely get rid of Alfonso?" I asked.

From behind me I heard. "I don't know how polite I was. But I wasn't threatening, if that's what you mean." He stood and walked into the bathroom.

I moved to the bed, turned down the covers, removed my robe and climbed between the sheets. Alex came out of the bathroom wearing only a pair of navy blue silk boxer shorts. And, let me tell you, that was something to see.

He crossed the room, checked the connector to make sure it was locked, and then turned off the main light. The only light left in the room was on my bedside table.

As he walked to the bed, he said, "You know that little shit thought I was lying about our being engaged before my stay with the state?"

"I suppose you can't blame him. Remember Tony asked him and the other two to get acquainted in hopes of my marrying one of them. What did you tell him?"

Alex slid into bed next to me. It was king size, but I could feel his body heat from the other side of the bed.

"I gave him a song and dance about Tony not approving of your choice of me as your husband. That's close enough to the truth from what Tony said to me earlier, so I figured it wasn't too far out there. I also said that since I was away, Tony felt he might be able to persuade you to choose someone else."

I was sitting up with a mystery novel I'd found in the downstairs library. Not that I expected to get to read—it was more of a prop, really. "Not bad. Good improv. Did he finally take it?"

"No, the little shit said that you didn't have an engagement ring on your finger, so he thought I was just trying to dissuade him from his interest in you." Alex fluffed his pillows and laid back. "I'll call Sal tomorrow morning, first thing, and have you a ring before the party. Maybe that'll make him go away."

I put the book on the side table. "Don't take this the wrong way, but I wouldn't bet on it. He's persistent. I don't even know if a wedding ring would get him to leave it alone. I may have to get rid of the little shit permanently. Not that his father would be pleased, but the entire Merek family would definitely be better off."

I was only half kidding about getting rid of Alfonso permanently. I didn't like him.

Alex reached under the covers, across the bed, grabbed me and pulled me to him. His eyes, this close, were dark, almost black and the limited light didn't help. My pulse was racing.

"I don't want you doing anything like that," he said, "without discussing it with me. Once we're married, The Fallen Angel, Lucifer's Mistress and The Angel Devine are all retiring. Do you understand me?"

This man may be making my pulse crazy, but not my brain—at least not yet. "You don't get to tell me what I *can* and *can't* do. And tonight, while we're in bed, there will be no negotiating. One of us might agree to something we're not really willing to live with."

I could see this wasn't the answer he wanted, but tough shit. What did I look like, anyway? One of his "yes" men? I think not. I tell it like it is … or at least I try.

"If it makes you feel better," I amended, "I won't eliminate anyone, family-related, without your knowledge and a chance to change my mind." I thought that was more than enough to ease his mind, especially since we were talking about Alfonzo.

His hands slipped slowly down the silk of my chemise, one sliding underneath the front, up my thigh, the other slipping under my buttocks. "Fine, we won't discuss negotiations tonight. But, be forewarned. There are several non-negotiable terms and one of them has to do with your work."

I grazed my hand across the front of his shorts and he gasped. Two can play this distraction game. "Then you may want to think about how flexible the details are within those terms."

He was nibbling on my ear and his mouth was working its way down, while his hands were working their way up. Preparing to remove the chemise altogether. This close, I was too excited to be scared.

"We'll discuss it in the morning," he murmured in my ear.

His mouth closed over mine and we slipped into an evening that would take some effort to be surpassed.

CHAPTER 9

THE NEXT MORNING ALEX was coming out of the shower, wearing a towel at his waist, when I fastened my robe.

"How are you feeling?" He undid the front of the robe I'd just closed and slid his big hands around to cradle my back, pulled me close and kissed me.

He kissed me again. This time his tongue touched mine and we were gone again—off came the towel, off came the robe and onto the bed we went. It amazed me that he could become aroused four times in less than twelve hours. Prison may have been responsible, but I was definitely going to get my exercise being married to him.

When I returned from the bathroom, after taking a shower, I found that Alex was on the bedroom phone. I walked to the closet. Since it was raining, I pulled out a pair of jeans and a light brown lace T-shirt. I was sitting on the side of the bed about to pull on my work-boots when I looked up.

Alex had the phone in one hand and was frowning, presumably at my outfit.

"You don't like it?" I asked.

"I don't like the boots. Do you have anything else?"

"Actually, I own about two hundred and fifty pair, but they're all in *Italy*. I only brought six pair and these are all I have that go with this shirt." I do love shoes. For the most part, I hate to shop with the exception of shoes. I don't know why, but they just call to me.

"What about the ones from last night? They'd match."

"They're suede and it's raining. Are we going someplace? I mean,

71

if no one of importance is going to see me, does it matter? I'll change before tonight."

He held up a finger, motioning me to wait a minute. "No," he said into the phone, "I don't. Hang on." He looked at me and asked, "What size is your ring finger?"

I was confused. Then I remembered the conversation we'd had last night about my engagement ring. "Six."

He went back to the phone. Then I heard, "Okay, we'll be down shortly …" I guess that answers my question about anyone seeing me.

He turned back to me. "Could you change into something a little more 'uptown'? I know you don't normally dress that way, but until we're married, I would appreciate it. My family is going to be seeing you for the first time in years. I'd like them to think you've outgrown the work boots look."

What the hell was *wrong* with the way I dress?! Okay … so I look like I'm still in high school sometimes, or in the military at others, but I don't look like something that crawled out of an alley.

Then I relaxed and thought about it. I suppose he had a point. I really hated that.

This whole marriage thing was a real irritant. That is, with the exception of the sex—that I'm actually quite pleased with. I'm not even all that unhappy about Alex himself, but having to change myself to make myself presentable is just aggravating.

I changed my clothes while he worked on some calls he had to make regarding business matters. I slipped on a pair of cream tone, light-weight, low cut slacks, a loose knit beige sweater and cream tone four-inch heels. I added some jewelry and makeup; then put my hair up in chignon to get it out of my face.

"Better?"

Alex turned and stared. "Much. You look beautiful." He realized he was staring and went back to the papers he was going through. "We should go down for breakfast and then get to Sal's so you can pick out what you like."

"How are you going to pay for this with all your property still being held in limbo? I know Max will fix this as soon as possible, but it does make things tough at the moment. I could pay for it, but I'd feel weird buying my own engagement ring," I admitted.

"I'd feel even weirder," Alex agreed, "so no, you aren't buying it. Sal's family. He'll extend me credit until my money's released."

I grabbed my wallet and keys off of the dressing table. I never carry a full purse if I can avoid it—it just gets in my way. I usually carry my wallet in the vest pocket of my coat and that was downstairs.

We had breakfast, crawled into my Cooper, which Alex made fun of, and went to Sal's. Sal's was not only a jewelry store and jewelry pawn shop, occasionally he also offered custom jewelry design—work he did himself.

✳✳✳

I hadn't seen Sal since I was very young, but I remembered what he looked like. He was short, portly and balding. I noticed, when I came through the door, that not much had changed. My memory was still pretty accurate—he was just older now.

He appeared very pleased to see Alex and then took a few minutes to give me the once over. "So, you two are actually gonna get married? I'm surprised, I heard it through the grapevine, but didn't believe it. I never thought either of you would ever go for it. No offense, but you're both a little jaded. Some bookmaker in town is gonna lose his shirt on this."

He shook his head and laughed, opened the gate to the back and we followed him in. The door led to a small office where Sal proceeded to pull out a large blue velvet tray. He turned to the safe set in the wall behind us, opened it and pulled out two small pouches.

"Okay, young lady, what exactly are we looking for here?"

He acted like I'd done this before. How the hell did I know?

"Something," I suggested, "that isn't going to get in my way. Nothing bulky."

"Small? I'd say that may not reflect well on your future husband."

"Okay, how about something that looks impressive, but isn't going to look out of place at, say … a gun range." That seemed reasonable to me, but the look on Alex's face said he didn't agree.

But it got an all-out laugh from Sal. "So, you shoot a lot?" Then he thought about that—probably realizing who he was talking to—cleared his throat and sat up a little straighter in his chair. "Never mind, I don't think I want to know."

"I think," I offered, "what I'm trying to say is *practical.*"

"Okay, let's start by picking a shape." He sounded frustrated already.

He laid several in front of me. The marquis and pear were beautiful, but I didn't see them as overly practical. They would snag on half of my clothes and they looked so dainty. I'm small, yes, but I'm not a dainty person. The oval didn't do it for me at all.

"What kind of mountings do you have for the square and the round?" I asked. "The others aren't really me."

He nodded and went back to the vault and brought trays of mountings and more stones. The whole process took another twenty minutes. I finally decided on a princess cut, apparently that's what the square cut was called. It ended up being a *Lucida* setting. The diamond was four-and-a-half karats. It was huge, especially on my finger.

Now you, probably, much like I, might be wondering what the hell I was thinking? Well, I suppose mostly I was thinking that Sal was right. If I don't choose something impressive, it might reflect badly on Alex, and he was more than willing to spend the money.

We also selected our wedding bands while we were there and Sal said he'd mount the diamond and deliver it in time for the party tonight. I was amazed that he had the setting in stock, especially for a diamond that size. But then, New York City supported a huge number of jewelers—so if Sal didn't have it, all he'd have to do was drive across the river.

Alex spoke with Sal again, while I milled. I decided I should pick out a decent pair of earrings for tonight, since I was probably going to be wearing my hair up. I have some nice jewelry, artistic pieces, but like everything else they weren't here.

I picked a pair of one-and-a-half karat solitaire diamond studs. They were beautiful. I was about to pay for them, but Alex insisted they go on his account. When we finished, I drove Alex over to his brother's condo.

✳✳✳

Alex leaned across the car and asked, "Do you have things you need to be doing?"

That's when I spied the dark blue sedan out of the corner of my eye. It was outside the jewelry store and now it was on the road, presumably following us. It was generic, but had a slight ding in the right front fender.

I reached over and opened the glove box. I pulled out my two guns. The Glock I normally carry at my back and the .22 I keep at my ankle. It was a pea shooter, but it worked in a jam.

The car could be a cop keeping an eye on Alex, or it could be something not so simple. Like, for example, our over-stimulated friend from last night.

"Take the .22 and keep it in your pocket. There's a car back there that's been following us. I want you to have something just in case." Alex glanced back at the car.

I put the car in first gear and moved closer to the condo so it would be almost impossible to take a shot at him when he went in. "Make sure you're looking when you come out," I cautioned, "and try to stay away from the windows. Hell, maybe he'll follow me. That would make everything easier."

Alex looked at me, "Remember our conversation last night? No killing anyone." He hesitated and then added, "Well, that is unless you don't have a choice."

"I'm going to Ricca's. I need some clothes and, as you pointed out earlier, shoes. I'll be back at the house in a couple of hours."

"Alright, we'll talk then." He leaned over and kissed me, then got out of the car.

The car stayed with Alex which is what I was afraid of. I called

Mike's and let Alex know. I offered to come back and get him, instead of putting Mike in danger. He agreed. His brother was still young and he didn't want him getting hurt without good cause. At this point, our problems didn't qualify on that account.

✳✳✳

Ricca's was a fairly upscale clothing salon. I'd shopped there a few times in my younger years, but only for formal outings. As I browsed, I found several nice dresses. I settled on a cream fabric with a shear appearance. It fit like a second skin, with gold and silver beads embroidered into the low v-neck and along the bottom of the skirt. Nothing gaudy, just enough for flair. It was a beautiful pattern and hung to my mid-thigh.

I also picked out a pair of four-inch strappy gold-tone sandals and a gold hair ornament, that gave off an antique feel, to hold up my hair tonight. I'd be showing off the beautiful earrings Alex bought me this morning.

I picked up a few additional things while I was there, knowing Alex was not going to be keen on having me go anywhere dressed as I normally do. That meant I needed more clothes. He and I were going to have to negotiate my living situation and get my clothes delivered wherever I was living. This shopping from necessity was a pain in the butt. If I shop at all, I like it to be a spur of the moment thing, not one where I feel forced into purchasing things. I almost never find anything when I have no choice. I was thinking I was really lucking out today.

✳✳✳

Pulling up in front of Mike's condo two hours after I'd left, I parked next to the door and got out. I saw the car in the lot that was watching for Alex. I put on my nasty attitude and gave the driver a look, a long, "I see you watching" look. I reached behind my back for my gun. It was in its holster and the minute I did, the driver started the engine and drove out of the parking lot. I guess he didn't want to get shot. Good for him.

Alex came down the stairs seconds later. "How did you do that?"

"I scare people—you know that. The locals know I'm a shooter. I never used to worry much about who it was that I shot, either. You're the only one who knows I've promised not to hurt anybody in the local families," I said. "Without provocation, that is," I added.

"But you *wouldn't* have shot him?" he frowned, "Right?"

"Not without being shot at first, " I replied. "But he didn't know that, now did he?"

Alex laughed and got into the car. He looked at the packages piled on my back seat. "Did you buy out the store?"

"Remember this morning? I don't have a lot of nice clothes with me. I wasn't planning on getting *married* when I left *Italy*. I wasn't planning on engagement parties and family meetings. Honestly, I thought Tony wanted me to get rid of somebody … or to tell me I'd be taking over in a couple months … tell me to find a house and prepare for the move. I didn't *pack* for this. Which is another thing we need to talk about—my house in *Italy*. How much of my living situation is negotiable? I like living there. And if not, where exactly *are* we going to live—if we're living together."

"I would say that living in *Italy* while I'm here is completely out of the question. We can go by my place. I can't get in yet, but we can drive by. I have a very nice condo on the other side of the city."

Ewww!

"Condo?" I echoed. "No offense, but neighbors get a bit panicky when I start shooting off firearms in their backyards. I want a house. We need something more like Tony's, but homier, not so … you know what I mean."

He nodded. "Alright," he conceded. "But if I'm selling my place, then you're selling yours."

"Why?" I demanded. "I have a number of rental properties. I can get a property manager there; rent it to tourists for a week or a month at a time. My housekeeper would be more than happy to take care of guests. She likes being busy and we can use it occasionally for vacations. It's got great views."

He gave me a grin. "Fine. As long as it isn't just sitting idle. Otherwise it's a waste." He leaned back trying to make his big stature comfortable in my little car.

I'd been watching as we drove back to house—the tail didn't pick us up again. I really liked being menacing at times. It comes in handy, and my rep in town didn't hurt either.

When we arrived, Jason came out and carried my things up to our room. Alex and I still needed to have our negotiations. I was certain that was going to take all of my efforts, so the quicker the better.

"Can we get this over with?" I asked. "We only have four hours until we have to get ready, and to be perfectly honest, I'd like to spend some time relaxing before this evening's activities." While this conversation with Alex would take all my concentration, this evening would take all of my patience.

His arms wrapped around me and pulled me with him onto the couch in the front parlor. This was a room no one used except to greet unwanted guests. I think it may have been decorated with that in mind, because it was downright uncomfortable, and in my opinion, ugly. Alex nuzzled my neck and ran the tip of his tongue around the outside of my ear.

I realized we were going to get nowhere fast at this rate and pulled away. "Behave!" I commanded. "We have to get this done. The sooner we finish the sooner we go upstairs." That should provide some incentive.

Actually, negotiating with Alex only took a little while. We agreed that we should "run" our respective families independently, but cover for each other when necessary. We also agreed that this meant cross-training, which would take a while, as we got to know each other's "methods" better.

We agreed to buy a home here. I would return to Italy and have my important personal items shipped back. I'd also have some basics added to the house to make it suitable as a rental property. Unfortunately for me, Alex was non-negotiable on children. He insisted we have a minimum of two and would prefer more, but agreed to see how it went. I conceded, but argued that we postpone the first pregnancy, if possible, so I could learn the businesses while unencumbered by child raising duties. He agreed.

The final things we argued about had to do with my work. He wanted me to stop accepting all assassination contracts. He also wanted me to remove my tattoos. I refused. This resulted in a stand-off. I understood that compromise in marriage may be necessary. I just didn't think I should have to make all the consessions.

Agreeing to halt the government contracting (at least as far as the government would allow)—the work I performed as The Fallen Angel—was less than painful, actually. Lately, I was more or less prodded and guilt-tripped into accepting these contracts. I even agreed to stop the work I perform as Lucifer's Mistress—that is, all the privately contracted jobs.

However, I absolutely refused to stop my work as The Angel Divine. The Angel Divine is the work I do as … well … how should I put this … I think of this work as a public service. Ridding the world of dangerous vermin.

By the time someone approaches The Angel Divine, I'm typically the last resort. I "eliminate" people who are truly a danger to the community, those who prey on the innocent. This includes those the law can't find or can't prosecute: child abusers, drug dealers who peddle to children, and that sort of thing. I don't like them, and I take that crap as a personal attack on mine and others' rights to live peacefully in a healthy environment.

I only intervene when the police or the government can't, for some reason, handle the problem through regular channels. In fact, when I have valuable evidence, I've be known to send it to the proper authorities. But, if the problem won't go away—then I step in and make it go away.

Alex's argument for insisting that I quit my public service work—although he understood my motives as The Angel Divine—was that of family. He worried that if he agreed now, I'd continue once we had children. He wasn't willing to risk family.

"Fine." I conceded. "But for now, The Angel Divine stays in business. We'll revisit this issue when I become pregnant. Besides, it isn't as though I go out and kill a person every week, or even once a month. The Angel Devine has only taken three killing assignments in the last year-and-a-half. And, remember, I never kill if there are other options available."

"Agreed," said Alex, "on the condition that if you take one of these assignments, I want to know all about it. I also want a say in considering alternate options. Sometimes two heads are better than one, even when the one has the IQ of two people combined."

I agreed, as long as I got final say. He conceded.

The final problem had to do with my tattoos. I couldn't possibly get rid of them. I've had the one on my back for almost fifteen years. "Alex, I can't just get rid of it. That isn't fair. I've had it almost half of my life."

Again, his reasoning had to do with our children. He didn't want them endangered because their mother used to be a notorious assassin.

Okay, I was willing to give in on part of it.

"Fine," I said. "When I become pregnant, we'll look at having my back tattoo removed."

God, that was going to be painful—it wasn't small. I was betting it would hurt more than the childbirth. "But the little one stays," I declared. "It's part of who I am and I'm not getting rid of it."

"I want the big one gone *before* you get pregnant. I don't want you walking around, eight months pregnant, displaying that thing which announces that you're an assassin. It isn't as though I'm the only person in the world who knows the mark. You're risking our family by leaving that thing in place. The little one can stay as long as it stays covered while you're in public. And most of your wardrobe manages that."

"I'll have it removed," I sighed, "when we start trying to have a family. I'll look into the cost and procedure ahead of time. But let's get this out in the open. I don't *like* it," I grumped.

"I understand that," he said, "but it has to be done. Your displeasure is something we'll have to live with since making you happy on this matter isn't worth the risk. We have to be realistic."

He was right. I knew it, I just didn't like it. There were times when being a selfish brat by nature was hard to overcome.

When negotiations were complete, the only thing I was really unhappy about was my tattoo … well, and leaving my house, but I couldn't do much about either. I discovered, during our negotiations that Alex was far more conservative than I, and definitely more cautious. He avoided risks of any type whenever possible, while I thrived on them. But he'd been head of his family now for over ten years and I was betting most of his caution had to do with protecting others.

For many years now, I'd lived my life on the edge because I liked it that way and besides, I had only to watch out for myself. This was about to change and it was going to be tough. It was good for the Pascolis that I was marrying Alex, even if they didn't realize it.

I was something of a brute-force type person. There was no question that, unlike me, Alex was a diplomat; always able to look at all sides, seeking common grounds and compromise. I'd spent my adult years living life exactly the way I wanted. Compromise was never part of my lifestyle.

This marriage was going to be a rude awakening and I was feeling the nudge in my metaphoric sleep starting already.

Chapter 10

ALEX WALKED OUT OF THE bathroom, fully dressed with the exception of his jacket. He looked my way and came to a dead stop. My hair was piled up on my head, held in place with the gold ornament, and little strands were cascading down. I'd taken the curling iron to them. My new dress and heels, and the effect of the hair and my coloring set off my beautiful new earrings. I was still trying to decide on a necklace when I felt Alex watching me.

"Which one of these do you think goes best?" I held up my plain solid gold chain and a chunky faux gold piece.

He hesitated and then turned away. "Neither," he replied. "I picked you up something that'll go better."

I sat back on the vanity stool and Alex slipped the necklace around my neck. It was gorgeous. There were three diamonds of the same size, about a karat and a half each, arranged in a symmetrical design that displayed each diamond to its greatest advantage. They were ensconced on a gold chain as wide as the diamonds.

"When did you buy this?" I asked. "It's beautiful."

I was feeling euphoric. No one had ever bought me anything like this. The people in my life never had the money, for the most part, and those that did would never have thought a gift like this was right for me. Probably because I'm not what most would think of as feminine.

Alex walked to the bed, picked up his jacket and put it on. "I picked it out while we were at Sal's. It looked so good with those earrings, I couldn't leave it. And …" He reached into the breast pocket of the suit jacket. A small velvet box came into view. It could only be one thing.

He opened it and I gave him my left hand. The ring was glittery and very obvious. It was far from the practical thing I'd imagined going into the store this morning. But it was, without a doubt, a ring that Alex would have given his wife-to-be.

"Now that," he smile, "is perfect. It was meant for you."

"You better watch it," I said. "I'm starting to feel more like a fairy princess than a paid executioner," I added, only half jokingly.

I almost didn't recognize myself. I wasn't poor by any stretch of the imagination, but I rarely went anywhere that required dressing and primping in a lavish fashion. I owned some nice things, of course. But jeans, boots and T-shirts, were what I normally confronted in the mirror.

"Good," he smiled. "Maybe you'll get used to this and like it."

Alex pulled me close, bent and kissed me. There was no hesitation in his approach. I slid my arms around his waist and kissed him back.

Fifteen minutes later Alex ushered me into the limo. He didn't think my Cooper quite made the statement he was looking for. He wanted our appearance to reflect the perfect couple—wealthy, attractive, influential and a little unnerving. There was no question in my mind that this was exactly what everyone would see.

Alex poured me a glass of the champagne that awaited us in the limo's leather sanctuary. I took my glass and sipped. "Can I ask you a theoretical question?"

"Sure."

"Do you think it's possible to be happily married and still manage to be a dreaded, sociopathic bitch? I mean, I'd hate to lose my basic 'self' just because I got married."

Alex laughed—and not just a little, it was nice to see. "Yes, my little witch, I think it is possible. You just need to learn to drop that aspect of your personality when you're not in public or doing business." His smile wavered and he frowned. "But that isn't tonight. Remember, this is all *business*. We need to be our nasty, hard-ass selves. We need to be the epitome of strength, especially considering my stay with the state. People are going to be looking for chinks in the armor."

I sighed. "You're right," I agreed. "Our families are fine but the other area families need to get the message."

It was like dealing with coyotes—they could smell weakness.

"Then," I added, "we have the Alfonso and Derek problem as well. Did you bring the gun I gave you?"

He nodded.

"Good. I don't know who that was this afternoon, but I don't want to take chances. I have one in my purse and one on me."

Alex looked me up and down, making quite a show of it. I glanced at him while sipping my champagne and asked, "What?"

"Where is it?" he frowned. "That dress doesn't cover much."

I slid my hand under the hem of my dress and pushed it up. From where Alex sat, I knew he could see my cream tone lace panties. The gun was small, just another little pea shooter, but if aimed properly it worked just as well as any .44. It was strapped to my thigh, higher than most women wear garters. I, however, was bare legged. I always hated hose, they made me itch.

"Well, I must say, all things considered, I do like the view."

He slid his hand over my knee and slowly worked his hand up my thigh until he was stroking my bare skin next to the gun. I tipped my head back and his mouth was on mine. His tongue slipped between my lips and ran across my lower teeth, inviting me to play. The rest of our trip to the restaurant was completely lost for me.

I had no desire to get out of the limo when we arrived. We both sat for a moment, breathing hard. I pulled a tissue out of my bag, wiped off his lips and adjusted my lipstick. Then Alex stepped out and turned to take my hand.

We both set our expressions to create our own personal auras of menace. This was a power display evening and we needed to get the message out from the beginning. It was no surprise, that when I walked in on Alex's arm, ring on full display, that all heads turned as we made our entrance. Individually, we could get that reaction if we worked at it—together we didn't have to make an effort.

My brother was the first to approach me. He had brought Cara. He was a lot of things, but his total lack of fear around me was probably one of the strangest. Even my parents were somewhat wary, but never Marty. He was afraid of things I was involved in, but not of *me.*

Cara fawned over me. Made a big deal about how beautiful my ring was and how wonderful it was that I was finally coming home and settling down. I don't know if she meant it, but she sounded sincere. All in all, it was great that she'd attended. It looked good for my family and gave me, and them, a real appearance of family connections—the blood type, not the business variety. One is just as important, if not more so, than the other on an occasion like this.

My regular piano routine wasn't going to work tonight. Alex and I needed to be a couple, acting as one and socializing. I was never good at socializing so I just followed his lead. There were seven family groups here tonight. The upper echelons were all present and their appearance made for a tense room.

Everyone got along, more or less—these families had drawn their territorial lines long ago. However, there were little fish, bigger fish and sharks in the room. The little fish and bigger fish naturally get tense when the sharks are circling. Alex and I, being sharks, produced an inordinate degree of tension as we moved from group to group. But this was *business* after all. We weren't here to win a popularity contest. In fact, we probably managed to do just the opposite … and maybe a little too well.

Alex knew more about all of them than I did. Of course, that was only because I'd been gone for so long. He moved us about the room and eventually we ended up with my parents and Tony.

I'd been home for a month and had only gone to see them twice. I know—you don't have to say it—I'm a rotten daughter. But there's always an underlying sense of falseness and lack of approval when I see them. I've found it better, for my sanity, to avoid it.

My parents understand my family connections and that I work with, and for, Tony. But, they never understood why I'd work for the government. Tony had had problems with this as well. But he'd gotten over it later when he learned just what I was doing. I was still *family.*

I hadn't turned into some super cop who was going to come back and bite them in the ass. That was probably his major concern, initially.

My mother, however, had been devastated and never quite got over it. She and dad hoped I'd pursue any number of careers in life. But for some reason, government assassin just never made the list of top ten parentally approved professions. But I'd decided, long ago, I couldn't be all things to all people. I think it was a song by the late great Ricky Nelson that summed up my feelings.. He sang, very melodically, "Ya can't please everyone, so ya got to please yourself." I couldn't have agreed more.

Dinner was a very nice sit down and Alex and I were seated at the head table. Tony sat to the right of Alex and I sat between Alex and his father, Roberto, who was in a great mood all evening. I caught Alex watching him chat with one of the middle-aged widows sitting at the next table; there were several in attendance.

I leaned into Alex, "He looks like he's enjoying himself. You shouldn't worry so much. He's out. He'll get back on his feet in the next few weeks."

Alex slid his hand over mine on top of the table. "You're right. But those months were a lot harder on him and it wasn't a picnic for me."

"Maybe," I suggested, "he should think about going south. It would remove him from the immediate details of family business. I think Tony's moving to the islands when his tenure is over. He has a real thing for the Cayman Islands."

"I've been thinking about it," replied Alex. "But since Mike's here, I don't know if I could get him to leave. Now he'll be extra-protective of Mike because of what happened to Thad."

Thad … hmmm—that reminded me. I was going to have to do something about that "evidence." I still hadn't had time to sit down and go through it. But now was not the moment to discuss it.

"Are you planning on bringing Mike in?" I asked. "He's still so young. It might be best to wait a while or give him a legit business to run, rather than dragging him into … the other activities."

Yes, I'd been younger, but I'd also been very jaded and the jobs I'd done … well, I wouldn't put them off on someone that age.

"Trust me," said Alex. "I'll leave him out until I can't avoid it anymore. I'm giving him the construction organizations to oversee. I'll go over everything in detail—they're all completely legal. I don't have anything running through it."

"Good," I nodded.

Just then our waiter brought our food. Salad, Prime Rib (an inch thick), potato and some vegetable combination dish. It was all quite tasty … I hadn't eaten since that morning and this was perfect. Alex and I relaxed a bit during the meal, discussing the various people around the room. He filled me in on people I didn't recognize as well as those who'd moved up (or down) in the organizations while I'd been gone.

After our meal, Tony stood and announced our engagement. It went well, despite a couple of less-than-pleased looks on some of the associate family leaders' faces. I could understand this. The Pascolis and Sevellis were already larger than the others individually. Everyone in town knew our dominating personalities. This meant that, together, we would call the shots … and there wasn't much anyone would, or could, do about it.

I, however, had no plans for a city-wide occupation. I wanted things cleaned up and legalized as much as possible. I wanted time to pursue my work and, honestly, I didn't think it was good for one group to run everything. There are reasons that monopolies are frowned upon in our society. Too much power in one place is never a good idea.

Running my hand up the back of Alex's jacket, I leaned into him and whispered, "I think we need to go and convey our lack of interest in dominating the marketplace. I see a few very unhappy faces."

"You saw them too, huh?" he said. "Well, I agree. As soon as dessert is over, let's make the rounds and cover the ones who are the most important."

For the most part, everything had gone well. On the whole, we managed to convey our genuine lack of interest in "expansion" to the powers present. Some were initially skeptical, but they seemed more relaxed after our conversation.

They were worried that our pending marriage was arranged solely for the purpose of overtaking the market. Since Alex and I actually gave off the couple "vibe," we managed to ease that concern.

We had skillfully avoided both Derek and Alfonso, slipping from one group to another without ever having to be in the same group with either. It didn't appeared to be outright avoidance—just poor timing.

Oddly enough, Anthony Sheppa hadn't attended. Theo and Charise, Anthony's parents were there and seemed to be enjoying themselves. Luckily, they weren't taking my engagement to Alex as a personal affront—unlike Elli Merek and Constantine Sampini.

I found it odd that Anthony was missing only because all the area families had sent not only their leader, but also his successor. It was a normal procedure to ensure that both generations were included and acknowledged the new "arrangement." Events like this were always useful for conducting business … they weren't just nice chit-chat.

✳✳✳

Alex and I decided, around midnight, it was time to go. I was tired and so was he. To be perfectly frank, he was getting grouchy. He'd been free for less than thirty-six hours and there was no way he'd caught up on the sleep he needed in just the one night.

I glanced out and saw our limo pull up. We left and Alex slipped my wrap around my shoulders and held the door for me. We approached the limo and as he reached for the door, I heard it—a *click*.

I knew that *click*.

It was the hammer catching on a .38 revolver.

I grabbed Alex and pushed him to the ground with me, just as the shot went off.

Instinct took over. I grabbed the Glock out of my purse and fired back, down the street.

The yelp that followed was satisfying. Yanking off my shoes, I threw them and the purse in the the limo—I'm not one of *Charlie's Angels*. I can't run in high heels over three inches.

Then I took off after the shooter. The shot came from the corner, near the end of the block. I was a quarter of the way down the block when Alex grabbed my arm.

"Let it go," he said.

It wasn't a question. It was an *order*.

I don't take orders well—it was one of the reasons I left the government. Alex must have seen it on my face because he added, "You *hit* him. Leave it alone. He won't try again tonight."

He looked behind us where Tony and several other family leaders were walking in our direction. "Besides," he whispered, "we're drawing a crowd. Let's go home."

We approached Tony while the others stood at a respectful distance—far enough to give the illusion of privacy but close enough to hear the conversation.

"Are you two alright?" asked Tony.

"We're fine," Alex replied. It was a flat authoritative response.

"Ace, put that thing away before a cop shows up." He looked at Tony and said, abruptly, "We'll see you in the morning."

I was escorted back to the car. We climbed in and shut the door. What was he thinking?

"You know as well as I do," I protested, "that the shooter was probably the guy who was following us earlier. Why didn't you let me go after him?"

He looked tired. "How did you know he was there? I didn't see anyone, even when you were shooting at him."

"I heard the click of the hammer on the gun before it went off," I explained. "Little things like that have kept me alive in my business—instant reflexes are mandatory. And I didn't need to *see* him. I knew where the bullet came from by the sound of the shot and I could *feel* him standing at the corner."

Now, he was rstudying me, as though he'd just caught the real drift of what I actually was. I guess being told your future wife is a killer isn't quite the same thing as seeing her in action.

"You *felt* him?" he said in a tone of mild disbelief. He shook his head and rubbed his temples. "Well, you hit him so maybe he won't try again."

Yeah, right! And someday maybe pigs will grow wings and fly.

"If he doesn't, then someone will take his place. He isn't doing this for himself—he's a hired hand. You know that as well as I do."

I settled back in my seat and tried to relax for the ride.

CHAPTER 11

ALEX LOOKED AT ME AFTER a few moments of silence. "I couldn't just let you go shoot him. We had about a hundred other people coming out of the doors behind us. They would have all seen it. And what would you have done with the body? Leave it there? And what the hell would you have told the police if and when they showed?"

He took a deep breath and let it out. "If we were alone, I would have let you take care of it, but the gun didn't have a silencer and there were just too many witnesses." He was reaching over to the other side of the limo for a drink.

"The silencer didn't fit into this bag," I replied flippantly.

It was true. I'd tried to get it in, but no luck.

He glanced back at me, stopped, and thought about it. Apparently he found a good deal of humor in my remarks because he started to laugh.

✳✳✳

The following Monday Alex and I went our separate ways. I reminded him to keep his eyes open and to avoid being out in the open too much. He thought I was being paranoid since I'd hit the guy last Saturday night. He really didn't believe he was in any real danger. I didn't feel nearly so optimistic.

I spent the early part of the day with Tony going over our import businesses. These were completely legit—nothing illegal and totally licensed. However, like all the legit businesses, money was being washed through them. This was going to be a pain in the butt to clean up. I had to speak with Alex and see if he could help me separate as much as possible.

It was around three when the wedding planner arrived and I sat down with her to go over the wedding options. Since we wanted to accelerate the wedding event, we had limited choices of venue. There were only so many places to accommodate a group the size of our families and guests—a guest list of at least several thousand.

We couldn't exclude anyone because it would be considered un-forgivably rude. We had to include all distant relations; upper level management from our contact families, including various organizations in other areas of New Jersey and New York; three family groups from Philadelphia; and one group from Boston. They wouldn't necessarily all attend, but they had to be formally invited. This was going to be big.

Unfortunately, this left only three options: tents in the park, the mu-seum or the coliseum. The coliseum/expedition center would be more than big enough, but I thought it sounded less than appealing. Tents in the park are risky … what if it rains? Not to mention the exposure. You don't want that many families in one place at one time without some general security, and this would be a critical issue in the park.

The museum was my first choice. It was beautiful, securable and could accommodate the right number of people. And for commesurate remuneration, they'd be willing to close down early the day before as well as the actual day of the wedding. I had to talk with Alex of course, but I thought he'd agree.

Just as we were moving into the centerpiece options, Alex stepped into the room. "Alex, you're back. I wasn't sure if you'd be around this afternoon," I said, making room for him on the couch I was sitting on.

I introduced him to Kimberly Garrett, our wedding planner. I told Alex about our options and he agreed with the museum. We also agreed that, even though the ceremony would be Catholic (since we both were raised in the faith) the ceremony wouldn't take place in the church. This was chiefly because all the dates were taken. That, combined with the lack of seating in the church he and I had both attended over the years, settled the matter.

"We need to speak with Father Jacobs," I said. "But we need to set a time and date so that he can arrange his schedule. We also need Kimberly to make arrangements with the museum so that exhibits can be relocated wherever necessary."

Alex, Kimberly and I managed, pretty much, to work out all the basics in just a couple of hours. I think she appreciated how easily Alex and I negotiated the details and all but completely organized the necessities. By the time we were done, we'd picked invitations, a cake, and where we would register for gifts. We'd chosen an orchestra over other music options. We'd decided to rent small tables instead of the banquet variety, picked out linens, dishes and silverware and were pretty much settled on everything but the flowers. We told her that Mario's would be catering and she could contact him for any additional arrangements regarding the food. All we needed, now, were the colors for the floral arrangements, a final date and a guest list.

Kimberly gathered her things and said she would get everything started. We made a date to meet again at the end of the week. Hopefully, by then, we could set a firm date for the wedding, I'd have a preliminary count for attendants, and would have settled on the color of the bridesmaid dresses in order to determine the floral colors.

I glanced up at Alex. "Do I *have* to have bridesmaids? I'm not close to any cousins who live in Jersey and adding people to the wedding just means more personalities to contend with. Can I get away with just Marty's three little girls as flower girls and nothing else?"

"Fine with me, but a maid of honor is a necessity since I'm going to have Mike stand up with me. You can go out with Cara and select dresses for the girls … hey, maybe you could have Cara as your matron of honor?"

Perfect. That would make things easier.

"And I prefer darker colors," he said, "No peach or aqua, if you don't mind. I know I'm not supposed to have an opinion on that, but I do. It will most likely be a late afternoon/evening wedding and neither of us has a peachy personality."

I grinned. Peachy?

"Maybe hunter, navy, burgundy," I suggested, "or something in along those lines? You're right—mint or pink are definitely not either of us."

Kimberly stood suddenly and seemed a little nervous. She'd been that way since Alex had joined us. He seemed to have gotten enough rest last night that his menacing aura was still in place without much effort. Alex and I also stood. I reached over and touched Alex's sleeve. In response he slid his other hand over mine.

"Kimberly," I said, "I'll give you a call in the next couple of days and let you know what has been decided regarding colors so you can get started on the flowers. We'll go see Father Jacobs, settle on a date, and then see if we can coordinate with the museum."

After showing Kimberly out, I looked up at Alex and demanded, "Do you *have* to do that to everyone? I don't want her quitting because you make her jittery."

He smiled. "We could always find a replacement."

I gave his sleeve a tug on the way back toward the kitchen. "I don't *want* a replacement. She's very competent and comes with great references. The next in line wasn't even half as well-recommended. Besides, I think you'd make any of them nervous, so be nice to her."

I looked at him and his quirky smile.

"Okay," I admitted, "you don't have to be *nice*. Just try not to be scary. She'll pull this together in the short time we've allotted and I don't want your overpowering personality messing with it."

"*My* overpowering personality?" he groaned. "What about yours?"

"I can put mine in check when I need something from someone and don't want to scare the crap out of them," I snapped.

That always seemed like a better choice than never getting anything done.

CHAPTER 12

WEDNESDAY MORNING FOUND ME looking for dresses with Cara. She'd agreed that the kids could be my flower girls and said she'd be happy to serve as my matron of honor. I knew she was a bit hesitant, but I did exphasize that this was a one time deal. Once the wedding was over, she and Marty really didn't have any further obligations to Alex or me. I needed to mention this to Alex. Otherwise, he might ask something "inappropriate" of Marty or Cara at some point.

We arrived at Cassandra's Bridal around ten-thirty. The girls were at school and Cara and I decided it would be easier to shop without them. They still have problems standing still for more than twenty seconds or so.

Making the rounds through the racks, we found literally nothing we liked—nothing for me, nothing for Cara, nothing for the girls. So, we made another trip, this time out of town. Beautiful Bride was a much larger store, located west of the city.

In the parking lot, I reached in the back seat to grab my wallet when I caught a glimpse of the car that had followed Alex and me the day we went to Sal's. I thought I noticed it outside Cassandra's but hoped I was just imagining things.

So he *wasn't* dead. Wasn't that fascinating?

I had to think about Cara. I didn't want her getting hurt because of our problems. I decided to fill her in and gave a detailed description of what had happened on Saturday.

"Is that him?" she asked. She turned around and peered through the back window. "*There?*"

The driver behind us couldn't see anything because of the tinted glass on all my car windows.

I nodded. "Well, I think we have three choices," I said. "I can turn around and can take you back to Marty's. Unfortunately, he'll probably follow us right to the front door of Marty's office. Second, we can finish our shopping and just ignore him. Finally, I can take the gun out of the glove box and attempt to ..."

"No!" she gasped. "I don't want to be around when you kill somebody. I know it's just like breathing for you, but I don't want to see it."

She was terrified. Like Marty, Cara was completely aware of who and what I was. Hell, what I always had been.

She'd always accepted this, and me, because I never put her or her family in danger. That, and the fact that I took Marty's side when he left the family business, had a lot going for me with Cara. But this particular situation was actually involving her in a different way.

"I'm not going to *kill* him," I said, reasonably. "Chances are, if he sees me, he'll take off, just like he did at Mike's place on Saturday night."

"I don't know," she said, dubiously. "What if he tries to *shoot* you? Or, maybe, run over you instead? I don't think that's a great option. Could we just lose him?"

"We could, but that would mean a high speed chase. Are you up to sitting there while I do ninety on a side street?"

She crossed her stomach with her arms. She was feeling sick and I knew the whole thing was getting to her.

"I promise," I said, "after today, I won't put you or Marty or the kids in this position. I'm so sorry—I thought this guy was long gone. Initially, he only seemed interested in Alex. I'll try scaring him and then we'll go on and finish our shopping. After this, I'll make myself scarce. You and the girls can do all the fittings without me around."

I glanced her way. "What do you think?"

She gave me an affirmative nod. "Scare him if you can. But I'd rather you didn't kill anyone, okay?"

I smiled and reached for my gun in the glove box, "You don't need to worry. Alex has forbidden me to kill anyone without his knowledge—unless there are no other options, of course."

"Thank goodness one of you has some restraint."

I couldn't help but laugh.

Luckily, I was dressed for work today if it became necessary. That wasn't my intention, but it was probably a good thing. I wore jeans, black boots and a black tank top. I had my coat, if necessary, but for scaring someone, you want them to *see* your gun, not hide it.

Sliding out of the car, I put my bitch persona into place. I gripped my gun and walked slowly, but directly toward the car. When I got within two car lengths, I began to think I was going to have to put a bullet through the windshield to get him to leave. At that point, the driver got nervous and pulled out. He must have gotten in trouble for running away last time or he wouldn't have waited so long.

I went back to the Cooper and decided it might be better if we tried another bridal shop. Otherwise, we'd probably find our tail sitting there waiting for us. "I think we should try Loraine's," I suggested. "Does that sound okay with you?"

"Yes," she agreed. "I don't want him finding us again. Let's leave." She fidgeted in her seat, fingered her seatbelt and looked all around to make sure the car was gone.

I started the engine, put it in gear and pulled out.

About fifteen minutes later, Cara spoke again. "Did Alex really *forbid* you from killing people?" she asked. "I only ask because it seems strange. Alex isn't known for being a … compassionate fellow. It isn't as though *he* hasn't killed people." Then she looked a bit startled. "Please don't tell him I said anything. I don't want him upset with me or Marty."

I couldn't help but grin. She was so concerned over what was really nothing. "I won't say anything," I assured her. "Besides, Marty's my brother. He'd have to do something really bad to get himself … punished in any manner, much less killed. And, to answer your question, yes—Alex was very clear how he felt about my job. He even wants me to completely retire. It seems he's a little uncomfortable being married to an assassin."

That got a full smile from Cara. "Gee, I can't imagine why? Are you really going to quit? I never imagined you'd give a man, any man, even someone like Alex, the authority to tell you what to do."

"It isn't that I've given him *authority*, exactly," I explained. "It's just that all marriages require compromise and this one is no different. We both have to make concessions for this marriage to work. I agreed to give up a "portion" of my work, at least for the time being.

"My future plans are contingent on our having children. And the truth is, if we have kids, I *can't* work. There's just something wrong about being both a mom and an assassin. Alex was pretty clear that this was a non-negotiable point and I think he's right," I concluded, almost sounding as though I was convinced.

She opened her door. "Well," she whispered, "if it's any consolation, I think you're right—the whole killer thing and being a mom … they just sort of clash."

We went to Loraine's. Thankfully, Loraine was there and helped us find everything we needed. We settled on a deep rich red wine tone and managed to get Cara and the girls' dresses in similar styles and I found a wedding dress. Yeah! It was really coming along. I'd have to come back for fittings, but that was about it.

I dropped Cara back at Marty's office, where I'd first picked her up. There was no sign of my shadow anywhere. I said a little "thank you," skyward, and dialed Kimberly's office to fill her in. She seemed quite pleased to have so much done already. I got the impression that most perspective brides don't move along this quickly. We discussed floral arrangements and bouquet alternatives and the overall color scheme as I headed for St. Christopher's.

∗∗∗

Alex and I had an appointment to meet with Father Jacobs at three o'clock. I pulled into the rectory parking lot and headed for the door. Alex's car was already there. We'd had a car rented for him so that he had transportation of his own until we got his things released.

When I arrived I saw Alex was reading a magazine in the waiting area outside Father Jacobs' office. He looked me up and down and shook his head.

I slid into the seat next to him. "What? Go on, say it."

"You're here to talk to our priest about getting married and you look like a bum," he muttered.

I looked at my clothes. I didn't look like a bum exactly. I looked more like an escapee from a juvenile correctional reformatory. I was dressed a lot like the juvenile delinquent I once was. I had well passed "delinquent" some time ago, but my clothes just hadn't kept up.

"Well, I didn't dress for this. I dressed for dress shopping and try-ing on clothes. A tank top and jeans are better for that sort of thing." Okay, so that was a big fat lie.

"Uh-huh." He said it like he didn't believe it. Couldn't say I blamed him.

I really hadn't thought one way or the other about my clothes this morning. I knew I wasn't going to be spending most of the day with Alex, so I wore my regular clothes.

"I don't look like a bum. I just don't look dignified." We were more or less whispering since we didn't want to attract Father Jacobs' secretary's attention. I leaned back in the seat. I noticed that my huge diamond ring was a little strange with the outfit I had on. It didn't exactly go. I really hadn't noticed earlier.

"Dignified? You look like a sixteen year-old. We're supposed to be talking about a wedding, not heading to the mall for a little girl-time." He shook his head. He was being snippy. "When is the last time you saw Father Jacobs?"

I never "head to the mall for girl-time" and he was pissing me off. I'd beaten the crap out of people for saying things like that to me. It was some time ago I'll admit, but I was tempted. He was condescending and I didn't like it. I had two choices, let it go or put up the bitch aura and see if I could scare the crap out of my future husband.

Taking a deep breath, I closed my eyes and then let it out. I decided to let it go. Sitting in a church was no place to have a knock-down-drag-out fight about my clothing.

What I needed was patience. I took another deep breath, closed my eyes and asked God to hand some down because I didn't seem to be finding it on my own.

In the end I knew that pitting him against me would only make things worse. We needed to be a consolidated front and yelling at him in the church office was really not a good idea.

I leaned in so the church secretary couldn't hear me. "You're being rude and patronizing and I don't like it. So knock it off. And it's been about fifteen years."

Alex glanced over at the secretary and decided she hadn't heard a word we'd said. He looked back, leaned over and kissed me. "You're right, I was being rude. But do you think next time we have to do something like this you could try to dress it up a little? A sweater or a nicer blouse would have sufficed." It was his way of ending the argument—winning it but being diplomatic.

I started to open my mouth to say something not very nice when Father Jacobs' door opened. Constantine Sampini stepped out.

Constantine was Derek's father. He'd attended the dinner on Saturday night, but hadn't seemed very happy about our engagement. He was most likely hoping that Derek had made a better impression than he had. We were certain at the time it had more to do with the expansion concerns the others were also having, but now I was wondering.

We said hello and spoke with him for a short time before he departed. Alex and I looked at each other. I was pretty sure we were both thinking the same thing. That guy following us and the shooter may not have been working for Alfonso, no matter how convenient it may have been to accuse him.

We spoke with Father Jacobs and arranged the time and date. We had to confirm with Kimberly that the museum would okay the schedule, but I felt better. The down side was that we were going to have to attend marriage classes. He had all but insisted, and since Father Jacobs was being flexible with his schedule, we decided not to argue.

On the way to the door I turned back to Father Jacobs. "Father, I don't remember Constantine Sampini ever attending church here. I of course know him as one of Tony's associates, but I thought he attended over at St. Mike's? Did he transfer?"

"No, Mr. Sampini is not a member of this congregation." He said it with a slight sound of disgust. At the same time, he sounded grateful that Sampini had not joined our ranks.

"Oh, I was just wondering if he'd decided to join while I was gone. Thanks for everything." And out we went. It was just under an hour since I'd entered the church. On the way out to the car I told Alex about the dresses, my chat with Kimberly and the tail I'd had earlier.

"So you spooked him again?"

"I didn't have much choice. I couldn't let Cara get caught up in this crap. And, just so I mention it, my brother and his family are *never* to be involved in family business. He's on the outside and he's staying there. Marty isn't up to family work. He never has been. He runs his insurance agency and he and Cara are happy with things that way." I stated this clearly. I didn't want there to be any confusion on that front.

Alex looked over at me across the top of my car. "I wish I could get my brother to do that. Unfortunately, he's young and he wants in neck deep. It doesn't seem to matter what I tell him. Not even the time Dad and I spent in jail seems to have any impact on his interest."

"Marty never had the skills or the personality for our work," I replied. "He started in the family almost as young as I did, but when he went to college he met Cara and she made him promise to get out and stay out. There were a lot of confrontations at the time and I took on the majority of things he turned down. It got him off the hook more often than not. But in the end, Cara was right. He would have ended up dead or in jail and neither of those options would be good for his little girls."

"Not to change the subject, but why did you ask about Constantine in there?" Alex asked.

"Well, weren't *you* curious? I know I was. I wondered what he was doing there if he isn't a member of the church. I couldn't very well ask Father Jacobs." There was that whole priest confidentiality thing.

"Oh, I was curious alright. I was coming to services every few weeks until I got sent away, and I never once spotted Constantine. And there is no way Father Jacobs would have told you even if he wanted to tell you." He gave me a big smile. "He's kind of close-mouthed that way."

Alex turned from me and headed to his car. "I'll see you back at the house." He was standing about three feet from the rental car when he punched the automatic door opener and the lights flashed.

Right before he got to the car I remembered something. "That reminds me ..." I called out. Alex turned and walked back in my direction, "we need to find a real estate agent. Do you have one that's related, that we have an obligation to use? Our side doesn't."

Alex had approached my side of the car. Just as he opened his mouth to respond the rental car blew up. Alex and I both went down instantly, crouched together and covering our heads. The debris from the explosion was falling everywhere and I was going to be extremely pissed if anything happened to my Cooper.

The black on black with the darkened windows and the sports package without the stripes was tough to find.

CHAPTER 13

I HEARD A HUGE CRASH. SHIT!!! It was the glass in my Cooper. Something big must have smashed it. Alex reached over and grabbed me. I think he was making sure I was okay.

"I'm alright. Are you?" I asked.

He nodded. We stood up and looked behind us at the rental ... or what was left of it. The car was in a million blackened pieces all over the parking lot and what was left in its original location, the frame, had black smoke and flames billowing from it. My car had a charred fender in its front window and the hood was scrunched.

"Damn!"

I looked over and Father Jacobs was standing on the grass of the rectory, eyes wide and hand over his heart. I was praying he wasn't going to have a heart attack, I didn't feel up to CPR, I just wanted to cry looking at my car. Then the sirens came.

✳✳✳

Alex and I had to go through all the details leading up to the explosion at least a dozen times. We weren't released for four hours. The questioning became so incessant that I called Max from my cell phone after the first two hours. It had survived in the glove box of my car, along with my guns, which I quickly and quietly removed prior to the police arrival. I didn't want to explain my weaponry.

Max was used to dealing with the local police. I didn't want to pull out my badge and I didn't want to have to play lawyer with them. The less the police know about me the better. I hadn't been in direct trouble with them since I was very young (I believe I was fourteen). I got good, at an early age, at not getting caught. Max managed to get us released finally. Otherwise, they might have kept us there all night.

For some reason, the cops didn't seem to understand that we had nothing to do with blowing up our own rental car. They also were under some strange impression that, if we really hadn't done it, then we knew who had. It was very clear from their behavior that they hadn't gotten past Alex's release.

I, for one, could have given them several possible perps for the car incident, but I didn't know for a fact that any of them had actually done it. But now I had every intention of finding out who was responsible.

I called Jason and he came to get us. When he pulled up in front of the station, he had a less than happy look on his face, almost somber.

"You okay?" I asked. "You look like someone shot your puppy."

That got me a smirk. "I'm fine. Tony's in a mood. Apparently you two almost getting blown-up and fried is bothering him, and in a church parking lot no less. He's worried."

I slid into the back seat and let Alex have the front. "Nice to know he cares."

"Actually, he's furious. He was hoping you'd killed that guy on Saturday, but it looks like whoever it was, is still around."

"Why does he think the guy from Saturday is dead?"

"Didn't he tell you?" asked Jason. "Apparently not. Pikey Deveraux was found dead, bullet wound. He bled to death."

"Who's Pikey Deveraux?" I demanded.

I hadn't been around here for a long time. Names and associations change. I would think a name like Pikey would stand out in my memory.

Alex responded. "Pikey's an independent. He does dirty work no one wants reflecting directly on their own family. He's worked for most of us at one time or another. He has ... well, had ... no loyalties to anyone."

"Seems to me that just because I shot a guy on Saturday," I said, frowning, "it doesn't necessarily mean this was the same person behind both attacks. If I did kill the guy I shot on Saturday—let's say it was this guy Pikey—then that could just mean that the person who hired our dead guy went out and hired someone else to finish the job Pikey botched. Was Pikey just a shooter, or did he dabble in other elimination methods?"

"Shooter … almost always," Alex responded.

"That makes sense then. This new one seems to have other skills. Otherwise a well-placed bullet would have been sufficient."

"Do you think we could discuss something else?" Alex said, testily. "I almost got blown to bits. I'd rather not think about being shot in the head, too." He sounded tense, more so than in the police station. It was clearly sinking in, and it was about time.

When we got back to the house, I realized how right Jason was. Tony was in a state. I'd known him all my life, and better than most, but I don't think I'd ever actually witnessed this particular disposition from him. Freaked-out would be the best description I could come up with.

Alex and I adjourned to our room after Tony finally calmed down. I had promised Tony we'd sort it all out. I couldn't promise to eliminate the problem, mostly because I had to confirm everything with Alex. I could see this was going to get sticky at times.

I walked in, sat on my side of the bed and took off my boots. I then walked into the bathroom and started a bath. The tub was a huge garden tub and would take a while to fill. Alex was sitting at the desk staring at his hands when I walked back in.

"Are you okay? Really?"

He turned in his seat and looked at me. "No. I don't like that someone wants me dead. It's bad enough the police want me back in jail. Do you have any theories on how we're going to 'sort this out' the way you told Tony?"

I was in the process of stripping off my jeans for my bath. "Yes, but I'd feel better if you would just let me take care of it. That's what I do. I eliminate problems. I know you aren't comfortable with my career choice, but in situations like this, I really am one of the best."

He watched me strip down to my panties. Not responding to my comment. "Are you taking a bath?"

I looked down. "I kind of thought that was obvious. I smell like burnt car and I'm covered in a layer of ash. And from the looks of you, I'd say you didn't fare much better."

I don't think he'd even realized. We were both a mess and really lucky to have avoided being blown-up, much less to have come through completely unscathed despite the large pieces of car that rained from the sky.

"Do you want to share?" I figured it would be comforting and might take his mind off of the day's events.

He didn't respond verbally, but instead he started removing clothing. An hour and a half later we were lying in bed. We were both tired and snuggled under the covers about to fall asleep when there was a knock at our bedroom door.

"Yes," Alex called.

The door opened slightly, and I could see a very uncomfortable look on Jason's face through the back light of the hall.

"Tony thought I should stop up and see if you wanted any food sent up. You guys didn't have a chance to get dinner or anything."

I hadn't even thought of it. But now that he mentioned it, I was starving and said so. Alex agreed.

"There was vegetable lasagna prepared for dinner tonight. If I have it warmed up and bring up some wine and bread, does that sound good?"

It sounded like heaven to me. Alex didn't seem opposed, so Jason took off to get the provisions ready. I rolled back into Alex's arms and closed my eyes again. After a few minutes, "I suppose I should put on a robe at least."

"Why?"

"Jason will be back with our food and I'd prefer he didn't see all of me. I'm not bashful, but I don't like the idea that he knows what I look like naked." It was sort of like your brother seeing you naked—creepy.

Alex laughed, then slid out of bed. He slipped on his robe, turned on a light and pulled the small writing desk from the corner up next to our bed to set the food on.

"You can just stay in bed. He doesn't need to see anything." He then gave me a more lingering look. "And I don't want him seeing anything."

Alex climbed back into bed and we curled up until our food came. Jason and Dianne, Tony's maid/cook, brought up our food and left.

Eating lasagna in bed was a little strange, but it tasted good. We hadn't discussed our problems any farther until after our meal.

Alex and I were sitting in bed, drinking wine and finally he said it, "I've been thinking. I believe it's best if you take care of this problem. I don't want to get killed and if someone keeps trying, they'll either succeed or they'll end up hurting someone close to me. You can do whatever you feel needs doing. But," he turned his face to mine, "please try to be as discrete as possible. We don't need any more problems with the police than we already have."

"Fine. Tomorrow do you have plans?"

"I have to meet my uncle and then I'm supposed to go see Mike. Why?"

"Because I'm going to follow you, I'll tail you until I spot our mystery player. Then I'll follow him. I still want you to be careful though. Just because we have a shadow and someone has tried to kill you twice, doesn't mean they're one and the same."

"You mean there could be *more* than one person who wants me dead. I don't think I like that. Actually, I *know* I don't like that."

Yep, that would definitely suck, but that wasn't my thought process.

"No," I cautioned. "I'm just wondering if the person following you is a *state* employee. I'm thinking that maybe the D.A. wasn't happy when his case vanished before his eyes and now he's got someone following you. I just don't want to leave you vulnerable and unaware of the possible danger while I'm off chasing your shadow, who may, in the end, turn out to be completely innocuous."

"Why don't you think they're the same person?"

"Because the guy following us doesn't seem very good at hiding his car and it's the same car. It didn't change. If it had changed I'd be more likely to believe he's the one trying to kill you. I just want to confirm my suspicions."

I finished my wine and put the glass on my night table. I snuggled down onto my pillow. "But while I'm off confirming, be careful." I took a moment and thought. "Actually, do you have someone who could play chauffeur? Maybe stay with your car while you're doing your errands?"

"I could get someone. Do you think I should? I could just be putting someone else in the line of fire."

"No, he wants you and he's less likely to plant a bomb if there's someone staying with the car at all times."

Alex set his glass on top of the writing desk, next to our plates. There was a knock. It was Jason again, he'd come to take the plates. We said our good nights and he was gone with the dishes.

Alex slipped off his robe and pulled me up close. He wrapped his arms around me and we both drifted off to sleep.

Chapter 14

THE NEXT MORNING THE FUN began. Now I was carrying, not only my guns, but my badge. If you want a state employee to disappear, the best way to make it happen is to pull rank. I just needed to substantiate what I believed was taking place.

When Alex pulled out of the driveway, driven by his younger cousin Rob, there was no one in sight. I let my car (actually it was one of Tony's), a blue Mercedes, fall back far enough that no one would ever know I was following. I had a tracking device on Alex's ride and could follow at a distance. The line was clean until we hit Stevens Street. That's when the shadow showed. He was still driving that same generic car.

Alex arrived at Uncle Joseph's and made his way up the front walk. The shadow pulled into a spot three houses up and parked. I kept going to the next cross street and parked on the side of the road.

I had to get to the shadow's car in broad daylight without him seeing me. Now that was a pain in the butt. Instead, I decided the most logical option was to be straightforward about the whole thing. I started the car again, made a U-turn and headed to the driveway directly behind the shadow's car.

The house that this driveway led to gave the impression of being empty, everyone was probably at work. The car on the street was only about twenty feet from my own. I got out, pulled my gun and aimed at his tires. I shot out the two on my side before he even realized I was walking in his direction. That's one of the benefits of using a silencer.

I made my way to the driver's side just as he was starting the engine. I put out the other two tires, went to the front door and yanked it open before he could get at the gun in his side holster.

"Well, isn't this interesting." I had my gun pressed to his temple. He stopped moving altogether.

"Lady, you don't understand," he stammered, fear permeating every word.

"I think I do. Did you know that someone tried to blow up my fiancé yesterday?" He nodded aggressively. "Funny how you've been spending so much time following him and all of a sudden his car blows up. One might get the impression those two things were connected." I reached inside his jacket and took his gun. "Now get out of the car."

He slowly slid out of the car and I shut the door. "Now, turn around slowly and put your hands on the roof of the car. I want to make sure you don't have any more weapons."

"Lady, this may not be something you want to hear, but I'm a cop. And I didn't blow up your boyfriend's car." He was quiet for a few more seconds and then continued. "You can't just *shoot* me. I mean, my boss told me to follow you and your boyfriend."

I took his handcuffs, they were attached to the back of his belt, and cuffed him. "Well, isn't that just the biggest shock I've had all day?" I said sarcastically. "Where's your badge?"

Turning him around to face me, I should have known that there would be be some confusion. "You aren't surprised at all," he muttered. "You *knew* I was a cop. You shot out my tires … Oh, God, you're gonna kill me aren't you? Shit! I knew I should have given this assignment to Kolby. He wanted it so bad. He'd deserve to be shot. They all said the families were trouble and you—hell—every one of the old guys said to stay clear of you. They said you were bad news. Shit!!"

"Are you done whining yet?" He looked down at his feet, probably realizing the spectacle he was making of himself. I pulled his badge out of his left inside pocket. "Okay, Detective Steven Morrey. I looked at yours now you can have a look at mine." I pulled out my own and showed it to him.

My ex-boss had never wanted it back. He said it came in handy on the rare occasions I had to do work for the government and needed access, and I wasn't one to use it without pressing necessity.

"As you can see," I said calmly, "I have no intention of killing you." I thought I should probably clarify that.

"Not that I won't, so don't piss me off. I'd just rather not. Dead cops are hard to explain. Now, we can do this the easy way or the hard way. You can leave this case voluntarily, while I look for the guy who tried to kill Alex, or I can arrange for you to leave this case. I can arrange the kind of pressure that makes a vise squeezing your nuts seem comfortable by comparison." Not that I thought he was being given a choice in this, but better to deter him from continuing once I officially got rid of him.

He winced. Private-parts in a vise was a rather colorful thought for most men, I had to admit.

"You act like I'm doing this because I like it," Detective Morrey whined. "Do you have any idea how *boring* it is following your boyfriend? He doesn't do anything. Hell, at least watching you I got to drive around and look at wedding dresses."

I lifted an eyebrow at that. "Do you like wedding dresses?" I asked. For all I knew, this guy liked to wear women's underwear in his spare time. You just never know about people.

He turned beet red. "No, but at least it was scenery."

"Fine, then you should enjoy this, because you're getting a new assignment shortly."

I took his boss's name and rank, and *his* boss's boss's name and rank. I then called my ex-supervisor and asked him to take care of the pressure. I got a hard time about breaking into the courthouse and destroying evidence—apparently Phil had heard about that. He wasn't complaining about Alex's stuff, but rather the other two cases that were ruined along with it. Apparently killing Thad and getting rid of all the evidence against Alex and his dad wasn't a problem. But interfering in other cases was a completely different issue for Phil. He thought I'd been messy.

I didn't admit to doing any of it, especially in front of shadow-boy. But Phil knew me too well to believe it could be anyone else.

"Alright already. I accept the criticism if I have to, but would you please get the locals off my butt? I have bigger problems. Someone tried to flambé Alex and I have to keep an eye on him. If I have the state's people all over him, it makes it just that much more difficult to sort the bad guys from the good. I don't want to take out a cop by mistake." I knew that would get his help if nothing else.

Phil groaned. "Why are you doing this?"

I wandered away from my temporarily detained detective and spoke in almost a whisper. I gave Phil an overall of my relationship with the families and my present situation. I'd never really felt it necessary to bring up my family affiliations before. He knew I was dysfunctional. Wasn't that enough?

I heard something on the other end of the line that sounded like snickering.

"Let me see if I got this right," said Phil. "You're taking over a crime family … one you've been related to your whole life. And now you're marrying into another family, so as to avoid a possible power struggle within the local families. But you think one of the other prospective husbands, one you didn't want, is pissed and trying to kill the one you broke out of jail. You've threatened this cop more than once and you've shot out his tires. And to wrap this up, now you want me to get the cops off your back so you can go look for the mad-bomber." At that point, he was laughing so hard he could barely choke out the last sentence.

He was finding my life funny. It was, I suppose. Just not from where I was standing.

"More or less," I conceded. I wasn't smiling. I felt like crap having to tell Phil this. He was never going to let me live it all down.

"Angel, only you could have a home life more dangerous than your work life. You do know you can't run a crime family? You're part of law *enforcement,* not law *breaking.*"

"I *used* to be part of law enforcement," I replied. "I *retired.* Remember? Now, I'm an independent. And, if it makes you feel better, if I have to take over, I'm planning on cleaning up the family. And, truth be told, most of my fiancés' family is already clean. I just need you to refocus the state's attention."

I thought about the best way to get Phil on board. "Besides," I pressed, "this whole thing looks a lot like harassment. This cop, Morrey, has no reason to be following Alex or me. I could have Alex file a lawsuit instead, but I'd rather not. It's too time-consuming and muddies the waters."

Phil had a thing about frivolous lawsuits. He could go on and on for hours on the subject. "Don't you even think about it!" he growled. "You don't need to be any more of a local attraction than you are right now, and neither does he. I'll work the pressure. You should be able to get free in an hour or so, provided I can get to the people I need to speak with."

"Sounds good, Phil. Thanks."

"And Angel, take the *handcuffs* off the cop. They don't like it when they get their own cuffs slapped on them and their gun taken away. They feel stupid and you know where that leads."

"Yeah, yea, slap a hornet ... I know the saying."

The saying is something Phil often alluded to. It goes something like: If you slap a hornet you shouldn't be surprised when it gets pissed and stings you in the ass. He meant, of course, that the cop might just continue following me because I pissed him off. And that was true and not something I wanted to deal with.

I un-cuffed the cop and gave him back his gun, without the bullets of course. I didn't want a standoff with him; then I'd have to shoot him and that was nothing but trouble waiting to happen.

"Now my dear detective," I said, soothingly. "You should be getting new orders shortly. You can just sit here 'til then. I'm sure Alex won't be out until around noon. You'll probably have to call a tow truck for the car, though."

"Why did you have to shoot out *all* my tires? How am I going to explain this?" He was walking around the car looking at his flats in disbelief. "I can't tell my boss what really happened, I'll get laughed off the force."

If he knew who I really was, he wouldn't have to worry about getting laughed off the force. Hell, they'd probably give him an accommodation for bravery. But I had no intention of filling him in.

"If I hadn't shot out the tires," I explained, patiently, "you would have high-tailed it out of here so fast I would never have gotten any information out of you. And if I didn't get the information, you were just another question mark. I don't have time to be chasing cops when I have more serious things to take care of. Besides, I had to be sure you were a cop and not the nut who tried to blow Alex up. And, for an explanation … you could say you left the car to get a closer look at Alex and when you came back they were all flat. You said it yourself, following him gets boring. Or you could have it towed to a local garage and send me the bill. But either way, you should be pleased. You won't have to follow him anymore."

"Right," replied Detective Morrey. "Don't take this the wrong way, but I'll believe it when I see it. My boss is really pissed because he's getting all kinds of crap since your boyfriend got out." He glanced up from the car at me. "You didn't have anything to do with that, did you?"

Shadow-boy wasn't nearly as stupid as he looked. And, I might add, he looked like a slob—wrinkled pants, a T-shirt that appeared to have spent time in the dirty clothes pile, and beat-up sneakers. This was topped by a blue windbreaker with rumples the size of the Grand Canyon. If he looks like that when he's working, I'd be afraid to see him at home.

"Do you really want me to answer that?" I asked. "I mean, consider the type of person who could have done all those things in order to get Alex released. If I were such a person, then that would make me an extremely dangerous individual—not to mention highly skilled. And, to top it off, I carry a badge. Knowing would really not be in your … best interest."

Complete understanding suddenly crossed his face. "You're right." he agreed quietly. "I like breathing. I don't want to know anything."

I heard a small chirp. He reached for an inside pocket and pulled out a phone.

"Yeah … oh … okay." He looked up at me, smiled and shook his head. "Yeah, don't worry about it. I'll start back to the precinct to fill out the rest of my paperwork. See ya later."

He was still watching me when he hung up. "I don't know what the hell your guy did, but it worked—and damned quick, too. I don't work here anymore." He reached in his glove box to grab the tow truck number.

"I highly recommend," I reminded him, "that you forget about this entire conversation. It might be best, not just for me, but for you as well. I still have a bad guy to catch and it would be to everyone's benefit if I didn't have additional problems while looking for him."

"Not a problem for me. I don't want to remember you," said Detective Steven Morrey, "this conversation, your badge or your boyfriend. The two of you are like a bad dream," he muttered.

He turned to his car and sat in the driver's seat. "I know it's none of my business, but I was wondering," he probed cautiously, "what's gonna happen in this town with the families? It's been quiet for years. There are no problems at the moment. Everything is peaceful. Everyone has his own territory and no one fights. My boss seems pretty upset, but I think this has to do with you coming back into town and the rumor that you're taking over for Tony Pascoli and marrying the head of the other largest family organization in the area. Everyone's afraid that we'll see an increase in, not only crime in general, but homicide … if you know what I mean? I hope you and the hubby-to-be aren't planning on changing anything … growing the family, that sort of thing."

Boy, now that was a big thought process for someone who looked so stupid and dressed so badly. I was impressed to discover he did have a brain, after all, under that slob attire.

"No," I assured him. "Alex and I are getting married to keep things stable … not to rock the boat. Neither of us wants warring factions in the families. We're hoping to keep everything floating on an even keel."

Detective Morrey nodded happily. "Good, because the more problems the families create, the more dangerous my job is. We got enough

trouble with gangs. We don't need the families starting turf wars, too."
He glanced down at the little card in his hand. "Well, I'm just gonna
call for a tow and a ride. I'll be out of here shortly."

I stood up and walked back to my car. Then I drove down the street,
said hello to Rob, and knocked on Uncle Joe's door. I spoke with Alex
and filled him in on recent events.

Then I climbed into the Mercedes and pulled out of the driveway.
I made my way around the block and came back full circle. Now *I*
was Alex's shadow. But I needed to keep my eyes open … that bomb
didn't plant itself. Someone would try again. And I wanted to be there
when they did.

∗∗∗

My cop friend, the-shadow-that-was, was absolutely correct. Following Alex was beyond boring, I wanted to take a nap by three in the
afternoon. Luckily, Alex went home before I started snoozing.

I pulled in a few minutes or so behind him, parked the car back
in the garage and went inside.

When I reached the hall, on the other side of the kitchen, I heard
voices. One of them was Tony. The other voice was familiar but I
couldn't place it.

Being the busybody I can be on occasion, I stopped outside the
library door and listened. The door was solid and if it hadn't been
slightly ajar, I wouldn't have even known there was a conversation taking place. I leaned my ear into the opening. I would have preferred a
listening device, but the old-fashioned way worked pretty well.

"… you're really going to let her *marry* him? He's a killer and, with
his connections and strength, he'll take over the Pascolis. He'll take them
over and clean them out. They won't even be run by one of their own.
Alex is a menace. The best thing that could have happened was for him
to have stayed in jail. I can't imagine why you helped him get out."

Well, now. This was an interesting conversation to stumble onto.
I wondered what the chances were that Tony had left the door open
on purpose.

"Would you calm down?" Tony replied. "I didn't help him out of jail … I don't know *how* he got out … but I have my suspicions. He and Angelica made their decision to marry long before his arrest. I offered her other options while Alex was away, but she wasn't interested."

Boy, Tony was a good liar. Of course I knew this firsthand—it wasn't like he'd never lied to me. But he was always totally believable.

I felt someone approach. I hadn't heard anything but I definitely felt a presence. I turned my head slightly and looked up at Alex, his left eyebrow raised quizzically. His expression said "shame on you." I raised my finger to my lips and pointed at the door, gesturing for him to "Be quiet and listen." I moved over slightly and we both tuned in as the conversation inside continued.

"… expect me to believe that she's marrying him without your approval?"

We heard Tony laugh … actually, it was more of a soft chuckle. "You think I have some say in who she chooses to marry? I couldn't even stop her from working for the government, all those years ago. Do you think she's *less* head-strong now?"

There was a slight sigh.

"No—I have no say in this matter," said Tony, firmly. "I gave her criteria and she chose within those guidelines. As you, and all the others should probably have guessed, years ago, Angel is excessively intelligent, extremely dangerous and determined to make her own choices. Since she's been overseas, she's actually become *more* dangerous and independent. *She* chose Alex. I couldn't force her to choose someone else. She will do as she pleases. You and the other family leaders are quite well aware of her general disposition in matters of this nature."

"Yes, we are. That is one of my key points in all of this; her disposition. She isn't likely to want to stick around and run the Pascoli operations and Alex is going to end up with both large families under his rule. Ace is brilliant, no one would dispute it. She's also devious and she walked away from here years ago to avoid family issues. What makes you think that once you retire, and she and Alex marry, that she won't just walk away again? That could be why she didn't even consider the other three you offered her. She knows Alex can manage it all."

"You're right," said Tony. "And that was one of the main reasons she chose him—his strength. She believes that if something should happen to her, or for some reason she should need to leave for a few days or even weeks, she can trust Alex to keep things running smoothly. She is family and honor-bound and before you ask, yes, she does know the meaning of honor; probably better than most of the others running their families, and without a doubt better than me. However, with all that said, she and Alex have chosen to get married for reasons beyond family obligations. They seem to genuinely care for one another. I've seen it myself over the last few days. They share a room and from all accounts appear to be in love. I believe this is not merely a convenient marriage for family work purposes. I think they'd be getting married even if I weren't pushing for her to make an alliance."

"Is that supposed to make me feel better or worse? What you're saying is that not only will she stand by him in business, but she'll do so blindly. She has no business inheriting the family if she isn't going to run it."

The sound of Tony's voice said he was getting pissed. "Angelica knows her responsibilities to the family. *Her family*. She came home for exactly that reason. She would have stayed in Italy if she didn't feel it was necessary for her to take the reins at some point. But she knows, and I know, that she is the best and most appropriate choice to influence the Pascolis. She is devoted to the family and will do what needs to be done, with or without Alex. And I can absolutely, without a doubt in my mind, say that she will not allow Alex to run her over, or her family. Ace may be in love, she may be extremely soft on Alex, but she will draw the line if it needs to be drawn."

I heard a chair move inside. It sounded like Tony's desk chair. Then there was the clinking of glass. He was pouring himself a drink. I couldn't blame him. If the situation were reversed, I'd be doing the same.

"But you know he killed his first wife don't you? What makes you think he won't do the same to Ace and just take everything?"

Tony started laughing so hard I thought he might choke on that drink.

I glanced up at Alex. He was smiling and watching me.

Tony continued behind the door. "I'm sorry, I shouldn't be laughing. Murder is a serious matter, after all. But you have to understand, Alex may have killed his previous wife, but Angelica's made a career out of killing and for far less serious reasons than Alex had. Alex would have a very hard time getting rid of her. As a matter of fact, I'm far more concerned for Alex's safety if he upsets her. My little Angelica is far more likely to turn to killing as an option than Alex is. She is, after all, one of the best in her field."

There was silence for a moment. Tony's diction changed. "Well, maybe you've heard the rumors through the years about Angelica's chosen profession? She's never confirmed my suspicions as to which government agency she was associated with, but since she's been living in *Europe* for many years now, I've decided that the CIA makes the most sense. It's just a matter of putting two and two together. I'd say that her exceptional skills and government connections would be proof enough of her past … undertakings, and behavior outside of the family."

I frowned. I wished he hadn't known that much. The question was how much more did Tony guess at. It wouldn't take a genius to place my tatts. Alex was right, sooner or later someone in our field would place me and that would cause problems for our future. I hated that he was right. I glanced at Alex. His face was the mirror of what mine must have looked like.

"You mean to tell me that Ace is a government spy of some sort and you are letting her take over your family? Are you crazy? Not to mention the implications of putting someone like that with …" He stopped. "You really don't know who got him out of jail?"

"No. I have no confirmation as to who it was. But, as I said, Angelica and Alex were engaged prior to his being sent to jail. "

"Am I correct then in assuming you suspect it was Ace?"

That was the end of that conversation. I knocked on the door and opened it before Tony could answer. Alex and I both put out our nasty attitudes for full view and feel. Sitting in the chair in front of Tony's desk was Constantine Sampini.

The expression on his face was one of awe and shock. I suppose being face to face with a government spy/assassin and one of the scariest killers on the East Coast might give a person pause, particularly when you know she's about to get married and merge two crime families.

"There you two are. I'm sure you both remember Constantine." Tony knew we did, of course.

I nodded in Constantine's general direction and Alex shook his hand. He could be so diplomatic when necessary. I, on the other hand, was not quite as pleasant and for once, neither Alex nor Tony gave me a dirty look about it.

I slipped off the oversized denim shirt I'd worn as a jacket so that, when I turned my back, my guns would be in full view. Since Tony had already unmasked my other existence, there was no reason not to play it up. I was wearing a pair of low rise Levi's and a black tank top covered my tattoo. Constantine already knew more than I wanted.

Making my way over to Tony's liquor cabinet, I reached for the scotch. I took out a glass and made myself a drink. I stood in the corner sipping and doing my best to make Sampini uncomfortable. I watched his reaction to me as he and Alex were discussing pleasantries and then the bomb that had claimed the rental car.

He had been at the church yesterday. That alone was odd. But Constantine wouldn't have risked planting a bomb himself, if he was even capable of making one and wiring it to the locking system of the car. I had reservations there, too. He was a shooter by reputation and, to my understanding, didn't dabble in other types of elimination himself—not even in his prime, which he was now long passed. I also had doubts that he could actually scooch far enough under the car to reach the necessary mechanisms to plant the bomb. He had a rather large chest and stomach—an operation like this required a certain amount of speed and agility.

After another twenty minutes of discomfort, seat shifting and jerky eye movements, mostly directed at me, Constantine took his leave. Jason suddenly appeared in the door to show Constantine out. Tony must have some sort of buzzer under his desk.

Tony turned to me when the door to his library closed behind Constantine. "So, how long were you out there listening?"

I lifted a brow at the comment. A nice "Who me?" look.

"Don't even think I didn't notice your timing … right as he was asking me if you'd gotten Alex out of jail?" He gave me a tisk-tisk finger waggle. "No, you were listening. That's the reason I left the door partly open. I heard Alex walk in and up the stairs, just after Constantine arrived. I figured you'd be soon to follow."

"You shouldn't have told him what I was. It creates problems that Alex and I were hoping to avoid. Actually, Alex wanted me to remove my tattoo for just that reason, to avoid identification." I turned and made Alex a drink—he looked grim and probably needed one.

"I still want it removed," he said flatly. "He hasn't identified you, just your arena of work. You do see now that it's necessary? Since our lifestyles are a little less than orthodox, I'd say we stand a good chance of people sniffing around your past, especially regarding the time you were gone. If it becomes common knowledge that you are The …" I turned to Alex when he cut his speech. He looked at Tony and then back to me. "Well, who you are, then. We could be putting not only our future, but any children we have, in danger."

"Yes, I see it. I don't like it, but I see it." I walked over to Alex and handed him his drink. "I'll have the large one removed soon. My past though, would be impossible for anyone to get at. All of my previous work would be considered highly classified. The majority would be denied access, even at the top-most levels."

Tony leaned forward onto his elbows. "I only mentioned your government affiliations because I felt it would make you appear stronger. And that was the concern that Constantine was voicing. He's afraid Alex will run you over … but I seriously doubt that Constantine will tell anyone about you. He's scared, and you being what you are, it just makes you appear that much more frightening to him."

I didn't believe that for even a minute.

Alex spoke, "He may have been voicing those concerns, but I don't think that was what was bothering him. As for being frightened, that was obvious, but people who are scared of change can do very stupid things without thinking through all the possible ramifications."

Chapter 15

SINCE MOVING INTO TONY'S I'd been trying to check my e-mail accounts daily. At one time it was something I'd done every couple of hours. Now that Alex was out and I had a wedding to plan I was lucky to remember it once a day.

Over the last couple of weeks I'd turned down several Lucifer's Mistress projects, and hadn't heard a thing on either of the other two fronts. The Fallen Angel was, for lack of a better word, retired, so the only time I heard anything was when Phil was desperate.

With me getting married, he may just let it go and avoid using me altogether. Good thing, considering my obligations to Alex and my promise to leave the business. Then, there was The Angel Divine. Typically, someone made contact only once every three weeks or so.

The Angel Divine's charitable service was something that only a select few knew about, and those few were made up of a couple of politicians, a handful of police officers, several mercenaries and a scattering of private residents. These people were strewn throughout the world and when something became bad enough, one of them contacted me.

All of my contacts were aware that I had to approve the target. They were also aware that if I could use law enforcement to take the target in question off the streets, I would. It was a public service, after all, not an assassination freebee.

After my conversation with Alex and Tony I'd headed upstairs to check my mail sources. Sitting behind the little writing desk, laptop in front of me, I checked the first of the three accounts.

The Lucifer's Mistress account almost always had some form of correspondence in it. Today there were two job offers and a note from one of the contractors I'd rejected asking for a reference for someone I'd recommend in my place. The first two were easy. I just sent a "Thank you, but no thank you" note in reply. The third was more difficult.

I find it hard to recommend anyone in my field. There are competent assassins all over the place, some better than others. The problem is that most of them are in it strictly for the money and never use any moral guidelines when selecting contracts. How do I consciously select someone I know has no conscience?

As I started to reply and explain that I don't give professional references, I heard my bedroom door open. It was Alex, of course.

"Writing a friend?" He walked behind me to read over my shoulder.

Living with Alex, I was going to lose all sense of privacy with regard to my work. It felt a little strange, but I figured I just had to get used to it. I'd been alone so long that it wasn't startling that I had adverse feelings to sharing.

"Only if your friend wants to bump off a public official in Spain." I looked up at him.

"You aren't actually going to give this guy the name of someone are you?" He really looked offended by the idea.

"No, I don't do that. I just make sure I return all mail correspondence. I wouldn't want to be thought rude."

Alex smiled. "So, what are you doing other than not giving out references?"

"Turning down jobs mostly, I still have to check the other two accounts."

I turned back to the computer to do just that. I checked my Fallen Angel e-mail and there was a message from Phil. I looked up at Alex. "I can't let you read the correspondence from the government. No offense, but it is considered classified." Alex still had his smile in place, turned around and headed for the bathroom.

Basically, Phil told me he'd taken care of my state problems. He reiterated his lack of appreciation that I'd left the government, destroyed evidence and gone back to the "mob," as he called it.

He also said I wouldn't be hearing from him again via this channel. He'd delete the e-mail address and if he needed me, which he considered doubtful, our communications would be done by secure phone line only.

Phil complained regularly about my leaving the government. I wasn't at all surprised by his e-mail. Clearly, it was time to cut some of the strings—but I'd always assumed I would be the one to pick up the scissors.

I wrote back to say thanks and I'd keep in touch, and then clicked on the send button. So much for The Fallen Angel. I then opened my e-mail at The Angel Divine location. There was one message. I was feeling popular today. This was more mail in one day than I'd received all week. Just as I clicked on the message, the bathroom door opened.

"Are you done with the government stuff?" he asked satirically.

"Yes, it was just Phil complaining and telling me he was shutting down my government mail address."

"Shutting it down? As in, you don't work there anymore, right?"

"Yes and no. I hate to tell you this, but I'll never 'not work there.' I know I promised not to take assignments, but because of the type of work I do, or did, it's hard to just walk away completely, with no ties. However, considering my current situation—no longer a government employee, successor to a crime family and getting married—Phil will do everything he can to avoid approaching me. Pretty much every other agent on the planet would have to be dead or missing for him even to consider it. I could be looked at as an enormous embarrassment if anything went wrong." I proceeded to tell Alex about the phone call I'd had earlier with Phil in more detail.

"You used your badge this afternoon. Is he going to want it back?"

Good question, I thought.

"I don't think so. If he does ever need me again, and I believe those chances are almost nonexistent, he'll want me to have access and that's why I have it now. I can use it to gain help from law enforcement when necessary and I can use it as a direct link to the agency and to him. He's always wanted me to have that. I suppose he could ask for it back, but it isn't like I take advantage of it that often. He's only been contacted by outsiders checking on me maybe once in the last five years. I almost never deal with law enforcement, this afternoon being an exception. Most people take it for granted that if you show them a badge, it's real. Very few actually check."

Alex leaned on the back of my chair so I felt his chest touch my hair. "Remember, you promised no more of this."

"I know and like I said the chances of the agency contacting me are slim to none. Phil knows it or he wouldn't be shutting down my e-mail address."

It was time I refocused on the screen and the newest message in front of me.

I started reading and when I finished the final sentence I realized that Alex had also been reading it behind me.

"You do know that it's rude to read over someone's shoulder don't you?" It was a rhetorical question.

In response, Alex bent his head to my neck, slid my hair to the side and gave me a kiss. "Yes, I know. But you're going to be my wife and this business is not something I'm willing to allow you to keep private."

Allow?

"This isn't the eighteen hundreds and I would hope that you're aware that you don't actually get to *allow* me to do anything. I make the decisions as to what I'm willing to do and not do, all by myself. You and I negotiate and discuss things that you don't like and vice versa." That got me another kiss on the neck.

"It was a poor choice of words." I could hear the smile in his voice.

"Good, I don't want you getting too cocky."

He chuckled. "What are you going to do about this one?" He was referring to the plea for help on the screen.

The e-mail was from one of the individuals I'm affiliated with. He goes by the name of Garbo. That isn't really his name but he and I have never met. He'd told me on several occasions that he'd do almost anything for money. He has a military background, is presently located in Philadelphia and seems to be morally reliable when it comes to his choice of jobs. He does draw the line a bit closer concerning legal aspects and, unlike me, he has a real problem killing people. His one "mercenary failing" he called it on our first contact.

Garbo was writing to let me know about a couple of girls who had gotten snatched several weeks ago. Apparently he'd been hired by the parents of one of the girls and hadn't had much luck. The girls were in their early teens and had similar features, but had nothing else in common. This job was a lot closer to home than usual. I usually had to catch a flight to get to my jobs.

"Well, I'd like to help, but I gather evidence and kill people. I don't look for missing people as a general rule. It isn't really my thing. Besides, I have to worry about our explosives expert at the moment. I don't want to go to Philadelphia and leave you exposed. I'll do some research for him, double over what he has and see if I find anything from this end without actually going there. If we clear things up here, I'll think about going down then."

"That's fine, but like you said, we need to clear things here. We need our life settled before we can worry about other people's lives." I felt him turn from my back while I sent my reply to Garbo.

"Speaking of getting us settled, did you speak with the real estate person?" I was anxious to get out of Tony's house. I really would prefer some privacy and personal space bigger than our bedroom.

"Yes, but I can't buy anything until my funds are released," he reminded me.

"I have plenty of money. We need to get out of this house so I don't constantly feel like I'm being monitored. It's getting old. I've already contacted my housekeeper in Italy and told her to start getting my things boxed up and ready for shipment. So if we find something we can get my things here in short order."

Alex cracked a big grin. "It would be nice to have a whole house to ourselves. I'll speak with Jenna; she's been doing real estate for the families for years. I thought you wanted to go back to Italy to get the things packed yourself?"

Inwardly I groaned. *Jenna?*

"I did, but with things the way they are, I can't leave. I can manage everything from here. I don't really need to go back and with so much occupying my time it isn't realistic. I should tell you though that I offered to let the young man who works for me back there come with my things. I sent Phil an e-mail yesterday to see about getting him work papers in the states."

"How long has he worked for you?"

"Six years. He's my housekeeper's son. He knows who and what I am and is extremely loyal. His name is Miguel Corlini. He's all of twenty-three and very bright. He speaks fluent English and should fit in just fine here."

I took a pause and shut down my computer. Then turned back to Alex, "Is there someone else we can use other than Jenna?"

Okay, this was bad. But I *knew* Jenna. *Everyone* knew Jenna.

She was sort of the town tramp, but with money. Women don't usually like her and she's slept with just about every prominent male in town, married and un-married. The question was—had she made it to Alex's bed? Honestly, I didn't think I wanted to know the answer to that question.

Alex gave me an odd look. "But she does all the family's real estate business. It would be extremely rude if I didn't use her."

Crap!

"Well, if I remember correctly, Jenna isn't someone I'm going to get along with. As I recall she has a tendency to ignore women *and* their opinions. Even when dealing with a couple, she focuses completely on the man. I'm pretty sure that, unless that's changed, she and I are going to have some extensive problems during our business with her."

I don't like having my opinions ignored, especially about a house I'm going to be living in. "Besides, I don't think she makes her sales based strictly on real estate services … but also on other services rendered. As I recall most women in town call her the real estate prostitute."

Alex started laughing. "Yeah, I think I've heard that a couple of times myself. But, considering your family position and reputation, I don't think we'll have a problem. Besides, you are more than capable of scaring the shit out of her if she doesn't fall in line. I'll call her and tell her what you want if you make some kind of list for me. Then we can go looking at whatever happens to be out there."

"Fine, but if she acts up don't be surprised if I lose my temper. Patience may be a virtue, but no one has ever accused me of being a virtuous woman."

Chapter 16

TWO HOURS LATER I'D MADE A fairly accurate list of the things I wanted in a house. Some were negotiable, but several were not.

I wanted lots of privacy. I wanted a place that felt comfortable, homey, not stuffy. Tony's place made me feel like I was always under dressed. I wanted a place where boots and jeans felt appropriate.

Alex called Jenna that night. The next morning she had a list of twelve reasonably appropriate properties to look at. She knew that we would be willing to spend a fortune if we found the right house.

I dressed in navy slacks and a silky navy tank sweater and matching shoes. And set it all off with pearls. I knew I had to look the part today, but wasn't feeling all that thrilled about dealing with Jenna.

We had agreed that taking one car would make things easier on all parties concerned. Jenna behaved herself for the most part. She did occasionally paw at Alex. When she did acknowledge my existence, it was all for show.

She'd smiled unrelentingly, which of course was just bringing out the worst in me ... not to mention her patronizing attitude. I don't like people who kiss my ass, or anyone else's for that matter. They can't be trusted. Alex of course knew how I felt and was doing his best to console me.

We went through one huge monstrosity after another. I felt like I'd been castle hunting instead of house hunting. I didn't even know there were this many houses in town like this, much less this many for sale. By the time we'd reached the tenth one, I'd all but given up.

I was toying with the idea of buying land and building. This was just not working.

As we pulled into number ten, I didn't even look up. Jenna started in with her saleswoman voice. "Now this isn't nearly as nice as the others, I doubt this is what you're looking for, but it does have an inordinate amount of privacy. That's the only reason I put it on the list. It's an extended villa style home with a Mediterranean feel."

My ears perked up immediately.

"It does need some work. I don't think anyone's lived here in over two years. It has a property manager and he takes care of the basic necessities. The home was built in the nineteen forties."

The driveway was gated and long, the trees and brush could use some trimming, but when we got up to the house I knew I was home.

It was a huge villa done in a brick and light terra cotta stucco. The front was accented by a big beautiful fountain. The walkway used hand-laid pavers. Some were cracked but that just made it homey. The doorways were done in arches rather than squared off and most of the rooms were open and airy. It was a sprawling home, covering a lot of territory. It was perfect.

On our way out to the back patio where there was a beautiful view of overgrown gardens and large rolling green lawn, I grabbed Alex's hand. I leaned up and whispered, "I like this. It needs some paint, fence repairs, a better alarm system and another garage, but it feels comfortable and I can see us living here."

"Thank God. I was starting to think we were going to end up living in one of those big ugly palaces we've been walking through all day. You haven't said a word one way or the other about any of them." He had his arm wrapped around my shoulders.

He was right, I hadn't said anything because, like him, I thought we were going to get stuck with one of them since there was nothing else. Building was an option but it would take forever.

"I hated them. I didn't say anything because I might have had to choose between the lesser of the evils." We were walking through the back courtyard. There was another large fountain and a building beyond that held an indoor swimming pool and cabanas. "Do you like it? I don't want to force you to live someplace you don't like, but it feels comfortable, doesn't it?"

"Mmm, it does, and I think it's a perfect place to raise a family. There's lots of room and it's quiet. You can't even hear the city from here."

It was totally peaceful, not a sound from the city, or from neighbors for that matter. It was a large property and the neighbors were some distance away. Yippee! I'd be able to set up a shooting gallery on the property and no one would hear it.

Alex told Jenna that this was the house for us. The shock on her face looked a lot like paralysis. She certainly hadn't expected us to choose this house. It was slightly more expensive than most of the others, it needed a lot of work and was outside the main city area. She'd expected us to just pass. What she didn't count on was my desire to live outside the city on a large piece of property. Apparently when I said privacy, she didn't equate that with land. I, of course, did.

Finalizing the purchase was almost a given since we were willing to pay the full asking price and it had been on the market so long. We were on our way back to the real estate office to make our bid official when my phone rang.

It was my housekeeper calling from Italy. She was beside her-self—weeping, sobbing and jabbering in Italian. When she gets upset, speaking English is completely out of the question. Apparently, she had cleaned out the entire house and everything was ready to be shipped. She was, of course, upset about my moving, but she was more upset that Miguel, her youngest, would be leaving with my things.

Louisa Corlini had five children. Two older sons, both married, lived in France. Louisa's two older daughters, also both married, lived, respectively, in Italy, about four hours away, and Germany. Her only real tie now was with Miguel … and he was leaving.

Louisa calmed down when I offered to let her come with Miguel. She could work for Alex and me as our housekeeper. I needed to call

Phil again and get another visa worked out, but that shouldn't be a problem. Phil owed me more favors than he'd ever be able to repay, so we'd both stopped keeping track long ago. By the time I hung up I realized we were already at Jenna's office.

Alex opened my door for me and took my hand to help me out of the back seat. It was very gentlemanly and a rarity for the men of my acquaintance. "So, who is Louisa and why is she coming to live with us? I didn't catch all of it. My Italian isn't quite as sharp as yours."

"Well, you haven't been living in *Italy* for the past few years, as I have. Remember when I told you that Miguel was coming with my things? His mother, Louisa, was my housekeeper. She's a nice woman and Miguel is her youngest. She's a little distraught that he's leaving because all her other children live far away and she'll be by herself if she doesn't come."

Alex held the door to the office for me. "And her husband?"

"He died about ten years ago. Besides, she's a good housekeeper and an exceptional cook and she knows about being discrete. Do you have a housekeeper already?" I probably should have thought about that before.

"Just a woman who comes in twice a week, but she doesn't do anything except the basics. And since the house was seized I haven't been employing her. So Louisa does cleaning, laundry, dishes, errands, cooking—everything?"

I nodded. "She does pretty much everything and anything. I usually leave the errands to Miguel, but they are both full-time and live-in. That's part of the reason Miguel ended up working for me. He was already living on the premises with his mother. Louisa will probably even help with our kids when we have them."

We were now in Jenna's office and the comment about "kids" turned her around rather quickly. Apparently she didn't think we were planning on the kind of marriage that included children. Considering our reputations, that shouldn't have surprised me. She probably thought we were marrying strictly because of the families, not because we planned on having a real marriage and our own family.

I'd thought the same thing not all that long ago, but our relationship seemed to be moving in more of a true marriage direction, not just business or negotiation tactics.

Initially, I didn't expect to be happy about the way things were progressing; but Alex and I felt comfortable. Spending the rest of my life with someone I hated or couldn't talk to would have been awful. Especially since Tony had given me that rule about not killing my future husband.

We sat in Jenna's office, filled out the paperwork, put in the bid and, in fact, had a confirmation for the sale in less than half an hour. Apparently the person acting as property manager had been given the authority to handle the sale.

"I assume you'll want to get a short-term mortgage to cover the purchase until your properties and finances are released . I have several banks that would be more than happy to handle the loan," she said.

I cut in on Jenna's banking commission speech, "We don't need a loan. Alex's money is the only cash tied up at the moment—mine is just fine. I'll have the money wired to my local checking account tomorrow. It should be here in plenty of time for the sale."

Jenna looked appalled that I, a woman, would be paying for our home. I don't know why. It isn't as though I don't plan on living there too. But some women have a thing about the man paying for everything and Jenna was obviously one of them. I figure, if we're getting married, then it all becomes joint property anyway.

I phoned my real estate attorney and asked him to handle the rest of the sale on our behalf. Zach had handled a lot of property purchases for me when I was younger and we had stayed in touch over the years. When I'd needed legal advice, help with my law school work, or just had something of interest, I'd go by and discuss it. Max was a great criminal attorney but Zach Limstein was a prize in the real estate and contract fields.

Technically, I could have handled it myself but I had too much other crap to take care of. I may find law fascinating, but title and land transfers are boring as all get out—not to mention that I'd rather not see Jenna again if I could avoid it.

Alex and I went outside as Rob pulled our car up. He was acting as chauffeur again.

I needed to have a home inspector out to the new house to analyze all the things that needed fixing. I had to contact my bank in Zurich and have the appropriate funds wired for the purchase along with money for fixing up the house. I wanted to be ready to move in by the time our wedding took place, sooner if possible. That didn't leave much time for our fix-it guys to get in and get things done. But it wasn't impossible, and I'd pull every string I could to make it happen.

"So, are you happy with the house?" Alex asked. He was sitting next to me, watching me think about all of the things that needed to be accomplished.

"Yes, I just need to make a list of things to get done. Do you know a good decorator? One who actually listens to what you want rather than just doing it all their way and forcing you to live with it?"

Alex wrapped his arm around me and pulled me close. "We'll get into the house soon. Just relax. Did you happen to see the look on Jenna's face when you told her you were paying for the house? It was priceless." I could feel him laughing.

"I don't think Jenna pays for anything herself if she can get some man to do it for her. I doubt she could possibly understand not being a kept woman."

"If I remember correctly; one of her many admirers paid for her home," he said. "And several others paid for the furniture. You're right, she really is awful. I was proud of you. You didn't lose your temper with her once and I know you wanted to a couple of times."

"It would have served no purpose and we wouldn't have found our house today if I had. I can manage my temper when necessary. I just don't like confining my irritation for long periods of time."

It's like pressure behind a cork. I hold it in and hold it in until I pop. Then ... well, look out.

"Have you finished with the wedding arrangements? Or are there more things that need to be taken care of?" he asked.

"I spoke with Kimberly yesterday evening and the museum has confirmed the date. We've chosen everything else, so all I have to do is go to a dress fitting and buy shoes. It seems everything else is done. "

Shifting in my seat so I could get a good look at Alex, I added, "Garbo sent me an overnight package with all the info on that case he e-mailed me about yesterday. I need to stop and pick it up at Mario's. We could just stay and have dinner there if you like."

"Sounds good, I'll call the house and let them know we won't be home."

Chapter 17

WHEN WE ARRIVED AT the restaurant, Mario was vibrantly pleased to see us. He was smiling from ear to ear and almost skipped along as he led us to a small dining area in the back of the restaurant where we'd have plenty of privacy with our meal. We ordered drinks and Mario brought my package.

"Do you mind if I go through this information while we're waiting?" I didn't want to be discourteous, but I'd been thinking about it for the last twenty-four hours.

"No, not at all. I'm a little curious myself."

To make room, Alex and I moved most of the items to the small table next to us. Then I opened the package.

Inside were copies of police reports and pictures of the girls. There was a full notation of all of the information that Garbo had collected during interviews with various people and a letter to me about what wasn't in the package along with his "feelings" about the case. Sometimes feelings work better than evidence and in the past Garbo had been right-on with gut instincts.

Each of the two girls was in her early teens, shared the same hair color and general build, and stood between five-foot-four and five-foot-five-inches. They were slim and well-developed for their ages. They went to different schools, different churches. Their parents had no reason to know each another. The girls shared no interests or extra-curricular activities. But Garbo thought they were linked cases. He also believed the girls were still alive. He had no reason to believe this—he just *felt* it.

"Felt it? Do you usually consider an opinion rather than fact to solve cases like this?"

My future husband, ever the pessimist. "Yes, when there's no real evidence or other leads, we follow our instincts. Garbo has really good instincts."

"So you'll assume they are connected cases and that the girls are alive?"

I nodded.

"You've worked with this guy a lot?"

"I never work with anyone. I've never met him. But he and I have communicated, over the years, regarding projects."

Alex looked confused.

I leaned forward on my elbows. "It generally works like this. I'm contacted by e-mail. I investigate the project. Then I respond with a yeah or nay. If it's a yeah, I give the person a location to leave all the info for me. I then take over the project. I never have face-to-face meetings and I never use the phone. For all Garbo, or any of them knows, I could be a man. During my investigation as The Angel Divine, I generally keep in touch with the individual who asked me to look into the case, just so they don't think I've jumped ship on them."

"Are you certain this Garbo is really a … mercenary and not a cop?"

"Of course," I said. "I did some research the first time I heard from him. He's exactly what he says he is. I don't work for people who lie to me. If they lie about the little stuff, they are bound to lie about the bigger stuff."

Besides, it wasn't as though cops hadn't hired me in the past.

Mario brought us each another drink and some garlic bread. We sat and went through the information in detail. While we were reading the interview information and the police reports, I suddenly had the feeling someone was heading in our direction. I turned in my seat to see Detective Morrey heading to our table. Mario was fast on his heels, as the detective came through the curtains that separated the back room from the main dining area.

Morrey was once again dressed like a slob. He had on a wrinkled T-shirt and jeans, along with those same beat up sneakers and a zip-front sweatshirt. He was really out of place here. But looking at him now, I realized there was "something" about him.

There was something familiar about the way he looked. I never forgot a face and yet it wasn't the same face I'd seen. But it was similar to someone I'd met or knew.

I didn't notice this the last time I'd seen Morrey. I told myself that was due to the fact that I'd been otherwise engaged. But now this was going to bug me.

"Ace, I'm sorry. I tried to stop him, but he is the police. I wanted to announce him, but he wouldn't wait." Mario looked scared I might do something rash.

"It's okay, Mario. The detective and I know each other." I glanced up at Detective Morrey. "Would you like Mario to get you something to drink?"

"Yeah, how about a beer?"

"Mario, would you please get the detective a beer." Mario nodded and took off.

I was a bit annoyed by Detective Morrey's presence, but not nearly as much as Alex was. "You do know that this is intrusive, yes?" The look I got said he knew but he didn't care.

"Never mind. Detective. Have you met my fiancé? You followed him for a while, but I don't think you were ever introduced."

After making introductions, I rearranged my papers to put them away. Morrey sat to my right and leaned over the case files.

"What are you doing with police reports? And why would you be interested in a couple of Philly missing persons?" He really just sounded inquisitive and was trying to read the scattered pages.

I turned abruptly to look at Morrey. "I know you didn't come here to get yourself involved in my hobbies, so what can I do for you?"

Mario had already returned with Morrey's drink. I inclined my head slightly and he took off.

Mario never did well with customer confrontations.

"No, I didn't. I was just wondering. Hobby, huh? Interesting hobby." He leaned back in the chair. "I thought you'd be interested to know that I'm back following you and your boyfriend. My boss wants me to keep it covert, but I don't want to get shot so I thought I should let you know I'd be there."

"Didn't you get yanked when the pressure went on? Why is he putting you back?" I demanded.

This was simply unheard of.

"He knows someone applied the pressure and he's doing it without authorization from the higher-ups. He could seriously get screwed if someone in the brass finds out, but it isn't worth me getting shot by mistake." He sipped his beer.

I watched the way his eyes moved when he spoke. He was telling the truth. I just scared him and he wasn't willing to die for following Alex. "Fine, I don't want to shoot you." Yet. "But if you get irritating I may have to file a complaint against the department to get rid of you. Of course, that means you're boss will probably get canned. I hope you don't like him much."

He shrugged his shoulders. "He isn't bad, but he takes it all too personally. Not that it isn't personal to me—it is. But it isn't *him* sitting in a car following you two, now is it? He wasn't the one handcuffed with four blown tires."

I remembered how much he seemed to enjoy following us and grinned complacently. "Just stay out of my way while I'm looking for the bomber. You might even serve a purpose. If you're watching Alex that means that the bomber won't try anything. That gives us extra coverage." Just in case I need to take some time to do other things.

He was looking back at the information I still had on the table. "So, about that hobby. Is it an official investigation or personal? I didn't think the CIA got into that stuff. And I've been thinking, isn't it a little strange for one of the upper crust in a family organization to work for the government?"

"It isn't personal *or* business, and it definitely isn't government work. If you know what's good for you, you won't mention seeing any of it.

As for my employment history and the family … it's a long story and not one I feel like getting into right now."

He was really mistrustful of me and my intentions. It was written all over his face—that face that had so many familiar traits.

"So why investigate something that isn't any of your concern?"

It was easier to tell the truth than sit here with Mr. Suspicious.

"If you must know, I'm doing a friend a favor by looking it over, that's all. Someone thinks these two missing Philly girls are connected and wanted me to look at what he had. He was hired to find one of the kids but can't get a lead. If you happen to hear anything, it would be nice if you let us know."

Again I got a suspicious look, so I continued. And I knew I recognized that look, but on someone else. This was going to niggle at me 'til I figured it out.

"I know what you're thinking. Why would I, being the family member that I am, do something for nothing, right? Even a favor?" That just got me a slight head nod and a glimmer of a smile. "Well, in my opinion, we all need to perform a civic duty now and then and I'm not old-school family. I don't always expect payment for my favors. When asked by members of my acquaintance, I often help if I feel I can be of assistance. Does that answer your questions?"

He nodded. "All but one. Why don't you want me mentioning that you were looking into it?"

"Because it wouldn't be good for my reputation as the successor of my family, now would it? For people to know that I still work with certain authorities, or with people who are working with the authorities, on things like this—it might be construed as a betrayal to the old-school family way of life. I don't want anyone thinking I don't have a heart of ice. In my position, being kind and compassionate, even to the plight of two missing girls, is dangerous. It calls into question my strength."

"So you wouldn't have really shot me, would you?" He had a big glowering grin that I wanted to slap off his face.

"I shot out your tires and if you really piss me off enough … well, let's just say you wouldn't be the first person I'd gotten rid of. I did that sort of thing for the government. I wouldn't object to doing it for my own personal relief."

"You may not want to push her," Alex announced.

With all of this newfound information, the irritating detective left so that Alex and I could eat in peace. Half-way through the meal Alex glanced up from his food.

"You were almost completely honest with him. Do you think that's a good idea?"

"I don't see any point in lying," I shrugged. "There isn't anything I told him that could put either of us in jeopardy legally. There isn't anything there that he couldn't have guessed. It's easier to tell the truth whenever possible. This keeps the lies I do tell fresh in my mind."

Chapter 18

ALEX AND I HAD AGREED TO LET Rob leave and come back. That way he didn't have to sit out in the car while we ate. However, when we walked out of the front door, there was no Rob to be found. Alex thought he might be waiting in the parking lot, so we made our way around the side of the building to the small lot in the rear.

There was no moon and just a single light at the far end of the lot. I managed to spot the car—it wasn't all that hard as there were few cars in the lot. I also spotted a shadow moving around the front driver's side fender. That wasn't Rob. Rob was much too small to make that large a shadow.

I lifted the back of my silk sweater and pulled out my gun. It hadn't left the cleanest lines, but I felt safer with it than without it this morning when I'd gotten dressed. I then opened the small clutch bag I was carrying—it had my silencer and a few other useful items, but wasn't large enough for the gun. I didn't want to hear any crap from Alex about police this time.

Alex pulled me toward him. I leaned into his ear and whispered as quietly as possible. "Someone is screwing with our car." I pointed toward the car. "Stay here."

Slipping off my shoes—they made too much noise—I moved forward. Using whatever cover I could, which wasn't much, I proceeded. Before I knew it, I was standing over the lower half of the shadow's body. The upper half was under our car.

He moved quietly, but so had I, and he hadn't heard me. As I stood there, my gun ready, he slowly eased himself out from under the front quarter panel. By the time he realized he wasn't alone, there wasn't much he could do about it. I grabbed him by the sleeve and yanked him to his feet.

I didn't recognize him, not that this surprised me. I hadn't known the shooter either.

"Who are you? And what, exactly, are you doing under my car?"

He tried to pull away and I pressed the gun to his temple. His eyes shot up and spotted the silencer. It seemed to register that I could shoot him, right here and now, and no one would see or hear anything.

"I don't know what you mean. I wasn't doing anything."

Oh please! "Really? So I didn't just pull you up from under my car? How stupid are you?"

Just as I was pushing him up against the back bumper, he reached into his jacket. It was so fast that my only reaction was to pull the trigger. And it was a good thing that I had. As his body collapsed, a Glock pistol hit the ground next to him.

I glanced around but no one had seen anything. Alex was next to me in an instant. I grabbed my bag from him and found my picks. A girl should never leave home without a brush, lipstick, mascara, lock picks and a gun ... and a silencer if she can fit it in the bag.

I popped the trunk and tossed our newly dead friend inside. Turning to Alex, "Where do you think Rob is?"

Just then I heard someone coming along behind us. It was Rob and he was carrying a doggie bag from Mario's.

I rolled my eyes. What can you say? Just unbelievable. So I gave my attention to finishing the matter at hand.

"Can I borrow your coat?"

Alex handed his over and I laid it on the ground next to the car where the bomber had been just a few short moments before. I slid in as far as I could and reached up and to the left. There, on the ground but still unattached, was the device. Apparently he hadn't slid out from under the car to leave—maybe just to get a tool to attach it properly.

Gently taking hold of the device, I carefully slid out from under the car. When I stood up, I heard Alex giving Rob a butt-reaming ...

as was appropriate since we'd all have been dead if it hadn't been for some lucky timing.

I set the device on top of the trunk and examined it. It was a very basic design with a five-mile radius remote trigger. Flip a switch and we were toast. I removed the detonator so that it was safe to move. I wasn't taking any chances trying to travel while leaving it assembled because the trigger could be anywhere. We could go over a bump which might jostle our corpse-in-the-trunk and next thing you know we'd all be corpses. No, that was not a great plan.

"Let's go. I want to get home, change my clothes, and then find our friend a nice place to rest," I stated.

"What friend?" Rob interjected. Apparently he didn't understand why Alex was so upset.

"The dead one in the trunk—the one who wouldn't have tried to put that bomb there," said Alex, pointing, "under our car, if you had *stayed* with it like you were supposed to. Did you think we had you driving us around because we were too lazy to drive ourselves?"

Rob was not looking so good and couldn't take his eyes off the bomb. "I was only inside a couple minutes. I didn't think …"

"You're right—you didn't. Now, let's get out of here before someone finds it strange that we're all standing here chatting in the dark," Alex growled.

That night Alex and I found a nice place to bury our burden, far outside city. Actually it was just before the Pennsylvania line, up in the hills. Between the two of us we managed to dispose of our unwanted problem quickly, quietly and permanently. There was not a chance in hell of anyone finding him.

Chapter 19

UPON OUR RETURN TO TONY'S that evening I went up to our room, grabbed my laptop and headed for the library. I wasn't ready for bed yet and I needed time to work on the case Garbo had sent. I didn't see any more leads for the problems with Alex's enemy now that I had disposed of two of the hired hit-men, and I needed something else to focus my thoughts on.

I opened the case file again and spread the information on the desk. I poured over the details again. I was sure it was here. I just wasn't looking at it right. I could feel it.

The answer had more to do with their similarities than their lack of contact. And who would take a teen-age girl? Logic, and my education and experience, said it had to be a man. No question about that. But both girls were snatched from their homes at night. From their own rooms. He'd had to have been watching them. It was logical. But what else?

My psychology classes did come in handy at times, but psychology is generally founded in logic. So what was the logical conclusion of what I'd read? It was too strange that the girls had no connection at all. They lived in the same city. They had to, at one time or another, have spent time, if not together, at a mutual location. Like eating at the same restaurant, getting their hair cut at the same beauty salon, shopping at the same stores … the mall. It was like a bell went off in my brain … girls go to the mall. That could be a connection.

An hour and a half after coming to this conclusion, I'd gone through the detailed interview sheets that Garbo had sent. The sheets said nothing about activities over the *weeks* prior to their abductions, just the couple of days preceding the abductions. But if someone were going to line up a girl, one he plans to keep, it would take longer than two days, wouldn't it?

"What are you working on now?" Tony stood over the desk.

"It's just a police case from Philly. Nothing family related," I said dismissively.

Something moved behind Tony. It was Alex, but Tony was completely unaware of his presence.

"I thought you were going to leave this stuff alone. You have plenty to keep you occupied here, and there isn't any reason that you should be working a police case of all things." He sounded disgusted just by the association.

"You have an assassin to find and a wedding to plan, Alex just told me you bought a house today and it needs to be renovated and decorated. All of your things are being moved here, along with two servants, and you have the house in Italy to lease. All of these things, along with the family business and your own businesses, should be more than enough to keep even you supplied with entertainment. Why are you doing this?"

He was restraining himself. He wanted to scream at me—I could see it in his eyes. He had hated my involvement with the authorities from the first day I left home. It apparently hadn't lessened over time.

I looked past him to Alex and said, "This is another reason I want to move into the house as soon as possible."

Tony was immediately offended, but I don't like being dictated to. I never had and Tony was containing his temper because he knew if he didn't remain civil, neither would I. "I like a certain amount of personal freedom," I added, "and I don't like explaining my behavior to someone else."

Tony's attention was now on Alex. "You know she's working with the police?"

"She isn't working with the police," he replied. "She's helping a … detective of sorts, to locate two girls who were taken from their homes in Philadelphia. She's reviewing his information and providing him with some possible insights to take the investigation in a new direction. The police and he have come to dead ends so far. We were looking it over at dinner and I think she's gotten hooked."

Alex then turned to me. "You've been in here for quite a while; we should be going upstairs soon. We've had a busy night. Have you come up with anything new?"

He obviously hadn't told Tony about our dead guy. He probably felt it was a "need to know" bit of information and Tony certainly didn't need to know.

"Well, the girls were taken two weeks apart."

I needed to bounce my idea off someone.

"Why don't you sit down? I need to see if this makes sense to anyone but me." He did as I asked, as did Tony.

"Okay, if you were going to snatch a girl—one you planned to keep, since we've decided they aren't dead—wouldn't you look around a little? Make sure she was the one you wanted? Then, wouldn't you learn her routines, where she lived, her overall behaviors, that sort of thing?

"I think he stalked them both before he snatched them. In Garbo's notes, he claims that these girls had similar personalities and lifestyles. Both were living in ranch style homes, so there was no problem getting into their first-floor bedrooms. Also, he *knew* where their rooms were, rather than having to go through the whole house."

I stood up and started pacing. "I think that he spotted them in the same place. He snatched one. That went well, so he went back to the same place and found the other."

Alex nodded. "Yes, but didn't the paperwork say they didn't have anything in common except basic physical characteristics. Where did he do this *girl selecting*?"

"Yep, it did. But there's something that isn't in the notes. The obvious—they were both girls. That alone says something. Girls like to go places together. They like to hang out in cliques. Girls go to the mall. And a strange man stalking a girl from a distance would be hidden well in the crowds at a mall. He wouldn't stand out. I'd bet both girls were spotted at the same mall, probably in the company of friends, and had gone there shopping within two weeks or so of their individual abductions. I wonder how long they keep surveillance footage at a mall."

"I have no idea, but why in the company of friends? Do you think this guy would have been that selective to prefer one that wasn't accompanied by a parent?"

"I think he'd be attracted to a girl who appeared to be a woman, but wasn't. The reports said both girls were young, but well-developed. Physically, they looked like women, but were young enough that our abductor didn't feel threatened. Parents make a girl appear to be a girl, even if she develops early. Also, the behavior of a girl that age is different around her parents than with her friends. Actually, girls of any age are different around parents and peers, but it is truly noticeable at that age. Around parents they act like children. Around friends, they act like young adults. I think her presence would feel different to him. Does this sound credible?"

I leaned back against the front of the desk. "It makes sense to me," I said, "but that doesn't mean it's right." The question was directed to Alex.

"It seems credible, but all you can do is relay your thoughts to Garbo and see what comes of it. He can follow up with the parents to determine if the girls were shopping at the same mall shortly before they were snatched. Then he can then follow up with the mall security and see if the tapes are still available. Of course, there may be somewhere else they both went, but no one has considered this possible link."

Alex continued, but with more thought in his eyes. "Also, if he was stalking them ahead of time, as you've suggested, someone may have seen a vehicle in the neighborhoods but not have realized it was relevant."

"Good point. I'll send this over and continue thinking on it. Maybe there's another possibility, but I can't see one right now."

Alex stood and headed to the door. "I'm going up."

I peeked over the laptop. "I'll be right behind you. I just want to send this to Garbo."

Tony stayed behind while I sent my message. When I closed my computer and gathered my papers, Tony spoke. "I can't believe he's letting you continue with your contract work. I was certain he'd see to the end of it." He looked tired and a bit irritated. "How did you manage to convince him to let you continue with it?"

"I didn't convince him of anything. We negotiated terms, just like you told me. This particular type of work was negotiated in my favor. I agreed to do no more paid contract killing, private or government. Of course, the government can force the issue, which he knows, but I will do my best to make sure I don't have to resume it. But public service work or favors are completely different. He wants to know about any projects I'm considering, prior to accepting them, of course. Alex's main concern is that I won't jeopardize myself and/or our family. This particular project does neither of those things. I won't even be in the city where the case is taking place. I'm just helping someone facilitate an investigation. Therefore, Alex felt there was nothing wrong in my providing assistance to the individual who asked for it."

Tony put on a wry grin. "So you need his permission before taking a project?"

"No. But I agreed to discuss any projects ahead of time, I did not agree to my needing his permission. If he can give me a reasonable argument for not taking on a particular project, then I'm willing to listen. I'm not going to argue if he can provide valid reasoning." This seemed obvious to me.

"You've given him a certain amount of power over you," said Tony, frowning. "Do you think that's wise?"

First, Tony was irritated because I chose to do an outside project and Alex hadn't stopped me. Now he was irritated because I was giving Alex a say in my outside projects. Sometimes, with Tony, I just couldn't win.

I was getting exasperated. "As I said to Cara, marriage is compromise. I'm just allowing him the opportunity to convince me I need to rethink, and possibly compromise. That's all. In the end, I'll make up my own mind as I've always done. Alex is going to be my husband, not my conscience. But my actions affect him and both families, and because of that he has a right to ask me to reconsider certain decisions.

"I'm used to being responsible for only myself. I'm not accustomed to having my behaviors affect other people. Alex is." I picked everything up and headed for the library door. "Now, if you'll excuse me, I'm going upstairs."

"Angelica, I just don't want to have lied to Constantine about your being able to stand up to Alex."

Why should he *care* about that one little lie? Tony lied constantly?

"You didn't lie—at least not about that—but I'm not going to pick fights over little crap. If Alex and I are going to have arguments, at least they'll be over things that are worth arguing about. Being realistic, this isn't one of them."

"Yes, but are you the one doing all the compromising? Has Alex made concessions as well?"

"I'm doing most of the compromising at the moment, but I think that it's because of the situation we're moving into. He's already set in his role with the family business operations. I'm leaving my old life, moving a great distance, and starting a new one. I need to redefine things while Alex is already pretty much there."

And the whole thing was very frustrating—not that I thought I should share that with Tony.

"He's made some concessions. He accepted my requiring a house outside the city, rather than living in his city townhouse. He accepted that my two employees will be coming with my furniture and will be living with and working for us. He was willing to let me continue this part of my work at least until we start a family. And the requests he's made, although annoying, mostly because they constrain my freedom, are more than reasonable based on the reasons he's given. This is all compromise based on reasoning, not dictation."

I turned and leaned against the doorjamb. "I may be a genius by technical standards, but I tend to think exclusively of myself and my own needs. I've never had to consider any influence my behavior might have on others. I know you don't see me this way, but I'm actually quite selfish."

The only word I could use to describe the look in Tony's eyes was disbelief. "You are far from selfish, but I do see where you get that impression. As you say, you've never had to worry about anyone else."

He nodded and then stood. "You were correct to allow Alex a say in these events. He does know better than you about keeping the families safe. And, although I've never experienced it, I believe you are correct also in assuming that marriage is a partnership. Just make sure you stay *equal* partners. I would hate to see Constantine be proven justified in his concerns."

Chapter 20

THE MONDAY THAT FOLLOWED WAS going to be filled with work. My work.

I contacted Miguel and had him hire a property manager to oversee the leasing of the house in Italy. I also asked him to check about purchasing everything including furniture, sheets, dishes, etc. I wanted the house to have anything renters might need when vacationing. Although I wanted to keep the present contents, I wasn't thrilled with the idea of strangers sitting on my extremely expensive furniture or eating off my antique dishware or possibly running off with my artwork. Forget it.

This assignment was something new for Miguel and I thought it would make him feel valued to oversee a task that was financially significant to me. I was right. He was thrilled with the request and said he'd take care of finding an agent and the home furnishings immediately.

I then set up a time to meet with my present property manager to review my various local properties. I'd done some of that during the first weeks I was back, before I'd gotten Alex out, but there were still plenty I hadn't had a chance to review. I had mostly taken care of those that were not, at present, under lease.

They had needed some updating. All needed replacement items like carpet or various appliances. Some needed more, a new roof in one case. Three units needed exterior painting, two needed countertops and two others needed their bathrooms redone. All of them needed interior painting.

Now that those items were taken care of, the six unleased properties when I arrived all had new tenants. I was a bit ticked with the property manager, since I relied on him to maintain these properties. In my opinion, that included telling me when they needed repairs and then scheduling them. Since I now knew I couldn't trust him to do that competently, I needed to examine all units currently rented.

You might be surprised. Some renters won't say anything when there's a leak in the roof, the toilet is cracked, or the carpet is fifteen years old and worn. I don't like the idea of being a slum-lord, so I thought it was time I took a look at what exactly was going on at my properties.

Alex had planned on working from home today, so I doubted he'd need me around to watch over him. I put on my low-rise jeans and a loose navy v-neck T-shirt and my work boots. I pulled my hair up and grabbed my jacket. I was gathering my rental files when Alex came into our room.

"Where are you going today? You look like your planning to work at a construction site?"

"Close. I'm going out to look over some of my rental properties. I haven't had a chance to examine them in years and I'm not thrilled with what I've seen of the property manager's efforts at the ones that I have seen. He doesn't seem to mind being a dump manager, but I do. He let some of the properties fall to a state that I would never have allowed if I'd been here to do it myself. Unfortunately I wasn't, and now I need to get them cleaned up."

"I was wondering what Tony meant Friday night," said Alex, "when he referred to your businesses. He implied that these were separate from the family."

"I own a number of real estate investments, as I told you. Most are residential. I also own a couple of businesses, but I don't interfere in them. Their managers send me financials and I receive an annual payment from them. I have them audited occasionally, but that's it."

Sliding my arms into the jacket, I continued. "When I left the states, I hired the real estate agent I used earlier to be my property manager. He was completely trustworthy, fair to the tenants and knew housing. He also knew what I expected for upkeep. Sadly, he was older and passed away five years ago. I had to hire the current person from a distance—one of my cousins interview him. He's nice enough, but he has no idea what he's doing. There's a good chance that when Miguel arrives I'll train him to take care of the property management and replace this person I have now."

"You trust Miguel to do that even though he's so young?"

"As far as I'm concerned, age has nothing to do with handling responsibility. There are twelve year-olds who are more responsible than some forty year-olds I know. So it has nothing to do with age. Miguel is mature and bright. He's trustworthy and he asks questions when he isn't sure of the appropriate remedy to a situation."

Alex had the hints of a smile at the edges of his lips. "If I change, do you mind if I join you?"

Okay, that's weird. Why would he want to look at old and—unless I missed my guess—beat up, buildings? But, hey, whatever toots his horn.

"If you want," I replied. "But it's going to be tedious and time consuming. The agent arranged for me to go through the ones in New York today. I'll have to have him arrange for the others in groups. I can only do six or seven a day. Luckily I only have four properties in New York."

"Well, it shouldn't take that long. Are they condos or houses?" He was at the dresser looking for a pair of jeans.

"I own three walk-up buildings. Each of the walk-ups contains four apartments. The other property is a brownstone, single residence. So we have to go through thirteen residences. That means we'll be busy. Are you sure you want to come? I'm not trying to dissuade you, but it can be a crappy job going through these places. I just don't want you having any illusions about what to expect from the day."

"No, I want to come," he insisted. "I'm curious."

We left the house at nine. By one o'clock we were going through the last apartment in the second walk-up. The first building needed new paint everywhere, new carpeting in all of the apartments, and various other items in each of the apartments. It also had a crack in the front stairs that needed to be fixed, along with the entry and stair tiles needing replacement before someone stubbed his toe, fell on his butt and sued me. And the second building had been far worse.

These people were living in a residence that I wouldn't even consider living in, paying a fortune and not complaining at all. Why? I know apartments in New York are hard to come by, but this was ridiculous.

"If you don't mind, Miss Pascoli," asked the property manager, "I thought we'd separate for lunch."

Why would I mind? This guy was pissing me off every time I walked into one of my buildings.

"Since I was in the city, I thought I could have lunch with an old friend. We could meet around two-thirty at the next walk-up. I'm sure the brownstone will take nothing at all."

"Actually, that sounds good. That way my fiancé and I can go over this morning's efforts," I replied.

We said our good-byes and headed to a small Chinese restaurant for lunch. The activities of the morning had my temper up, but also my appetite. I was starving. When we were directed to a table I sat down with a humph. Alex sat across from me at a table for two. It was a very quaint little place, with an intimate feel. The waitress took our drink orders immediately and brought menus.

Staring at the menu, but not seeing it, made me realize that I didn't really need to think about what I wanted. I wanted shrimp fried rice, lemon chicken and egg drop soup. I looked over the top of the menu at Alex sitting on the opposite side of the table. He hadn't said a word after arriving at the second building. Of course, in his defense, he had to listen to me bitch all the way there about the first building.

I told him what I was ordering and we agreed to share. So I'd get some of his General Tao's chicken as well. The waitress came back with our drinks and noodles and took our orders and we sat there looking at each other.

The entire day had been completely rotten but it was clearly necessary. "Are you going to say anything?" I asked Alex.

"I've been waiting for you to start in. The last building was, by far, worse than the first. And you wanted to beat the shit out of your manager after seeing the first one. My guess is he's lucky you don't have a gun on you."

I did have a gun on me, I always have a gun, but it wasn't worth killing him over. I honestly believed he was just inept. I hoped so, but maybe I was being naïve. I, for one, believe that when I pay someone to manage my property, I don't want them to collect rent and take care of complaints. I want them to manage it.

"Do you think I'm expecting too much from him?"

He tipped his head to the side and then nodded. "Yes and no. I think you expect him to treat the properties like you would. But they aren't his. He's only the manager. At the same time, he has let them slide, especially based on the pictures you showed me, taken prior to your leaving. They're going to need work."

The pictures were part of the files I'd maintained over the years. They included original renovations of each of the properties when I'd first bought them and then subsequent fix-ups supplied by my old managing agent.

"I just want them to be decent places to live. If you don't provide reasonably decent places to live, you attract icky tenants."

He smiled. "Icky?"

"Yes, icky. Drug users, low-lives, people who live like pigs, that sort of thing. I wanted my rental properties to be family- and young career people-friendly. That's why they were reasonably priced." Or at least reasonably priced by New York standards. "I didn't want them to turn into slums."

"You bought them with young career people and families in mind?" He was crunching down on a noodle.

"I went to school here remember? I had a lot of friends who lived in dumps because they couldn't afford anything else and it was usually two or three of them going in together to rent the dump. I bought the brownstone, lived there and fixed it up. That's why it's a single residence. I didn't like the idea of living in dorms or in an apartment.

I wanted space, but that didn't last long. By the time I graduated I had four other girls living there with me. They stayed until each of them graduated. I wasn't going to pitch them out just because I finished early." Somehow that had seemed wrong, but I was certain most people would have told them to leave.

"After that I rented it to a young family. The guy was going back to grad school and had just found out his wife was expecting their second child. He couldn't afford to buy anything and the standard rentals were too much for him. He would have had to leave school, live in a one-room apartment, or commute some ridiculous distance. I felt they were the most appropriate for the property."

"When did you buy the other three buildings?"

"During my second year at school. I picked up the first one during the first semester and the other two the second semester. I spent all my spare time working on them and hired a select group of students to do the painting and help with the fix-ups. They needed the money and I needed assistance. When they were completed, I rented them to young career people who couldn't afford to move into anything comparable elsewhere, and young families. I think some of those people are still living in the same apartments."

"Okay, so where do you want to take this from here? The places have obviously been neglected, at least by your standards." He quirked an eyebrow at me. "There are worse in this city you know?"

"I know, but I don't have to sleep at night knowing that I own them." I'd be sick to my stomach thinking about those people living like that if I didn't do something to fix it.

Our food arrived and we started dishing out helpings. "As for what I want to do … I think the best approach is to replace all the carpeting, paint everything, and then work on the individual issues for each unit. Some need a lot more than others. I'll make a schedule so that I can get a deal on certain things.

"A number of them need new linoleum in the baths and kitchens, some need their wood floors refinished. Several need countertops and new appliances. I should be able to get a better deal if I have a bulk order. The buildings have already paid for themselves more than twice, so it isn't like I don't have the money to renovate them again. They're worth every penny."

"I agree," said Alex. "We'll go through the other two and then we should be able to use family contractors to get it all at reasonable prices. It shouldn't even take that long. We'll try to fix up the individual units and then we can work on the common areas."

I nodded. At least we had a plan for the renovations. Now I just needed to get it all down on paper and schedule it. We finished our meal and headed for the next destination. I was thrilled when it was over and completely exhausted. From the looks of him, so was Alex.

We'd been extremely careful during our outing. I'd parked the car in a garage and put a motion detection system under the car so that I'd know if someone tampered with it. I figured, along with the alarm system, that should be more than enough to keep us safe from another bomber.

Detective Morrey had started out with us this morning, but turned back at the state line. Apparently he didn't want to tick off the NYPD if they found him messing around in their city. It was probably a good thing. He would have been bored stiff and would have most likely complained about the whole thing later.

✳✳✳

Wednesday morning I spent in Tony's library. I'd received an interesting e-mail back from Garbo. Apparently he'd checked yesterday with both sets of parents. It seems both girls had gone to the mall with friends, just as I'd suspected, but they'd also gone to the movies at the same theater in town. Both visits were approximately a week and a half prior to their abductions. That was the reason no one thought about them. He was checking on both and would let me know when he got more.

Yesterday, I'd created a spreadsheet of required repairs for all the buildings. The third building was in better shape than the other two, but it still needed some basics. It was in better shape because I'd hired a live-in maintenance person who actually took his job seriously. The brownstone was in decent shape, but it did need some updates and the wood floors needed refinishing. There was also a roof leak Alex spotted which needed to be fixed as well.

By lunch time, I'd contacted contractors in both families and scheduled repairs. Then I let the property manager know, so that he could make my tenants aware of the dates and the repairs that would be taking place. While I spoke with the contractors, I also scheduled them to come out to the house we were buying so they could start repairs there as well. The sooner these were made, the sooner Alex and I could move in.

Things were moving along. The only thing I wasn't pleased with was the progress of the family business situation. I didn't like how things were set up, and the more time I spent with Tony, the less pleased I was. How the hell did I get myself into this mess? For that matter, how did Tony get the family into such a mess? I'd been in bar fights that seemed more organized than our family businesses. I was really starting to get worried about taking over things.

Alex was standing in front of the desk when I looked up. He'd spent most of the morning on the phone as well. "Are you about done for the day?" he asked.

I nodded. "Yep. I got work for the rentals scheduled and I also booked them to go out to our new place as well, to make repairs."

"Good," smiled Alex. "I have to meet Max at The Finish Line." The Finish Line is a sports bar in town. They have pretty good food and it's a relaxed atmosphere. "Do you want to come?"

Chapter 21

"GIVE ME A MINUTE TO GET my jacket. Or do you want me to change?" Alex always looked put together. No matter what he was wearing he managed to look neat.

I was another matter. I was in my usual, jeans, T-shirt, and boots. My hair was in a pony tail and I was sure that I wasn't looking my best.

"I'd prefer if you at least changed the top and let your hair down."

I stood up and headed to the library door. "Okay, I'll be down in a couple of minutes."

Alex caught me before I made it to the door. He pulled me toward him. The closer I got, the better he smelled. I slid my arms around his neck and kissed him. That seemed to have been his plan from the response I got.

Things between us had become far more entangled than I'd envisioned, especially in such a sort time. I was probably closer to him than I'd been to any man I'd ever dated. Part of that was the result of my constant need to keep myself separate from the person I was with and I could never really be honest.

You'd be surprised how men react when they find out you kill people for a living. First there's disbelief; then a settling into the idea; and finally real fear when they discover what you're actually capable of. I'd seen it long ago and had just stopped putting all of me into my relationships. And since relationships are supposed to be based on honesty and trust, well, let's just say mine never lasted very long. They always knew I was holding back, keeping something separate.

With Alex, it was different. I could tell him pretty much anything. And I could just be myself and it didn't throw him too far out into left field. I was becoming very fond of this man who was going to be my husband. I just wasn't sure if that was a good thing or not.

He ran his hand down the curve of my back and then lifted his head. The look in his eyes said he'd rather come upstairs with me, than let me go alone. But if he did that, we'd be extremely late.

"I need to go change if we're going to get there on time." I slid myself away and went to change into something presentable.

Rob dropped us off at the front door. I still wanted him to play chauffeur. I was certain there would be another attempt eventually and just in case it happened to be another bomber, it didn't hurt to have someone with the car. Rob was also a bit more leery about leaving the car, thanks to how close we'd all come with the last one.

Upon opening the front door I was hit with the bar noise. There were several televisions going and the place was crowded, considering it was after one. I'd expected it to be somewhat less busy.

I looked toward the back where the tables were and saw Max. He was his usual business self, sitting in a back corner.

As we arrived, I realized Max hadn't expected me to come with Alex. He was surprised, but pleased. He stood and gave me a hug.

"Ace, I'm glad you came. I thought with the wedding and everything you'd be busy." We all sat.

"No, we've got almost everything taken care of and the things that are left are being handled by the wedding planner."

Our meal was good and filled with interesting conversation. Most of it consisted of business and legal issues. We learned that Alex's funds and properties should be released sometime in the next two days and that the District Attorney's office couldn't come up with any new evidence, or even recreate what they'd had so they were letting the matter go. Max had managed to cut a six-to-eight week time span to less then four weeks; Alex was extremely pleased.

Somewhere along the line, Max and I started a debate about a new piece of legislation that was being considered at the state level. Our debate lasted more than forty minutes before we realized how long we'd been going at it. When I looked over I saw a big smile on Alex's face. I couldn't quite decide what the expression was for.

"What?" I asked. "Why the grin?"

"Nothing," Alex replied. "I know you have a law degree, but I didn't think you were keeping up with state politics. I'm just amazed at how easily you can debate the relevant legal nuances of state legislative policy considering how long you've been gone and all the other things that have been happening. You just don't look like a lawyer," he said.

"I may not look like one, but looks can be deceiving. And I've always kept up with state policy, mostly because I have to in order to maintain my license. Also, I own so much property in New Jersey that it's in my best interest." I sipped my cola.

Alex gave me a perplexed glance. "License?"

"I'm a licensed attorney. I thought you knew that?"

Max took this opportunity to jump in. "Speaking of which, have you given any thought to coming to work with me?"

"I don't know if that's a good idea, Max—not if I'm taking over for Tony. Besides, I like to keep a very low profile. I've done my best to avoid attention most of my life, you know? And, of course, I wouldn't be interested in anything that involved actually arguing in court."

"I remember all too well how you avoided attention," Max replied. "Your father did everything he could to get you to try out for the Olympic team and you refused. And your mother, she was heartbroken when you refused the pianist position you were offered with that symphony group out west. I never understood that—you always loved music. But both your parents just about died when you took to the underground."

Alex cut in, "*Olympic* team? Symphony?"

"Women's gymnastics," Max explained. "Her parents and her coach tried to persuade her, first in her early teens and again, four years later. She refused to do it. The symphony position was offered back when you where what … nineteen or twenty?"

"Okay," I sighed.

There are things that Alex doesn't need to know; I don't want to be pestered about them after all this time. I had my reasons for refusing both and I still think they were valid reasons.

"First, the training schedule for the Olympic team would have been a nightmare and I don't follow orders well. Second, I like my joints just the way they are. All that training beats the crap out of your knees and back. Third, I don't like being the center of attention. I never have and that's also the reason I passed on the music gig. I was in college and it seemed a better choice for me. Now, can we leave my youthful lack of aspiration alone and get onto another topic?"

What I didn't say was that I didn't want to leave my brother to handle Tony on his own. And, if I'd left, that's exactly what would have happened. Heaven only knows what would have transpired from that.

Max smiled. "If that's how you feel. Where was I? Oh yes, I just wanted to let you know that one of my associates is leaving the firm and moving to Tennessee to be closer to his relatives. He never goes to court and spends most of his time in the law library, writing briefs, that sort of thing. I thought that might appeal to you."

I could never live in Tennessee myself, but each to his own. As for the idea of spending most of my time in a law library, well, I thought that sounded pretty good. My two favorite places are the shooting range and the library. Odd combination, huh? But Tony would never understand if I decided to take on both working for Max, and taking over his work. Besides, with the way the family looked right now, I wasn't going to have time for the next ten or maybe twenty years.

That must have been exactly what Max read on my face when he said, "Just think about it. You don't need to give me an answer yet. But considering your background and my clientele, it would be a good match. You wouldn't have any problems ... managing them."

After Max left I ordered another drink. I wasn't in a hurry to leave, so I was hoping that Alex wasn't either.

"You just keep coming up with new ways to amaze me," said Alex.

"First the Olympic gymnastics thing and then the pianist thing. I knew you could play well, but being offered a position with a symphony *any-where* says something. And then the lawyer thing. I'm almost speechless. Is there anything else I should know? I mean, I never thought you'd consider working for Max, but you almost look disappointed because you can't." He frowned and took a swig of his beer.

"This may shock you, sweetie," I replied, "but there are a lot of things you don't know about me. And, I *did* tell you about the gymnastics thing back when I told you about who I was. I also have a master's degree in criminal psychology. I found it useful later in studying my prey, but I studied law because I found it interesting as well. There's nothing like working on the background of a good case. It's like solving a really in-depth puzzle. I know where it starts, and I know where I want it to end. All I have to do is fit the pieces to link the two and get the correct outcome. Of course you have certain criteria to fit into that puzzle-bridging—the evidence."

"You make it sound like a game."

"It is. But I never liked litigation or court cases. I have problems arguing with conviction when I know, or even suspect, that the individual is guilty. It was my biggest flaw in school. I'm a great liar, but I can't hold that level of conviction when I don't honestly believe in the cause."

"So you were better with prosecution than defense?"

"No. Again. I really had to believe in the charges being levied. If I honestly believe the individual being tried is guilty, and that the crime deserves punishment, then yes. But just because someone goes to trial doesn't mean you have to believe he's guilty. And, since it's the job of the courts to determine guilt or innocence, I'm sure plenty of innocent people get tried. Do you see what I'm getting at?"

He nodded.

"And to top that off, I have to believe it's worth trying. Just because something is illegal, doesn't mean I agree that the act committed deserves punishment."

He was grinning again. "Would you care to give an example?"

"Well ... let me think." I took a minute. "Say a woman finds out her husband has been abusing her child, or for that matter he's been abusing her. If she kills him, plotting his death in advance, technically it's premeditated murder. But I happen to think he had it coming. I'd find it very difficult to prosecute her with any degree of enthusiasm for the case."

"I see your point. But if you weren't taking over the family, would you consider working for Max?"

"If I weren't taking over the family, I'd still be living in *Italy*," I reminded him.

He accepted that as an answer and we left. There was no point in discussing "what if's." Things are the way they are and I can't change that. If I could, I'd be headed back to my beautiful house in Italy, reviewing contract options and going about my life as it was before.

I'd miss Alex, but I didn't want to move back to this city and there wasn't much that could make it appealing enough to stay without the family commitment tied to it. Not that the commitment was appealing—it was just that I never ignore my responsibilities.

Chapter 22

THE REST OF THE AFTERNOON consisted of paint color selection. The apartments were easy. Everything was going to be more or less the same color, beige. Boring, yes—but also clean and effective. The house was a completely different matter. I decided it would be best to wait and do the selecting when I had more time.

I scheduled a private consultation at the house so I could see how it looked with the light that would be available. We also stopped by the appliance store so I could pick out the replacement pieces for the apartments. We also managed to decide on our own pieces for the house. Most of these appliances had to be special ordered, but we were told they should arrive by the beginning of next week.

We made it home just in time for dinner and then I took myself upstairs for the night. I was tired. I don't usually get the kind of tired I was tonight, but I figured a long soak in a bath and a book would do wonders.

After fifteen minutes of absolute luxury I opened my eyes to find Alex sitting on the side of the tub watching me. I all but jumped. I don't ever remember a time in my life when someone could sneak up on me like that. My brother had tried when we were kids, but he never succeeded.

I never knew why this was—the smell of skin, the sense of another living thing, or maybe it was just the sound of a heartbeat, but I always *knew*. Alex, however, had managed it more than once. I was finding this very unnerving. Maybe my edge was slipping. It might be a good thing I was retiring.

"What are *you* doing up here already? I wasn't expecting you for at least a couple of hours."

He reached out, tracing his finger down my arm through the bubbles. "I wanted to talk to you."

"Anything interesting?"

He stood and started to remove his own clothes. "If you don't mind, I think I'll join you."

He climbed into the tub and lay back next to me with his arm around my waist. I leaned my head back onto his chest and closed my eyes again. It was quiet and comfortable.

That is, until he felt the need to share. "What would you say if I told you that nothing is what it seems?"

I didn't move. "Is that a riddle?"

"Not exactly. I think I'm feeling a little guilty. What if I were to tell you that moving back to take over the family was just an excuse? That Tony really just wanted you home to get me out of jail? And … while you were here, he thought it was time you settled down?"

I really didn't like the direction this conversation was going. I'd been lying here perfectly happy and he had to come in and ruin it. He'd better be kidding.

"If that were the case," I snapped, "first of all, I'd be extremely pissed."

I thought about it for a minute before I spoke again. "But that isn't really a plausible possibility anyway. If it were, Tony never would have presented those three nincompoops as suitors. He'd have known better than to think I'd even consider marrying any of them. Wanting me settled or not, he wouldn't want me settled so badly that he'd offer me such inappropriate husband material." I was still trying to relax, but it wasn't working. The more I thought about it, the more tense I became.

Alex must have felt it. He pulled me over and started rubbing my shoulders. "What if I told you that he and I had an understanding, prior to your coming home? That the families were working together on … certain things? Things, I don't really want to talk about—it's really a discussion for another time. But, that you were required more to get me, and Dad of course, out of jail rather than to take over anything, and getting you married was, in Tony's mind, an added benefit.

"I'm not saying Tony couldn't seriously be considering the idea of you taking over now, since you *are* here and more than capable of handling it. But—what if the main reason you'd been lured back here was because Tony knew you wouldn't have any problem with a little murder and B and E? It could also be possible that he chose you specifically for the job because he wanted you home and settled."

He seemed to think on it a moment. "He probably could have gotten someone else to get me out of jail. But, then again, he knew he could trust you and your skills and contacts are pretty hard to come by."

If any of this was true, I was going to have to seriously consider beating the crap out of Tony. "If that were so—" I replied, "and I'm not saying it isn't possible—Tony can be a shit and using me wouldn't be that far a stretch for him." Stretch, hell, he'd made it a regular part of our relationship over the years.

"But, wouldn't it have been easier just to *ask* me to get you out rather than playing this game? I mean, throwing those three guys at me and hoping I didn't pick one? Not to mention pissing off the other three families involved, since they probably feel snubbed by the whole thing. Hell, I'm the one who chose you. I'm the one who insisted on getting you out of jail, not Tony. He didn't even bring your name up."

I thought about all that had proceeded thus far. But in just asking, Tony wouldn't have gotten me settled. He needed a reason for me to marry, a reason for me to stay.

"No," I said, "Tony's manipulative, but he always wants to know what the result will be before he starts and with me he never does. I'm always the wild card. I've almost never done what was asked or what was expected …"

That is, without a little coercion or guilt. Could Tony have foreseen that? That I'd go for exactly what he'd said not to? Initially, he'd said "No" to Alex as a husband prospect. I'd been the one to suggest Alex, but Tony might have known I'd ask. He was the only local leader who was single and even remotely appropriate as a husband: age, position, skill and appearance. Alex had a reputation and one I would be capable of handling. It was possible, but not probable.

"He had no way of knowing I'd decide on you," I said.

"You don't look at all certain. Are you? Besides, I don't know that you were supposed to decide on me. You were just supposed to get me out of jail, not necessarily marry me. Tony may have been serious about the other three."

I glanced over my shoulder and that same smile was there. But this time I wasn't finding it charming. "If you're trying to tell me something, I wish you'd get to it. I don't like being strung along."

He pulled me back down toward his chest again. "If I were, would it change things?"

"It would definitely change things between Tony and me. I also think it would have an impact on our relationship since the main reason I agreed to this was because of family responsibility. I liked living in Italy. I had a beautiful house and I don't like living in the city. I liked my job. It can be morally challenging at times, but I always have a choice. Are you going to tell me if this is just some sick game Tony's playing?"

He chuckled. Now that was irritating.

"I liked the part about your job being morally challenging," said Alex. "I'm sure it was. As to whether or not I'm going to tell you, well … after this conversation I'm thinking that wouldn't be in my best interest at the moment, so it will wait until after the wedding. I want to make sure you don't jump ship on me." He moved my hair to one side and kissed my ear. "I think we're going to be happy together and I don't want to screw it up, but if you really like the idea of working for Max, you may want to keep it in mind."

I liked the snuggling but I was still mad enough that it wasn't distracting me quite as much as Alex anticipated.

"And what makes you think," I demanded, "that I won't jump ship after the wedding?" Tipping my head back I looked at Alex. The smile was gone.

"You wouldn't do that. Marriage is a commitment, not just to me, but to my family, and you are a big one on keeping up with what is required of you. Besides, we have an agreement between us and it has nothing to do with Tony or your perceived Pascoli obligations."

He slid me off of his lap and stood up. I guess we're getting out.

He dried himself off and then took another towel down to dry me. He turned slightly to look in my eyes as he wrapped the towel around me. "You do know that if you felt the need to run back to Europe, I'd have to go get you and bring you back."

Pushing past him to the door, I moved to the dresser to get my pajamas. "You're assuming you could bring me back if I didn't want to return. I never do anything I'm not willing to do. I think it would be unwise for you to forget that. I don't like being dictated to. My behavior is of my own choosing. It could be a costly error in judgment, on your part, to ignore that."

I felt him standing behind me as I finished. He took my arm, not harshly, but he knew I was pissed so he was holding more tightly than I might have liked. "I hope that wasn't a threat."

Yanking my arm away from his hold, I responded, "No, just a statement of fact. I don't like being screwed with and I don't take orders of any kind. Ever. I would have thought that was evident by my background."

"It is. And I didn't screw with you. If, and I use the term *if*, Tony called you back under false pretenses, then he's the one messing with you, not me. You presented me with an opportunity. I marry you, and you get me and Dad out. Your situation with Tony is not something I created."

His arm wrapped around my waist. "You publicly accepted to be my wife, in front of all of the families. I expect you to go through with it, even if Tony has lied. Besides, one way or another the family will be yours, sooner or later. Tony has been clear about that, yes?"

I nodded and slipped away from him to put on my pajamas. I needed to think about this little revelation. If I wasn't going to run the family, what the hell was I going to do with my time? I'd agreed to give up my work. I'd be bored stiff. Even working for Max wouldn't fill all of my time.

✳✳✳

After putting on my robe, I left our room. My bare feet on the stairs, I went to the library. It was quiet in the house and I needed to be alone for a while.

The piano, my solace, awaited me in the library. I closed the door and sat in front of the keys. Tony had the house designed so that when the doors were closed, it was impervious to sound. The piano wasn't just my escape from family gatherings, it helped me think and evaluate the life issues that came up.

I thought about making myself a drink, but since I'd been home, I'd been trying to deal with my problems in a bottle. This problem wasn't going away and a drink wasn't going to help. A clear head was what I needed. And from here on out drinks were not an option.

Now, to evaluate my situation, how do I really feel about all of this?

First off, I'll admit, I don't want the family obligations. Not having to contend with the mess that Tony had made sounded pretty good to me. I never had wanted it to begin with. It was just one more responsibility I didn't want, and a big one at that.

And I suppose I could see Alex's viewpoint. I'd offered myself in exchange for his release from jail. As irritated as I was, it wasn't because I felt like I was getting the short end of the deal, even though I'm pretty sure I was.

If I'd been in any way inclined to take a husband, Alex was perfect. But I hadn't been so inclined and I'd been tricked. I felt used, but not just used, vulnerable? Vulnerable!

Only my family could put me in a position of vulnerability. It was a feeling I wasn't used to having. I don't think I've felt vulnerable for years. Last time it had happened I'd probably been … one of Tony's enforcers. Why is it that that seems so ironic? I leave for twelve years and haven't had one moment of vulnerability, even considering my industry, but send me home to my family and I'm getting screwed over first thing. Ugh!!

I felt more than vulnerable though, I felt … stupid. Yep, that was that feeling, stupid. I should have known I couldn't trust Tony. I mean, I could trust him not to kill me, or send me to jail, but I couldn't trust him to tell me the truth. I never trusted him before. That was one of the reasons I'd gone to work for the government.

Tony had lied to me too many times when I was young. Which of course now made me wonder why I'd done it. What emotion had possessed me to make me willing to compromise myself, my safety, my sense of well being, to put my trust in someone I knew couldn't be taken at face value? There was always an ulterior motive with Tony.

Maybe I was getting old. Maybe I thought things had changed, because I had changed. But in hindsight, I hadn't trusted him, had I? I'd known he seemed to be up to something. Why hadn't I pursued that mistrust? I'd known right from the first meeting at Mario's he was up to something.

There was no point in chastising myself. I couldn't very well change any of it now. I'd have to decide how to proceed. There were only a few options available. I could kill someone. That was always an option, but sometimes it didn't solve anything. If I kill Tony, I end up with the responsibility I don't want and Alex for a husband. That doesn't achieve anything of benefit, other than maybe making me feel better for about five minutes.

I could kill Alex. That would be the only way to get out of this wedding. But then I'd leave his entire family messed up. His little brother would be left in charge without the skill to handle his responsibilites—not to mention that I like Alex and don't want to kill him.

Confronting Tony was an option, but then he'd just lie to me again. It doesn't take much imagination to figure out what he'd say, either. He'd tell me that Alex just wasn't privy to the knowledge of his retirement and he only told Alex what he needed to know. But then I'd be stuck with the job because I'd put him on the spot. And he'd retire just to keep the peace.

One thing was certain, whatever I did, I needed to be out of his house. I'd be vulnerable the entire time I was under his roof. There was no question about that.

"What are you still doing down here?"

I just about leapt off the bench. Again, I hadn't heard Alex enter the room.

"I thought you were just coming down for a drink or something to eat. You've been down here for almost an hour." He was walking over to me from the doorway.

"Has it been that long?" I replied. "I feel like I just sat down." I turned back to the keys. "We need to be out of this house by the end of the week. If we have to move into your place while the house is being finished, that's fine. But if I have to, I'll go to a hotel."

"I think you may be overreacting."

He didn't know the history. All the manipulation I'd left behind. He had no idea why I'd left—no one did. No one knew how close I'd come to taking over for Tony the old-fashioned way … murder.

I was absolutely calm. But this had dredged up all of those old issues.

"No, I'm not," I replied. "Tony's lied to me more times over the years than I care to remember. But then I always knew I couldn't trust anything he said.

"I think I forgot somewhere along the line. Maybe I've been gone too long. You may not think that this particular lie is a big issue, at least not to you. To me, it just reminds me of the main reason I left." I glanced in Alex's direction. He was sitting in one of the overstuffed chairs near me.

"Tony will tell me anything he has to in order to get me to do what he wants. Keeping me under his thumb as much as he can, I feel like a pawn. His family loyalty isn't usually in question, but he has very little individual loyalty. If I were you, I'd be very careful when dealing with him. Do you remember the day that Constantine came to the house and was speaking with Tony?"

Alex nodded.

"Tony said something about my being family and honor-bound and how I knew the meaning of honor better than most of the others who run the families, and without a doubt better than he did? He wasn't just saying that. It was the truth, even if the rest of his conversation with Constantine was crap."

I stopped playing and looked at Alex full-on. "I knew that first day he was up to something. He was underestimating me. He may have done it growing up, but he never did it once I got older. He knew I had the skills to get you out and I knew that he knew. But the whole notion of my taking over the business overrode everything else in my brain. I think he knew it would throw me off."

My fingers slowly began to flow over the keys. "The question is why? Why go to all of this trouble? To get me married? What purpose does it serve to marry me off, one way or another? He may have wanted you out of jail because of an arrangement you had with him; or, for that matter, just for his own reasons. Your brother certainly wouldn't stabilize the area family units. He's too young. But all he had to do was ask me to take care of it. There has to be a reason, but I don't know what it is. And until I do, I won't be taking anything he says at face value. From now on I'm going to be on full-alert where Tony's concerned. For all I know, he needs a patsy for something and I'll kill him before I let him run me under."

"You'd actually kill him? After all these years?" He was shocked I'd even imply it.

"Alex, don't ever underestimate my ruthlessness. It could prove fatal. And no, that wasn't a threat either, just a reality. Tony and I are alike. If the shoe were on the other foot, he'd be saying the exact same thing. Neither of us would like cleaning house, anymore than you did with Thad, but if push comes to shove, we won't sit back and watch someone, no matter who it is, screw us or the rest of the family over. If that's what he's up to—but with Tony, you never know until it hits the fan. The truth is that this distrust is the biggest reason I left. Tony was using me, continuously. It got to the point where I had to choose … so I left. I wasn't ready to make the alternate choice back then. But I am now."

"And what choice are we talking about?"

I laughed. Marty had asked the same thing thirteen years ago, when I first started seriously thinking about leaving. I turned back to the piano. "The choice is to have a life I choose or one that is forced on me by the actions I take and the responsibility those actions create. Many people have their lives forced on them by their own actions. It isn't like I'd be the first. If I kill Tony, I have to accept the role of leader for this family. Or, I can turn a blind eye, pretend I know nothing, and just let him screw with everyone, including me.

"The difference between now and then is that I no longer have it in me to walk away from someone who tries to screw with me. I'm not twenty-three. He should have a certain amount of respect for me by now. And the only reason I didn't stay and do him in back then was that I was too young, or at least I thought I was, when I left. Running the family scared the crap out of me. Hell, it still does, but I don't scare off nearly as easy these days."

"You actually thought about killing him?" said Alex. "And that's the real reason you left?" The shock in his voice was evident.

"No," I said. "there were a number of reasons. I didn't like being a prime target for every family in the tri-state area. Being Tony's successor and assassin put me in that position. I didn't like always being involved in some hair-brained scheme. You'd be surprised at the number of stupid things I got myself into, or, I should say, Tony's guys got me into. I didn't like my parents always looking at me like I was some huge disappointment and constantly harping on me. I'm sure you recall the life-picking I told you about. I didn't like having everybody in town know my name. I'm notorious here, but there are places all over the world where I'm just nobody. I didn't like being treated like a guy by just about every member of my family. I'm not a guy, in case you missed it. But because I could beat the crap out of any and all of them, I got treated like a guy."

Alex laughed.

"Do you really want me to continue on this little rampage?"

"No, I'm too tired," he said. "We can discuss it in the morning." We started for the door. "I didn't realize you and Tony had such a volatile relationship. But I suppose I'm not the only one who doesn't know this, am I?"

"Well, we don't air our dirty laundry in public. What's between us always stays between us."

Chapter 23

THE NEXT MORNING, SITTING at the large round table in the library, I spotted an e-mail from Garbo. He informed me that the mall did hold their tapes for an inordinately long time. The security director was a stickler for documentation. He actually held them all for three months. That was unheard of in most retail establishments I'd dealt with. It was lucky for the girls that the director was so meticulous.

The kidnapper was right there on their tape. It only took them a couple of hours after that to locate the girls. Apparently he was a known nut in the area. Both girls were examined last night and sent home this morning. They had both been sexually assaulted. It couldn't be undone, but at least they were alive. I sent a thank you to Garbo for letting me know and then logged on to Lucifer's Mistress's sight.

There were two messages. The first was from Phil. He'd shut down the Fallen Angel site, so now he was going to use this one? Whatever.

He wanted to let me know that both visas had been taken care of for Miguel and Louisa and that I should be ashamed of myself for the problems I was causing for the D.A. here. Apparently one of the other case files that had gone up in the fire was related to a murder trial.

The man in question was accused of killing his wife, cutting her into small pieces and then disposing of her body parts in various locations throughout the area. Many of those parts were still missing. Phil was pissed because I'd destroyed several pieces of evidence in the case that couldn't be replaced. Clearly, I was going to have to look into fixing that problem.

I couldn't be seen having assisted in getting a man off the hook for an excessively gruesome murder. The guy, if he did it (and there wasn't much doubt), was nuts and shouldn't be on the street. I was going to have to find at least one of the other missing body parts and hope there was additional evidence to be found with it. Gross, huh? But a girl has to do what a girl has to do and I have to fix the mess I've made.

Replying to Phil's e-mail, I let him know I'd try to make things right before the trial came up. I also asked for a copy of the files so I'd have something to work from in my search for additional evidence. Then I moved to the next e-mail.

The second correspondence was one of those things that only enhanced the strangeness of an already not-so-wonderful twenty-four hours. It just about floored me. "What ... the ... hell?"

Alex was sitting on the opposite side of the library getting his things boxed for moving to the condo. "What is it?"

"You are not going to *believe* this. You really need to read it for yourself. It's just ... bizarre."

That was an understatement. I wasn't even sure how to react. Maybe I should be grateful that the contract had come to me instead of some-one else. Maybe I should laugh out loud because it was too weird. Or maybe I should just be sick to think that someone wanted him dead so badly that they were willing to pay that kind of money.

Alex leaned over my shoulder and read the e-mail. Then he looked at me. His eyes went back to the screen. He was in shock. Couldn't say I blamed him, either. If someone was willing to pay a half-million to get rid of me, I might be a bit shocked, too. Well, not if they wanted to get rid of me, I guess. There's probably someone out there who would pay three or four times that for me. But for anyone else, a half-million is a pretty sizable contract.

"Why do you think they're willing to pay so much? They could have offered half of that and gotten some decent candidates. It seems a tad excessive, doesn't it?" asked Alex.

"Well, it depends. If they want to guarantee that the Mistress would take it, they'd probably be willing to hike the price. It's pretty common for me to get an offer after someone else screwed it up. And, let's be honest, they don't know that *I'm* the Mistress. But one thing is definitely clear—someone wants you dead. People don't contact this address and offer me money like that unless they are extremely serious."

"I assume you don't plan on taking it?" he said. It was only a half-jest. He was clearly concerned that I might still be irritated about what we'd discussed last night.

"Well, if I don't take it, they'll just offer it to someone else and I'll have to kill them, too. And, since the bodies are already starting to pile up, I don't think that's such a great idea. It just makes things more difficult," I said and began to type an affirmative reply.

"Do I need to be worried when we go to bed tonight?" Again, a half-jest.

"No," I smiled. "Actually you should be sleeping better at night—at least we know who has the contract. I'll have this person wire-transfer a down payment for services; that's how I normally operate. Then I'll trace the account number back to its source so we can find out the name on the account—if one's available. Then, if we're really lucky, we can narrow down which family we're dealing with. "

"What are you going to do with the down payment?" Alex asked. I glanced back. "It just makes me wonder. I have a problem believing you'd take money for services you have no intention of performing."

He *was* still concerned I was going to kill him. He was looking at me with extreme discomfort. Now doesn't that just figure?

"I'm not going to kill you," I said firmly. "Would you calm down? You're going to get on my nerves if you keep it up. As for the money—things like this have come up before … well, not things *exactly* like this, but jobs that I've accepted just so that no one else would. As a rule, I just give the money to a significantly appropriate charity."

I turned back to my e-mail response.

"Once, when I did a project related to the clergy, the money went to a local church. When I did a project related to kids, the money went to a local orphanage … that sort of thing."

"And where are you planning on sending this money?" Alex

asked.

"I'm not sure yet, but I'll come up with something. There are always charities looking for generous benefactors."

"True enough." Alex moved away and back to his chair. "How are you going to track the account number? Don't banks have security programs to keep people from accessing their customer's accounts?"

"Of course," I said. "If they didn't, people wouldn't give them their money. However … everything can be discovered with the right skills or contacts." I gave him a big smile and went back to my computer. Phil was useful for many things and this was certainly one of them.

✳✳✳

Alex and I arrived at the townhouse at four-thirty that afternoon, after getting the go-ahead from Max. Everything had been released and there was absolutely no reason to stay with Tony any longer. I felt much better about that.

The townhouse was large. Not compared to Tony's home, of course, but it was well over three thousand square-feet. And since it was just going to be the two of us, this was more than enough room.

The house just screamed Alex through and through. It was completely decorated in a very masculine style. All the wood furniture was dark and so were most of the fabrics used throughout the house. There was no full-time housekeeper or cook. It looked like Alex just fended for himself or went out to eat a lot.

Alex had contacted his occasional housekeeper and had her come by to get the house ready for us. So everything was cleaned, dusted and waxed. But there wasn't a speck of food in the fridge or the cabinets, not even salt or pepper. I'd better check for pots and pans. With a single man, one just never knows.

Amazingly there was a full set of very expensive pans in the cabinet, along with a food processor, coffee maker and several other necessary items. Good—I didn't want to have to buy everything I needed tonight.

"We need groceries. I'll make a list and then go shopping," I said.

"I usually just eat out," Alex said. "Can you cook?"

"Now, what sort of good Italian girl would I be if I couldn't cook? My mother would have thought it sacrilege if I hadn't learned. Besides, I've lived alone for a good bit, sometimes in not so friendly areas. It was either learn or starve."

Alex laughed.

We discussed food, including his preferences and mine, and then I made my list and headed to the store. I noticed Detective Morrey in my rearview. Maybe I could put him to work pushing the cart. It wasn't as if he was going to enjoy sitting in the parking lot any more than pushing a cart.

I parked and walked over to his car. He let the window down.

"Evening," was the greeting I got when I approached.

"Why don't you come with me?" I asked. "I'm sure you could use a little exercise considering what you've probably been up to all day."

He rolled up the window and climbed out of the car. Today, his rumpled shirt was a navy blue with some sort of slogan for a bar called Pound Down. Sounded like a real upscale joint.

He stretched his entire body. My guess was he'd been in that car all day sitting outside Tony's, and then again, outside Alex's townhouse. I turned and headed for the store with Morrey following.

"You should watch it," I said. "You spend too much time in that car and your ass will get wide and flat."

He snickered. "Yeah, well I'm more concerned with ever having feeling in it again. Every time I get out it's numb."

I grabbed a cart and passed it off to Morrey. "I take it I'm working during this outing?" he inquired.

"You might as well be useful," I replied.

The first stop was produce. We didn't say anything for a good four or five minutes. That's when Morrey must have gotten a sudden need to chat. "So, I hear they found those girls in Philly. They say that some P.I. found them. I take it he was the friend you were helping."

I didn't say anything. I glanced at him, then put my bag of onions in the cart and moved to the bell peppers.

"I was tempted to say something to one of my friends when he told me, but decided not to. There's obviously more to this than you just wanting to have the families believe you're vicious and cruel."

"There is," I confirmed. "That P.I. doesn't know who I really am. All he has is an e-mail address and a contact name. Needless to say it isn't my real one." I started sorting through the sweet potatoes. "There are reasons I use aliases and it would be very," I paused and looked at him, "very bad if someone could put my real name with the alias." I went back to eyeing the spuds.

"So he isn't really a friend?"

"I suppose that depends on how you define the word 'friend'. He's a legitimate business contact who works toward the same goals I do. He asked for my help and I gave it to him." I selected four sweet potatoes.

"But, you don't actually know him and he doesn't know you, right? So, if you ran into him on the street you'd never know it?"

"Actually, I'd know who he was," I explained, "he just wouldn't know me. He isn't hiding his position in Philly. He works with the law enforcement there on a regular basis. He has no reason to pretend to be someone else."

"But you do."

"Yes."

We started up the first aisle. I was selecting bread when I looked up and saw my Aunt Geraldine. Great, now comes the life-picking. I can only be grateful that it wasn't Ruth or I'd be hearing about every aching bone in her aging body.

"Angelica, sweetheart, what are you doing in a *grocery* store? I'm certain you have plenty of people to do this sort of thing. It just isn't right that you're out doing these little daily things. Hasn't Alex provided you with a housekeeper?"

"Hi, Aunt Geraldine." I leaned in and gave her a kiss. "No, Alex and I don't have a housekeeper yet. My housekeeper is coming over with my things from Italy and neither she nor the furnishings have arrived yet.

"We've been staying at Tony's, but Alex and I wanted some privacy, so we moved into his townhouse. I'm shopping because there's no food there. Besides, I'm more than capable of shopping and cooking for Alex and me, at least until Louisa arrives. I'm not above doing daily chores."

"You are just amazing," she said, making it sound like rocket science. "You'll make a wonderful wife and mother. I just can't wait for those children. So, have the two of you discussed when we can be expecting some little ones? We can't have you putting it off too long—you're not getting any younger and neither is Alex. You'll want him to be an active father I think, so the sooner the better."

I'm not even married yet and they're already trying to get me to reproduce. "We've discussed it and will start trying in a year or so. We need some time to settle into our new home and get our lives in order before we add a baby."

She looked at Morrey. "And who is this? Oh, Alex must have been worried about you going out by yourself and sent a personal bodyguard." I thought I heard Morrey snicker. "He is so thoughtful! Worrying about you … not just any man worries about his fiancée like that."

I should hope not.

"No," I agreed. "Actually, this is Detective Morrey. He follows Alex and me occasionally to see if he can find evidence to send Alex back to jail."

The look on my aunt's face said, unequivocally and without a doubt, that *she* did not approve of Morrey. And, I was pretty sure that Morrey was none to happy with that explanation, either.

"Since he was just following me anyway, I figured he could push the cart," I explained.

"You're not serious? You wouldn't actually spend time with someone who wants to send Alex back to jail? Whatever would he say about such a thing?" my aunt scolded.

"I don't think Morrey is being given a choice in his assignments. Otherwise, he'd have chosen something more interesting. In any case,

Alex is quite well aware of his existence. Now, if you'll excuse us, I have a million things to buy and if we don't get going I'll be here 'til midnight."

She pursed her lips, making her look even more perturbed. "Well, I suppose I'll be seeing you later. And you," she pointed at Morrey, "you should be ashamed of yourself, following our lovely Angelica around like she was some sort of ax murderer."

I'd never actually used an ax ... too ... gross. But Morrey was probably wondering. I got another kiss on the cheek and she was gone. We headed for the meats.

"Did you have to tell her all that?" he whined. "I was waiting to be hit with a purse."

He had a point. It wasn't impossible to imagine an attack on Morrey by Aunt Geraldine.

"I just told the truth," I shrugged. "You are acquainted with the truth, yes?" I gave him my Miss Innocent smile.

"Very funny."

I'd selected several boneless chicken packages and was headed for the beef when I asked, "Since we're here, maybe you could fill me in on the Hitchigan case?"

He glanced at the meat and then at me. "You do know you're sick, yes?"

"No, the red blood just reminded me. So do you know anything or not?"

"Such as?"

"Such as, why he is supposed to have ... done it? Where they found the evidence, what type of evidence, what was destroyed in the fire, who's heading up the investigation, that sort of thing?"

It took him a minute and then he said, "What was destroyed in the fire? You wouldn't be feeling guilty, now, would you? I mean, we both know you're probably the one who started that fire at the evidence locker ... maybe you're feeling rotten because you screwed up two cases other than the one you meant to screw up? Is that it?"

I gave him a dirty look. "If you don't want to answer the question, that's fine, I have a copy of the files coming to me tomorrow. I just thought … if you had any first-hand knowledge and, since that nut is probably going to walk, according to my sources, due to the lack of evidence, you might want to discuss it."

He was watching me while I selected a pork roast. "Another hobby project I suppose? Well, there isn't any reason *not* to tell you. It isn't like it's a big secret. We have the basic circumstantial stuff. The guy was having an affair, he was known to have slapped his wife around, he had a nice life insurance policy on her and we don't believe his alibi."

"Why not?"

"He changed it. First he said he was out with friends. When he couldn't get any of them to back him up, he said he was with the girl-friend. But who else is going to cut up his wife in the house? And we do have the evidence that it was done in the house. There were traces of blood found in the tub, on the shower stall, around the drain and on the bathroom floor."

"So, what got destroyed that was so vital to the case?"

"The DNA evidence that linked him to the murders. The test's answers can be reprinted, but the physical evidence was stored inside the lockup—vials of skin cells taken from under the woman's fingernails. It was all him. The problem now, is they can't use the results without the actual evidence."

"So, I take it they found an arm if they found the skin cells under her nails, yes?"

"Actually, all we found was the left hand and forearm. It was severed from the upper arm." He stammered slightly. "Man, this is just too gross to be discussing in the meat section. Can we move to another aisle?"

"Yes, I think I'll go to the butcher for the rest of what I need. These don't look that appealing." And, when I don't feel like puking up my last two days worth of food. It all looked totally gross. He was absolutely right.

"You know it could be the conversation," he suggested, smiling.

I moved to the first central aisle—baking goods and seasoning. Things I definitely needed.

"Okay, so all the physical DNA evidence was removed from under her nails in order to do the testing? There must not have been much to begin with or they could go back and do another scraping."

The body parts would be kept refrigerated to preserve the evidence, so the matching DNA must have been removed just to make the ID or they'd have more to use as backup.

"But it was her left hand," I said. "If she were right-handed then there might be more conclusive evidence. It's still out there, right?"

"That's what I hear," he replied.

"So, in order to gain the same type of DNA evidence, we need to find the right hand and hope that there is more under those nails, yes?"

He stopped as I continued down to the cake mixes. "Are you going to go looking for body parts?" he demanded.

I kept walking. "Do you know another way to find that evidence?"

"No, I guess not," he mumbled.

"The guy is still in jail and will be there for a bit longer, so we have some time." They'd held him without bond and, with the circumstantial evidence, had managed to keep him behind bars. At least, so far he was still there. "When I get a copy of the police file, I hope it has the locations where they found the pieces. It will make a search much easier."

"We? That isn't my case. I'm supposed to follow you and Sevelli. I don't want to go looking for body parts," he groaned.

I grabbed a box of yellow cake mix. "Well, Alex is now back at his own residence and will be running his businesses from there. Therefore, the only person who will be going out, for the most part, is me. And I'll be looking for body parts. I don't see why you shouldn't help. It's your job, after all, to solve crimes, right?"

"Yes," he admitted, "but not *that* crime."

"Do you want that sicko back on the street? Because that's exactly what's going to happen if the evidence isn't replaced. He won't be convicted on circumstantial evidence. In fact, it may not even go to trial."

"And whose fault is it," he asked, pointedly, "that the original evidence was destroyed, hmm?"

Smartass. "It isn't like we can reverse time and fix it, now is it?" I countered.

"Are you actually admitting you screwed this up?" he asked. "I get the feeling that this doesn't happen often."

"I'm not admitting anything …" I said, "other than wanting to fix this problem. Now come on, I need to hit up the canned fruit aisle."

After too much shopping, over two-hundred dollars worth with almost no beef, I finally made it home. Morrey followed and helped me bring in the groceries. Needless to say Alex was a bit perturbed to see the detective in our home.

"And what is this?" he asked.

"Groceries naturally," I said. "Or are you referring to my assistant?" Alex nodded. "He helped me with the shopping. He was already there, after all, and volunteered to help schlep bags. I think he gets bored."

Morrey walked in with two more. He was bringing them in and I was putting everything away. Alex went to help with the carting in of the bags.

When he returned after the second trip he said, "How much did you buy? It looks like enough to last months."

"We're going to be here for a couple of weeks at least and most of this stuff is staples."

"Staples?"

Men. "Yes, mayonnaise, mustard, ketchup, syrup, flour, sugar, salt, pepper, that sort of thing. There is literally nothing in your townhouse. There isn't even coffee. I don't think either of us could survive a morning without coffee or, at the very least, tea."

"That's because what was here was so old. Mrs. Smitts just cleaned it all out and trashed it. It's better than food poisoning."

"I agree. But that meant buying everything over again."

Morrey walked in with his last bag. "That's it for me. I'll see you tomorrow."

"Tomorrow?" Alex asked.

I glanced up. "Yes, we're going body hunting. Sound like fun? You're welcome to join us."

"Why don't I like the sound of that?" said Alex.

"Because it's gross?" suggested Morrey.

"What body are you hunting? And I assume it's dead, since the detective here seems to find it 'gross'?"

"Yes, it's dead," I assured Alex. "I'm sure you heard about the guy who killed his wife and chopped up her body and left the parts all over the place. Well, it seems that some of the DNA evidence was destroyed in the fire downtown." I gave him knowing look. "I've decided to see if I can find the missing hand to replace it."

Alex looked green. "Missing hand? I have a future with a woman who looks for missing corpse hands? Isn't this one of those things we should have discussed before you decided to do it?"

"If you can persuade her to not go looking for the missing parts of Mrs. Hitchigan," interjected Morrey, "I'd be grateful. I don't want to rummage around in the woods looking for body parts. I'd rather sit in the car and follow you someplace boring, like I've been doing."

Morrey was just pathetic.

"You'd rather have a nut released to kill again, right?" I snapped.

"No, but I don't have a strong stomach." He put a hand to his stomach like he was going to be sick just thinking about it.

"How did you make it through the police academy? Don't they screen for weak stomachs? You must have had to look at half-rotted corpses—I did." I was still putting things away .

"Well, yea," Morrey admitted, "but those were pictures. The real thing is much worse. And it usually smells awful," he added, rumpling up his nose .

"You … are … a … wuss!"

"Fine, I'll go with you," he said grumpily. "But I hope you have some idea of where to start. All the other pieces were found completely by accident."

"Then, that means he wasn't hiding them very well, now doesn't it? You said they have six pieces. That should be about half of her. And if he wasn't careful getting rid of one half, he most likely wasn't careful getting rid of the other. They just haven't been stumbled on yet."

"Yeah, but you're being picky about the piece you want. It might take finding the entire other half of her to find that one piece. I'm gonna have nightmares if I start thinking about this too much. I'm going home."

"See ya'. Thanks for bringing in the bags."

"Yeah," Morrey mumbled. I heard the front door shut.

Alex was watching me. He was right, I should have told him before I started on this. But it was my fault that Hitchigan might get off. I put away some canned peaches, turned and looked at him.

"You know I have to fix this," I said. "I don't have a choice. It's my fault that the evidence got destroyed. And the case in question isn't a nice little assault and battery or corporate theft. He chopped up another human being and distributed her parts throughout the greater New Jersey area. He's psychotic. He can't be allowed back on the street. If this fails then I'll probably have to kill him, just so I can sleep at night. It's better if I look for evidence to replace what was lost in the fire."

"You really feel that strongly about this?"

"Yes. Like I said, it's *my* fault. And we know there won't be another attempt on your life for the time being. I'm still waiting for something to move forward with the banking info. The contact said they'd send over the deposit within ninety-six hours. That could be as much as four full days. So, I might as well look for body parts."

"You're right," Alex agreed, grumpily. "It's our fault that the evidence got destroyed and the guy clearly has a few screws loose. I guess investigating the missing body parts isn't a real problem. But we did agree that we'd discuss these things from now on. So, why wasn't I informed that you planned on doing this until you had already made plans with Detective Morrey?"

"Well, I got a message from Phil on the Mistress' site this morning. He sort of bitched me out for screwing up the evidence for this case."

Again.

"I would have told you," I said, apologetically, "but there seemed to be other, more pressing, matters at the time."

"Like someone hiring you to kill me," Alex replied.

I nodded. "And when Morrey and I were at the meat counter, it reminded me that I needed to do something about Mrs. Hitchigan. Actually, I think it was just a matter of timing."

Alex stood and smirked. "Yeah, right. But, I think you forgot you were supposed to discuss these things with me. You just made the decision by yourself."

"Maybe," I agreed.

He slid his arms around me and I leaned my head on his chest. "You know, I'm not used to having to discuss things first. Honestly, I wasn't avoiding talking to you or trying to get around you. I just didn't think about it."

He kissed the top of my head. "I know. But you need to try to remember. And I don't want Morrey to become a fixture in our house. He is still a cop and one that was assigned to find more evidence on me. We don't want to make it too easy on him."

I tipped my head up and smiled at him. "Yes, I know. I thought hunting for body parts would keep him otherwise engaged."

"Weren't there three cases that were destroyed? What was the third?"

"It was an embezzlement case. I don't feel bad enough about that to do anything."

If the D.A. can't remake the case, tough crap. At least I knew that the embezzler was unlikely to go out and lop off someone's head.

"I wonder how the evidence for these cases is arranged?" mused Alex. "I mean, there were three cases: one involved murder, another embezzlement, and then mine, which was full of everything but murder. There doesn't seem to be a common thread."

"There isn't," I confirmed. "They're simply sorted by docket number. These numbers are assigned according to the order of the court filing, not by case content."

And that reminded me, I really needed to do something about that evidence I had stashed.

Chapter 24

THE FOLLOWING MORNING I started the coffee, then trekked my way into the dining room to access my laptop, hoping that the police file would be there to download. I'd taken over the dining room as my temporary office. I figured that Alex and I wouldn't be entertaining any time in the near future and the dining room was big enough to accommodate my maps and paperwork while still leaving room to get at the computer.

I logged in, checked my e-mail, and there it was; along with a little note from Phil expressing his overwhelming appreciation for my taking responsibility for the mess I'd made and trying to fix it. I set the file up to print and went back to the kitchen to make breakfast.

I'd thrown together a fruit salad the night before and made scrambled eggs and toast this morning to go with it. I always use a little cinnamon in my eggs; it gives them a little flavor.

Just as I was setting up the breakfast table Alex came in. I was tempted to go and get the file I'd just printed, but I was certain that I'd regret it once it was on the table. Furthermore, I was sure Alex would not appreciate my putting that sort of thing in front of him while he was trying to eat. I could turn off a lot, but severed body parts were not among them.

So instead, I refilled my cup and we both sat to eat.

An hour later I was poring over the reports, fourth cup of coffee in hand. It was only eight o'clock when the doorbell rang.

I heard voices. "What do you want?" asked Alex.

"Remember?" was the response. "Your wife-to-be wanted to go

look for hands and such. That's why I'm here." It was Morrey. There was no mistaking that voice.

I stepped into the hall. "Alex, honey, let him in. I'm working in the dining room on an area map to see if I can detect a pattern for the parts that were found. Morrey might be able to help. Just as soon as I have someplace to start, we'll leave," I promised.

Alex turned to me, complete disgust written on his features. "Do you have a general time frame on that? People come to see me here and I don't want cops in my house while they're here—some of them would be uncomfortable." He looked at Morrey. "No offense intended."

"None taken, I'm sure," Morrey grumbled.

"We should only be about a half-hour," I said. "I think I already see a loose pattern."

Morrey took a look at the police reports I'd scattered everywhere. "You see a pattern?"

"It's not really a *pattern*." I replied. "It's more of an organized splatter than a pattern. But when you put all the pins on the map, it looks like a loose pattern of sorts." I'd actually marked them in red felt tip pen, not pins.

"This is how I see it," I explained. "I figure he took her in one trip. I mean, who wants pieces of dead body hanging out in his house? How could he sleep at night? That would make him even more bizarre than I already think he is. The official report says he was driving a dark blue Taurus. Now, assuming he took all of her in one trip, he would have put her parts in the trunk. This makes sense because only a total freak would be comfortable driving around with hunks of his wife stored in pull-tie garbage bags on the back seat."

Can you say *yuck*!

I leaned into the map. "So, most likely he took a single route, distributing body parts along the way, and getting rid of them as quickly as possible." Morrey was looking intently at the map. "Since body parts were located *here*, at the edge of town on the north side of the road, I think it's likely he was headed *away* from town because, from the passenger side, it's easier to pull off on the right side of the road.

"Right about here," I pointed to the map, "he jumped out, pulled a garbage bag from the trunk and quickly hid it.

"We got a lucky break because these body parts were stumbled on by hikers. That means he had to hoof it up the hill and hide the bag under the leaves where it was found—if we follow the forensic reports."

"So far that makes sense."

"Well then, following this assumption, I think he was headed *back* into town when he dumped these three body parts." I pointed to the red dots on the map, noting they were all on the same side of the road. "The only way I see to connect those two roads is here, here, and here," I said, indicating three separate crossroads. "But one part was found here, in the tree line along this road. It was near the end of the road, but I think we can assume that's the way he came." I highlighted the path I'd indicated on the map.

"Okay," said Morrey, nodding, "since you think this was his path, then we should look for a pattern in the distribution along that path."

"Right. However, Hitchigan placed the first two body parts further back from the road, in the woods. That might make it difficult to start from that end. However, we can probably suppose that he was more picky about where he placed the bags when he began his disposal route than near the end."

I grabbed my map and began to fold it. "That's why I think we should start at the *end* of the trail and work our way back. You can see how he just dumped those last three pieces less than two miles apart and not even very far off the road. He was clearly getting lazy."

Morrey blew out a long breath, grabbed the map from me and pointed to one of the little red dots. "So, we should start about a half mile or so west of this dump site," he said, indicating the third dumpsite near the end of the route.

"Yep. I think that way we can make sure we don't miss any-thing."

I told Alex where we were going, so he couldn't accuse me of keep-ing secrets. Then Morrey and I packed ourselves off. It was going to be a long day.

The weather was positively beautiful. The temperature was in the mid-eighties, clear sky, or at least as clear as it gets in this city. I'd dressed for this outing. I knew it was going to get hot after a while with possible hiking in the woods. So a pale blue tank top, jeans, and boots seemed logical attire for the work ahead.

Two hours of walking along the south side of a moderately scenic rural road later, we spotted a small black piece of plastic under a fallen branch. It was about four yards in from the side of the road and almost brown from the dirt and leaves that had accumulated on top of it.

"Do you think that's one of them?" Morrey asked reluctantly.

We were now approximately a mile and a half from the nearest known dump site. "I hope so. I was beginning to think maybe I had it all wrong. We can't touch it, exactly—if we do we could contaminate the evidence."

"I am a professional, you know?" said Morrey. "I do this for a living."

I raised an eyebrow. "Fine, be that way. We'll just see if it's one of those thirty gallon pull-tie trash bags. It's the right color for it."

We were both very careful to watch our feet and make sure we didn't step on anything that might be evidence. Then I slid on a pair of plastic gloves and gently lifted the branch that was lying on top of the bag. The bag had been punctured by the branch where it had fallen and when the piece of tree was removed, the bag let out a smell that left nothing to the imagination.

"Dear God, put that branch back exactly like it was," said Morrey. "We need to call this in."

He looked at me closely. "I didn't think about that before. How are we going to turn these things over to the department since I'm pretty sure you don't want credit," he said.

"Well, I didn't think you'd want credit either," I replied. "This isn't exactly where you're supposed to be."

He shrugged.

"I'll call Max. He'll call the D.A.'s office and then they'll call the officer in charge of the case," I said. "That way no one knows we're out here." I pulled a yellow flag from my pocket and tied it to a branch above the bag.

We turned away from the site and headed back. "Let's go up the road about three quarters of a mile and start looking again."

"Hey," said Morrey. "That bag could have the *hand*. If it is, then we won't need to find any more pieces. Why don't we wait until we know?"

There are times when Morrey reminded me an indolent ten-year-old. "I know you don't like this," I said, "but that process could take a bit longer than I have. Remember, there's still someone trying to kill Alex and I have lots of other things to do. Come on, let's move away from here because I don't want to call Max until we're out of the area."

At approximately twelve-thirty, we were just under two miles from the body piece we'd found when Morrey suddenly came to a stop. He was looking into a drainage gully that ran under the road.

"That could be one," he said, pointed down at the piping and the slick blackness that was hidden inside. "What do you think?"

I looked down at a messy little ravine covered with various litter and slime. Only two to three feet deep, it could be a good hiding place for what we were looking for. If we hadn't been on foot, we'd never have seen it.

"Yep," I replied. "That's it. Those yellow pull-ties are pretty bright in all that gunk." I pulled another flag from my back pocket and tied it to the overpass rail.

"Two down," I beamed, "and, hopefully, only a couple more to go."

Morrey whined like an exasperated puppy needing attention. I tried to ignore him.

"I take it we're going to move down another mile or so?"

It seemed to me that Hitchigan's pattern was expanding. "We'll go down about a mile and a half this time. Chances are the next one is at least two miles from here."

"Okay," he muttered.

We climbed into his old blue dented Crown Victoria and headed further down the road.

"Can we stop for lunch in a little while?" he asked. "All this walking is making me hungry."

"How can you think about food while we're looking for body parts?" I was a little shocked he'd even asked.

"I'm trying *not* to think about what we're actually looking for," he said, grumpily. "That makes it easier."

"Okay, if you see a little place to stop. If not, we'll go for food after we find the next one."

Just up the road, less than half a mile on the right-hand side, we saw a food truck. Actually, it was more-or-less a hot dog stand inside an RV. Morrey got two dogs, both with extra kraut, mustard, chili and onions. That should make him pleasant to be around this afternoon. I'd have to remember to stay upwind.

I had a dog with onions and mustard and a diet cola. After our impromptu meal, we headed up another mile and Morrey pulled off onto a scenic-view parking location and we started our walk. This time it took less than fifteen minutes to spot the half-opened bag.

There it was … out in the open and only seven yards or so in from the highway. It was in a clearing between tree sections. It was remarkable that someone hadn't seen it before now. Through the top of the bag we could see maggots and some seriously tainted-looking, decomposing flesh.

"I think I'm gonna puke up those dogs," moaned Morrey with his hand over his nose and mouth.

I could completely understand his stomach retching because I wasn't far from it myself. "Go over there and find me a sturdy stick. We need something to tie the flag to."

He'd been more than happy to get away from the bag. From what little I could see, I could tell this was definitely not the missing hand. It looked like a piece of rib cage, from the bones I could observe without actually touching the bag. Again, I didn't want to contaminate any evidence. And, on top of that, I wasn't all that sure I wanted to see it.

Tying the flag to the stick, I put it five feet or so to the left of the bag.

"We found three bags. Can we call it a day yet? That last one was just *nasty* with a capital *N*." He started making gag sounds.

"No," I said firmly. "But I should call in the first two right now so forensics can start working on them. Otherwise, it will be dark when they come out. Besides, we're going up about five and a half miles from here. They found a piece just under three miles from this location and I'd say, based on the scatter pattern, there isn't much chance of one being in between."

I dialed Max's office and his receptionist put me right through.

"Ace, how are you and Alex getting on together? I'm sure you're pleased to be in your own place for a change."

"We're doing just fine, Max. The idea of having privacy was becoming a foreign concept. I love Tony." More or less. "But he has far too many people in that house to suit me."

That was the truth. Tony had his maid, cook, Jason and his wife, a gardener, a mechanic and, of course, the enforcers. They were all there most of the time. It was a bit crowded even for a mansion.

"I can understand that," Max replied. "I'd hate being monitored every time I came and went and Tony is a big one for security. So, what can I do for you? I'm sure you didn't call just to chat."

"No, I didn't. I was calling because I need you to act as intermediary with the D.A. and/or the police."

He groaned. "Ace, what are you doing? Please tell me you aren't going to get yourself into a mess after all this time."

"Absolutely not," I assured Max. "I'm not in the middle of anything. But," I glanced at Morrey, sitting with his eyes closed, "you remember the evidence in the Hitchigan case that was destroyed by an electrical fire? Well, I thought I might go out and find something to replace it."

"You're feeling guilty, Ace," said Max. "Can't say I blame you. I felt pretty bad myself when I found out. Hitchigan is a few fries short of a Happy Meal, if you know what I mean?"

I explained about the DNA matter and the missing parts. I also explained my theory on Hitchigan's disposal and locations.

"And since you had this theory you decided to go see how accurate it was?" he asked.

"Exactly. No point in having a hypothesis and not trying to prove it, now is there? We found three of the bags, but I only want you to call in the first two right now. We're going to keep looking and I don't want a bunch of cops following us around while we do it. This way, we'll be more than seven miles from where they're working."

"Who is *we*? And you really found three bags of ... body parts?" He sounded a little grossed out by the idea.

I explained about Morrey and his reluctant but dutiful monitoring of me and Alex. Max responded exactly as I knew he would. "I could file an official complaint if you want. It would make his boss think twice."

With a mental image of Phil, his face beet red and screaming, if he found out, I said, "No, don't bother for now. If it becomes a real problem, I'll let you know. In the meantime, if you could call the D.A. and let him know about these two bags—I marked both with a yellow flag. We tried not to touch anything. Just don't give him the name of your informant, please. There would be a lot of questions."

After hanging up, Morrey and I headed to the next possible site. We parked on the right-hand side, next to the river, and headed across the street. We must have walked for well over an hour before we saw the next bag. This one was more than three and a quarter miles from the nearest known body-dump site and set back in the woods a bit. Hitchigan must have parked here for a while to get the bag back this far. I was betting all the bags, from here on out, were placed further out of sight.

There were a couple of claw marks on the bag, and again, it was really foul. This bag was bulkier than the others we'd found and it stunk to high heaven.

Morrey was looking greener than he had when he'd seen the maggots earlier. "Are you okay?" I asked. "I don't want you puking here—it would screw with the scene. If you can't hold it then go across the street."

"No, I'll keep it together," he replied wearily. "How the hell do people work around this stuff? … and who in his right mind chops up a body?"

"You get used to the smells and learn to accept it by tuning it out. You try not to think of it as a person. But as for cutting up a body, I'm pretty sure that Hitchigan isn't in his right mind." I grabbed another flag out of my pocket and tied it to a tree limb above the bag.

"Come on," I said. "I think we can go a good three miles this time."

"We've found four body parts today," whined Morrey. "Can't we stop now? I don't know if I can take anymore of this. That last one … well, it just went beyond average on the scale of disgusting. I didn't think I'd hold down my lunch that time." He glanced back where the bag lay in the lightly wooded area and then turned to me. "What part of her do you think was in the bag? It was awfully big."

"I don't know and I don't want to know," I said flatly. I opened my door and looked at Morrey. "And if you were honest with yourself, you should admit you don't really want to know, either." He wasn't the only one who was going to have nightmares about this. But I'd be damned if I was going to throw up in front of Morrey no matter how repulsive the scene.

I called Max.

"Max, you can let them know about the third piece now. We just found a fourth." I gave him the location of the third flag.

"Matt is pissed because I wouldn't give him a name," said Max. Matt Laren is the D.A. these days. "But he *knows* it's you. He said so, Ace, very clearly. He said he hopes that, since you're sticking your nose where it doesn't belong again, that you manage to find the other hand. They have it on good authority that she was right-handed and she probably put up a hell of a fight. He said it was the least you could do, considering … He also said he couldn't prove it, especially to a jury, but he knows you're the one who started that fire in the evidence lock-up. Of course, I reminded him that saying such things could be considered slander, but he didn't seem to care."

"He can't do anything," I replied, "without proof and he knows it. All he has is a gut instinct. You didn't confirm anything?" I asked, though I figured I could assume that.

"Of course not! You know better than that. I simply told him that I had a concerned citizen who had found a couple of the bags he'd been looking for, that's all. But you are marking them with flags, just like a member of law enforcement … not that I'm complaining. I'm sure it makes it easier to find them. But you are sort of giving yourself away. Matt Laren knows where you went when you left, remember. He also knows what you were before you left. He isn't stupid."

"No, he isn't," I agreed. But he couldn't prove anything one way or another and that was all that mattered. "I'm trying to find the right hand. Morrey and I assume that in order to replace the lost evidence, we need it. We'll keep looking, but let them know about the third piece, okay?"

"Okay. Just let me know when I can give them the fourth."

We hung up and I looked at Morrey. Good thing he couldn't hear the other side of the conversation, but I was sure he'd guessed at most of it by now. He also wasn't stupid, despite his appearance.

"Laren's figured out that I'm the one looking for the parts. He knows that when I left here, I went to the FBI. He knows more about me than most law enforcement people, but I was hoping he wouldn't tie me to this. Now, he'll be asking me all kinds of crappy questions … and I don't want to deal with it," I said slumping into the seat of the generic cop car.

Laren actually knew about my education and my licensures, mostly because he'd given me a letter of reference for the licensing boards in several states. Actually, he'd done that because we'd been dating at the time. Small world, huh?

"So you know our prestigious D.A.," said Morrey. "I'm surprised you didn't just call him yourself, instead of going though your attorney. Or are you two on the outs?"

Morrey was taking advantage of not having to walk around out in the heat. He was, at the moment, drowning himself in a bottled water.

"The D.A. and I know each other, but he would hound my butt about not handling the matter through proper channels. Also, he'd probably give me the third degree about the electrical fire that took the original evidence. I just don't want to hear it." I couldn't imagine anyone in my position feeling differently on that matter.

That was a vague version of the truth. I'd left out a few other things he'd chew me out about. Laren would have jumped all over me about Alex, the mess I'd made of the other cases. And he would have given me a good set down, even if he couldn't prove it. It would have been worse than one of my mother's long, drawn-out, life-picking sessions.

"Okay, so now what?" asked Morrey, less than enthused. "More Mrs. Hitchigan, right?"

"Yes."

Three miles down the road, the only place to park was what looked like a Park Ranger pull-off. "In there," I said.

We climbed out. There was literally nowhere to hide anything for another mile down the road. There were sloping hills straight up from the roadside. The pull-off had a path that led back into the forest. We followed it. It was evident that no one had used this path in years; it was overgrown and dark from the trees blocking the sky. Morrey and I continued for about a quarter-mile, periodically ducking into the trees that lined the path on either side.

"Ace, I found something! Come over here."

"Is it another bag?" I called back.

"No," said Morrey, "it's a dead body—all in one piece. I think I'm really going to be sick, now. My stomach isn't up to this. All these dead smells and … oh God!" He started gagging. He was going to be sick.

"Just imagine what the county coroner has to put up with," I said as I made my way over to him. "If you're going to puke, do it as far away from the site as possible."

"No, I'm good. I have it back under control." Morrey had turned away, but pointed to direct my line of vision. I glanced a couple of feet in front of him and there was the body of a young boy. He was most definitely dead.

"I'm beginning to feel like I attract this crap," I whispered. "How about you?"

My eyes went back to the boy. He couldn't have been there long. He'd only just started to decompose. He was partially covered in a white sheet with pink and green flowers on it. "Don't go anywhere near him," I cautioned. "Back up the same way you came in. This is a fresh scene and we don't already know who did this. They're going to need everything they can get to find out who killed him."

"You act like I've never done this sort of thing before," he groused.

"Well, you're the one who keeps prepping to lose his lunch." I pulled out my flashlight and scanned the area. Our bag was less than ten feet from the boy. "Look over there, to your right."

"Is that what I think it is?" he asked.

I nodded.

"How are we going to phone this in without letting them know it was us?"

Good question. I think it's definitely time to call Phil. Crap!! I looked at the boy and the only thing that ran through my head was, "Things could be worse."

First, I called Alex. If I were going to contact the authorities, he needed to know. I wasn't sure if Phil would let me get away with leaving the scene and avoiding the authorities altogether. Alex put up an argument, but the young boy won out in the end. I hit my speed dial.

Two rings later, I had Phil on the phone. I gave him a full accounting of the new body bags we'd found. Although Max was acting as an intermediary for the body parts bags, I asked Phil if he could call the local FBI field office with this newly-discovered body information.

"I can," he said, "but shouldn't we contact the locals, Angel? Otherwise, they're going to feel like they're being overstepped."

"I'm not worried about anyone's feelings here," I replied. "I'm worried because I stuck my nose in this evidence search in the first place. The locals will already have their hands full and I don't want this kid taking second place to the Hitchigan mess. Besides, the local authorities probably have their best people out working on the bags we phoned in earlier. If you give this to them now, the kid will end up with the second or possibly third string. I don't like that. A child deserves better."

"I know you have a soft spot for kids." Phil groaned slightly. "And you're probably right. I'll call it in. Will you be there when they arrive?"

"Not if I can avoid it. Also, tell them there's another piece of Mrs. Hitchigan, about ten feet to the right of the body. I doubt that the person who dumped the kid even saw it, it's so dark in there. I don't know anything about how the kid got here. All I did was find him. I couldn't help them even if I stayed."

I gave Phil a better description of the area so that the unit would be able to find the location.

"I'll flag the entrance with a yellow marker. That should make it easy enough to find. I think I'll call it a day and go home and take a shower. I'm feeling a little ... out of sorts at the moment. And Morrey has been complaining since we found the first bag." Of course, now I was also being bitten by mosquitoes.

"Make sure you have that attorney of yours call in the fourth bag you found."

"I will. I'll talk to you later."

I leaned against the steel gate that blocked the path to the entrance. I dialed Max.

"Hi," I said, none to brightly. "It's me again."

"Did you find another one?" Max was sounding excited about all this cloak and dagger crap.

"Yes, but there is a bit of a complication." I explained about the boy and the scene. I told him I was calling in the Feds and they'd take this scene.

"That means the D.A.'s office will have a piss fit. They don't like the

Feds taking over their stuff," he reminded me—as if I weren't already aware of that.

"They have more than enough to do right now with the four sites they have to secure. They'll just have to deal with it."

"I don't think they'll have a problem getting the bag from the unit that shows up here. They're being warned that the bag is here and what we believe is in it."

"I'll call it in and do what I can," said Max. "Are you staying at the site or moving on to look for more body bags?"

I was tired. Too tired to even think about continuing. The sickened feeling in my stomach still hadn't dissipated—I thought it was probably the dead kid.

"No," I replied. "I told my contact I was leaving. It isn't as though I can do anything but help bag evidence, anyway. I don't know what happened here, any more than they do. And we can't continue with our body hunt because, no matter where I am on this road, someone will find me now. I'm surprised the cops haven't come looking for us yet." I gave a low sigh. "I'm sure I'll be hearing back from you when Laren gets wind of it all. I'll talk to you later."

"You did a good job today," said Max. "Who knows if those body parts would have ever been found—or how long it might have taken for someone to come across that boy. Go home and have a glass of wine. I'm sure you could use it."

That was exactly what I planned to do.

Chapter 25

MORREY DROPPED ME AT home. I filled Alex in on the events thus far and then headed upstairs for a shower. I felt yucky. All I wanted to do was lie down and cry. I don't get that way often, but when I see a young life snuffed out, it makes me just want to cry.

Alex was lying on the bed with his hands behind his head, legs stretched out and ankles crossed, when I came out.

He sat up. "You're looking beat. Do you want me to order takeout and have it delivered?"

I was still drying myself off. "No, I'll make something. It'll take my mind off all this." I walked over to my suitcase and pulled out my olive green silk pajamas and my robe. The feel of the silk on my skin was wonderful. Cool and soft and worlds away from the day I'd had.

Alex and I made our way downstairs to the kitchen. I decided that something comforting and warm for dinner was best. And for me, comfort was one of two things: pastry or pasta. And since pastry isn't really the makings of dinner, I decided on chicken fettuccini alfredo. It was rich and fattening and tasty, all the things that make a great comfort food.

Half-way through dinner preparations, and still nursing my first glass of wine, the doorbell rang. Alex went down the hall to answer it. I heard the door open and then I heard the strong tones of raised male voices. I took the food off the burner and peeked down the hall.

Ooh, Matt Laren. Lucky me.

"Alex," I said, intervening, "let him in. He won't go away, no matter how loudly you ask. He can be a real pain in the ass." I went back to my dinner preparations. I put the noodles into the boiling water and continued stirring my sauce.

Matt entered the kitchen, bringing a hurricane of frustration that could probably be felt next door. "What the hell," he demanded, "do you think you're doing calling the Feds in on this?! I'm going to have to *negotiate* to get that piece of Mrs. Hitchigan away from them! They don't play nice with the locals and you know it!"

Matt Laren was still a fairly attractive man, if you go for that type. He was one of the "suits" of the world. Physically, he was six-foot or so, and slender; blonde, blue eyed, short, well-manicured hair and nails. And he wore the standard attorney attire: a plain suit, tie, white shirt and wing tips. In other words ... boring. He could have been an accountant or an insurance salesman for all the difference it made. I don't go for that look anymore and it almost scared me that I ever had. He and Alex were like night and day.

Instead of responding I pulled another glass out of the cabinet and poured Laren a glass of wine. "Drink this and calm down."

He looked into the glass as though he wasn't sure—it might be poisoned after all. Then he grabbed it and stomped over to the table. I could feel Alex in the doorway, even though he hadn't said anything. He didn't seem to like Laren. I suppose the fact that Matt had thrown him in jail might have something to do with that. I don't think I'd be happy, either, to host the person who tried to have me incarcerated for the rest of my natural life.

I gave it a few minutes of peace and continued with dinner.

"Well?" Laren asked in a not-so-friendly tone.

"I'm not saying anything if you're going to start an inquisition about the events leading up to my activities today. Do you think you can manage that?" I glanced at Matt. He seemed to be considering this. He looked as tired as I felt.

"Fine," he snapped. "Then I won't ask. It isn't as though it would get me anywhere, anyhow." He hated this stipulation, but gloomily accepted it.

I pulled the sauce off the stove and took out a loaf of Italian bread.

I love garlic bread, especially with lots of butter and garlic. As I sliced the bread, I continued.

"The decision to call the Feds," I began, "was made because every police officer in this city worth his salt was already tied up with the discovery of the other four bags. You even had to call in the Staties. Your main forensic crew, homicide primaries, and most related experts were frantically working on the newly-discovered Hitchigan evidence. In order to make certain nothing got rushed in the case with the dead boy, I thought it best to call in a new team."

"What boy?" demanded Matt. "Max didn't say anything about a *boy*. All he said was that another bag was found, but that his 'informant' felt it best to call the Feds."

"I assumed Max would tell you the rest," I replied calmly, "and I'm sorry he didn't. There was a boy, pre-teen, about ten feet from the fifth bag. He was quite dead and, from the looks of the body, fairly recently. Now, I certainly understand why your people want that bag as soon as possible.

"However, I also believe that *any* child homocide deserves very special attention. I was afraid this case might be jeopardized in the scramble to retrieve the evidence in the Hitchigan bag. We needed a fresh team to carefully scope out the crime scene, search the surrounding area, and so forth. I was sure your guys were already exhausted from the day's activities. Frankly, I wasn't willing to risk turning this over to an already overworked group. I wanted to make absolutely certain that they discover who killed this child and why."

Alex walked across the kitchen and got himself a glass of wine. He'd probably been wondering all day how we were going to stay out of the middle of this. And now he knew—we weren't, or at least I wasn't.

I reached for the noodles, which were now done, and took out my colander to drain them. Matt was apparently stunned by this new information because he didn't say anything.

"You should be able to get that fifth bag from them," I said, "if you're polite and explain just exactly why you need it quickly. I don't think the dead boy can possibly be related to the Hitchigan case. Mrs.

Hitchigan has been dead for several months now. The boy, as I said, was killed quite recently. I'm guessing that this was just a convenient place to drop the body."

I looked at our local D.A. and continued, "The truth is, *no one* would have found that kid any time soon if we hadn't been looking for those bags." It could have been much longer, I thought, and the elements have a way of destroying evidence which Laren knew very well.

He seemed to be coming back to himself. "How did you know where to look for those bags?"

"It wasn't that hard to figure out," I replied and then explained in detail how I'd guessed the pattern.

"So, the rest of them should be along that same route," said the D.A. "I can send out people to look—I'll have them start first thing in the morning. You won't need to continue *helping*. We know there are at least three more bags—not including the one the Feds have." He stood, apparently getting ready to leave. And none too soon either, dinner was ready.

"When you talk to the agent in charge," I said, "keep in mind that the individual who contacted him would undoubtedly have informed him that the bag found at the murder scene was part of your ongoing case. My contact at the government would never have failed to pass along this information. Hopefully, neither did the person who contacted that agent directly."

"Okay," he replied, somewhat mollified. "I won't say I agree with your assessment of the situation, but I do understand it. My crews were extremely absorbed with the work they already had today. In the future, though, try to stay away from my cases. I don't want you involved. You know, as well as I do, that your presence discovered anywhere near one of my cases, taints it. Not literally ... I know you were good with the law and probably when you worked for the government, as well. However, the public's perception of you here is not one of a law *enforcement* officer. They see you as the head of a crime family, or future head, anyway." He glanced at Alex. "And as future wife of a crime family leader, I'm sure you'll understand why I don't need that kind of publicity."

He walked to the hall door and paused, "You said 'we' before. I don't suppose *he* came with you?" he said, nodding at Alex.

"No," I replied firmly. "Alex has plenty of other things to do with his time. Actually, I was accompanied by a Detective Morrey, one of our city's finest. He's been told by his boss to stalk me and Alex.

"I figured that if he was just going to follow me around anyhow, he might as well do something to earn his keep. Max thinks I should file harassment charges. You may want to look into that before I have to humiliate the entire department because of the poor choice of one senior officer."

I received a look of disgust. "I'll look into it," he promised. "I'd rather you didn't do anything rash. Any time someone files charges against the police, it makes it harder for us to do our jobs and that creates problems for every citizen who lives here. How do you think this detective's senior officer would feel if he knew that your detective, the one who's apparently supposed to be looking for dirt on you, was making nice with his quarry?"

"At least he was doing real police work for a change," I said, "and not wasting the city's money sitting out in a car watching our home, following me to the bridal shop, to the grocery store, shoe shopping, and so on. So, I think that Morrey has just earned his keep for the last couple of weeks or so, of doing absolutely nothing. Morrey's boss might not be happy, but if he hadn't helped, it would have taken that much longer to get your evidence. Right?"

I turned back to dinner. "So, if I were you, I'd be looking out for Detective Morrey a bit on this matter. He could be useful to you later, especially when the time comes for the police to tell how they found the new evidence. You may need him. He was there. That's just a suggestion of course."

He nodded. "Fair enough. Let's hope we don't see much of each other in the future."

Turning slightly, I lifted my glass to toast that idea. "We can only hope to get that lucky."

He left and Alex followed to make sure he'd actually gone while I managed to get our meal ready. I was getting silverware from the drawer when Alex stepped back in the room. I served the food, brought the rest of the wine, and sat down across from him.

Alex started digging into the pasta bowl. "So, are you going to tell me what the deal is with you and the D.A.?"

What did he mean by that? "What deal?"

I got a let's-not-be-stupid look from him.

"I mean it," I protested, innocently. "I have no idea what you're talking about." I dipped my bread into the cheesy alfredo sauce. Mmm … yummy.

"I get the feeling you two go back a ways … from the way you spoke to each other. I can see that you two aren't exactly strangers." He made "mmm" sound. "By the way, this is really good."

Manners. You really have to appreciate good manners in a man. Not all men have them.

"Thank you," I replied. "And, yes, years ago, I dated Laren for a short time. It was in the interim between the FBI and graduating from law school. It really wasn't very long. He gave me a couple of references for the licensing boards, but that was because I was a good attorney not because I was seeing him. I could have gotten any of a dozen other lawyers to give me the reference. He was just easier access."

Alex's fork was now resting on his plate. He was looking at me like I was a complete stranger.

"What?" I asked, surprised. "Are you going to tell me you never went out with anyone who was totally wrong for you? Women do it all the time. We often refer to it as a *phase*. I, for instance, was going through my boring-suit-man phase."

I don't have a lot of experience with men, but what I do have isn't really all that memorable.

"No," Alex said. "I've gone out with some less than long-term types, but I guess I never thought about you having ex's here, in the area. You were so young when you left that I never considered it."

He was jealous. Why? Heaven only knew. Comparing Alex to Matt was like comparing lobster to a fish stick. It just wasn't even close.

"You don't need to think about it now," I said. "It's been more than a decade. And I'm certainly not attracted to Matt. Honestly, I wasn't really all that attracted to him when we were young. It was more that we shared a common interest in the law and had a lot to talk about … mostly philosophical stuff as I recall. But let's be realistic, how attached could I have been? I don't even think we should classify him as an 'ex.' After all, I applied to the FBI after the first month, left after a whopping three months, joined the FBI and never spoke to him again until just a few minutes ago in our kitchen. It isn't as though we've been pining away for each other."

I contemplated what I'd just said for a moment. "I don't even recall pining when we were actually dating," I added. The truth was, I'd totally forgotten he even existed until Tony mentioned that he was the current D.A.

Alex laughed. Apparently my sarcastic tone had had the intended effect. We continued eating while discussing a couple of Sevelli family issues that had come up during the day.

I picked up our dishes and started cleaning up when Alex said, "I don't suppose you remembered to call your doctor about the tattoo removal … and also for your blood test?"

As a matter of fact, I had remembered, but not for either of those reasons. "I phoned on the way out to the first site today. I told Dr. Martz's secretary that my appointment was for the blood test, but I'll speak with him about the tatoo while I'm there. I don't think everyone in town needs to know about this. My appointment is Monday morning. And, since Laren wants me to stay away from his evidence, I thought I'd go out and see how the house is coming along. My furniture and belongings should be released from customs shortly and I want to ship it all to the house rather than leaving it in storage."

He carried his plate to the sink. "You're going out by yourself?"

Did I need a babysitter? "Yes, unless you want to come with me."

"You haven't spent five seconds even considering that maybe you should be working with Tony, have you?"

"No, I haven't," I agreed. "We only moved out yesterday afternoon. It may have been a long day and a half, but it was still only a day and a half. And let's be perfectly frank … I don't want that job. If Tony was just using it to pull my stings, then fine, he's done it. But, if he really expects me to take over, he'll come looking for me—I won't have to go to him. It's a good way to assess his stance without actually asking."

Alex headed back to his office. He was still trying to put things in order after the authorities had rummaged through it. Also, a number of things were gone because he'd had Mike arrange to get rid of most of it so the D.A. couldn't recreate any of the info destroyed in the fire. Now he had to put everything back together from memory, or using the few pieces still available.

I rinsed off the dishes and put them in the dishwasher. I put the leftovers into two airtight containers, grilled chicken breast in one and noodles and sauce in the other and put them in the refrigerator. It would make a good lunch tomorrow if I happened to be home. Sauce is always better the second day.

The rest of the evening was peaceful. I actually set myself in front of the television. I seldom watch television, but I was bone-tired and soul-weary after my day. I lay down on the couch with a big chenille throw. Alex's couch was wide and cushy. It was really deep and lying on it was like resting on a cloud.

I caught about twenty minutes of some romantic comedy with Meg Ryan and drifted off to sleep. The next thing I knew, Alex was lifting me to carry me up to bed. I snuggled into his chest and let him. It isn't every day a girl gets carried to her room. You need to take full advantage when these rare occasions occur. Besides, I didn't see a reason not to let him. Walking required a great deal of effort and energy I didn't have at that moment.

Feeling his breath on the side of my face, I could tell that it was clear and even, all the way to our room. Apparently carrying me was no worse than, say, carrying a child. I wasn't big, by any stretch of the imagination, but I would have thought he'd have to extend some exertion.

When Alex and I were both tucked comfortably under the covers, I snuggled up against him and drifted off again.

Chapter 26

AT NINE A.M. ON MONDAY morning I was sitting in Dr. Martz's office. I hadn't seen him in years, obviously. I sat there for twenty minutes before I was called. The nurse did the usual, asked me a crap load of questions that were, in my opinion, not only none of her business, but also completely unrelated to the reason I was here. She weighed me, checked my blood pressure and then said the doctor would be with me shortly.

Shortly turned out to be another twenty minutes. Why is it that doctors make appointments for one time but don't actually see you 'til a good forty minutes later? Just one of those mysteries of life, I guess.

The door opened and a tall, elegant-looking fifty-something man walked in.

"Hey Doc," I said. "It's nice to see you looking well." Martz had only gotten better-looking over the last twelve years. He'd added a scholarly appearance to his already nice features.

"Same to you." He opened my file and sat on a stool next to me. "So, you're getting married. Is the blood test the only thing you wanted to talk to me about?"

He knew me well. I hated telling the front desk staff what my real reason for seeing him was. Several of them are known blabber-mouths. They get good info and next thing you know, the entire city knows your business.

"Well, no, actually. First, I'd like you to look at the tattoo on my back and tell me what it would take to remove it." I lifted my shirt and turned around for him.

He studied it for a moment. "Angelica, this can't be removed in one sitting. It will take a number of extremely painful laser procedures, over a long period of time … and I don't think you'd be happy with the results. It will probably leave a very unpleasant scar. Why do you want it removed?"

I turned around and slipped my top back on. "It has to come off, or at the very least, be altered in some way. The real issue is that this tatoo is like neon lights screaming 'Hired Gun Here' I might as well put a big sign on my forehead."

I wasn't worried about what I said to Martz. He knew who and what I was. He'd treated a number of family members and had never revealed anything, including bullet wounds, which by law, he was required to report. He even made house calls, believe it or not.

"Why not just alter it? You could go down to the artist who made it, and have him develop a plan to change it so that it isn't the same tattoo that everyone recognizes. It would be less messy than a complete removal, and a lot less painful. I really think you'd prefer the end result."

"Okay, I'll talk to Alex and see what he says."

He sat back on his stool. "You said 'first.' So, what else do you need?"

Okay, now to confront the topic I'd been trying not to think about this last week. I wasn't ready to deal with it, but I had no choice. It was going to come to light sooner or later and I needed to be prepared.

"How soon after conception would a pregnancy test be accurate?"

I was more than two weeks late.

Although Alex and I hadn't planned on my getting pregnant for a year or so, we weren't actively avoiding it. Which, now that I think about it, isn't all that different from trying to get pregnant, is it? I hadn't mentioned the possibility to Alex yet, although I was certain the sick feeling in my stomach was only going to get worse when I had to tell him.

"Almost immediately. When was your last monthly?"

"A week or so after I came back to the U.S., approximately six weeks ago. I wouldn't be worried except, as I'm sure you remember, my body runs like clockwork, and even a day late is unusual. But I don't want anyone knowing about this test. That means your reception crew and nurses. Can you run it without them knowing?"

"Of course. I just need a urine sample." He handed me a cup. "I'll be right back."

The test took almost no time at all. Before I knew it I was sitting in the parking lot in my new hunter green and black Cooper. I'd had to replace the black one. There had been more damage than was worth fixing. Alex had laughed at it, but hadn't argued about my choice of vehicles, as long as he didn't have to drive it.

✳✳✳

I was feeling a little peaked. The sick feeling was still there, but now a definite sense of turmoil had joined it. I didn't want to go home yet. I wasn't ready to face the inevitable.

Alex had Roberto and Mike at the condo this morning, going over some of the construction business financials. He was hoping to impress on Mike the finer points of financial forecasting and growth analysis in the construction industry.

For the first time in ages, I actually wanted to go see my mother. But going to see her would be a mistake and I knew it. I couldn't take a session of "your're just not worthy or living up to your potential" right now. Instead I called Marty.

"Ace, how are you? I haven't heard from you since the family dinner."

"I sort of promised Cara I'd keep a distance for a while, until things were running smoothly. But I was wondering if you were busy today?"

"No, not at all. It's just another dull day. However, I'll have you know that I had the office painted and re-carpeted. The walls are something called Mocha Mist and the carpet I got is a 'burr-burr' with gray, light brown, a little white and some darker brown in it. It looks really good. I kept most of the gray furniture, but I replaced the front chairs with a pattern that goes with both the gray and the light brown. It looks classier and it didn't even cost that much. I got Perk to put in the carpet for about half what it would have cost from a regular carpet store and Derm did all the painting. He said that since you were having your entire house and all of the rentals done by him, he'd give me a discount."

Perk ran one of the Sevelli businesses. He was called Perk because of the quantity of caffeine he required. He'd been a caffeine addict most of his life. Alex and I had decided to use him for the carpet in just about every rental property I owned. There wasn't any carpeting in the new house—it was all tile, wood floors and stone.

Derm on the other hand was all Gabella. The Gabellas are related to Marty and me on our mother's side. She was never that close to them, but Marty and I had forged decent relationships with several of our cousins. And now they were a good alliance to have.

The name "Derm" came to him at a young age and, unfortunately for him, it stuck. He'd had bad skin when he was young and when one of the Gabella enforcers heard a big word like "dermatitis," naturally he couldn't help but use it … over and over again, even when he was pronouncing it incorrectly. Derm's skin cleared up later but the name was still going strong. My guess was that no one knew where it came from any longer. The guy who originally put the name out there was long since dead.

Derm ran one of the three painting companies owned by the Pascolis, not the Gabellas. I'd dragged him into the Pascolis mostly because he was having problems finding anywhere to fit into the Gabella group. The Gabellas are exactly what you think of when you think of crime families. They have their hands in more than anyone has a right to and they're in the heart of New York. Or at least that used to be the case when T. was running it. Some things had changed over the years.

My Uncle Geraldo, my mom's brother, had always wanted me to take up with T. and that side of the family, but I never had a hankering to get involved in Gabella business. As far as I could tell, especially back then, it wasn't a place for Derm either.

He's hard, but he can be a nice guy. Nice guys are few and far between in the Gabella family tree. Mostly it all came down to the bottom line. If you couldn't increase it, you were considered a bottom feeder for life, and more or less worthless. If you decreased it, you might as well kiss your ass good-bye.

"Great, it sounds like you've been busy. I take it the office isn't nearly as depressing anymore?"

"No, not even close. So what are you up to today?" he asked.

"Well, I'm going up and look at the progress on the house. I was wondering if you'd like to come and have a look? You haven't seen it yet."

"No, I haven't, and I'd love to come."

"I can pick you up if you want. I'm here in the city," I offered.

"Sounds great! I'll be ready in ten minutes or so."

I stopped and picked up a bottle of water at the convenience store and drove to Marty's. I checked out his office. It looked good; it needed some matching wall hangings, but all in all, it was a thousand times better than the pink and gray. The secretary still looked almost the same, but she had at least touched up her roots since the last time I'd seen her.

Marty went on and on about the girls and what they'd been doing at school as we headed to the house. The oldest had decided to take drama and was going to be in a play three weeks from Friday. That would be the week after my wedding and I wasn't sure if we'd be here or not.

Alex and I hadn't discussed a honeymoon. Come to think of it, I was beginning to think we hadn't discussed a lot of things. I was getting nervous. Not that I wanted a honeymoon—I didn't. I just wanted to know where the hell my life was headed. I didn't think that was too much to ask. And now I was gonna be a mom! How the hell did *that* happen?!

I mean, I *know* how it happened. God must be getting a good laugh out of this whole thing. I felt like I was in the middle of a joke and I was the only one who wasn't finding it funny.

How do you go from killing people to changing diapers? I'm not the most maternal person in the world. Hell, I'm barely female. I don't even carry a purse regularly and when I do it's to carry lock picks, guns and gun accessories. How am I going to be responsible for another living being and carry around a diaper bag?

These are the occasions when you really want a drink. But, being pregnant, that wasn't an option. I was wondering if I could find a bad guy soon, just so I could take out some of my frustration on him. Of course I'd have to make sure he didn't hurt me ... I couldn't risk the baby ... hell, this was just not going to work!

We arrived at the house, turned in at the gates and drove down the stone-paved drive. The mason had fixed the cracked pavers and replaced the ones around the fountain out front. It was just beautiful. I needed to check the fountain pump to see if it worked. If it didn't then I could always turn it into a koi pond. That was exactly what I planned to do with the one in back.

Marty was enamored with everything. "I can't believe this place! It's great. I thought for sure you'd end up in some place like Tony's. Big, palatial and cold ... but this is just amazing. It's big, but it seems so ... I don't know ... family friendly."

All the stucco was gorgeous, especially with the red tile roof, no matter how impractical this was in New Jersey. The colors inside were warm and friendly, and my furniture was going to fit perfectly. But, looking at it now, I realized that Alex's furniture would look good here, too. He and I both had a thing for darker-toned woods which would serve as a complimentary contrast to the soft colors throughout the house.

The pool still needed filling and the guest house out in back also need to be completed but Alex and I could move in as soon as the security team finished with the cameras and security center in one of the lower rooms. We also needed to have the front gate wired with an intercom and automatic gate opener so that not just everyone would be showing up on our doorstep. They assured me the work would be finished early next week. That meant we could move in well before the wedding. Yeah!!!

"So when do you move in? Marty asked. "It looks ready to me."

"Next week," I replied. "Louisa and Miguel should be here by then and my furniture and things will be out of customs. We'll have to move Alex's things immediately afterward, but that shouldn't take long."

I took a seat on a stone settee in what had been the neglected, overgrown garden. Now it was cleaned out and blooming in a color-ful array of flowers. The scents were overwhelming. Not in a noxious way, but you'd never be able to walk past and not be overtaken by the perfumes. Whoever Alex hired to take care of the landscaping had done a fabulous job. It was a peaceful place now, with the light sound of the brook running in the distance and the birds singing in the trees. The only word that did it justice was splendid. It was a girlie word, but it worked for the garden.

I told Marty what Alex had said regarding Tony's resignation.

"What are you going to do?" he demanded. "The only reason you agreed to marry Alex was because of the family. You don't have to go through with it now."

If he only knew. "It isn't that easy. Alex and I are getting married and, oddly, that doesn't bother me nearly as much as it did a month ago. But now I don't know what to do about Tony."

"I see your point," Marty agreed. "If you confront him, he'll resign to keep the peace. But you definitely don't want the job if you can avoid it, right?"

"Right. And that's the problem. I figure I'll just avoid him until the wedding and hope he decides to tell me he's changed his mind and wants to stick it out for a couple more years. The longer he stays in control, the better."

"But you're still going to marry Alex," said Marty. "Isn't that a little … I don't know … unnecessary. It seems like a high price just to make Tony happy."

"I'm not doing this to make Tony happy," I admitted. "I suddenly realized that, although Tony pushed me into this, I'm actually not un-happy about it. I'll never give Tony the satisfaction of telling him so, though. I figure I'll just let him sit and stew for a while."

And if I could turn up the heat a bit I just might, for spite.

"So now you *want* to marry Alex?" Marty said. "I guess this shouldn't seem so strange to me. You and Alex look as though you'd be quite compatible. I just never thought of you as the marrying type. I guess I figured you'd keep going along, single, content with your work and free from all entanglements. That sure seemed like what you wanted."

It was. It is, but I tried to share my thoughts. "It's hard to explain. Of course I don't like the entanglements, as you put it. I don't like having to tell Alex everything. It's not that I'm such a secretive person—it's just hard for me to remember that he wants to know everything. It's also difficult because I've been on my own for years in a profession which requires a good deal of … discretion. Having to worry about someone else is totally foreign for me."

And now there was going to be *another* someone to worry about. Oh, crap! I could just throw up.

"Then there are the family obligations," I continued. "I've been away from those for so long that they now just seem like a burr in my ass. Every time I turn around, I have to worry that what I say or do might affect the family. That part, I can honestly say, sucks."

"Well, there must be something positive about it," Marty replied, "or you'd just pack it up and head out. I *know* you. If you were really opposed to this, then nothing anyone said would force you to go through with it."

True, I thought. I am a force to be reckoned with when I stand in total opposition to those around me. I don't take crap from anyone, not even Tony. But lately I've noticed that I'm taking more than my allotted share … and I don't seem to be doing anything about it. What the hell was wrong with me? Maybe it's baby hormones? Does that happen this soon? I'm out of my depth and have no idea what I'm doing.

I calmed myself and considered the question. What I came up with was, "Well, I do like having someone I can be honest with. Someone I can talk to about things that require a little more depth and understanding me and the things I do. Alex is smart, not overly judgmental and can be very sweet. He seems exceedingly tolerant and, so far, hasn't asked anything unreasonable. And the fact that I find him incredibly attractive and feel comfortable with him doesn't hurt either."

"I think maybe you're …in love," Marty stammered, "or at least *your* version of love."

He looked at me cautiously, as if he were worried I'd take offense. "What I mean is—you're not exactly the valentines, flowers, choir singing on high, cupid's arrows and all that type. But, I'd bet the description you just provided was …love."

He gave a little snort. "I never thought I'd see the day." He shook his head. "I will say I'm glad it finally happened. And if this means you'll be leaving your old profession … then it's all that much for the better."

I was hoping we'd change the direction of our chat shortly. I'm not good with talking about my feelings, even with Marty. And right now, I had more feelings than I knew what to do with. Normally, I don't think about my feelings, much less discuss them.

Sensing my confusion and uncomfortableness, Marty suddenly changed the subject. "Are you selling Alex's place?" he asked.

"I don't know," I said. "I'll have to speak with a real estate agent and see if it's profitable to rent something that size. It's a pretty big place and we don't want to keep it if it isn't going to pay for itself, you know? We'll have to see."

I was leaning against the back of the settee with my eyes closed.

"And the place in Italy? Did you sell it or are you renting it?"

I explained that Miguel had arranged to have it refurnished for rental and secured a rental agent for me.

"Is it going to be a vacation rental or a long-term lease?"

"Vacation rental, I think that would work best. There isn't much demand for a long-term lease, mostly because of the location and cost."

Suddenly, I knew something was up with Marty. There was almost a physical change in the air. When I turned to him he was looking at me sheepishly.

"What?" I demanded.

"Well," he said, thoughtfully, "I've always wanted to take Cara to Italy, but she's never liked the idea of leaving the kids at home with relatives. You can understand that, considering our relatives. But if we stayed at your place, outside Florence … well, it's big enough to bring the kids and there's a pool and a spa and a million attractions nearby and … from the pictures you sent …" Marty paused and then managed to complete his thought, "it actually looks perfect."

He continued, "I've asked Cara at least a hundred times about visiting you there, but you know how she is about your work. I think she was afraid we might get caught in the middle of something … but now … well, you aren't living there and you've more or less retired. Would you consider letting us use it for a week or two?"

I smiled warmly. "Of course, Marty! Just let me know when you want to go and I'll check with the leasing agent to make sure no one else has booked that time."

"You really don't mind?"

"Why would I mind? Assuming that it's not rented, it would just sit there unoccupied. You might as well go and enjoy it. I already pay for everything—pool and grounds maintenance and everything else—whether someone rents my unit or not. I know you don't make a fortune and the plane tickets for the whole family will cost you more than enough. Renting a hotel room would be a waste of money and probably uncomfortable for the kids."

I sure wouldn't want a vacation like that. For an entire family, with extremely active children, even renting two hotel rooms, would be tight.

Marty planned to speak with Cara about it tonight.

Suddenly I felt the hair on my neck go up. I whipped around and there was Alex, leaning against a tree and looking quite comfortable. I suspected he'd been there a while. Most likely he'd listened to our entire conversation.

Chapter 27

"HOW LONG HAVE YOU been standing there?"

He smiled at me. He knew what I was thinking. "Oh, long enough to know that Cara would enjoy seeing Italy."

He looked at Marty and walked to the front of the settee. "I can't blame you for wanting to see it. I've only been twice myself, for a total of three weeks, but there was so much to see and do. I didn't even come close to seeing a quarter of what one should see on a trip like that. It's an amazing country and with so many profound historical sites. You should definitely take advantage of the opportunity to go. If leasing the house doesn't work out then eventually we'll sell it, so you should make plans during the next year or so, just in case."

He turned back to me. "I thought you were coming up here alone."

"I was," I said, "but I realized that Marty hadn't even seen where we were going to live."

He glanced back at Marty. "And what do you think of it?"

"I love it. It's warm and comfortable, big, but not ostentatious. It's nothing like Tony's mansion. And the grounds are just like something out of one of my girl's fairy tales. It's so quiet, I could lose myself back here for hours." Marty didn't seem as uncomfortable with Alex as he'd been at the family gathering a few weeks ago.

"I agree," said Alex. "I think it'll be a perfect place to raise our family. The large yard is great for children. There are just a couple of things left to be done."

"And what are *you* doing up here?" I asked. "I thought you had visitors this morning?"

He was standing over me. He pulled me to my feet. "I brought them with me. Like your family, mine hasn't seen the house, either. I think we may have to have a party for the whole family after we move in. Preferably before fall—that way the whole family can take advantage of the yard."

Alex slid his arm around my waist and we all walked back to the house. I could see Roberto and Mike making their way toward us.

Alex leaned into my ear. "There were several messages for you on the machine at the house. One from Kimberly, making sure you remembered your appointment for your final fitting and to make sure Mike and I remember to pick up our tux's from the alterations person. Then there was a message from your mother complaining that she hadn't seen you in almost a month."

Marty must have heard that because he started to cough. I knew he was covering up his laughter.

"And the third," said Alex, "was from Dr. Martz leaving you a referral. Was that for the tattoo removal?"

Right now was definitely not the time for this conversation. "No," I replied. "It's a bit complicated to discuss right now. Can we talk about it when we get home," I looked at him pointedly, "and are alone?"

"We are home and I can arrange for us to be alone." His voice no longer a hush next to my ear,

"Mike, you remember Marty, Ace's brother? Why don't the three of you go check out the pool house? I need to speak with my bride for a few minutes."

Okay, so much for putting it off. I sat on the side of the backyard fountain. I looked inside it and saw patches in the bottom where the mason had replaced tiles. With water in it, and the small water plants, it was going to be breathtaking.

"So what happened today?" he inquired.

"You're pushing you know?"

His look was intense, but his voice was complete calm. "I realize that, but I'd like an answer." He took my hand.

"Well, the tattoo can't be removed for at least a year, but even then, it will be problematic. According to Martz, even the best laser surgeon would leave some unpleasant scars. Instead, he suggested having the tattoo altered. That would mean going back to the original artist and having him change it. Or, I can have some parts removed via laser and then have the artist alter the scene so that it's no longer the Avenging Angel.

"In theory, that would probably be best. Otherwise, every wise-guy in town who already knows I have a tattoo, even if he doesn't know what it is, specifically, will think it's odd if it suddenly disappears. Removing it might attract more attention than changing it. If it's altered gradually, no one will know but us."

"Why a year?" asked Alex. "Why can't you go down to this artist tomorrow and start the process?"

"Well, I may go down and have him copy the angel so he can see about redesigning it. But I can't have any laser work or tattooing done for about a year."

"Why?" he said irritably.

"Well," I cleared my throat. "In my present condition, the doctor said that any form of physical trauma was a bad idea."

"And I repeat, why?" said Alex. "What, exactly, is your present condition? You're okay, right?"

"I'm perfectly healthy," I assured him. "It's just that … umm, remember, during our negotiations, when we agreed to wait a year before actively trying to start a family? Well … it seems that we won't be waiting a year," I trailed off quietly.

Alex's dour expression, from the time we'd started this conversation, suddenly disappeared. He was beaming. The smile couldn't be described in any other way. It was so big that I thought his facial muscles might revolt.

"Well you can't be very far along. When …"

Calmly, I replied, "It must have been during the first week we were together. I didn't start worrying until last Wednesday. I thought all this stress and change might have affected my regular cycle. But

Martz confirmed that that was not the case. The referral from Martz is for an OBGYN in New York. I don't want everyone around town knowing yet, and if I go to a local, everyone will. Once people know, it puts me in a less than favorable position. So, can we keep this secret for just a little while? I'd like to clean up this whole someone-is-try-ing-to-kill-you thing, move into our new house, and get through this wedding business."

He literally picked me up, sat me on his lap, wrapped his arms around me and kissed me. Clearly, he was adjusting to this business much better than I was.

Personally, I hadn't decided how I felt about my situation. I did feel a little trapped and sick to my stomach. I decided to chalk it up to panic—hoping for the best.

Cheek to cheek, he whispered, "Sure, we can keep it a secret for a while. When were you going to tell me? It wasn't going to be here, I could see that."

"I would have waited until tonight when we were alone."

"Are you sure? I wonder if maybe you planned on keeping it from me a bit longer so that you could avoid the inevitable curbing of your activities."

I glanced up and Alex looked so smug I wanted to kick him. "No, I wouldn't have kept it from you. And I know some of my activities will have to change, but I want to get settled. I hate this constant feeling of things being left unfinished. Don't you feel that way?"

"Yes, I do. But it looks as though the work on the house will be completed next week.

"So, if you can just trace your payment to the originator of the contract, then we can eliminate him and be done with it."

I really hated bringing this up. "In theory, yes," I said, "but what if it's someone we *can't* eliminate?"

Apparently he hadn't thought of that possibility. "Such as?"

"Well, for example, Derek Sampini. I don't, for even a moment, believe it's him. I'm just using him for a 'what-if.' He's the *son* of one of the family heads. We can't kill him without risking retaliation, providing, of course, they learn that we did it."

Alex groaned.

"In a case like that, we'd need alternate options. For example, we could dig up some dirt and arrange for delivery to the D.A."

That got me a "look" from Alex.

"Okay, but *dead* can be a problem if not handled properly … I suppose he could have an accident."

"Instead of two at the back of the head?" He was being sarcastic. "I think an accident would be better, no matter who it turns out to be."

"Okay, then, for sake of argument, what if it's Elli Merek? If we kill him, we end up with a conniving vicious weasel in his place. Do we have both father and son share an accident? We can't very well leave him in charge."

Alex frowned and said, "I see your point. Let's discover who it is first. You should receive that wire transfer soon, so we'll deal with it then." He gave me a squeeze. "You know, it's going to be almost impossible to keep this news to myself."

He was glowing and if he didn't tell, someone might guess.

"I know, just try to hold on until the wedding. Hopefully, by then everything else will have fallen into place."

CHAPTER 28

IT WAS TEN AFTER NINE when I woke up. I was becoming extremely lazy. I had no energy and didn't even want to get out of bed. I decided it must be the pregnancy. Okay, it was a little early, but it was still a good excuse.

I had to get up. I had things to do. Dress fittings and shoe purchasing, I'd put that off as long as I could. Kimberly wanted to meet at the museum today and go over the finishing touches. I should go to the meat market and I had to make my first prenatal appointment.

Dr. Martz said it wasn't urgent that I make my first appointment immediately. We'd found out early and that gave us a little flexibility. I wanted to wait until after the wedding for the actual appointment. I had enough going on and if there wasn't any hurry, I wasn't going to push.

I got up, showered, brushed my teeth, dressed and headed downstairs for breakfast looking pretty good. Martz had told me I should give up caffeine and alcohol. This was going to be a problem.

I could live without the alcohol, although yesterday had been a trial. I'd given up cigarettes years ago so I should be able to handle that. However, caffeine was another matter. How do you just stop drinking coffee and tea, not to mention soda? I would have to try out some decaf everything. Hopefully, that would do the trick. If not, then I'd probably be an extremely unpleasant person to be around for a while.

Alex was in his office with the door mostly shut. I heard him talking. Leaning in to get a look, I saw someone's back in the chair in front of him.

We apparently had a visitor. Good thing I'd gotten dressed. Not all that interested in Alex's work, I headed for the kitchen. Just as I reached the doorway, I heard a scuffle from Alex's office.

Crap!

I headed back and pushed the door open. There, I saw Constantine Sampini fighting with Alex over a gun in Sampini's hand. Lovely ... this is just the way I wanted to start my morning.

Walking behind Sampini, I kicked the back of his kneecap and down he went. He wasn't a big man, but Alex had been grappling with him while leaning across his desk. It made for a very awkward stance.

"Okay, which one of you wants to explain why my breakfast has been delayed?" I looked at Constantine. "You have no idea how crabby I am before I get my coffee."

Alex had the gun. He emptied the bullets, returned it to Constantine, and explained, "We had a disagreement regarding the combining of the families. Sampini thinks I should bow out, rather than marry you, and give one of those other 'lucky guys' a chance at taking over the Pascoli's."

I glanced at Constantine. "Are you completely deranged? You came here to try to call off my wedding right before it's scheduled? Do you have any idea how it would look if I had to call off the wedding because of you? I'd look like a fool! I am not looking like a fool to please you, or anyone else for that matter. I should probably kill you for even considering interfering in my personal life. I don't let my *family* interfere in my personal life."

Both of them were watching me as I walked in the general direction of the door. "And, you have no idea how lucky you are that you didn't shoot Alex. For interfering in my life, I might just kill you. But for shooting my future husband and making a fool of me, well ... I'd have had to hang you by your feet and skin you alive. I have a very sharp knife I picked up in Germany and I've used it in the past for just that purpose."

That was a big fat lie. I'd never performed any execution that was gruesome. My motto was always, "Do what needs to be done—do it right—and do it as quickly as possible." Drag it out and you run the risk of getting caught. Besides, one's mental stability should be questioned for peeling off someone's skin. Skinned bodies! Yuck!

I was almost to the door when I decided to embellish a bit. "It's the way you'd peel the skin off an apple with a pairing knife. You try to take as much skin as possible in as few strokes of the knife as possible." I shot him a sick smile. "It's like a game."

Constantine was as white as a sheet. He looked like he'd do anything to get out of Alex's office and our house. This was the reaction I was after. Looking him up and down, I peeked at Alex, who wasn't sure if I was serious or not.

"I was just going to make breakfast and now I'm hungry for bacon. Have you eaten yet?"

Alex came very close to losing his composure. He wanted to laugh, but his visitor wasn't finding it funny. "No, I haven't. Make enough for both of us. I'm certain Sampini is leaving shortly." He raised a brow at the sheet-white Constantine who, if a strong breeze had been present, might have been knocked on his ass.

"I'm leaving," he said. "You're both … crazy," he stumbled. "I can't believe Tony is giving his business to a mad woman. Does he have any idea how unstable you've become? I doubt it, but let me tell you, he'll hear about it!" He stood, finally back to his old self.

All I could say was, "More power to ya'. I'm sure Tony will enjoy your story." I left the room and headed for the kitchen.

I didn't really want bacon, as a matter of fact; it sounded greasy. I wanted pancakes with fresh fruit and eggs, so that's what I set about making. I was stirring the buckwheat mix when Alex came in.

"Did you have to mention skinning him? Alive? That was a bit excessive." He stopped for a beat. "It *was* a joke? I mean, you wouldn't actually do that? Would you?" he asked. "For that matter, you haven't actually done that?" The look on his face showed concern. "Right?"

"Of course not!" I assured him. "What kind of sicko do you think I am? But, don't you think he deserved it?" I went back to stirring the pancake mix. "He pulled a gun on you in your own house. For that, he deserved to be shot and dumped in the woods—not frightened out of his mind and then set free."

"True," Alex agreed, "but at least we know who's trying to have me killed."

I hated to tell him this. "I doubt very much that Constantine Sampini is behind that contract."

Alex was digging in the refrigerator for juice. "What do you mean? He clearly would like to see me dead."

"Right. But if he thought you were already under contract with Mistress, he wouldn't bother killing you himself—in your own house no less."

"Maybe he thought he'd save himself the money?" Alex suggested.

"No, I don't think so, honey," I replied. "If someone has the balls to pull a gun on somebody in their own home, when they know someone else is there, he isn't going to bother hiring an assassin. He could have taken you out in the middle of Times Square, for all he cared about getting caught. Someone who hires an assassin does it to remain anonymous. Either he doesn't want anyone to know, or he's incapable of performing the job himself. Neither of those situations fits Sampini."

"So, there are two people who want me dead?" he groused. "Well, that sucks. Do you think maybe the banking info came today?"

"Maybe. I'll check after breakfast."

I made pancakes, chopped some strawberries and made scrambled eggs. Alex wouldn't let me have any coffee so I got juice and milk instead. I was going to have to get that decaf stuff—breakfast just wasn't the same without something warm.

I went in and checked my e-mail, "Nothing here yet. I'll check again later."

"What are you doing today?" asked Alex.

"I have my final fitting and after that I'll meet Kimberly. I still need shoes for the dress. After that, the meat market and the grocery store. I really can't wait until this day is over. You could come if you want, but it's one boring day I have ahead of me."

"Yep." He leaned against the counter where I was rinsing our dishes. "I guess it's hard after hunting and killing people, dumping bodies, looking for pieces of other bodies, then finding out you're pregnant. Final fittings are usually a big deal to most women, but I can see how it might not rate very high compared to your last few weeks." He had a big smile on his face.

Pain in the ass. "I don't like having to stand around looking like *Bride Barbie* while a woman who reminds me of *Mama Celeste* stabs me with the occasional stray pin."

"Don't get huffy," said Alex, laughing. "I'll come with you. That way, at least I can keep an eye on you. It seems that whenever you're out of my sight, you tend to get yourself involved in events I'd rather you weren't."

"I think you're overstating. I only went out once and got myself into "something." Just when I went to the grocery store the other day—you knew about everything else." I dried the dishes and put them away.

"That isn't completely true," said Alex. "Yesterday you went to the doctor. You hadn't told me you thought you might be pregnant, so it that was a surprise. Not a bad surprise, but a surprise all the same. Last Friday, you found a dead boy which brought the D.A. to our home. The day before that, you brought a cop into our home to haul groceries. Then you told me you were both going body hunting."

He gave me a knowing look and continued. "The day before that, you told me we had to move out of Tony's house because you didn't trust him, that you've had problems in the past with him telling you the truth. That same day, you threatened to leave me if Tony had lied to you. Finally, you spilled a lot of info over these past weeks that I had no idea about. And I'm not even mentioning your contract to kill me or bumping off a shooter and, later, killing a bomber and dumping his body." He turned to walk out of the kitchen.

"In just this past couple of weeks alone," he continued, "you've shaken our lives so much that I'm thinking I should probably go with you this afternoon in case you're tempted to shake it up a bit more."

Alex was out of sight now, down the hall, but he concluded, "I don't want anything happening to our child."

I knew he said this partly in jest but I had to face the facts. Alex was going to be extremely possessive and protective from now on, at least through my pregnancy. Considering the things that had been going on, I guess I could understand, but I was getting tired of being understanding. It was incredibly inconvenient.

"Oh, I forgot," he yelled. "We have our final marriage class with Father Jacobs this afternoon at two, so we'll have to move through the rest before then. Will you be ready in fifteen minutes or so?"

I slid the last glass into the cabinet. "Yes," I replied. "I have to be at the bridal shop in forty minutes anyway. We'll meet Kimberly at the museum at eleven. Maybe we could do the shoes in between and the grocery and butcher afterwards."

CHAPTER 29

THE FITTING WAS ALMOST unnecessary. It fit perfectly. I'd chosen a very plain gown, no ornamentation at all. I intended to wear a couple of nice pieces of jewelry so, between that and my flowers, I'd have enough to give off a simple, but elegant appearance. The less is more philosophy.

I let Alex see the gown on me. I know it's bad luck, but I don't believe in that crap. You make your own luck and if your marriage doesn't last, it isn't the fault of bad luck. It's usually a cheating spouse, high utilization of alcohol and/or drugs, or the inability to handle money. It rarely has anything to do with luck.

Alex said it was perfect and that he'd have picked the very same one if he'd been choosing himself. I was glad he liked it. That meant the families would approve and considering what it cost … don't even ask. Let's just say that a family of four could live quite comfortably for a good four or five months on what this dress cost.

I stood there looking at myself in the three-way mirror while the *Mama Celeste* look-a-like checked the seams. I'd have to pick out a pair of three or four inch heels for this dress to look right and not drag on the floor. I could see Alex's reflection sitting behind me.

"I'll be back in one moment Miss Pascoli," Mama cautioned. "Don't move."

I nodded. I knew from previous experience that if I did move, it would most likely end in pain and possible blood being shed.

"Alex," I said. He looked at my reflection in the mirror. "I'm feeling a little rotten about the money we're spending on this whole thing. By the time we're done, I could have bought another very nice investment property. It seems like such a waste for one day."

"I know," he agreed. "But in order to accommodate everyone, we need a major to-do. It'll be over soon enough. Just think of it as a business expense. That's really what it is. We're making all our business associates comfortable while they're visiting."

"If you say so," I said, frowning. Then I caught a hint of a smile. "I know we have money, but just because you have it doesn't mean you need to spend it wastefully. Personally, I prefer nice art work or real estate."

Or shoes, actually, but I didn't mention that.

"Please tell me that isn't why you drive that Cooper."

He really had a thing about my car. "No. I drive it because it's fun." I looked down at the silk flowing from my waist. It was beautiful, even if it cost more than my car.

We finished my fitting in no time. The shoes came without much looking. After a quick stop at the convenience store for something to drink, we got to the museum a whole fifteen minutes early. Imagine that.

✳✳✳

It was only eleven and I was pooped. This being pregnant thing was wearing me down quickly ... or was it just stress? I didn't want to think about what it was going to be like in a couple of months. All I could hope was that my body would get used to it.

We spoke with Kimberly for a short time and wandered through the museum.

I had a nice art collection of my own. Some were considered significant pieces, and not just from an artistic stand point, but from a financial view as well.

My collection included oils, water colors, charcoals and several sculptures. I've never been big on modern art. It just isn't my preference. I preferred the impressionist period—Monet, Renoir, Pissaro, Saurat, Cross and Cezanne, but almost any type of art, other than modern, calls to me.

We sat in a small chamber displaying several eighteenth century religious representations. They were all very well designed and displayed beautifully.

"You said earlier that you prefer spending your funds on art and real estate. I'm aware of the real estate acquisitions—I think we covered those. But I don't think we've discussed the art work."

I nodded. We'd reviewed the full listing of my properties the day we'd gone to look at the New York residences. He was now completely abreast of my residential and commercial holdings and Alex had agreed that the work required to maintain these properties would keep Miguel quite busy. Those responsibilities, along with running errands, would be practically a full-time job.

"I don't want to be nosey, but if we're going to combine households, I need to know what the financial profile on your side looks like," said Alex. "Then we can go over mine." He said this as though he were almost afraid I'd be offended by the idea that he wanted to know how much I was worth.

He was right about one thing. I hated discussing money. It wasn't a comfortable subject for me—maybe it had to do with the fact that my parents were never well off. Maybe it was because Tony was quite affluent and, when I'd been at his side growing up, I noticed his distaste for discussing his fortune.

There was one thing I did know, however. I absolutely was not embarrassed about my wealth. It was just the idea of discussing my estate was … I don't know … disconcerting. However, this certainly was a logical conversation for us before the wedding actually took place. After all, we'd be seeing Max's business associates about our prenup in just a couple of days.

We sat in the gallery discussing our finances in hushed tones. While we were technically in a public place, there wasn't anyone here at this time of the day, in the middle of the week. We had the place to ourselves.

It was quiet here, and they had a fairly impressive gallery. I'd seen bigger, but this particular museum gave off a quaint, comfortable feel rather than the austere cold of some displays I'd seen. This certainly wouldn't be the last time I visited this place.

Chapter 30

I MADE MY CALL TO DR. MARTIN in New York and scheduled my appointment for five weeks from Friday. I scheduled it around Alex's calendar so he could also attend.

I connected my laptop to my cell phone and got on-line to check for e-mails. There it was, big as life. Money, money, money … recently transferred to my account. I sent Phil an e-mail and asked him to backtrack this deposit. Maybe he could find out where it came from. I also told him why because I didn't want Phil to think I was being overly pushy lately. He may owe me big, but it's always better to space my requests out. Lately, it seemed I needed one after another.

Once that was done, we headed to the church. Our visit with Father Jacobs was short and sweet. He thought we'd covered pretty much everything in order to be properly prepared for marriage. Fat chance, but you don't tell your priest that.

"So, is there anything the two of you would like to go over, before the rehearsal?"

I looked at Alex and shook my head. I didn't have anything, but Alex was about to bust a seam. "Can I tell him?" he whispered. "I know it's a secret, but he is a priest. He won't tell anyone."

I blew out an exasperated sigh. "You are terrible. You can't keep a secret to save your life."

"That's not true. I'm just having problems with this particular secret."

"Fine." I looked to Father Jacobs. "But I'd appreciate it if you didn't say anything until after the wedding."

"Not at all." He assured me. "Now, what's this about?"

"Angelica is expecting," said Alex. "We just found out yesterday."

The glowing pride in his voice was amazing. He could have been more excited today than he'd been yesterday and that was hard to do. Now, why couldn't I muster up a little excitement about the big news?

"That's wonderful!" Father Jacobs said. "It would have been better, of course, if you had waited a few weeks, but you're old enough to understand the responsibilities of parenthood. Maybe we should meet again in a few months. That will give the two of you time to settle in and discuss the implications that a child will bring to your lives."

Oh goodie, just what I needed … to discuss my feelings … again. Alex agreed readily and I agreed in general acknowledgment that there was no graceful way not to.

Alex and I stood to leave when Father Jacobs asked if I would stay for a moment and speak with him privately. Again, this wasn't something I could get around gracefully, so I accepted it. Alex went to wait in the front room.

"Angelica, I've known you since you were born. And I know when something is bothering you, even if Alex doesn't. You don't seem pleased about this pregnancy."

So much for hiding my feelings. It looks like we get to discuss them now, too … whoo-hoo, big fun.

I sat back down. "I just don't think I'm up to this," I said. "I'm not capable of being a mother. I'm not the type—that nice, normal, well-adjusted children have. I know I'm going to screw this up." I put my elbows on my knees and my face in my hands. Then I pushed the hair off my face and looked up.

"Hell, you know my own mother screwed it up and continues to do so. How am I supposed to do better? I'm even less suited to this than she was. I'm just not … prepared to be somebody's mother."

I stood up and started pacing. If we were going to get at it, I might as well just keep on truckin'. "I just don't know what to do. When Tony suggested that Alex wanted children, he recommended that I get a live-in nanny—because of my lack of parental inclination. But I feel as though that would be stiffing the child. I mean, I should be able to take care of my own child, shouldn't I? I'm not stupid. If my mother had pawned me off on a nanny, I might have turned out better, but I sure as hell would have resented it. I would have felt unwanted."

Well, I still did feel unwanted, but the resentment might have been worse. Personally, I felt that this was a natural response to being shoved aside.

"I don't want my child to feel unwanted, but I don't think I have a maternal bone in my body. And, of course, I've been killing people for more than eighteen years. How do I turn off that person? I can't be who I am and have a child. It just goes against nature. Do you see where I'm going with this?"

I stopped pacing and looked at our priest. He was far more calm than I was. How did he manage that? He always seemed calm. Well, minus the blown-up car incident.

"I know you, Angelica," he said, smiling. "You are perfectly capable of handling anything you choose, including parenting. You may need to do a little research on the subject and I'll be more than happy to help in any way I can. As for your previous "profession" … you know I don't approve, but even I can see that you have your own code of ethics. Not the ethics I would like to see within you, but you do have morals, Angelica." He stood and walked to my side.

He took my hand in his. "And I do *not* think a nanny is a good idea. I believe a nanny will allow you to distance yourself from your child. Once this child is born, you'll develop a normal sense of maternal awareness. All new mothers experience these feelings, Angelica. It will get easier for you as time passes."

"Your mother," he said frowing, "is another matter. It isn't that she was a bad mother or that she didn't care. Actually, I believe she cared too much. She smothered you so that you turned to Tony for acceptance. She didn't mean to to make you miserable. However, she doesn't accept what really happened when you were growing up. You haven't even seen her since you've been back, have you?"

I shook my head. "Not for any more than a passing conversation, surrounded by others. I just can't put myself through her 'you're not worthy and look at the mess you made of your life' speeches."

He nodded. "I hope that the birth of your child will allow your mother to realize you're not the disappointment she's led you to believe. Not that I think she truly believes that. Rather, I suspect she would simply have preferred that you chose a different means of … employment."

He gave me a hug and said everything would be fine. If only I believed that. But I did feel somewhat better after having put voice to my concerns. There's something about saying thoughts aloud that lessens most fears.

Alex was waiting for me, looking a little more worried than he should have. As we left, he said "Is everything okay?"

"Fine."

"Do you want to talk about what you discussed with Father Jacobs?"

"Not really. But I could use a slice of cheese pizza; extra grease."

Alex laughed. "Yeah, I suppose I could go for one of those myself."

Chapter 31

THAT EVENING WHEN ALEX and I arrived home I checked my e-mail. There was a note from Phil. It more or less stated that the account used to pay my fee came from an account in the West Indies. The account was in the name of Theodore Marcos Sheppa.

Now that was confusing. Why in the name of heaven would Theo Sheppa want Alex dead? That just made no sense at all. From what I saw at our engagement party he wasn't upset about our marriage or with us, or about *anything* for that matter.

A little voice at the back of my head asked, "What if it isn't related to your marriage? What if it isn't actually Theo? Who else has access to his accounts?" I needed to think on this. My little voice was often right. I closed up the machine and saw Alex watching me.

"What was it? You look confused," he said, "like you're trying to work something out."

"The money came from Theo Sheppa's off-shore account. I just don't know why he'd want you dead. Do you have some relationship with him that I don't know about?"

"No, I don't …" Then he nodded, remembering. "Yes, actually, I did. But I don't think it would impact this. There certainly isn't any reason to kill me because of it."

"Let me be the judge of that," I replied. "What is it?" Sometimes you don't see what's right in front of your face unless someone else points it out.

"It goes without saying that this stays between us, right?"

I nodded. What the hell did he think I was going to do? Go blabbing to the cops?

Alex sat down. "Well, Theo's people did some transportation for me for a few years. It was very profitable for both of us. I was between reliable transport providers and needed someone to fill in. He supplied the drivers and trucks."

"What were you transporting?"

"Well, you know—the Sevelli "usual." Guns. It lasted about three years. Then, just as Theo was getting uncomfortable with things, I came across another transport operation that wanted to take over."

"So Theo wanted out?" I asked.

He nodded. "He was only using the transportation funds to finance his new business operations' start-up costs. Once those operations were in the black, he wanted out and I found someone to replace him. But, as you can see, he wouldn't hold any of this against me. It was just a business agreement. In fact, he's the one who brought it up."

I had a nagging suspicion that, although it seemed this wasn't the problem, it really was. Where else could I find the information?

***

The phone rang.

Alex answered, said a few words and handed the phone over. By the time I got off I was furious.

"I have to call Jason and a few of the guys. I need to get the old house cleaned out before tomorrow night. That dumb-ass property manager has rented my old office. I told him if he found someone who was interested, I'd need a week to move out. Well, he told *them,* but never bothered to tell *me*. They're scheduled to move in two days from now," I groaned. "I can't wait to hand all this over to Miguel."

"You shouldn't be lifting things," said Alex. "We'll just send a moving company over and have it all moved to the guest house in our new place."

If it were only that easy. "Most of the stuff would be fine to send with movers, but I have a couple of boxes of guns, knives, ammo, and etcetera." I cringed. "Then there's the evidence I snatched from the D.A. and the law office when I got you out."

"You *kept* it?" he replied. "What the hell were you thinking?! Shit, we have to get rid of that stuff. Why didn't you burn it?" He was turning red.

"Don't get mad. I wanted to go through it. I wanted to see what they actually had on you. I wanted to see what the evidence was, the testimonies they'd taken, all of it. It isn't a good idea to marry a criminal if you don't have any idea what he's been involved in. I just haven't had a free minute to go over there and go through it all."

I stood up. "But one way or another, we have to get that stuff. Some of the weaponry has been used in some pretty high profile cases. I have a lot of the Gabella evidence from the takeover. Ari didn't trust her own people to take care of it all. And then, of course, there's always the Hand of Vengeance."

"You have the *Hand of Vengeance?*" Alex moaned. "Shit! If the cops ever got their hands on that thing … I don't even want to think about it."

The Hand of Vengeance was used by my cousin as well as the present family leader of the Gabellas, Ari. She'd taken over her family after killing her uncle. A majorly sick man, he was my uncle as well. He was a freakin' nut—money was all that drove that man, no matter what he had to do to others to make it.

I may seem messed up, but Ari was much worse. T. Gabella, as he was called most of his life, was a very disturbing influence on her. Not that my own Tony wasn't disturbing, but nothing like T.

Ari had used the Hand of Vengeance, a steel representation of a hand, that fit over a human hand like a strapped on glove of sorts. The fingers were braced steel, made to bend with the joints of the hand. But the ends extended past the fingertips, like long talons. Ari had used it, literally, to rip a man's heart out of his chest. She said it was to make a statement, but the only statement I got out of it was … *eewh, yuck*! In my opinion a gun is faster and much less gross.

The last time it was used was on a rival. She'd attempted to tear the man's spine from his body. I was glad I wasn't there … Apparently Caster, Ari's older brother, shot the guy in the head during the process because he couldn't take the screaming. Ari was indeed something else—something amazing, but also something very scary.

But I don't think Ari is as sick as she used to be. Even though Ari's husband, David, was the one who brought me the "Hand," saying it was not something that should ever be used again, I had the feeling that the "spine experience" had finally affected Ari. Maybe even more than bumping off her uncle, and that had been extremely difficult. No matter how much better off her family was now, she'd taken it all on herself to fix their problems—and at the time she was only twenty.

The stories of the *Hand of Vengeance* traveled, like some sort of wise-guy boogieman tale. So I wasn't at all surprised that Alex knew about it.

"I'm not trusting anyone but us to get that stuff," he said. "I am *not* going back to jail." He was growling. Alex resembled a large jungle cat prowling the house for someone to tear apart with his claws. Sadly I was the only one around.

"Let's go over to the house tonight," I said. "We'll get anything that could be considered incriminating and then we'll let the movers do the rest. Why don't you call Mickey's guys and see if they can do it tomorrow?"

He growled again, but went to the phone to make the call. I headed upstairs to change into something a bit more lurk-in-the-dark and dirt friendly. I was sure we were no longer being followed, so we could just take the car over, load up and bring it back. But neither of our cars was big enough.

"Do you know for certain where all the evidence is?" he asked from down the hall. "All of it—not just mine."

Well, what kind of crook did he take me for? "Every good gunman knows where he keeps his damaging evidence. I have a "removeable" section of floor in one of the side bedrooms. That's where I store the guns and related items. Your boxes and other paper evidence is behind the stacks of leases and miscellaneous stuff."

"Right out in the open?"

"Of course not." I shook my head. There was no explaining it. He'd have to see it for himself. "You'll see when we get there. Someone would have to be willing to dig through a lot, and I mean a lot, of paperwork before they ever found anything damaging."

Chapter 32

ALEX CALLED PERK to borrow his van. He didn't ask any questions but I had to give him my Cooper. Alex was not handing over his beautiful, almost new and very expensive Mercedes, that was for sure.

The smell of fresh paint in my old office permeated everything. I could feel Alex checking out the space around him when we walked in.

When he caught sight of the contents I heard, "Dear God, look at all of those boxes. There's an entire room of nothing but boxes. How do you find anything?"

"I never have to search but they are all arranged in sequence and labeled if I actually needed to find something. But what are the chances that someone is going to want to see a rental agreement from fifteen years ago?"

"Slim to none?"

"Exactly. And the sheer volume is why I wasn't worried about showing the house with all this stuff in here. No one would ever find anything." I moved forward to the back left corner of the room, three stacks from the side wall.

I'd labeled the paperwork that we were here for as well. They appeared to be more of my own dull business transactions. The only difference was I'd used black ink instead of the blue, red or green I'd used on the others. "These are your boxes, here on the bottom. Then these four over here are Ari's business records. That's it for damaging paperwork. I never keep any of my own. Start loading these and I'll go pull up the floor in the other room."

I walked into the next room. I was shocked that the rental agent found anyone willing to rent this place looking like this, but I guess you just never know. It was inexpensive and in a good neighborhood. The neighbors would probably be happy to have someone living here instead of it always being empty. Also, I'd had the kitchen completely updated when I'd set up the same work for the other homes. It's amazing what a good kitchen will get people to do.

I slid the crowbar I kept hidden in the closet inside a rolled up carpet, into the quarter inch gap in the boards. I shoved down and up came the board section, just like it always had.

I took out my flashlight and illuminated the space. There were several new spiders and webs. Considering I haven't opened this space in … oh … more than a decade, a few spiders should be expected. At least no rats or mice had invaded this place. I don't like rodents. They give me the itches.

In the hall I caught sight of Alex as he pushed a hand truck with four bank boxes through the door and out toward the van. Reaching down into the space, I yanked up one box at a time. They weren't light—more like apple crates than boxes. Heavy wooden squares with flat wooden tops.

The hand truck was a stroke of brilliance on Alex's part. I heard the squeak of rubber wheels on the wood floors as he returned for another load and stopped in the doorway.

"What the hell am I going to do with all of this?" I asked him. "I need to find a safe place to dump it all. We can't store this crap in our home. We're having a baby …" I gestured at the box.

There were a bunch of guns of varying sizes and calibers, automatic weapons and ammo, knives and even a couple of explosive components.

Alex lookied down iat the box. "What are those black things on the bottom? They look like match sticks."

"A specialized variety of detonator."

"You are absolutely right. That stuff can't come live with us. I assume all those weapons have been used in at least one violent crime?"

"Actually, most have been used in several. You see that knife there? That was the knife that punctured the lung of that visiting Chicago boss, Louis Tergas. And that gun with the white butt—that was used in the Carper hit."

I blew out a sigh. This was amazing. None of this was *mine* but I was the one who had to dispose of it all. "We need a safe dumping ground," I mused. "One that no one will look at even a hundred years from now. We could wipe them all down, disassemble the guns and scatter the pieces in various spots."

He grinned. "Like Mrs. Hitchigan?"

"Very funny. I was thinking more along the lines of … dumping some at the bottom of the river, some in a lake and others in various holes thoughout New Jersey. Hitchigan was clearly an amateur."

"We could wait until they pour the foundation on the new banking center downtown," Alex suggested.

"Or we could find a blacksmith and see if he could melt it all down?"

I sort of liked that idea, but where does one come across people who melt down guns and knives? I was going to have to think on it.

"Is there anyplace in the basement we can store these boxes until we can go through them and get rid of everything that isn't essential?" I asked.

"Yeah, there's a false wall in one of the basement sections," Alex replied. "I should have been storing everything there, instead of just the old unused files. And those should have been sorted through and destroyed. But the room isn't big and I was lazy. I should have gone through it all ages ago. We'll start tomorrow—sort through it all and destroy whatever we don't absolutely need. If the cops had known about the room in the basement and the files … let's just say Dad and I would have had a hell of a lot of company in our visit with the state."

"Fine," I agreed. "We'll go through it all tomorrow. I don't want to go after Sheppa yet, anyhow. I want to find the link first. I want to know positively that it was Theo, and not one of his people. I want some sort of motive for this. It just isn't coming together yet, but sleep might clear it up a bit."

We backed into our driveway, opened the garage and started loading boxes onto the hand truck. *Ca-thunk, ca-thunk, ca-thunk*, down the stairs to the basement, we went.

Alex stepped around the boxes and approached the wall behind the water heater. The basement wall there looked exactly like all the others, half cinder block and half brick. He reached under a piece of old rag hanging behind the water heater and presto, the wall opened. There was no gap at all between the floor and the moving section of wall, but it didn't scrape either. Whoever had designed it had done a fabulous engineering job.

"Cool." I was impressed.

"Yeah, it is," he agreed. "Now, let's get these in here so we can go to bed. It's late and I'm beat."

"I think I'm actually passed beat. I think I may be on the verge of collapse." I didn't know what was keeping me going at this point, it must have been adrenaline.

We brought down four loads, or should I say Alex brought down four loads. I rearranged the boxes already in the space so we could get the loads to fit. He was right. The space was small, about the size of a mausoleum.

✳✳✳

The light from the window was shining right in my eye the following morning. I rolled over and tried to go back to sleep, but there seemed no help for it. I was up for good. I slipped out of bed and got going.

On my way down the stairs I looked at the grandfather clock in the main hall. It was almost ten. Boy I *had* slept.

There was coffee in the pot, but not a sound about the house. No coffee for me, was my first thought. But then again, I did buy some apple cider at the store yesterday. And warm cider is almost as good as coffee. After warming the cider, I took my mug with me and looked around the main area of the house. Nope, nobody. I looked out the window and saw Mike's car. And it looked like my Cooper was back as well.

They must be in the basement. I made toast and headed in that direction.

Halfway down the stairs I heard, "Holy shit! Is that what I think it is?"

Then a voice I knew well, replied, "Yes. And don't touch it. That stuff isn't our problem at the moment. We need to go through these files."

I got closer to the door and heard, "But how many people do you think have ever even *seen* that thing? It's supposed to be a fabrication of someone's wild imagination. Isn't that what you told me when I was a kid? That something like the *Hand of Vengeance* wasn't real. It was just a fairy tale designed to scare young people into doing what they were told? Well, this looks pretty real to me. What the hell is Ace doing with it? She isn't the Guardian, is she? I mean she hasn't been ripping out hearts and stuff, right?"

"No, she isn't the Guardian, thank God. Ari Gabella is the Guardian … and I thought you knew that. Ace's been holding, or hiding, this stuff for the Gabellas—they're cousins. And no, my fiancée is not nearly unhinged enough to be ripping out hearts. Although, she did once threaten to filet Constantine." He stopped and thought for a minute. "No, I'm pretty sure she was just trying to spook him."

"Filet? Like a fish? As in cut into pieces?"

I joined the conversation. "Yes, but he deserved it. He pulled a gun on Alex here in the library upstairs. And I still stand by what I said then. He should have been shot and dumped in the woods, not just scared."

I looked down at the "Hand." I had to get rid of that stuff, and suddenly I knew how … fish.

"I think that stuff and I are going to take a boat trip out into the Atlantic."

"You think dumping it in the ocean will take care of it? Aren't you worried someone will spot you?" Mike asked.

"Tony has a good sized boat. I'll just borrow it and take it out as far as possible and dump it all over the side. Besides, if I go out far enough, the chances of anyone spotting me, much less thinking anything of it, are slim."

I moved further into the room. The only other alternative I could think of that would be permanent was melting it all down but I didn't know anyone who worked in an active steel works.

"That's not a bad idea, except I don't like the idea of you going by yourself in your condition."

My condition. Ha! Alex was so going to get on my nerves with this overprotective thing. "Well, I think my present condition is far more appropriate for this than it will be in a couple of months. And I want this crap cleaned up. Is everything being moved this morning from the rental house?"

"Yeah, I'm having it all sent to the guest house for the time being. We'll go though it when we move in and get rid of what we can. Otherwise it will just sit around taking up space and I know you wanted Miguel to have the guest house for his living quarters. We'll get it done as soon as we can."

"Who's Miguel? And what is your condition?" Mike asked, peering into my cup. "And what are you drinking, it smells good?"

Alex hadn't said anything to Mike, just as I asked. "It's hot cider, and Miguel is my … protégé—that's a good word for what Miguel does. He takes care of things for me so I don't have to worry about them."

I glanced at Alex, who finished my thought. "He's the son of Ace's Italian housekeeper. He's been with her since he was a kid, so she trusts him to take care of things. Both he and his mother, Louisa, will be coming in next week. And Ace is expecting."

Then Alex turned back at me. "You are not going out on that boat without me. We can borrow Tony's boat this week sometime and I'll come with you. We can make a fishing trip out of it." He looked at all the boxes again. He was disgusted.

I think Mike was still in shock. "You're expecting … a baby, right?"

I nodded.

"Awesome. That means I'm gonna finally be an uncle."

"We'd rather you didn't tell anyone just yet. We'd like to get through the wedding first," Alex added.

"Does Dad know?"

"Not yet." Glancing back at me, Alex said, "We really should have the immediate family over and tell them. This isn't going to stay quiet. I can ask Mike not to say anything, but he'll tell Dad, who will tell my aunts, who will tell absolutely everyone in the tri-state area."

"Are you saying I can't keep a secret? I'll have you know I keep plenty of secrets," Mike insisted.

"I'm saying you won't be able to keep this one from Dad. You won't be able to help yourself. You'll be sitting there, having a normal conversation, and next thing you know it will be flying out of your mouth. Like I said, you won't be able to help it."

Mike looked sheepish. Apparently Alex hit the nail on the pro-verbial head.

"If you want, you can come with us when we take the boat out. There isn't any reason you shouldn't be able to spend the day out deep-sea fishing. Dumping these boxes shouldn't take long. And after we finish going through all this, we'll need some time to relax."

I called Tony and he said we could have the boat tomorrow. I noticed he didn't even mention that I hadn't been to the house to go over work things since we'd moved out. He was definitely up to something.

Tony accepted the dinner invitation I offered for Saturday evening. Again, Alex was right. We needed the immediate family to hear the baby news from us. They would, each and every one of them, be majorly pissed if they found out from someone else.

I then began the long process of sifting though boxes in the library. Someone had placed a shredder nearby and I kept it busy until lunch time. A fire would have worked better, but it was the summer after all and it would seem odd if smoke were billowing from our chimney. We could shred it all and then do the fire thing this evening when it was dark and no one would see.

After I made lunch for the three of us, we all went back to the papers. Mine had only been the four boxes I was keeping for Ari. Since she was living overseas, and had been for six years now, I decided that the contents of these ten-year-old-plus boxes of hers could be mostly shredded.

I managed to get it all down to one box of necessary papers and none of these were illegal.

Then I started in on the stuff that I'd absconded with. The evidence files consisted mostly of business letters, banking correspondence, computer info from Alex's hard drive and several damaging witness statements. Amazingly enough, the most damaging of these statements was not from Thad. They'd gotten enough from him to make a basic case, but the worst was from a source I would never have guessed.

From the personality of this witness, I gathered it didn't take much to extract information. He wasn't exactly a tough guy and I was pretty sure that even the suggestion of being sent to jail would have gotten him to spew forth everything he knew. I didn't want to believe he'd do that to his own family, but like I said he wasn't a tough guy.

"I'd bet the house I just found the answer to our contractor problems." I handed the testimony to Alex so he could review it. "He's probably afraid that you'll try to kill him if he doesn't kill you first."

Mike was so curious. It was like watching a puppy. He wanted to be in the middle of everything but Alex kept the file out of his line of vision.

"Shit. We can't kill him can we?" Alex was resigned to that fact without my even saying it.

"I wouldn't recommend it," I said. "Besides, I don't think he wanted to do this. He probably thinks you know he ratted on you and now you're just waiting until things die down to get even. The police can't use him again for testimony because they can't make a reasonable case based on only that testimony."

Alex looked grim. "We have to go see Theo. He isn't going to be happy. We had to clean house. I should make him do the same."

"No, you can't ask him to do that. It's not the same as Thad ratting on you and Roberto. You aren't his family. And we don't know the circumstances. It's possible they didn't give him much choice. I could imagine Marty being bullied, or conned, into giving information on someone if he had it. That's one of the many reasons why he was taken out of family business."

Alex nodded. "Let's get this crap cleaned up. We have other business to take care of."

"Neither of you is gonna tell me what's going on, are you?" Mike said angrily. "I'm not a child. You can tell me. I'm not going to tell anyone."

Alex and I looked at each other. I patted Mike on the back. "That isn't the reason we aren't telling you. This is a difficult predicament we've gotten into. We could have the person who gave that report to the police killed, but he probably only did it out of fear ..."

"Or he was protecting his own," Alex chimed in.

"And now that Alex is out of jail, someone is probably afraid. We think he might have hired some thugs to kill Alex. I don't really think he wanted to. I don't think he has it in him, but he probably felt that if he didn't, he'd end up dead himself.

"And the fewer people who know who that person is," I explained, "the better. I'm fairly certain we just need to kiss and make up. If this information is floating around, then someone may perceive our lack of reaction as weakness. And with the major life changes going on here, with the marriage and new baby, we just don't want more publicity than necessary."

Alex stood up and stretched. "And now we have to go play peacemaker and hope it takes. Otherwise ... it's bad enough he was using Theo's funds to kill me. He made it look like Theo did this."

"I don't want to believe he knew about that. I'd rather think he just didn't realize that we could trace the account back to its source. Most people couldn't," I reminded him.

"True. I hope you're right. Go get cleaned up and changed we need to go visiting."

Chapter 33

THEO AND HIS WIFE OWNED a very nice home on the outskirts of town. Charise had great taste and the house was a testament to it. She was also on various committees and boards about town regarding both the arts and education.

When we entered the Sheppa house we were ushered directly into Theo's office. The Sheppa's are big on the hugging thing, like my family, so there were hugs all around.

Theo went back behind his desk and sat. "Please sit. I'm glad the two of you have the time to come and see me. I wasn't expecting to be able to see you until the wedding."

"This isn't exactly a social visit." I admitted, glancing at Alex. "Do you mind if we get right to it? I'm not good with the small-talk thing."

"Be my guest," Alex replied.

"Theo, you know what I do," I began, "or rather, I should say *did*, for a living, correct?"

"Initially, you were a family assassin," he smiled. "I assumed you had simply changed employers at some point. I know the Pascolis weren't pleased, but they seemed to accept it over time. In any case, we all knew you hadn't actually become a cop."

"Good. Then you understand my situation perfectly. Well, recently I was contacted, under one of my work identities, to eliminate some-one—Alex, to be precise."

His face dropped. "You have got to be kidding."

"No, unfortunately. But this was really a stroke of luck because, prior to soliciting my services, this person had hired two other assassins. Both managed to botch the job but that's been taken care of. Anyhow, we've recently discovered who hired these people—and why."

Theo looked puzzled. Clearly he was trying to discover the reason for this at-home visit based on what I'd just told him. But it wasn't registering.

I elaborated. "I had a government connection trace a bank transfer back to the originating account. The money was intended to be used as a downpayment for the job."

"This is all very interesting," said Theo, "but what does it have to do with me?".

Alex leaned forward in his chair and said, "The account the money came from was yours—the one in the islands."

Theo looked green. What is the appropriate response when one is told that he's been, more or less, accused of attempting to murder a business associate? What he came up with was, "I swear to you, I didn't hire *anyone* to kill you. I certainly have no reason to want you dead …"

I held up my hand to stop the sputtering of innocence that didn't need to be declared in any case. "We know it wasn't you, Theo," I said. "The *account* is yours, but the motive isn't."

Alex handed him the testimony transcript. "We believe it's Anthony. We figure he's afraid I'm going to retaliate because of his testimony. We just discovered it this morning in the evidence files that were "removed" from the D.A.'s office. Actually, today was the first chance we've had to examine them."

Alex and I leaned back and waited, giving Theo a few minutes to digest this information.

"It all fits, doesn't it?" moaned Theo. "I'll do whatever you want, but I'd prefer you don't ask me to have him killed. He's my only son and I don't think I could do it … and Charise … she would never understand."

"We don't want him dead, Theo," I assured him. "In fact, we're pretty sure the police scared the crap out of him in order to extract this information. But we need to be *realistic*. He just isn't family material and he certainly shouldn't be running the family when you retire. He doesn't have it in him. He didn't even hire competent assassins until he decided to hire me. And even then, he didn't anticipate the possibility of an electronic money trail," I explained.

Alex joined the conversation. "First, you need to find a new successor, Theo. And I want to have a few words with Anthony myself. I want to make sure he knows this is over. I don't want him to try it again because he's afraid I'm still clamoring for revenge. It might even be a good idea if he moved overseas for a while—that way the police wouldn't have access to him." Alex was being very diplomatic considering the recent situation.

"But you don't want him dead?" said Theo, amazed. "You had Thad taken out, so how can I believe you're willing to let my son live! When you killed your own brother?" Theo's voice was quiet but hopeful.

"They're two completely different situations," I explained, delicately. "Near the end, Thad had become a highly volatile entity. He was perfectly willing to sell out his family.

"We're not talking about business associates. He let his aged father go to prison just so he could dodge drug charges. Not only did he put Alex in jail, but he put their entire family's operations at risk, and everyone who relies on those operations, legal and illegal alike, for their livelihood. If Anthony had sold you out and put you and your wife in prison to avoid spending time in jail himself—time he rightly deserved—then I'd see it as the same situation. He may have sold out an ally, but we'd like to believe he had a reason. We don't want to think he's just a spineless coward."

"And I don't see," Alex added, "what would be gained by killing him. We've enjoyed good relations for a long time now and I don't want that to end. But Ace and I agree that Anthony is out of his element when making decisions involving family business."

Alex, ever the epitomic politician.

Theo sat in silence for a moment and then nodded in agreement. "I don't think he'll be overly disappointed when I tell him he won't be taking over. He never did take to this whole thing anyhow. My nephew might be a better replacement."

Then events went well enough. Theo called Anthony in and we all had a very long, strained discussion about his behavior. But in the end, Theo and Anthony promised there would be no more activities of this nature. And, as devastated as Theo was to hear the truth from his son, he managed to hold it together. I could never see Anthony doing that. He'd have had a breakdown under similar circumstances. He practically got down on his knees and begged Alex not to kill him.

It was a bit embarrassing, not just for him, but for Theo.

Anthony did explain that, near the end of his four-hour interrogation, the detective in charge finally threatened him by saying that the police had incriminating evidence concerning his father. If he didn't cooperate with the Sevelli investigation, they would arrange for his father to be charged and imprisoned just like Alex. Anthony felt that he had no choice when confronted with this information.

I felt somewhat better knowing he'd done it to protect his father—not that this made Theo any happier. But in my eyes he was protecting his own, doing what he felt necessary to keep his family safe. I could live with that.

Anthony agreed that a few months … or years, of travel might not be such a bad idea. He also thought his girlfriend, Shannon, would enjoy living abroad for a change. He confessed that he didn't really want to take over the family business, but always felt he wasn't given a choice in that matter.

I could understand that well enough, since it was exactly what I experienced in my own situation.

Chapter 34

WE CLIMBED INTO THE CAR in front of the Sheppa house. "Well, that's over," I said. "They never asked for their money, though. Should I give it back?"

"I didn't even think about that," Alex said. "I'll call Theo from the marina tomorrow morning and see how he's doing. I'll ask then."

"OK. We should get going early. Who are we bringing with us?"

"I thought we'd bring both my dad and Mike. Dad could stand a day of fishing and needs to get out. Neither of them will mind that we're really going out to dump weapons."

The following day was a series of relationship trials. First, Alex acted like a mother hen the entire trip. I wanted to kick him overboard. Then Mike kept insinuating that we didn't trust him. Roberto, bless his heart, had brought a girlfriend and was doing his best to ignore the boys' behavior.

I stopped the boat about twenty miles out. The depth meter said that no one would be casually diving in these waters. Once the boxes were dropped over the side, even if someone wanted to go down there they'd need special equipment. It was too deep for a conventional dive suit and tank—the pressure at these depths would kill a person.

Alex knew the basics of sailing and could probably negotiate the boat, but he'd never piloted anything this large. He generally stuck with speed boats and smaller sailboats and decided that leaving it to me was wise.

It was a calm day and the sun was out—really a perfect day for boat-ing. Everyone was at the front of the boat, so I went below and started hauling up the two wooden crates of crap I had to get rid of. I looked up the stairway that led from the engine compartment, where we'd stored the crates, to the main galley. Alex was glaring down at me.

"You shouldn't be lifting those things," he scolded. "They're heavy." He took the box from me and hefted it up the stairs. Then he returned for the second one.

We took the two boxes to the back of the boat and tied the lids down tightly. Then we looped a rope over the edge and attached the boxes, one at a time, and gradually dropped them into the water. Once they hit the water, I sliced the rope and watched them sink.

"Well, that's that," he muttered watching the last one disappear.

"That went off without a hitch," I agreed. "Now if only everything else can work out that well." I was thinking about the move and the wedding.

We spent the rest of the afternoon fishing, lying in the sun and just generally enjoying the day. Alex tried very hard to be nice about Roberto's new friend, but he couldn't sound sincere. The girl kept checking out Mike, which pissed Alex off. If you're going to be a cheap floozy who dates old men for their money, the least you can do is pretend not to be blatantly interested in his twenty-something son. It's tacky.

***

The next few days went pretty well. I notified Ari that I'd disposed of certain items and gone through the old Gabella files. She didn't have a problem with it. She was glad I'd finally disposed of the weapons. She always worried something would happen and her old activities would come back to haunt her or someone close. I wished I couldn't relate, but I could.

We discussed the wedding. She said she wouldn't be coming, that things in Europe had heated up and she was in the middle of something. She didn't mention what and I didn't ask. I told her about the baby and the silence on the other end of the phone pretty much covered it.

"You're actually reproducing? I didn't even know if we were capable of something like that."

Ari, Riella and I were far more alike than any others in the family.

There was always Nella, but she was just a bit perkier than the three of us could muster.

"Yeah, it's possible," I assured her. "You and David don't have kids by choice, right? I mean you're using birth control?"

"Naturally, I was never willing to test the theory. Can you imagine me a mother?" Ari laughed.

"I can't even imagine me as a mother. I don't want to think about you. You're even harder than I am. Riella was the one I thought would get to this first." I took a drink of my decaf iced tea. It wasn't bad. "But she never did get married. You're the one who settled down first."

"I think that depends on how you define *settle down*. You know David and I married chiefly to stabilize the family. I was too young to take over on my own, or at least that's the line of shit those old guys fed me."

The old guys were our uncles and her father. David was at one time Ari's mentor in the enforcement area. He watched her back and kept her from doing anything that would have ended in almost certain death—not that she didn't fight him on every occasion possible.

"The old guys brought around a group of prospective grooms," Ari explained, "but David wanted to kill them, one and all. Do you have any idea how many stupid men exist in the families these days? I swear the gene pools just went to shit."

"Tell me about it. I got the opportunity to meet several of the moron variety before I gave up and decided on Alex. He has a lot going for him. The others were in a totally different league. It was like comparing a high school basketball player to an NBA All-Star."

She snickered. "Yep, David blew a gasket. Told me there was no way in hell I was marrying one of them and to go pack my things. The next thing I know we're in Vegas and I'm Arrianna Gabella Passerini. He and I had never even shared a stick of gum before that night, and next thing I know we're married."

"At least I'm getting a little time to get used to the idea," I said. "But, as I recall, you didn't have any to spare. There was a revolt going on after T. ... passed on."

"Passed on" wasn't exactly the way one would describe what happened to T. "Passed on" sounds serene or peaceful; but there was a hole in his head so big you could see through it.

"Well, that's history," said Ari. "I'm glad. David, Caster, Nella and I now spend most of our days in leisure. That is, with the recent exception—but you don't need to hear about that crap."

"Just so you know," I said, "Riella gave my wedding a pass as well. I don't think she wants to come back to the old stomping grounds."

"No, probably not—too much history," said Ari. There was silence on the other end of the line for a moment. "I should go. David just came in."

We said our goodbyes and hung up. As I headed for the door I noticed Alex lurking there. "You have a gift for eavesdropping," I said. "Has anyone ever told you that?"

"Was it supposed to be a secret?" He had a smirk on his face, again.

"No, but it's rude to listen to other people's conversations when they don't know you're there."

All I got was a smile in response. He knew it was rude. He just liked keeping tabs on me.

Chapter 35

WE MADE ALL THE dinner party calls and everyone accepted. I wasn't sure if that was good, or bad. I was running into that feeling a lot these days.

Alex and I hadn't entertained at all yet and Louisa hadn't arrived from Italy so I was a bit nervous. I was cooking for the entire party. I mean, I *can* cook—I just don't normally serve anyone other than myself and now Alex. I made a seafood alfredo using the fish Alex had caught earlier in the week along with some choice lobster pieces and shrimp and served it over angel hair pasta. I also offered a huge Caesar salad, made with my own signature dressing, and fresh bread from the bakery. Finally, I managed to produce a triple layer chocolate cake filled with chocolate mousse and strawberries. It all looked very tasty. This was an informal meal, but I hoped everyone was hungry because I made enough to feed an army.

My mother and father arrived with Marty, Cara and the kids. One big happy family, ha! If only. Marty had as many problems with our parents as I did, but it appeared that his progeny had gotten him off the hook. Maybe I'd get lucky and it would do the same for me. Not much chance there, I thought. Although I hadn't mentioned it to Alex, I was concerned that it might do just the opposite.

With my mother you never know which way the wind may blow. She didn't want me to be what I am, but she didn't want me to be what Tony and everyone else seemed to accept as my fate. She seemed to live under some delusion that I might become something more … someone famous or world-renowned. I just didn't have a famous-world-renowned bone in my body.

I'd had plenty of chances to become that person and I think this fact made it that much worse for her. She couldn't fathom that I didn't want to be a public spectacle. In contrast, I wanted to be a *shadow* on the face of society, not a front-runner. And now, it was possible that she'd view my pregnancy as the absolute and final end of the fantasy life she'd always envisioned. That life never had a chance, but mom wasn't likely to accept that. Seeing me for what I was had never been one of her strong suits.

They were followed by Roberto and Mike with Tony almost immediately behind them. We hadn't included any other family members. It would be fine when they heard, secondhand, that we were expecting a child. They would understand that those present would naturally know before anyone else.

Alex made the announcement after dinner but before dessert. For the most part, everyone seemed pleased. I was pretty certain that Roberto had already been told because he didn't look all that surprised to me. Evidently Mike did have a few problems keeping things from his father. My side of the family just seemed pleased that I would be settling down.

Apparently my pending marriage wasn't enough to convince them that I was going to stay put. My unexpected pregnancy did it though. Tony looked like the cat that swallowed the canary, as though he'd accomplished the impossible. And maybe he had, but I still wanted to know what he was up to.

Mom didn't look all that happy. Dad, on the other hand, seemed genuinely pleased. I wasn't sure how he was taking this whole, me-getting-married thing. We don't talk much. He's one of those distant fathers. He's there in a crisis, but otherwise, well, he's a lot like background noise. And I don't mean that disrespectfully. He's just never been involved. Of course, my mom was always deeply involved and perhaps he thought there wasn't any room for him. I have no idea and psychoanalyzing my family is not an easy thing.

I needed cake. Apparently the girls did too, by their comments. I brought it to the table and the girls helped me serve.

For the most part, the evening had gone quite well. My mother was the exception, but what was I going to do? She was what she was and I couldn't do anything about it. So I was prepared to forget it.

We said goodbye and called it a night. Before he left, Alex spoke with Tony for a few moments and then came upstairs. I was lounging in the tub, again.

"You take one of those almost every night now."

"Yep, and your point is?" I have every right to soak my body in a tub as often as I like. And poo on him if he doesn't like it.

"I don't know. It just seems odd," he said taking a seat on the little chair in the corner.

"My body feels yucky and I'm tired. A nice soak makes me feel better." I laced my fingers through the bubbles.

"Can I come in?" he asked.

I looked at the tub—it was a huge garden tub. I don't think it had been used until I'd moved in here. "If you want to."

He stripped down, climbed in and slid beside me. He gave a slight groan as he leaned back. I knew that feeling—I'd had it myself.

"I'm starting to think these next couple of weeks are never going to end," he said with his head leaned back and his eyes closed.

"Isn't that the truth? I spent an hour-and-a-half on that cake today and it was gone in ten minutes. I don't think we even had one piece left."

"Mmm, but it was good." He grinned down at me and pulled me closer. "The whole dinner was amazing. Everyone complimented it, including your mother."

I harrumphed. "Until she found out I'd made it. Then she said that next time I might want to try a little more pepper. I can't do anything to please her. That's why I gave up trying when I was sixteen. It wasn't worth the effort."

"She didn't look happy about the baby," admitted Alex. "Her reaction surprised me. Your dad almost glowed. I don't think I've ever seen him that happy or that relaxed."

"With mom, it's not that there's anything wrong with my having a baby. It's just the death of her dream. She wanted me to be ..." How does one explain it? "something more, something beyond a wife with children. Not to say I'm not more—I am—just not the *more* she wanted. And even though I could have achieved the "more"—that dream of hers—any number of times, I kept turning away from that path. She never could accept that her dream for me wasn't *my* dream."

"The difference being?" asked Alex.

"She wanted a daughter who was 'someone.' You know, the first female president of the United States, a Pulitzer Prize winner, a noted pianist, an Olympic gold medal winner, that sort of thing. I wanted to be left the hell alone."

I felt a rumble of laughter in his chest. "I can't see you dealing with notoriety. Even as an assassin, you used multiple names to keep yourself as anonymous as possible. I don't think you could take living in the spotlight. I'd think she would have understood that by now. You turned down the Olympic gymnastic trials twice and then refused that symphony job."

I snickered. "She, for some reason, has a selective block there. I don't even socialize at family gatherings. For that matter, I'm going to have problems standing in front of our wedding guests and getting married. I don't like being the center of attention."

"Don't worry about the wedding," he ran a hand down my arm, "you won't be standing up there alone."

As strange as it may seem, that made me feel better. I wasn't in any of this alone. He'd be there through all of it.

Chapter 36

ON MONDAY LOUSIA AND Miguel arrived. They were given rooms in the condo for the next two nights but we were hoping to relocate after that. My jewels went in Alex's safe for the time being. They'd come with Miguel for safe keeping.

Alex's response to seeing my personal choice of jewelry was far from positive. He about had a bird. "You can't wear these," he insisted.

"Why the hell not? I've been wearing them for a few years now."

Like most women, I have a few really nice pieces of jewelry. The most select I purchased at estate sales, bank auctions and antique shops where I got exceptional deals. They were antique, yes, but they were all I owned in the way of good jewelry with the exception of the few pieces I had here. I couldn't very well not wear any of them, and what good would they do locked in a safe?

"Ace, honey, these items should be in a museum, not hanging on you. What if you lost a stone? Do you have any idea how hard it would be to get something like this repaired?"

"Well, this and the pieces I had before these arrived are all I have. I don't have a lot to choose from, so I wear the ones I own."

"I'll buy you new ones. We'll talk to the museum and see if they're interested in displaying these. Do you have any documentation on them?"

From my perspective, he was being annoying. I didn't want to hear what he had in mind for my furniture. "Yes, of course."

The bulk of my furniture was scheduled for delivery first thing Tuesday morning. I wanted to be there to direct the unloading. I told

Miguel about my intention to move him into a more hands-on position regarding my real estate. Naturally, I also told him it would come with a significant increase in pay, since the position would require much more responsibility. He seemed elated. I could almost feel the little ripples of energy coming off of him.

Since they were actually members of my home, I told Louisa and Miguel about the baby. Lousia was beside herself. She cried and exhibited a lot of hand gestures and hugging. And everything she managed to say was all in Italian. After she calmed herself, she went to check out the kitchen. We'd only be here for two nights, but she wanted to know what we had.

Alex gave me a look after Louisa left the room. "She does speak English, right? I mean, I sort of assumed it."

"Yes, of course. But when she's tired, upset, or excited, it's harder for her. She has problems remembering the right words, so it usually comes out in Italian." I leaned into him. "Look at it as an exploration into your ancestry. You're a full-blood Italian-American yes?"

He nodded.

"Well, by the time she's done with your Italian verbal education, you could be an Italy-born and raised Italian and no one would be able to tell the difference. You never know when that might come in handy."

Alex laughed.

"And Miguel will teach you some new words, too," I assured him. "His are usually best used outside the general public's hearing, though."

Alex's laughter continued.

✳✳✳

The following morning we started the moving process. The truck pulled up and around the circular drive. It was a group of museum movers. For my belongings, most of which were antiques, I don't trust anyone else. They were packed by museum movers and will be unpacked in the same manner. They take their work seriously. They cost a fortune but they were worth every penny.

Three hours later, they were back with the second load. Alex gave me a dirty look.

"What?" I asked.

"Two full truck loads. How much did you pay to have all of this shipped?"

I started to uncrate another painting. "You don't want to know," I said, wrinkling my nose. "Besides, it isn't like there's that much more stuff than the average person owns. It just has to be packed more carefully. Because of this, everything takes up more room—hence, one truckload of things becomes two truckloads of things. And remember, there are two pianos to be moved in here as well, and those won't be coming until tomorrow."

He grumbled something that sounded like "Dear God." Then he surveyed the boxes of paintings along the wall. "I don't think you mentioned having quite so many of these. Are they worth anything?"

"Yes," I confirmed, "and they're all insured. Most of them are contemporary European artists so, while they're worth something, mostly I own them because I love them. There are only two pieces that I'd consider masterpieces and they're over there. Those are the ones I had the special security installed for. I had wiring placed over the fireplace in the living room and another here, against the outer wall."

"I think we should ask that guy Linier, from the museum, to stop by and see if he'd be interested in displaying any of these there."

I sighed. Why did he insist on trying to change my lifestyle? "But I like having them in the house. I like living in a place that has a 'gallery' feel."

"Yes, I know, and you can keep any that he isn't interested in. But the security here is nothing compared to that of the museum. It's only fair to think about public display of any 'masterpieces' for others to see."

Shaking my head at my fiancé's paranoia at being robbed, I turned and began uncrating another painting. I spent all morning and most of early afternoon directing furniture and belongings, and occasionally getting the opportunity to uncrate art.

Alex came into the music room looking for me.

"Ace, honey," he said.

He may have called me "honey" but that was clearly not the endearment he had in mind.

"There are twelve," he continued, "four-foot high by two-and-a-half-foot wide boxes in our room. They're labeled 'shoes.' You cannot *possibly* have twelve giant boxes of shoes. No one has that many shoes. What are in those boxes?"

"They are shoes, actually. I sort of have a thing about shoes. I don't buy anything else—with the exception of gun ammo maybe—that I buy the way I buy shoes. It's not as if they are expensive shoes—they're just shoes. Boots, heels, sandals, sneakers. I have a number of everything, in every color."

Now he really was looking annoyed.

"It could be worse, you know," I said with a deprecating smile. "I could collect jewelry. Lots of women do, or I could collect handbags, or ... Precious Moments."

The last one got me a relieved look. "I can say that if you collected Precious Moments, they wouldn't be coming out of the box. But Ace, we don't have a place to put all those shoes."

"Yes, as a matter of fact, we do." I stood up and guided him past our bedroom to a door located on the opposite side of our master bath. I swung it open and Alex stepped back, amazed.

"Was this here before?" he asked, a slight shock in his voice.

"Nope. This was part of the renovations I ordered. This whole room is our walk-in closet. I decided we didn't need all those bedrooms ... and we can use this door." I showed him, opening the door that led to our master bath, "to go to our room and back. Besides, the little walk-in closet for the master bedroom would just barely hold your clothes. We needed this."

"I had no idea," said Alex. "You're right about the other closet. I was wondering if we were going to have enough dresser space to make up for it. And looking at the furniture in here, we do." He glowered at me as we entered the bedroom.

The room contained my dark mahogany set. The bed was from the mid-eighteen hundreds. The mattress was new; and was specially made for the bed. The posts at the corners were round, hand-carved and ten inches in diameter. Two of the bureau chests were six feet high and had six drawers each; then there were two night stands, a dressing table, a regular dresser with mirror and a matching blanket chest at the end of the bed. It was a good thing the room was big, because it needed to be so that the bedroom wouldn't be overwhelmed by the furniture.

"I know it seems a bit much," I admitted. "Just give it a while, until we get our personal effects moved in. If it still feels like too much, we can move one or both of the chests to the walk-in. I just hate to do it. I like the feel of it all together. They've been with this set since it was created."

"Which would be when?" he grouched.

"From what I gather, between eighteen-forty and eighteen-eighty, I haven't been able to pin it down any closer. I know who made the set and his working life span. He started on his own at twenty-six and died at sixty-four. So it had to have been made sometime in those forty years."

"I'm going to say this again. These should be in a museum. I should not be sleeping on something like this. It's priceless."

"No, a good antiquarian could tell you what it was worth, within a few dollars," I replied, being a smartass of course.

I turned around to leave the room. Every time we discussed these things we both got annoyed. "I'm going back to my art. I need to see how everything fared in this move. I want to make sure none of the frames are chipped."

"Ace, you're avoiding this conversation."

"Only because I don't see a point in arguing, What I own is what I own. I'm not selling any of it and I have no intention of moving my furniture into a museum. They don't make furniture like this anymore. It's durable, it's solid and it never goes out of style. I don't have to worry about replacing it and I love old things, so I'll never get tired of it."

"You won't budge on the furniture will you?" said Alex.

"Nope," I said agreeably. "Do you want to help me uncrate the paintings?" I asked, hoping to move the conversation to something else.

"Am I winning that battle at least?"

"We'll need to speak with Mr. Linier and see if he's interested in taking any for display in the museum. However, I want to know exactly what the security arrangements are. I'm not handing them over if it isn't up to par."

He was following me down the hall to the music room, where I was going through the art. "I won't argue that point," Alex said. "It wouldn't make sense. Security's the main reason I'd feel better if at least the more valuable ones were at the museum."

Alex about had a fit when he finally saw the "collection," as I like to call it. I think he may have wanted to strangle me for not being a bit more forthcoming regarding these "pieces." Needless to say, he called Mr. Linier immediately after all the crates had been unpacked.

✳✳✳

The following morning, Mr. Linier was there, waiting at the gate when we arrived. I didn't know what Alex had told him, but he looked ready to pop. The excitement in his stance, the merriment in his eyes was a little unusual for someone who was normally so subdued. He normally came off as a cross between a mortician and his client, but not today.

Alex and I headed into the music room to show Mr. Linier the collection while Miguel unpacked boxes for his mother to enable her to set up the kitchen in the manner that best suited her.

We stood there for a good ten minutes before Linier said anything. Then I heard the standard, "You do have provenance don't you?" No museum would show anything without it.

"Of course. They wouldn't be being considered for museum lending if I didn't," I replied.

"Mr. Sevelli mentioned that you also own several jewelry pieces that you might consider lending. He said you may consider a long-term display placement for them."

"I might consider it for a few of the pieces, yes. Alex isn't comfortable having such valuable pieces in the house for any lengthy duration. I've never had a problem, but he'd sleep better knowing they were as safe as possible."

"Oh, I completely understand. If I owned pieces such as this …" he motioned toward the paintings I'd lined up against the wall, I'd separated them from my less valuable pieces, knowing they'd be the ones he'd show the most interest in. He finished the thought, "… security would definitely be my primary concern. But pieces such as these were exactly what museums were originally designed for. These are just amazing. How many are you considering lending at this time?"

"Four of the sculptures," I motioned behind us. I'd set several on a table and the others around the room. "Four of the paintings and my jewelry. That is, if you're interested, have the security and can handle the insurance. I understand if this is an issue. We can reduce the size of the loan …"

"No, *please*," he said, practically jumping at me. "We would love to have all these pieces, if you're willing to lend them." He was referring to those of more prestigious origin. "I'll need to speak with our board, not that I think this will be a problem. Maybe we could call this group the 'Angelica Collection' or the 'Pascoli Collection,' or," he stopped and thought for a moment, "now it would be the 'Sevelli Collection' wouldn't it?"

"I'd prefer if you kept our name as a very minor side note. Actually, I think it best to simply treat this as an anonymous loan. I'm just a minor side note, and seeing as I live here, I don't think I want everyone in town knowing it was me." I looked to Alex for support.

But what I got was, "Ace, honey, if you put your name on it, your mother might be happier."

What? Crap! I never thought of that. He was right. My mother and her five minutes of fame.

"Fine," I relented, "but no more than a quarter inch in height. And please don't use our last name. 'Angelica' is more than enough, should you decide to use it."

The doorbell rang. "That's the movers," I explained. "The pianos are coming into this room."

I'd moved everything to the side to make space. In fact, that was the reason the paintings were up against this sidewall.

Miguel came in and opened the French doors for the movers. The pianos were brought in. They were both fully boxed.

"Since when do they fully crate a piano?" Linier asked.

I walked up to the first smaller crate. But Alex answered. "Since it's an antique … or at least one of them is, I think. Ace, which is which?"

"This one," I pointed. "The smaller of the two belonged to the Earl of Brakenridge. It was originally purchased in 1878. He had it specially made for his daughter to celebrate her sixteenth birthday."

The side came off as the museum movers brought in the second, much larger piece. They put it in place and came over to help me with the top of the crate.

"And the other?" Linier asked with baited breath.

"It's a grand piano, originally made in 1892. It was the property of the Bartelli Opera House in Rome until they went out of business in 1936. At that time it was sold to an aristocrat in the area named Edwardo Bartelli. Rumor has it, or at least Edwardo's wife had it, that Edwardo was the illegitimate great-great-grandson of Petri Bartelli; the original owner of the opera house."

"It was said that Petri, although married, had a long-time mistress, an actress from the opera house, who gave him four sons; a feat his wife never managed with only one daughter to call her own. Because of this, and the lack of social ostracism in Rome at the time for this sort of arrangement, Petri recognized all his boys and gave them his name as well as financial support. Then his oldest son, Renold, had a son called Petri, named for his grandfather. Petri then had a son Ellis, who later sired Edwardo. When Edwardo died, about six years ago, his wife, at this time in her late seventies, asked me if I would like to have it. She offered to give it to me because she knew I loved music and antiques. Her own children would never want it, so she thought of me. But I couldn't just take it for nothing. So, I checked around and paid her a reasonable sum for it."

"How old was Edwardo when he died?" Alex was paying attention.

"He was ninety-nine. Two months short of his one-hundredth birthday. He used to tell me he'd never make it. I guess he knew what he was talking about. He was in his twenties when he purchased the piano."

Finally the uncrating was finished and the pianos were free. The benches had also been packed away in a similar manner.

"Are those the original benches?" Linier was looking like he might just salivate on my keys.

"This one is." I was sitting at the bench in front of the smaller instrument. "The other had to be replaced several times during its life. An opera house is a very busy place and things break. The bench for the other is from the same time period and was made by the same craftsman."

I set my fingers on the keys. I knew they were probably out of tune, but I had to do this. It had been so long, too long to be away from one of my main life forces. Music filled me with energy, it flowed into my body though the keys. It was the most amazing relationship I've ever had with anything.

Music wafted over the room. The tones weren't nearly as off-key as I'd expected. I'd have to find a tuner who dealt in antique pianos. I asked the museum movers if they knew of anyone who had an older instrument that needed regular tuning. They recommended two people and gave me names and a general location of their homes.

Linier stood there drooling over my pianos when the doorbell rang again.

Chapter 37

"DON'T WE HAVE A gate?" I asked, looking at Alex.

"Yes, but since we expected the movers and we were going to be here anyway, we didn't shut it." He glanced down the hall to the entryway and then back at me. "But I think it's time we did," he grumped.

Miguel entered and said, "You have a visitor. A Detective Morrey. He looks like a person who lives in the park."

Odd, that was one of my first observations about Morrey as well. I rolled my eyes. "I know. Send him down here."

A few moments later I heard, "Damn! This place is nice ... a whole lot nicer than Tony's. Does he know you have a nicer house than him?"

Then he saw the pianos. "Damn, and nicer music makers, too. I wouldn't think he'd appreciate knowing you were doing so much better than he was."

But when had Morrey been inside Tony's house? He sat outside, yes ... but inside? Hmm? ...

"Let's not be stupid," I replied. "Tony couldn't care less where I live and his house is just as nice. It's just suited to a different type of person. Tony likes things crisp and elegant. We like comfortable and sprawling. So what do you want?" I asked curtly.

"Now, that's not nice," said Morrey. "I haven't done anything to make you mad at me ... at least not lately," he muttered. "In fact, I helped you look for dead bodies."

That sure got Linier's attention. His little head was up and looking around, like a bunny in hunting season.

"And then I helped out the D.A. for you. You shouldn't be so mean." Now he was looking at the artwork scattered about the floor. "Nice pictures," said Morrey. "Worth anything?"

"As a matter of fact, they are. That's why Mr. Linier is here," I snapped. "He runs the museum downtown. That's the building with all the stairs, next to the Department of Education."

He rolled his eyes. "You may find this hard to believe, but I've been to that museum."

"They let you in with the way you dress? They must be hard-up for patrons." Miguel was right, Morrey looked like a bum again today, rumpled everything. "Do you even own an iron?"

"Damn pregnancy has not done nice things for your attitude," Morrey observed. "You've gotten mean."

I thought about the conversation. I *was* being mean … and pretty much without cause. I blew out a sigh. "You're right. I'm sorry. I just have too much going on and this move has sent me over the edge."

I turned to Miguel. "Would you please ask Louisa if she could bring something to drink to the sitting room, since it's the only one that's actually put together. Then maybe you could show Mr. Linier around the house."

Miguel came back a few seconds later, "Momma said she was making some of that decaffeinated iced tea for you. She will bring in a pitcher."

"Thanks. If you could show Mr. Linier the furnishings in the rooms, the antiques, I think he would find them interesting. And you can answer most of the questions he might have."

"All of the antique furnishings? That could take days," he said with a smirk.

Alex laughed.

"No, just the older ones." I shook my head at him. He was being a smartass and he knew it. And now that there was another male around, he was going to be impossible.

***

Morrey, Alex and I moved to the front sitting room. The furniture there was from the nineteen-twenties—a low-back sofa and two sitting chairs in the same style. The tables were another matter. They were all pre-eighteen-hundred, but somehow it all worked.

"I'm sorry I was rude," I said as I sat down. Alex sat next to me and Morrey sat in one of the chairs. "I've just been overwhelmed with things lately. And who told you I was pregnant?" It had just dawned on me. I hadn't mentioned it, so someone else must have.

"I heard it through the grapevine," Morrey shrugged. "One of the D.A.'s people mentioned it. Why? Am I not supposed to know?"

"Stupid me. I wanted this info to stay in the family until after the wedding. I guess that didn't work." I glanced at Alex. He looked guilty.

"Who did you tell?" I demanded.

"Chester Watkins," Alex said. "He's my accountant. And … his office is in the same building as the D.A." He grimaced.

"And now I can't even blame the family, can I?" I groaned. Oh well, what's done is done. There's no fixing it.

Louisa brought in our tea and glasses. I put down a place mat so that the tea wouldn't leave a mark on the table and poured each of us a glass. Then I handed them both coasters. And they'd better use them, or else.

"So, what *are* you doing here?" I asked, using a much nicer tone. "I don't think you came out here to congratulate us on the baby."

"No, but congratulations anyway. I came because Laren is throwing a fit. Apparently, he went to talk to one of the witnesses who originally gave testimony against your beloved over there," he said, nodding at Alex. "… only to be told by the housekeeper that he was no longer in the country. Laren seems to think the guy is either dead, and you two killed him, or he left because of a threat."

It had to be Anthony Sheppa, there was no one else. "He's looking for Anthony?"

"Yeah, what happened to him?"

Alex answered before I could speak. "I think he went to Italy or someplace in Europe. Or at least that's what he told us. You could probably check the airlines if it's that important."

"Why would he leave like that?" Morrey asked suspiciously.

Now, Alex left it to me. "Well, Theo decided it wasn't in the family's best interest for Anthony to take over."

"Why after all this time? That's been planned since he was born, right?"

"Have you ever met Anthony?" I asked.

"Yeah."

"You don't think he's a little … overly kind for the job?"

"Kind?"

"Not family material," I replied.

"I don't know," Morrey said. "I didn't think about it. Besides, some people are just better at hiding what they are. You never know when it's just a good act."

He did have a point, of course. "Well, Theo told him he was go-ing to give the job to Anthony's cousin, so Anthony was off the hook. From what I understand, he wasn't all that disappointed. Last we heard, Anthony and his girlfriend decided to move to Europe for a while. I'm sure he'll be back. It isn't like he's been banished or anything."

"But why move away? This reeks of you two interfering," said Morrey, scowling.

"Have you ever had the stress of family obligation hanging around your neck like a noose?" I demanded.

He shook his head, but something passed through his eyes. I knew those eyes. Again, this was going to annoy me. I should just ask him about his relatives in the city. It would be easier than trying to figure it out.

"Well, trust me, it sucks," I assured him. "He probably chose Europe because they speak English there and it's an entire ocean away, just in case Theo changes his mind.

"If Tony let me off the hook, trust me, an ocean or two away would sound real good if I weren't getting married. Hell, it would sound good, even married. I moved to Europe for my job, but a group of my cousins all left when their family obligations were paid up. I think it has to do with starting over fresh. No expectations, no past recriminations. No one knows you. It can be very rehabilitative after a long time under someone else's rule."

"Well, I guess I can understand that," said Morrey. "... not that Laren will."

"Like Alex said, he can go check the airline passenger listings and find out where they went. Or he could probably just go see Theo. I'm sure he knows where his son is staying. Anthony is his only son and he isn't likely to lose touch with him," I said.

I took a sip of the tea. It was good. Louisa had added some lemon. "Why does Laren want to talk to Anthony anyway? No matter what he might get out of him, it's probably hearsay and I don't believe you can build an entire case on it. And since we don't intend on making it easy for Laren to put Alex and Roberto in jail, I don't see what he plans to do with Anthony's testimony."

Morrey smiled at me. "But you knew about the testimony?"

"Yes." There was no point hiding it.

"How? It was a well-guarded secret. I mean you probably didn't look through the evidence you stole before burning it all, so how did you know?"

"I didn't burn any evidence," I said, indignantly. And that was the truth. I shredded it and let Alex and Mike burn the remains later.

Clearly Morrey didn't believe me. "Whatever," he shrugged. "Are you gonna tell me?"

"Is this for your own personal curiosity, or is it for the D.A.?"

"My curiosity. You always know things you shouldn't. I just wonder how."

"Well, you remember the little problems we were having with someone trying to kill Alex?"

Immediate recognition. "Shit! It was Anthony? But why?"

"He was afraid that Alex might take revenge for his testimony," I explained. "So he thought it was a kill or be killed situation. It was all just a big misunderstanding. One that has now been happily rectified on both sides with no hard feelings."

"Are you sure you didn't kill him?" Morrey pressed. "That's a pretty good reason, you know?"

"I'm positive." I assured him. "Go see his father if you don't believe me. And you didn't answer my question. Why is the D.A. after Anthony?" He'd dodged the question.

"He wants to see," said Morrey, "if he can get him to spill the beans on a few other wise-guys."

I glanced at Alex and he responded this time. "Well, that changes things. I don't think it would be wise for you to go to Theo's. Not if you want to live. Laren's trying to get Theo's only son killed and Theo won't stand for it. I think the best thing Anthony could have done was to leave. Hopefully he'll stay away for a while."

"What do you mean Laren's trying to get him killed?" asked Morrey. "He just wants him to testify against some family thugs. That isn't going to get him killed if they go to jail."

I couldn't stand it. "Can you really be that naive, Morrey? You must know that if you rat out a family member, you're going to be a prime target. The main reason Alex and I accepted the situation was because the detective in charge coerced him into his testimony by telling Anthony they had something on Theo and they'd throw *him* in jail. I'm pretty sure the detective was full of crap, but it put Anthony in a bad position. Also, our families have excellent rapport. We don't want to jeopardize that. But most family members would just kill his ass and not be bothered about details. Laren knows this perfectly well. He's being irresponsible with that kid's life." I was annoyed and sickened.

"And when Theo gets wind of this," Alex said, "and he will, you better be wearing a bullet-proof vest if you show up looking for Anthony on his doorstep. He'll shoot first and ask questions much, much later."

Alex was one hundred percent right about that. Protecting his son was something that, no matter how mad he was at Anthony, Theo'd never stop doing. "Maybe you should just go back to tailing people. I'm thinking it might be safer," I suggested.

"You and me both," he grumbled.

Morrey finally drank his tea, thanked us, and left. I did warn him that next time the gate wouldn't be open and he'd need to press the buzzer to gain access. He just smiled and said okay.

Just as he was leaving, I caught sight of Miguel showing Linier back into the music room. I pulled Alex along behind me.

***

Finally, two hours later, Linier finished and left. He'd made the selection of pieces he wanted to show and was hoping to have the museum ready in the next month.

He needed to present his idea to the Board of Directors and was going to call a special session before the end of the week. I think he was concerned we might change our minds and go with one of the larger New York museums if he didn't hurry it along. He'd mentioned that it was rare for their museum, because of its size, to receive loans without having to actively pursue them. They were always in competition with larger facilities, making it difficult to lure donors like ourselves.

While Miguel showed Linier to the door, I stood in front of the pictures. I was thinking … but not about Linier, not about the art that I was looking at, or the museum. I was thinking about Morrey.

"What's wrong?" Alex asked. "You worried Linier can't pull this all together, or are you upset about giving them up?"

I looked Alex in the eye. "I think I want more information on Morrey," I said, thinking aloud.

That was not something he'd been expecting. "What the hell for? I don't even want to know what I *do* know about him."

"He said the house was nicer than Tony's. Did you catch that?"

"So?"

"So when was *he* ever in Tony's house?" I started pacing. "He sure as hell wasn't invited by one of us. While he was following us, he only pulled up to gate and sat outside the drive."

Alex sat down hard on the piano bench. Good thing they were made well. "He also mentioned that the pianos were nicer," he mused. "That means he's been in the main house, not just the foyer. You think Morrey and Tony are up to something?"

I wanted to scream.

"Yes!" I snapped. "And I don't think he heard about my pregnancy from the D.A.'s office, either. Somehow, he's tied to Tony. I just don't know why or how."

I headed out of the room. I still had a ton of unpacking to do. I thought I'd start in our bedroom.

Turning back to face Alex from the doorway, I said, "I may not know what the connection is right now … but I will." Then I headed out of the room to get started with today's work.

But tomorrow, now that was an entirely different story.

Chapter 38

THE FOLLOWING MORNING brought a new perspective. I could attack this thing with Morrey from one of two directions. I could go through Tony's side, but that would be full of brick walls. If I went to Tony directly, he'd lie. He was an excellent liar. He didn't even need a good reason to lie. It was second nature to him and sometimes I thought he did it just to confuse people for no reason.

The other alternative was to go through Morrey's side. I could check him out through his police files and his general background, or I could simply go straight to Laren because Laren owed me. He wouldn't like it, but he did, and I could make him pay up.

That seemed the best approach. Hit up the D.A. for info. He was gonna be pissed, but I didn't care. He didn't want me around him. I made him look bad. Ha! It was those cheap suits he wore, not *me*. Besides, I wanted to give him a piece of my mind about Anthony Sheppa.

I called the D.A.'s office only to discover that Laren was in court this morning. I asked and was told he'd be on the second floor of the courthouse. They gave me the name of the case so I could track him down.

The case being tried was minor. The defendants apparently had gone for a joyride in a car that belonged to one of the town council members. But unfortunately for the defendants, the council member was an attorney so it was being treated a bit more severely than if the car had belonged to an average every-day citizen. Which is why I suspected Laren was bothering with such a minor violation.

When I entered the courtroom, it was clear that they hadn't expected any more guests to this particular party because everyone turned and stared. I looked for the defendants' attorney and found Max. It figures. He stands by every criminal in town.

They were all still staring so I waved at the group and sat down behind Max's defense table. To my surprise, Max asked for a moment to confer with his associate. Then he walked over and handed me the case file. Apparently I was the associate.

"Do me a favor?" he whispered. "Please look through that quickly for anything out of the ordinary. I know I'm missing something. This judge is usually friendly but the car belonged to Attorney Tanner. He's on the town council."

I noticed the old fart sitting on the other side of the room. I also noticed that Max was not looking good today. From the looks of him, I'd guess the flu. He was sweating and blotchy.

I quickly scanned the file. The trial, for something so minor, seemed a bit overzealous. They were actually calling for jail time for this crap. Like prisons aren't already overcrowded. Next thing you know they'll be pitching in graffiti artists. Unbelievable.

According to the file, the evidence was all circumstantial. They didn't even have prints on the vehicle. They had no confession. They had nothing but the word of one person who said he'd seen the boys in the car. Other than that, there was absolutely no evidence.

The witness was one Mark Teller, a well-known fibber. But since the D.A. liked the fib this time, he was accepting the souce. Doesn't that just figure?

"Mark has been convicted for perjury three times," I said to Max. "What's he getting out of this BS testimony?"

"Good question. I asked and was told that it was immaterial."

"Yeah, right," I grumbled. "Can I work this? Or is Laren gonna have fit?"

I wouldn't have asked, but studying Max, I concluded he needed a break. He looked like he was going to fall down if he didn't sit down. Clearly he was running a fever or he would have seen the giant holes in this case—they all but jumped out of the folder.

"You have a plan?" he asked, hopefully.

I nodded.

"Well then, let's see." Max turned to the judge and asked if I could continue the case in his place.

Laren objected, of course, but the judge overruled it. He was watching Max with concern. Like Max said, the judge was normally friendly.

"I want to call Mark Teller back to the stand," I announced.

Laren objected again, and was overruled. Next thing I knew, Mark was in the witness chair being reminded he was still under oath. Not that it mattered to him.

Mark looked at me carefully. Now he recognized me. He started to fidget. Like I said before, everyone in town knows me.

Laren stood up immediately. "Your Honor, Ms. Pascoli is intimidating the witness."

Although that was probably true, I wasn't doing it intentionally.

"Laren, she hasn't even said a word yet. Please continue," said the judge, looking at me.

Laren sat down and I went to work on the little ferret in front of me. "Mr. Teller, I'm not going to suggest you were lying when you identified the defendants—those boys over there," I began. "But I think you may have made an error. It says in this file ..." I said, glancing down. I didn't really need the case file. But because I don't like being the center of attention, I tend to do better with a prop. "... that you observed these three young men driving the stolen automobile down Corrington Street at nine-thirty in the evening. Is that correct?"

"Yes," replied Mark, with uncertainty. He didn't believe it and neither did I.

"Well, unless things have changed dramatically on Corrington, the lighting on that road is non-existent. Has that changed?"

He faltered for a moment, then looked up at me. "No."

"Since it would have been totally dark by nine-thirty on the evening in question, and this automobile was going ... what does it say here

... forty-five to fifty miles an hour," I looked up from the notes and gave him a quizzical look, "I don't see how you could possibly have identified your own hand much less three boys in a dark car. Now, are you absolutely certain you want to say that you're *positive* it was these boys? I mean, really look at them. They look like students ..."

"I object,"

"... they don't look like hardened criminals."

"I object,"

"Are you sure you want to send them to jail if ..."

"I object,"

"... you aren't absolutely positive? You know from first-hand experience ..."

"Your Honor!"

"... what happens to young boys ... innocent young boys ..."

I heard Laren in the background screaming and the judge pounding his gavel. But the look I gave Mark Teller pretty much said it all. If he was lying, he was dying. I'd kill him if I found out he'd sent those boys to jail for no reason.

"Your Honor, I object!" howled Laren.

"Ms. Pascoli," admonished the judge, mildly. "I know you haven't been in a courtroom in some time, but you should reassess your examination of the witness. You must adhere to the standard question-and-answer format. I'll give you one more chance. Use it wisely."

"Yes, Your Honor," I answered.

I turned to put the case file back on the defense table when I spotted Alex, and even more oddly, Morrey. We seemed to have a full house.

I returned my attention to Mark with a dead stare. "Now, Mr. Teller. Are you absolutely certain that these are the boys you claim to have seen? Could you possibly have been mistaken?" I was providing a convenient "out" for his previous testimony and he (and everyone else) knew it. I could have come right out and accused him of perjury. Again. But I had no wish to make his problems any worse.

Mark, tentative and shaky, darted his eyes from me, to the boys, to Laren, to the judge. Then he stopped. He looked up at the judge and, clear as day, said, "I didn't see these boys. It was dark. At the time, I thought it was them, I really did. But I could only see the outlines of the faces. I didn't actually get a good look. It was real dark and the only light was from the moon and the radio inside the car. It wasn't much."

He kept looking up at the judge for acceptance of his testimony. And he finally got it. The judge nodded, and threw out the case. I had just refuted the prosecution's only piece of evidence.

Chapter 39

LAREN WALKED UP TO me and bellowed, "What the hell are *you* doing in my court room?"

"Really?" I replied calmly. "Your courtroom? And to think that the judge thought it was his."

He grunted. "You ruined this case."

"You didn't *have* a case and you know it. There was no evidence. You remember that stuff, right? The solid building blocks of any case." This was a quote he'd given me back in the earlier days.

"Very funny." He looked at Alex in the back of the room. "And you have a lot of nerve … you not only come here, interfere in a case with which you have no connection, but you also bring your own personal criminal."

"Would you knock it off?" I said. "You didn't need this case. If you had, you would have put more into it. Besides, I don't really think those kids stole anything. Look at them," I instructed.

The boys were standing on the other side of the room with their parents. One of the boys was actually crying.

"On top of that, maybe you missed it, but Max has the flu today. I should have him come over here and breathe on you, just for the fun of it."

"This is a court of law. I don't care if he's sick. Besides, he only defends the guilty," he said and headed back to his table to clean up his mess. I followed.

"That isn't true and you know it," I argued. "He still defends some who aren't guilty. Besides, if he doesn't defend them, then someone else will. And everyone deserves good representation. I'm thinking this public position has turned you into a monster. I want to know why you think those kids did it? You have nothing on them, so why?"

He studied the papers in his brief case and then said, "They were spotted less than a mile from the abandoned car and they were all stoned." He blew out a sigh. "And you're right, I may be turning into a monster ... but you beat me there years ago."

"Quite possibly," I agreed, "but I don't send innocent kids to jail and irrevocably ruin their lives."

Sadly, I abruptly remembered why I was there in the first place. I wanted information out of him. Now, if someone were to ask me, "What is the best way to get information out of a district attorney?" surprisingly, my first answer would probably not be "insulting him." But for some reason, I just couldn't help myself. He inspired me to argue. Maybe that was the lawyer in me.

"I didn't come down here to fight with you," I said, truthfully and genuinely apologetic. "I didn't even come to argue that case." This served as a reminder and I glanced at Max who still looked like crap. "Incidentally, does Max have any more cases today? He really should go home. If he passes out then he isn't going to be much use to anyone."

Laren sent his associate to find out and try to talk Max into re-arranging anything else he might have. He then leaned back against the small separator that divided the courtroom proceedings from the spectators.

"So you didn't come to argue, or try a case? Interesting. What *do* you want?"

I decided that, with Morrey sitting in the stands, this wasn't really the time to ask. And, considering how mean I'd been, maybe I should wait for the background info on Morrey after all.

"I wanted to talk to you about Anthony Sheppa," I said. "I want you to leave him alone. He left specifically to get away from the family situation. I'm afraid you're going to get him killed if the wrong person discovers that you're looking for him."

"You can't ask me to do that," said Laren. "I *need* him for a case. He knows things. He told me …"

"I know he gave a written statement to the police about Alex. I also know that this information was coerced. Anthony was threatened by his interrogators who claimed to have incriminating evidence about Theo, his father. You don't have anything and we both know it. Otherwise you would have already filed charges."

"What do you mean they coerced him?" Laren sounded genuinely surprised. "I was told that statement was provided of his own free will?"

"After four hours of constant questioning and innuendo," I said, "followed by the threat against his father—this was far from free will. Anthony absolutely will not testify. I doubt if he would have taken the stand even if you'd actually brought Alex to trial. Anthony may have left the country just to get out of it."

"Shit!" he slammed his fist on his closed briefcase. "You really know how to ruin my day don't you?"

"I do my best," I admitted. "But that wasn't why I came here. This was just an added benefit …"

"I don't mean to interrupt," said Laren's assistant.

She was a cute little blonde in a blue suit. She looked like she'd just graduated from law school and was working her way up. Soon she'd finish her time at the D.A.'s office and move into a private practice making six to ten times what she made now.

"Max has a trial date setting in an hour," she said to me. "He refuses to reschedule. He looks terrible. Do you think you could take it for him? He said he knows you don't like being in the courtroom, but he really needs someone to cover. His other two trial attorneys are in major cases right now."

I glanced at both Morrey and Alex. "Yep, tell him I'll take it. I just need the case file." She turned and went back to the defense table.

I'd take the file, get him to fill me in and then send him home. Good thing I'd dressed to visit court today. I might not be in the standard law garb, but at least I didn't look like a bum.

"I have to check on Max, find out about the case and see what Alex is doing here." I was more than a little curious.

"He feels guilty because he missed his opportunity to go to jail," said Laren. "You felt bad enough to help with the Hitchigan stuff. You wouldn't want to produce a box of new Sevelli evidence would you?"

"Sorry, I only look for crazy people evidence—the kind who will harm others if released. Besides, haven't you heard? I'm pregnant. It wouldn't do to send the father of my child to jail now, would it?"

Laren physically collapsed into the chair. "You're what?"

Uh-huh, just as I suspected. Morrey hadn't heard this from the D.A.'s office or Laren would know. "Pregnant, with child, knocked up, bun in the oven ... you know ... reproducing."

"Who would have thought it was possible?" he muttered.

"Now you sound like Ari."

That got his attention. His head shot up. "Gabella?"

"Yeah, I talked to her the other day and she was a little shocked. She and David still don't have any kids."

"Don't take this wrong," said Laren, "but I don't think it would be wise for those two to have kids. They're both a little ... messed up."

"Understatement there," I agreed. "But she is my cousin and David is probably a lot saner than most people give him credit for. After all, they completely redesigned the Gabellas and legalized everything in less than two years. Shut everything down and started all over. They can't be totally screwy."

I glanced back at Max. He had his head on his briefcase. I had to do something. In the next ten minutes, Max gave me the highlights of the case, told me the room number for the hearing, and handed me the case file. I had a bit of time before it started so I could brush up a bit.

I crooked my finger at Alex. He came so far and then stopped. He looked at the defense table and told me he'd rather we talked on the other side of the partition. Couldn't blame him I suppose, but I noticed the big smile on Laren's face.

"Ace, honey," he asked, "what the hell are you doing here? You left this morning and didn't tell anyone where you were going."

"So how did you find me?"

That just got me a grin.

"You put a tracking device on my car didn't you?"

Again the smile.

"You stink, you know that?"

That got me a kiss.

"I have to fill in for Max at a hearing in forty minutes. He looked terrible, did you see him?"

"Uh-huh. He looked like he had the flu."

"I think he does. I was here out of pure coincidence. I wanted to see if I could get Laren to dig up some info on Morrey. But I finished up the last case because I was afraid Max might pass out."

"Do you think Laren will look into it?"

"No. Actually, I never asked. I pissed him off and decided it would be best to pick a time when he felt better about dealing with me. But one thing struck me. Laren didn't know I was pregnant so I have a hard time believing that's where Morrey found out."

Alex just growled. "Are you going to be here for a while? I have a couple of things I have to do."

I glanced down at the folder. "Yes, I'll be downstairs. I have to review the case file and I don't need a babysitter."

Alex stood up, kissed the top of my head and said, "I know. I just worry." As he walked up the aisle he called, "I'll be back to take you to lunch." Then he was gone.

Chapter 40

BY THE TIME I LEFT the courtroom Morrey had gone without saying a word to me. I headed downstairs to the bench outside the room where the hearing was to be held. After reading the paperwork I wanted to beat the crap out of Laren. I looked up and saw him and his associate sitting two benches down. He and the newbie were chatting over a file.

"Laren!"

That got his attention. "What?"

"I think we should discuss this before we go in to the judge."

"Why? You want to pre-negotiate a plea?"

He wished. "No, you fool." I let my eyes sweep the hall. It was just the three of us here. "I want to keep you from making an ass of yourself … again."

He stood up and came over. He sat down and looked sick. He knew I'd found something or I wouldn't be saying anything at all. "What did you find?" he asked.

"Too many rights violations to count. You'll never get this all the way to trial. Why are you proceeding with it? This guy, Juan Ricando, doesn't speak English. He was held for eight hours before a translator was brought in. He was never read his rights, or at least not so that he would understand them, even after the translator arrived. They could have been speaking gibberish for all he knew. And he was interrogated for three hours by some cop who didn't believe he didn't speak English, so he tried to beat it out of him."

I pulled out an envelope. "From these pictures in Max's file I see bruises and marks from a beating that the defendant claims the detective caused because he couldn't answer his questions. How the hell do you think a judge isn't going to throw this out? You're wasting tax dollars and your time bringing it to trial."

Tentatively Laren looked at the pictures. Then he said in a hushed tone, "Eight hours? That does seem like a while."

"Yes," I agreed, "and if you try to say that it took eight hours, in this city, to find someone who spoke Spanish, one of the foremost languages in the world, much less the U.S., I'm going to have to say you're full of crap. There's no excuse for that sort of delay and even less excuse for those bruises. He should have been kept in a holding cell until a translator could arrive. And then the first thing he should have been read was his Miranda rights. But as you can see, this was not the case."

"Shit." He was getting good use out of that word this morning.

"I *know* your department is overworked, I know the police in this city are overworked. But there isn't any reason that this man should have been treated like this. And, when you discovered these facts, why didn't you ask for a dismissal? You'll be lucky if Max doesn't file a suit against the police for beating the crap out of his client."

"Shit!" said Lauren, thunking his head into his hands.

"Who's reviewing these cases before you get them? Who's looking for problems?"

Tilting his head so I could just see one eye, he replied, "Do you have any idea how little we pay our recruits? Do you have any idea what law firms are paying new recruits? Hell, *I* don't even make crap. It isn't as though I get first pick of the graduating class. I settle for whoever is left after the private practices have their pick. Which means, of course, the bottom of the barrel."

He glanced up at his assistant who was lurking nearby. "I don't mean that quite the way it sounds," he said. "Sometimes people who don't do well in school or graduate from lesser-known schools turn out to be really hard workers. Like Sissy here," he said, nodding at her. "She works sixty-five hours a week. But most of my staff members aren't quite there. They put in the hours, but it's more like a paper mill than a law office. The big cases eat up so many of my qualified resources that smaller cases, like this one, sometimes get this far when they never should."

"And what exactly," I asked, "*were* you working on just now? You looked as though you were doing something, but it wasn't this, was it?"

He groaned, head still down, "No," he agreed. "I was looking at the evidence the FBI submitted for the body of that boy you found."

"You found him?" said Sissy. "Really, that's too weird. I'm so glad I've never seen a real dead body," she added and gave a little shiver for effect.

Oh yea, weird. Personally, I saw it as an omen. Stay away from assisting law enforcement or you'll find dead people.

"Well, you need to focus on one at a time," I said, "and this is the one coming up next. If I were you—and this is just a suggestion, seeing how I won't be the defense attorney later, if the case goes anywhere—I'd ask the judge to dismiss this case.

"If Max has to take this to court," I reasoned, "he'll rip you and the police department a new ass. And not just in the courtroom either. He'll take it to the media. You do not want that happening."

Lauren finally sat up. "No, I don't," he agreed. He stood and stretched. "I'll ask if the judge will see us in chambers first. I don't want any spectators if I can possibly avoid it."

We proceeded upstairs. Judge Cline was pissed that the case had gotten this far but was happy to dismiss it. I called Max's office to see if anyone could arrange for Juan's release. Sandy, Max's paralegal, said one of the associates would meet me downstairs in the court house to take the paperwork and get Juan released.

Yay! I didn't have to visit the jail. I always worry they'll find a reason to keep me.

Alex arrived while I was still talking to Max's associate. He thanked me for taking care of Max's load for the day and said he and the others would cover for him until he was up to snuff again.

Alex looked confused. "What happened? Your case is over already? I thought it was supposed to start five minutes ago?"

"It didn't actually amount to anything," I explained. "After speaking with Laren, we agreed that he didn't really have a case. We asked the judge to dismiss it."

"So the guy's off the hook?"

"Yep. Can we eat? I'm hungry!" I said.

He smiled. "Of course."

I looked over and saw Laren running down the hall toward me calling, "Hey!" He glanced at Alex, and did his best to pretend he didn't see him. "I wanted to thank you," he said. "Max would have eaten me alive in front of the judge. I really do appreciate it."

"I don't see why I'd need to rip up at you in front of anyone," I said, smiling.

He smiled back and nodded. "But, thanks anyway."

✱✱✱

Alex and I left for lunch. As we walked into Jack's, another small Pascoli restaurant, I spotted Franky and Barry. That meant Tony was here.

Franky went straight to the back room when he spotted me and Barry, oddly, blocked the back entrance.

"What are they up to?" I asked Alex.

I didn't realize I'd said it out loud 'til Alex responded. "I guess they think Tony doesn't want to see you. Maybe we should go someplace else?"

"No. Not yet." I flagged down Blu, who runs the joint. He seated us near the back of the restaurant where I continued watching the boys' odd behavior.

Barry looked nervous. It is never good when the enforcer looks nervous.

"I think I'm going to check on Tony," I told Alex. "I want to make sure they haven't done something they shouldn't have. Barry's acting weird."

Alex's hand was on my arm. "Make sure you don't get hurt. Remember, it isn't just *you* now."

"I know," I assured him.

I walked up to Barry. Toe to Toe. It was physically impossible to be eye to eye, but I managed to get my point across.

"Is he here?" I asked sarcastically.

"Yeah, but he don't wanna be disturbed." He was clearly unnerved. And he should be. I beat the crap out of him when I was only twenty. I'm betting he's gotten slower over the years, but I've gotten faster.

"If you don't mind," I replied, "I think I want to make sure he's okay. You're acting strange."

"He don't wanna be disturbed," Barry said again. Apparently he thought I was deaf.

"Barry," I explained, "I'm going to move you if you don't move on your own."

"Please don't," he replied. "I know you're gonna have a baby and I don't want Tony to kill me for hurting it. But he told me not to let anyone in."

Okay, I know, I should go easy on him. He's big, he's stupid and he's already said he doesn't want to hurt me. But I'm not that nice. I slid my hand under the back of my shirt and pulled out a stun gun that I was now carrying because the real gun made Alex uncomfortable. Besides, it isn't nice to shoot your own guys, even if they don't listen and have the IQ of a stone.

"Whatever," I shrugged. "I'm hungry. I just wanted to see if Tony was coming for the rehearsal dinner, but I'll call him later." He looked so relieved that by the time he realized he was getting zapped, it was too late.

As Barry landed, his head hit with a *ka-thunk*! His huge falling mass parted the curtains and I saw an interesting sight. Two sets of eyes peered out at me and the now out-cold Barry. The resemblance of the two faces now struck me, suddenly.

"Did you have to do that?" Tony asked.

"He wouldn't let me in," I explained. "Tony, you know from personal experience how I hate it when people keep things from me.

Almost as much as I hate it when people lie to me, and you two have been doing a shit load of both. I don't really want an explanation right now. But Morrey, if that's really your name, you should know that whatever line of crap Tony has filled your head with is most likely just that, crap. The only loyal and honest bone in his body is in reference, and reverence, to himself. He did put you in my line of fire. You might want to keep that in mind."

I turned around and walked away. Alex was standing over Barry and checking out the two of them watching me. I looked up at Alex and said, "Now we're leaving."

"What was going on in there?" he asked when we got to the car.

"It's been bugging the crap out of me," I explained, "ever since I met Morrey. I knew he looked like someone but I just didn't know who."

"Well? Who, then?"

"*Tony.* Didn't you *see* it? They have the same eyes, the same forehead and, now that I think about it, even the same chin."

"So you think Morrey's … what?"

"He has to be Tony's son. There's no other explanation. Even Uncles don't look that much like their nephews."

"Holy shit!" he said, flopping back against the seat.

"Yep, I couldn't agree more. Can we go eat someplace else? I'm still hungry."

He started the car engine. "I don't get it, you have a family crisis and all you can think about is food?"

"My family is a perpetual crisis. Haven't you noticed? We invented the term 'family crisis.' If I stopped eating because of every family crisis, I'd be dead from starvation."

He snickered. "True enough."

Chapter 41

TWO MORNINGS LATER, I FOUND myself walking across the lawn out in back of the house. It was a warm morning, having rained the day before and now it was getting muggy.

I had my guns and was headed to the back of the property to shoot at some targets Miguel had set up for me. I really liked having him and Louisa back in my life.

The shooting area consisted of a set of paper targets that could be moved back and forth on a pulley for positioning and replacement. I set up the first target and then moved to the second when I felt someone coming. Thinking it was Miguel, seeing how we have all this security, I didn't bother to turn around.

I hooked in the second target and then moved to set up the third. Each target was set back ten feet further than the previous one. I pulled out my gun, silencer in place and fired. I may not have neighbors, but why take chances.

"Nice shot."

I knew that voice. It was a Jersey accent, not an Italian one.

I didn't even bother looking at him. I moved to the next target. "What the hell are you doing here? I know you didn't come through the gate because no one would have let you in." I lined up my mark and fired.

"Now why are you so mad? What the hell did I do? And I jumped over the fence down on the far side of the lawn. You may want to have that looked at."

"Why am I mad?" I said, and moved to the third target. "I'm mad because I was lied to, by my family, again. Maybe you haven't had that feeling lately, but let me tell you it isn't all that pleasant." I pulled the trigger.

"Are you *sure* he lied to you? Maybe it's just a misunderstanding."

I pulled the gun around and pointed it at Morrey's head. "I know you don't believe this, but things with Tony are never what they appear. He can't be trusted. He manipulates the outcome of events to his liking, no matter what he has to do to make that happen. And, since an apple doesn't fall that far from the tree, I'm guessing you're probably not that different."

"Whoa!" He put his hands in the air. "I think you have totally misread things? I'm not trying to manipulate shit. I'm just a local cop. That's it. I barely know Tony."

"You suck at lying," I told him. "You need to spend more time with your father. He'll be able to teach you to do it so well that even a polygraph won't know."

"Father?" said Morrey. "My dad died four years ago."

"Really? So, the fact that you and Tony look so much alike is just a coincidence? There are no coincidences, Morrey; not with Tony. Tony lured me back here to get Alex out of jail. But then he decided, in all his great wisdom ... by the way, his wisdom isn't worth shit either ... that I should settle down. Of course, the only way to get me to do that was to marry me off. And the only way to marry me off was to make it look like a family responsibility. Then he, of course had to find a groom. And what better way to get a groom, than to bribe him into it. You wash my hands, I'll wash yours. It's an old game, but still effective."

I turned the gun from Morrey and went back to my target. "But Tony had one big problem. He needed me to believe that I had a *family* obligation. But, in fact, he'd already found a satisfactory successor." I glanced at the man who was now not sure if he should run and hide or stay and listen.

"He couldn't really give me the family," I explained. "I had a conscience. I always had. You can't hand a crime family over to someone who doesn't really believe that crime pays, or at least not enough to make jail appealing. I'd have legitimized everything. Tony's old school. Legal isn't his way and it doesn't pay enough."

I fired off two more rounds. "Believe it or not, I wasn't the quite killing machine everyone made me out to be. Hell, I'd gone to law school. I joined the FBI. Tony couldn't give me the family. It looked really bad, at least until recently, but like I said, he'd already found a replacement." I fired again. "So when did he approach you?"

Morrey was just watching me shoot. He hadn't tried to run. He had just listened. "Eight years ago."

"Is Morrey really your name?"

"It's my stepdad's last name and the one I was raised with. Tony wasn't around while I was growing up. He only came to visit a couple of times when I was a kid. He wasn't exactly father of the year material."

"No," I agreed. "He isn't even 'uncle of the year' material. He'll screw you over, if he hasn't already. He did it to me a thousand times when I was younger. I got a little tired of it."

"He's done it to me already, twice," said Morrey.

"Well," I sighed, "don't expect it to change. He always has a reason, an explanation. Too bad it's never the truth. Have you ever noticed that when he lies he picks at his watch?"

"No."

"He does," I said. "So, whenever you see this, always question the B.S. you're getting."

"I don't think," ventured Morrey, "that he intended, initially, for you to marry. At least he never mentioned it. He did say that he wanted you here in the area, though. He wanted you home to watch out for me. He doesn't think I can do it on my own. He thinks I was raised wrong. I'm not ruthless enough."

He leaned against a tree. "I also might add that Alex was not his first choice for a husband. Tony thought Alex wasn't in the family trades anymore and would only soften you. He was just a good ally by reputation, and Tony and Roberto go way back. When you chose

Alex, Tony went nuts. But I convinced him that with Alex as an in-law it made for a really good connection."

"Nice to know I still don't do what he wants." I pulled the empty clip out and reloaded. "It's a lot of work trying to piss people off. I like it better when it comes naturally." I started reeling out new targets. "So when is he going to announce you're taking over? It has to be after the wedding. He wouldn't risk my hitting the road."

"That was true until he found out you were pregnant. Now he thinks you'll understand that you can't run the family businesses, at least not by yourself, and be a mom at the same time."

I turned my evil eye on Morrey. "If that isn't the most chauvinistic thing I've ever heard. What the hell *century* does he think this is? I can't believe …"

"Ace," interrupted Alex. He could have been standing there since Morrey arrived and I'd never have known, "you don't want the family. Remember?"

I focused on the target and pulled off three rounds.

"That isn't the point," I replied. "That manipulative old fart thinks he can rearrange my life to suit him. He lies to me and then he insults my abilities. I'm sorry, but I take offense."

A few more rounds and I felt Alex standing beside me. He ran his hand over my hair and leaned into my ear, while removing the gun from my hand. Alex didn't like guns. He knew how to use them, but he didn't like them. He didn't even like having them around.

"Let Morrey have the damned family and all the problems that come with it. You and I both know you don't want it. We have our own things that should be taking precedence—and not just the baby. We have this house, your real estate, your art collection, my businesses and my family obligations. And then, if you want to go back to practicing law with Max … Neither of us wants the added burden of the Pascolis and you know it."

"I didn't say that I did," I countered. "I'm just pissed that Tony feels so free to screw around in my life after all this time." I snatched up the gun and went back to the target. "But maybe, now that he has another successor, I should just shoot his ass and be done with it."

I fired again.

"Ace, honey," reasoned Alex, "you don't really want to kill Tony. You're just mad, but it'll pass."

I pulled off another few shots.

Alex tried another tactic. "There will be no killing Tony. Understand me?"

"Whatever," was the only reply I could come up with.

"Is that an 'I won't kill him' whatever, or a 'don't tell me what to do' whatever?"

I stopped, replaced the gun in the holster and started reeling in the first of the spent targets.

"I won't kill the old goat," I agreed, "but he better stay clear of me. I don't want anything to do with him. I lived without him for more than a decade. I don't see that the rest of his lifetime should be such a problem to get through."

"Ace, it isn't like things turned out badly, you know?" said Alex. "You and I are good together, we have a nice house, we're starting a family—things are pretty good, at least from my perspective. I don't understand why you're so upset."

"That's pretty much it," I agreed. "You don't understand."

I pulled up the remainder of my paper targets.

I knew what was wrong, I just couldn't express it and I didn't want to try in front of Morrey. As far as I was concerned, he was on his own. I didn't come here to play bodyguard to Tony's illegitimate offspring. I didn't have anything against Morrey, other than his sire … and, of course, his wardrobe.

I just didn't care. If Morrey wanted to continue running that mess that Tony called a business, fine. But he'd do it without me. I'd just seen the light at the end of the tunnel and I was running for that light as fast as possible. Alex was right, after all. I had a million other things I'd rather be doing, and none of them was family related.

What Alex didn't seem to grasp, and I couldn't explain, was this. Even though Tony had raised me in the family, he'd also given me the understanding that I was part of him. That I was important to him. And every time he lied to me, it tore away what little affection I had left.

I saw our relationship as a piece of rope. Tony kept cutting into the strands of that rope, a little at a time. We were now down to something that looked like a piece of sewing thread which could be snapped with no effort. I was at the point where killing him might actually be the only thing that made me feel better.

I'd been more or less rejected by my mother and ignored by my father. The only emotional family ties I had with the Pascolis were with Tony and Marty. Marty's love was unconditional, of course, and always would be. Tony's, however, was a lie—the kind of lie that was essential to my being as a child because all children need love. But eventually, this type of lie is almost impossible to give up, even as an adult. It's so emotionally entwined into your being that you just can't let it go—no matter what facts or the truths you finally realize.

Tony had used me for years, lied to and manipulated me. I couldn't believe that he actually expected me to play blocker for Morrey. He had to be nuts. This whole family was just about to drive me over the edge. If I went postal and started killing people left and right, no one should be surprised.

"I'm going in." I turned to leave, bringing my swiss-cheese targets with me. "Morrey, go back and show Alex where you came over the fence so we can have it looked at."

Alex tried to talk to me over the next few days about the situation, but I was doing my best to ignore it as much as possible. Our wedding was next week and I just wanted to run away. It wasn't Alex's fault. I just didn't want to deal with my family issues, any of them.

CHAPTER 42

BY THE TIME OF THE REHEARSAL, Linier had secured his funding for the "Angelica Collection" project. Apparently the board agreed that the sooner the display could be in place, the better. He'd selected the pieces and contacted the insurance appraisers to make the confirmation of provenance.

The house was now fully settled for the most part. We'd gone through my files, condensed everything and put the remains over the garage. We finally managed to get Miguel moved into the guesthouse so he would have some semblance of privacy. I didn't want him feeling he wasn't allowed a life. Jason had had that problem for a long time and I didn't want Miguel to have to live that way. He was a young man and young men need space.

Before the rehearsal I went to see Father Jacobs for confession. Actually it wasn't really to confess, it was to try to get some things off my chest. I thought he'd be more likely than anyone else to understand my problems with the family and my apprehension at tying myself to someone for life. I was amazed at how clearly he always knew what I was thinking.

"Angelica, you can't allow these issues to color your view of marriage. I've seen you and Alex together. This is a good marriage. You're having problems with Tony, not the entire family. And, from what you've said, you don't even really know what his position is. You've been avoiding him."

He was right, but what could Tony possibly say to make it all better? I was pretty sure it couldn't be done. And to be frank, I doubted that I'd believe him no matter what he said.

Father Jacobs continued. "You said your father was pleased. Your brother and Cara are pleased. These are positive signs. Even Alex's family seems happy, yes?"

I nodded.

"Your mother, sadly will probably never be pleased, but that isn't your fault, or your problem. It never has been. It is not your job to make her happy. And as for Tony, well, in his own way, he does *care* for you. He's just so self-involved that I don't believe he sees how his actions affect you. This young man you told me about, Morrey. He was most likely better off being raised by his mother and a stepfather. Tony would have done more harm than good with him."

"I know I shouldn't say that," Father Jacobs chuckled, "but it's true. I often think that Tony doesn't see past himself. But that is his problem, not your problem. Again, it is not your job to make things right for him, or to fix him. You are getting married. You'll be a wife and then, in a short time, a mother. This is what you must focus on. And, if you want my honest opinion of this matter, you're better off."

Father Jacobs had taken my killing the two hit-men far better than I had expected. He hadn't made a judgment call. He used to yell at me and tell me I was going to go to Hell if I didn't straighten myself out. But I guess the fact that they were trying to kill Alex made a difference. We did turn the other cheek, as it were, when it came to the Sheppa's. I think it was kind of a moral break-even, but he did feel the need to say that I should try to stay out of trouble now that I was with child. I noticed that with pregnancy, people often felt the need to remind me of the obvious.

Alex was outside waiting when I left Father Jacob's office. I didn't bother asking how he'd found me. I knew it was the tracking device. I should be irritated that he wanted to know where I was twenty-four hours a day. I knew it was going to annoy me eventually. But he was just concerned and I couldn't muster up enough irritation to override my happiness that he cared enough to keep going out of his way to find me.

He slipped his arm around my waist as we made our way out to the parking lot. Neither of us had said a word. Alex was the one who broke our silence. "I would appreciate it," he said, "if you would please let someone know where you go. I worry when no one knows where you've gone."

"I don't want to fight, okay?"

"I wasn't looking for a fight."

Turning in his arms, I buried my face in his chest. I felt his arms come around me. He was practically big enough to completely enclose me and make me appear to disappear and that was what I wanted. I felt better about things, but not as good as I would have liked.

I mumbled into his chest, "Two days, right?"

"Two days?"

"I just have to get through two more days and it'll all be over, right? Then I can go back to my life. I can do what I want and there won't be any more of this ..."

"Stress?"

"Yes. I don't like this stress. Work stress is bad. People trying to kill us is bad. But this *family* stress is killing me. I'd be better with someone shooting at me."

As depressing as it was, I wasn't exaggerating. Full-scale war would be better than family problems as far as I was concerned.

He was stroking my back. "I know. It'll be better. Just two more days and then the wedding will be over. The business associates will go back to where they came from, the family will still be there, but hopefully they'll leave you alone and you can settle in."

I nodded into his chest. I still hadn't looked at him.

"Are you sure I can't kill Tony? It would make things better," I mumbled into his shirt.

Alex chuckled. "No, Ace. You cannot kill Tony. And it wouldn't really make you feel better. You just think it would. Besides, now that he has Morrey as a pet monkey, I'm hoping he'll leave you alone."

I nodded into the shirt. He was right. The wedding was two days off. I would handle this. I had a nice home. My real family was Miguel and Louisa. I hadn't needed anyone else in years. And now I had Alex and we were going to have a child and a life together. I could do this. I just needed to rally.

Father Jacobs was correct. Mom and Tony were the only issues I had and their problems were only mine if I let them be. Sadly there was this niggling feeling that was saying "not quite" in the back of my head. It was time to get on with my life and forget about everyone else's expectations.

"Do you want food?" he asked. "I know you seem to like to eat a lot lately."

I looked up at him. "That's rude," I pouted. "You should never comment on how much a woman eats. So I like food. I liked food before I got pregnant. It's just gotten worse and all I want to do is eat all the time. I've decided to blame the baby."

I thought about it for a minute. Could be all this stress. Or maybe I'd turned into a stress eater since I couldn't drink alcohol or caffeine.

Alex still had a big smile on his face. He cocked one eyebrow and asked, "So, is that a yes?"

"Don't be stupid, of course it's a yes."

Chapter 43

SATURDAY FINALLY ARRIVED. According to Kimberly, every-thing was taken care of. All I needed to do was show up. I was praying she was right, I didn't think that at this point I was up to much more than that.

I had stopped by the museum yesterday morning and it looked like a wrecking crew had come in and destroyed everything. But Kimberly swore that it was just the tear-down before she could get all the wedding rubbish into the rooms we'd use. Needless to say, I had been a bit concerned. But I decided it was her job and I didn't want to think about it.

So here I sat, in my room looking into the mirror of my dressing table feeling sick to my stomach, wishing this whole thing were over, and sadly, it had just begun.

The hairdresser would arrive in less than an hour, along with Cara and the girls. I'd had the forethought to have my manicure and pedicure yesterday, so at least that was over with. I still had the makeup person coming to do my face. I wanted to do my own, but apparently it was unheard of to "do your own" on your wedding day.

My dress was hanging in the dressing room and so was Alex's tux. At the thought my stomach convulsed. I ran for the bathroom. Unfortunately for Alex he was in there taking a shower. I managed to get to the toilet, just before everything I'd eaten last night came up.

The heaving sound must have brought my present situation to Alex's attention. "Ace?"

I could feel him standing behind me, dripping on the floor. I must have made quite a sight, crouched down on the tile floor, head hanging over the toilet bowl, and a skin tone closer to gray than "human." I was wearing my flannel red and black checked pajama bottoms and a red tank top, hair piled up on my head in a big mess. I'm sure this is how every man envisions his bride on the day of their wedding.

"Honey, are you okay?"

"No, I want to lie down here on the floor and die," I declared. I slumped against the wall and flushed the toilet.

"Are you sick? Maybe it's morning sickness? You haven't had that."

"Or maybe it's my nerves," I groaned. And that is exactly what it was.

In truth, the only thing bothering me was having to get into that dress and parade myself around in front of everyone and make nice. I don't do that stuff well and everyone would be paying attention to me.

"People suck," I said and closed my eyes

"Yeah, but tonight it'll all be over. Come on. I'd give you a couple shots if it weren't for the baby." He pulled me to my feet. "But you're just going to have to tough it out. Brush your teeth, take a shower and I'll have Louisa make you some breakfast and tea. I don't want you eating anything too heavy or you'll just be in here puking it up again."

"I don't want food." I started to pull out the toothpaste.

"You have to eat. You can't go without food. But we'll try for something light. Go on, get in the shower."

I brushed my teeth, undressed and climbed in. The water felt good. I tried to close my eyes and relax, breathing deeply, but it wasn't doing much, and my stomach kept churning. I needed an outlet and the only ones I had were music and shooting. Shooting sounded really good this morning, but I didn't think Alex would let me disappear long enough to achieve any stress relief .

The rest of the morning went along as well as could be expected. I managed to sneak into the music room for a few hours while Cara took the girls on a walk around the gardens and then had their hair done.

The wedding was scheduled for 3:00 and it was 2:00 when we finally left the house. Alex went to meet his brother and left me in Cara and Miguel's hands to insure I got to the museum on time.

Cara managed to remember everything from my jewelry to my shoes. I don't know what I would have done without her. She loaded Miguel down with everything we needed and off we went.

Alex had Sal find me something on the same basic design as the necklace I had originally planned on wearing. What he found me was a new ruby and pearl choker and earrings that were so beautiful I didn't complain about having to put my jewels in the museum. I suspect that was what Alex had planned. He also told Sal to keep his eyes open for anything exceptional since he wanted to put my 1920's jewelry on display at the museum as well.

It was all costume jewelry, but apparently Linier discovered their existence and more or less begged Alex to show them to him. I must have one hell of an eye because several of the pieces were now worth a small fortune. The escalated value had something to do with the designer of the jewelry I happened to be attracted to. He'd been some major designer in his time and an originator of the styles of that period.

To think, I'd been wearing them with jeans.

Alex had promised to replace the jewelry being sent to the museum with more reasonably valued items so I had nice things to wear, but he wouldn't have heart failure if I lost them or lost a stone out of one of the pieces.

We came in through the main door of the museum, but were sent to a room in the back that Mr. Linier had set up on the first floor for me to use as a changing room. Kimberly was there and assured me everything had come together perfectly. People were starting to arrive and we only needed to get me ready and in front of Father Jacobs.

Chapter 44

BY THE TIME THE DRESS WAS on, jewelry in place and my makeup touched up, they shoved a bouquet in my hands and off we went. I felt like I was having an out of body experience. Before I knew what was happening, I was standing next to Alex at the end of the aisle and looking at Father Jacobs.

I hadn't seen the girls or Cara go down the aisle, I hadn't seen any of the guests. I'd say I was in a trance. I finally awoke from it when my stomach grumbled. I'd only had fruit and a piece of toast and that was at nine o'clock that morning. I was afraid I'd be sick again and wasn't willing to risk it. I figured the baby and I would survive that long.

Apparently the grumbling was loud enough for Alex to hear, because he glanced down at me. Father Jacobs was in the middle of his sermon on the meaning of marriage, and I was hoping this wasn't going to take long.

I know, I know, I spent a crap load of money on this dress and the entire setup, but all I wanted was to get it over with. I wasn't even enjoying the money I'd spent. Something was wrong with that, but it didn't change the feelings I was having.

I noticed for the first time that Father Jacobs can go on and on when he wants to. His church sermons never take this long. Finally, we exchanged vows and rings, kissed and we were done. If only I could go home now.

We formed a receiving line at the entry to the dining area that Kimberly had miraculously transformed. The truth was, she had really earned her keep. The entire wedding setup was just amazing.

When Tony came through the procession, almost immediately followed by Morrey, I wanted to say something but didn't. This was my wedding, this was my family and even if I was mad at Tony, the reality was, although I hadn't known it prior to a few days ago, Morrey was my cousin. I wasn't going to make a scene in front of every other member of the family as well as the visitors.

We all ate and it wasn't bad. It wasn't Louisa's, but Mario's is always pretty good. The orchestra was wonderful. They played a variety of tunes and kept people on the dance floor. Thank goodness—it gave me fewer people to talk to.

I was making the rounds and just about to sneak off and go up to the galleries when my mother approached me. "I was speaking with Mr. Linier," she said. "We were talking about the art exhibit you're lending to the museum. I just wanted you to know how wonderful I think that is. He assumed, naturally, that I'd already seen your collection. Why haven't you mentioned this before?"

Just great; I thought, here we go.

"It just never came up," I replied. "Alex learned about my art collection and wasn't comfortable keeping so many valuable pieces in the house. So, when the collection arrived, Mr. Linier came to the house to examine the works and discuss the loan. It all happened rather quickly."

"But they are all at the house now?"

"Yes, but they're all just lying around in the music room. We aren't going to hang them since it puts holes in the walls and they won't be there long. I think Linier will put together a wonderful display. I'm not worried about that and my insurance company is checking out their security. It should all be in place shortly. Alex and Linier will both feel better when the display is here in the museum," I explained, giving the particulars of the items to go into the collection.

Amazingly, my mother was actually impressed. I can say that hasn't happened before. Her only complaint was that she and Dad hadn't been invited to the house before now. I told her that Alex and I had finally gotten the boxes unpacked from both of our previous residences and that we wanted to have both the immediate families over to the house before fall really arrived. That statement also was met with approval.

I was starting to feel as though I was in an alternate universe. Next thing you know I'd be wearing a pink tutu and dancing to *Swan Lake.*

I finally managed to disengage myself from my mother and turned to head up the stairs to the gallery. The gallery was closed, but the only thing keeping me out of it was the little red velvet rope across the steps.

✳✳✳

Slipping the rope off its hook, I headed up the stairs. I needed some peace and quiet before I screamed. Alex had been fulfilling the obligatory duties and was still making the rounds. He was also dancing with every little old lady in both families. I smiled to myself at that thought while I climbed the stairs.

There was a room down the hall that was especially peaceful. It contained landscapes of various countryside scenes. Lots of mountains, fields, rivers and the occasional animal populated these paintings. It was relaxing.

After what seemed no time at all I heard footsteps. Looking at the entrance hall I saw Tony and Morrey. God, didn't it just figure. I get a moment of peace and they need to screw it up.

"There you are! We've been all over this place. You can get lost in here."

I shushed Morrey. The halls resonated sounds and made him louder than he already was.

He strolled over to my side and asked, "What?"

"I'm tired," I snapped. "Voices carry in these halls and we aren't supposed to be up here. If a guard hears you they'll make us leave."

He sat next to me on the bench. "Sorry."

Tony took the other side.

Wonderful, now I had one on either side. That wasn't comforting. "What do you two want?"

Tony spoke, "What makes you think we *want* something? Couldn't we just be looking to spend time with you?"

Who did he think he was kidding?

"No," I said. It was gruff but honest.

Tony groaned. "You are still mad, that's obvious. But, be that as it may, we need to talk. I know you and Steven have talked and I understand that you are probably upset that I didn't tell you about him. But that doesn't change the fact that he is my son."

Was he nuts?

"You think I'm jealous?" I asked, perfectly astonished. But it had been obvious by the tone of his voice. "No, not even a little bit."

I stood up. "I'm upset because for some reason you keep thinking it's perfectly acceptable to lie to me, manipulate me and generally screw with my life. I couldn't care less if he's your kid. You and I had plenty of problems before I left and they certainly had nothing to do with Morrey."

I couldn't think of him as Steven, he was Morrey in my brain, not Steven. Even if he changed his name tomorrow, he'd still be Morrey to me.

"I don't recall problems," said Tony. "As I remember it, you wanted to go to the FBI to try something new."

"I lied," I said. "*You* should be well aquatinted with the process. You do it often enough. I left because you kept manipulating me. I got tired of it. I got tired of constantly trying to figure out what your real motive was, what the underlying truth was. I thought about killing you, but decided that would give me too much responsibility, so I left."

The look on Tony's face said he had no idea I'd thought about killing him. "You left," he said, "to get away from me?"

"Among other things," I said. "My mother was driving me nuts. My father had slipped into that shell of his so far he didn't even acknowledge me half of the time. The family obligations were suffocating me. I sucked at the politics. Marty was finally out of your grasp, more or less, my properties could be managed by someone else and I didn't need to be here. It all just tied together. I wanted out of it all and the government gave me that opportunity."

"And now," said Tony, "you still wanna kill me?"

"No, I don't want to kill you anymore. I just want to know what the hell is going on. Every time I turn around, you're at it again. It's as though nothing has changed. Twelve years go by and you're still pulling the same crap. You told me you wanted me here to take over because you were retiring. You told me I had to marry to keep peace. And you told me that I needed a strong alliance. Turns out that this is all a bunch of shit. You don't want me here to take over, not that I want it. I didn't need to get married. You just needed to get Alex out of jail. I don't need an alliance and we both know it. Now there's Morrey …"

"Steven."

"Whatever you want to call him is fine with me. Can I please continue?" I gave him a dirty look and went on. "Now you plan on making him the successor, but for some unforeseeable reason you couldn't manage to leave me the hell alone. I don't have a problem with Morrey …" I stopped and corrected myself, "Steven taking over, unless he screws up and gets my family in trouble. Then I'll kill his ass. But I still don't see why you couldn't just leave me in Italy minding my own damn business. It's as though you feel you have some license to screw with other people's lives. I haven't given you that right."

"You're right, you haven't," Tony agreed. "But I consider you mine, as I always have. You are not my child by parentage, but I consider you mine by arrangement. And since that's the case, I also consider your future my responsibility. I didn't like that you left and I made this clear when you did. However, now that I know the real reasons why, I'm glad I didn't push the matter or I might not be here right now." He cleared his throat and continued. "You needed to see the world, but I didn't like that you never came home. You settled in Italy, alone. You didn't marry or have children. You didn't see the importance of building your own family. I knew you hadn't been home since you left and that you'd never come back here by choice."

He stood and put his arm around my shoulders. "And, once I finally got you here, you would never have chosen to stay. I might add that the reason I sent for you was valid. I really did want Roberto out of jail. And, as you know, it would have taken much more effort for anyone else to have performed the task."

He was speaking in hypnotic voice, rich, calm, soothing. I knew what he was up to but I was willing to listen.

"You left me little choice," Tony continued. "The only way to keep you here was to either hand over the family obligations or get you to marry. As for the rest of the story—I'm not ready to retire and I have not told Steven that he is taking the helm when I do. I have not decided this question. But either way, it doesn't matter. He's not proficient in the way of the families. He doesn't have the gift for certain things that you do. You do not have the gift for other things that he does. Therefore, when the time comes, I will most likely split the family responsibilities between you."

He gave a little grumble. "Not that either of you, I've noticed, seem to want this honor and its responsibilities. You were both more than willing to give away your share to the other one. It's a good thing I don't plan on leaving any time soon."

"Yes," I said, "well, you're lucky Alex told me I absolutely couldn't shoot you. I was seriously considering it."

"I think Steven mentioned that," said Tony. "I didn't intend to make you this mad. I just wanted you settled here at home."

"You tried to marry me off to morons," I groaned. "It seemed that the result of my settling here would not have been worth the cost of spending the rest of my life with an idiot. You didn't think that was going to be a problem?"

"I didn't realize," Tony admitted, "that they were so bad. I hadn't spent any time with them myself. Their fathers are reasonable men. I never dreamed their offspring would be so appalling. Besides, you and Alex seem to be satisfied with each other and that was your choosing, not mine. I would never have chosen him for you, but I suppose that shouldn't bother me. You were always choosing something I didn't approve of. Psychology, law school, moving to New York, then the FBI …" He shook his head slightly. "I don't want to think about it. I must say, though, that Alex was a good choice, even if he was not mine."

"Nice to know you approve," said Alex, speaking from the doorway.

We both turned. Neither Tony nor I had noticed him. And Morrey hadn't said anything.

"Ace, you ran off," Alex explained. "We have guests downstairs. It's rude to have disappeared."

"I know," I said apologetically. "I just needed a little peace and quiet."

He lifted a brow, as if to say, "This doesn't look like 'peace and quiet' to me."

"They followed me," I explained, meeting Alex half way across the distance between us.

"Well," said Tony, smiling, "let us congratulate both of you. We'll be downstairs with the rest of the guests."

Alex nodded as Tony and Morrey left the room. "Are you okay?" he asked.

"Yes, but I'll be better when we can go home."

He wrapped his arm around my shoulders. We sat down on the bench.

"Did you get anything resolved?"

"I don't know," I confessed. "I'm too tired to know if he was telling the truth … or if it was just more of his crap. But either way, it doesn't matter. He said he isn't retiring yet and that he's a bit disappointed because neither I nor Morrey are the least bit eager to take his place. I guess Morrey and I have more in common than I thought," I said and smiled.

"It wouldn't surprise me if he's Tony's kid. You and Tony have an awful lot in common. I think that may be why you two have so many problems with each other."

Alex and I spent another fifteen minutes or so sitting there just talking. We hadn't had much of a chance to talk all day, so it was nice to catch up. We managed to make our getaway an hour and forty minutes later and headed home. Miguel and Louisa left as soon as I had mentioned wanting to go. They were headed home to put things in order for our wedding night.

Chapter 45

LYING ON THE BED TWO hours after arriving home, snuggled under the sheets next to my husband and feeling completely relaxed, I thought about the day. It had, for the most part, gone by in a blur. I'd been told by many that it was a wonderful event. Several brides-to-be had asked about the wedding planner and Kimberly had been pleased with the way it had all come off.

I also thought about Tony. He certainly had lied to get me here. But feeling Alex's leg next to mine under the sheets I realized, for the first time since I'd come home, that it didn't matter. I'd made the choices I'd made. I'd chosen Alex. If the choices had been those three nincompoops I'd never have done it. I was fairly certain that even if the choices had been others who didn't live up to my expectations, I'd have rejected them. Tony hadn't forced me into this.

He'd nudge and badger me, but he hadn't held a gun to my head. I could blame him for sticking his nose where it didn't belong, but I couldn't blame him for the choices I'd made. I was an adult and that came with certain responsibilities. One of them was accepting the consequences of my own actions. This marriage, and without a doubt, the conception of my child were prime examples.

Somehow that put my mind at ease. Alex, the baby, the house and the direction of my life had been my choice. I was still in charge of my life. I just needed to remember that when I felt events were out-of-control, no matter how much pressure was applied by my family, in the end the decisions were all mine.

I didn't have to take over the family. I didn't have to deal with my mother. I didn't have to do anything I didn't want to do. I didn't really even have to retire if I didn't want to. I smiled to myself. I was still the woman I'd chosen to be and no one was going to change that without my direct approval.

Now, that was comforting.

www.ingramcontent.com/pod-product-compliance
Lightning Source LLC
Chambersburg PA
CBHW021533250626

47154CB00006BA/2099